THRALL

DIVISION ZERO
BOOK THREE

MATTHEW S. COX

DIVISION ZERO PRESS

Division Zero: Thrall

Book 3 of the Division Zero series.
Second Edition

Original © 2014 by Matthew S. Cox
Revised edition © 2018

This book is a work of fiction. Any similarities to real persons, places, or ghosts is purely coincidental. No portion of this book may be reproduced without permission from the author.

ISBN: 978-1-949174-15-1 (Ebook)

ISBN: 978-1-949174-16-8 (Paperback)

CONTENTS

STALKED

Enchanted by a fleeting daydream of the perfect fairy-tale wedding, Kirsten watched imaginary guests mingling among the dark spots between trees. Evan grabbed her arm with both hands, shaking her out of the fog of an idyllic day. Fanciful organ music retreated into her thoughts, replaced by the reality of whistling wind and distant commerce. Alas, The tiny nature preserve of Sanctuary Park, five square miles of green contained in a flower-box of silver high-rise buildings, didn't offer an escape from the incessant jingles of ad-bots.

She blinked at him, as if surprised by his sudden proximity. The sight of the boy's defensive posture over Shani made her smile. The look of urgency in his eyes took it away. The little girl seemed confused at the sudden end to their play. Kirsten glanced to her left, as if an explanation for everything had been written on the sienna face of Nila Assad.

"K?" asked Nila. "Are you all right? You kinda zoned out there."

"Mom..." He pulled at Kirsten's arm. "Something's in the bushes watching us."

The genuine fear radiating from him grabbed her with a sense like she'd awakened from a momentary daydream. "Where?" She put a hand on his shoulders. "Did you see anything?"

Evan shook his head. "No. I just had a creepy feeling like something was there."

"Umm." Nila stared at her, reaching for Shani.

Kirsten frowned. "I don't think it's a..." She switched to telepathy. *Pervert. Shani didn't see anything. Evan's too scared. He wouldn't be this rattled if it was just a man.*

Nila relaxed a little.

"A what?" asked Shani.

"Living person," said Kirsten.

The glare Nila sent into the bushes melted to worry. Shani hopped up on the bench while Evan remained standing, arms folded, eyes fixed on the spot. Kirsten struggled to pull her E-90 out of her too-small purse.

"You know," said Nila, "you can wear it on your hip. You don't have to hide it. Besides, it's against policy to stuff it in a bag that tiny. What if you needed it in a hurry?"

Kirsten brushed her thumb over the molded grip. "I guess. I wanted to feel normal for one day this month." She rubbed Evan's shoulder. "Stay here with Nila, I'll be right back."

"You're not going alone, are you?" Nila put a hand on Kirsten's arm.

"What else can I do? Should we leave the kids here alone while we run off? Or bring them with us after who-knows-what?"

Evan turned so Shani couldn't see the frightened look he gave Kirsten. *Mom, you did kill that bad ghost, right?*

Kirsten stood. Her shoes meowed as they absorbed her weight. Evan cracked up giggling. She sighed, glancing down past her skirt at the pink and white Nomz. She suppressed a cringe at the memory of Seneschal's final obliteration. *Yes, I did. Did it feel like him?*

"Kinda." He bit his lower lip. "It's pretty strong."

She shivered. The thought of another abyssal stalking her son chilled her blood. The wind going up her skirt didn't help either. She smirked at Nila.

"What?" asked Nila.

This is why I don't wear skirts. I'm gonna get into a fight and it's gonna come off, or I'm going to go headfirst into something with my ass in the air. Kirsten blushed at the mere thought of it.

Nila grinned, hiding her face in Shani's hair to avoid laughing at Kirsten's mental grumbling.

"Stay here and protect Shani, I'll be right back." She winked at Evan.

"'Kay." He puffed out his chest.

Shani frowned. "He's just a kid too. Alls he can do is see ghosts." Evan floated off his feet, squealing from the sudden telekinetic levitation. He whirled around in a 180 and landed on the bench sitting next to her. Shani folded her arms. "I'll probably wind up protecting him."

Evan looked annoyed for a second or two before he held Shani's hand. "You can't TK a creepy spirit, and that's what's watching us."

After a reassuring squeeze to his hand, Kirsten went toward the edge of the wooded area with both hands on her weapon, aimed down and to the right. She felt ridiculous brandishing the E-90 while wearing a thigh-length skirt, white sweater, and cat-headed sneakers that meowed whenever she stepped too hard.

Great, I'm the cheerleader from hell.

The mood shifted as she neared the edge of the clearing. Forty yards or so from the bench, a definite unease permeated the area. Dozens of different ad-bot tunes collided at once amid the rustling trees. Whatever energy hung in the air here altered her mood, changing the sound into a sinister calliope that could accompany the carnival of the damned. Primal trepidation swam up her spine. With it came the feeling she wouldn't be able to find her way out of this forest.

Kirsten paused at the end of the grassy field by the trees, forgetting for a moment the nature preserve only occupied five square miles. It seemed endless, beckoning, as if a malevolence within wanted her forever. Wind fluttered her skirt; the cold air on her legs caused a shiver. It took her a moment, as well as a glance back at the three people she considered family, to gather herself.

Something is trying to freak me out.

Squinting, she searched the foliage for any sign of what caused the twisted mood. The presence clawed at the back of her mind, wanting to make her feel scared. Kirsten tapped her power, raising an active defense against the spectral ambiance. The fear lessened. *There's definitely a spirit here.* Her astral ward wouldn't have affected a living telempath.

Her confidence back, Kirsten straightened her stance and walked into the trees. The entity hadn't attacked when the kids were close to it, a chance moment when she would've been unable to intervene. If it had come to harm them, why hadn't it made its move then? Evan said it felt strong, which made her worry she missed an abyssal somewhere along the way. Many of them, at least according to her recent research, preferred weeks and months of slow maddening to murder. Certain spirits could derive untold amounts of pleasure from watching a mortal's slow descent into insanity.

She stepped over a root that encroached on the jogging path, wondering how deep the soil went before it hit the city plate. *Enough for trees, apparently.* The occasional holographic sign flickered into view as she moved, bearing reminders that park visitors were responsible for any litter. Continued tweaking at her mental defenses kept her on guard, but a presence still watched her.

To the right, a spread of debris outlined a space in the park claimed by vagrants. Three crude shelters ringed a nine-foot-wide metal dish filled with ash, a cover from an articulated cargo mover's wheel motor. Still, she found no larger trace of paranormal energy. Small bits of trash wrapped about trees, flapping in the wind. A bot the size of a shoebox orbited the camp, itching to issue someone a fine for littering. Detecting her motion, it came zooming over. By the time it reached her, its prosecutorial zeal had faded to a disappointed nose-down approach. A small holo-panel sticking out of its side displayed her face—her official ID image.

"Good afternoon, officer. Have you located the parties responsible for this code violation?"

Kirsten smirked at it. "Please tell me you're not just going to slap a littering fine on the first person you find who isn't a police employee."

The floating bot sagged. "Pardon my enthusiasm. I've been on this assignment for ninety-three hours now."

"I hate to throw sand in your lubricant, but the people responsible for that campsite probably don't even have citizen registrations. You should move on."

"I can't," whined a petulant male voice, "my program does not contain a logic gate for failure-slash-lack of suspects."

"Well, what will you do if you find the ones responsible and they don't have a PID transponder to fine?"

It trailed behind her as she walked. "In that event, I am programmed to use verbal compliance enforcement techniques."

Kirsten avoided another huge root. "You mean nag them to death?"

"*Hmmf.*" The floating brick pivoted away, as if offended. "I'll have you know I perform a very important function."

"I'm sure you do."

With a shake of her head, she turned away from the patrol bot and came to a halt. The induced fear was pervasive, omnidirectional. She could walk for hours and never find anything by sight. *Maybe who or whatever this is only comes out at night. Ugh, this is a waste of time. One more try.* She closed her eyes and reached out with mental energy. Her influence projected into the astral realm and mingled into the emanation teasing at the edges of her mood. She swept back and forth, hoping to feel some sense of direction that would lead her to an entity. After some time, she concluded the effect to be an imprint on the area rather than active radiance. A spirit had infused this section of the park with its desire to frighten the living away from its domain. That would also explain why she didn't see anything walking around.

She let her head sag backward and sighed at the treetops. "Well, not the first time I've chased my own tail."

"You there," said the bot. "The fine for littering is—" The pronouncement cut off with an electronic scream. "Assaulting a municipal patrol robot is a crime!"

When she opened her eyes, she found a face less than twelve inches away from hers. With a gasp, she leapt back and collided with another man behind her, who was all too happy to catch her by the arms and hold on. The sudden shock of a grab from behind left her unable to do much but squirm for a few seconds.

The bot glided up behind him. "Now the total fine is 4,942 credits. Please swipe a NetMini or await the police."

"Well, well," said the man in front of her, ignoring the nuisance behind him. "Candy cute. Do your parents know you wandered off alone?"

He didn't appear to be much older than seventeen with frizzed-up orange hair and wore a long, multi-pocketed coat. A glowing NanoLED tattoo wrapped around the right half of his face, a dragon drawn in red. The light darkened with his expression.

"Do yours know you're assaulting people in the park?" She stopped struggling. "You two should go back to school. Not much future in the UCF for people without advanced degrees."

They both laughed. A mix of warm and cool gathered at the left side of her neck as the man holding her pressed his face close and inhaled.

"Relax, princess. I got some stuff that'll make sure it doesn't hurt." He slipped his hand out of his coat, holding a refurbished, refilled autoinjector. "Or, if you'd prefer not to remember it at all…" His grip shifted, fanning two more injectors out from behind it like cards. The purple one still had dried blood on the end.

The way the man at her back held her arms prevented Kirsten from aiming the E-90 at the one in front, despite not wanting to kill someone that young. She tried once more to wriggle free, but found her strength lacking.

"This is normally where I would give you one more chance not to make a stupid mistake, but I'll settle for being happy you two idiots decided to try and grab me instead of some helpless kid."

"Whoa, Skeev, we found a freak. I think she likes it."

"Yeah," she said, as her eyes faded to flat white. "I'm going to love it."

Her thoughts wrapped around the sentience behind her head, and she pumped a Mind Blast into the cloud of thoughts that knocked the man into a stupor. She held back, hoping to only stun him. Skeev, or whatever his name was, backpedaled the instant her eyes glowed with white energy. Kirsten shrugged her arms free and raised the E-90, her eyes returning to their usual sapphire blue.

"Police, Division 0, on the ground, now."

Whether by panic, ignorance, or desperation, Skeev howled and charged. Not wanting to shoot him, and not feeling threatened by him, she spun into his attack and guided him face-first into a tree with a ju-jitsu toss. He bounced away and staggered to face her again, so she kicked, slapping him across the face with her sneaker.

Meow.

He flailed his arms to maintain balance. Kirsten advanced on him as he went for a knife, kicking it out of his grip before he had it all the way out of a belt sheath.

Meow.

Skeev backed off, cradling his wrist. He glared, reaching for a pistol.

"*Freeze.*" Light flickered in her eyes.

"Ssssomeone lose a cat?" moaned the stunned punk.

The psionic suggestion had such a profound effect on his weak mind that he ceased all motion—even breathing. Onset of a sudden pallor and cold sweat made her worry she'd stopped his heart.

"*Breathe.*"

Kirsten grabbed his shoulder and swept his legs, sending him chest-first to the ground. She swiped a hand at her belt, reaching for binders she didn't have with her. *Crap.* She went for her purse. *Back on the bench, double crap.* The gang punk had a NetMini, though its powder-pink case made her assume it stolen. She relieved him of three handguns, six more knives, and a retractable shock-baton—the cheaper civilian-legal cousin to a police stunrod.

"Bot!" she yelled. "Get over here."

"Not bad," said a voice to her left.

Something about the tone made her whirl. A man leaned on a tree, clad in a dingy pair of coveralls somewhere between orange and tan.

Copious amounts of black grime clung to him. He tapped a clod of dirt from heavy work boots and straightened up before taking a step. His bulk would have been intimidating, if not for the sense of his being a ghost.

Kirsten relaxed. "They're just kids."

The worker spirit laughed. "Kids with guns, knives, and an itch they wanted you to scratch."

She frowned at the stolen NetMini. "I doubt I was their first."

"Yes, officer?" The litter bot zipped over, orbiting about her head in a side-slide.

"Outside the trees by the park edge, there's a woman with two kids. Her name is Nila. Ask her to call for a Division 1 unit to respond to the park right away. When they arrive, lead them here. Tell Nila everything is fine, just some lowlifes."

"What about the littering violation?"

Kirsten sighed, pressing the cold E-90 to her forehead. "To hell with the littering fine, this is actual crime."

"But…" It wobbled. "He tried to hit me."

"Fine, take it up with the Div 1 officers when they get here."

The worker ghost laughed. As the frustrated bot raced off to carry out her request, she dragged the mind-stunned assailant over and flung him to the ground near his friend. Backing off, she kept her weapon trained on them. A pang of curiosity laced with guilt came on. She could poke into their memories to see what befell the owner of the pink NetMini, but hesitated to look. After a moment of pondering, these two idiots did not give her a murderous vibe. Chances are, the girl who owned it was still alive.

She peeked into Skeev's head, and instantly regretted it.

The other one moaned, sliding one hand to his face. "Ugh, what happened? Why am I on the ground?"

Kirsten got their attention with a laser blast in the dirt between them. "Police, Division 0. You two are both under arrest for attempted rape, assault of an officer of the law, and illegal sexual contact with a minor." She tried to keep a straight face. "And for attempted destruction of a municipal service bot."

"What? Minor? That's horseshit. If you're a damn cop, you're old enough!" Skeev seemed ready to cry, his bravado gone.

"I know about what you all did to your associate Blowfish's sister."

Blowfish glared at Skeev.

"I didn't say a fucking word, man, I swear. The bitch was cool with it."

Kirsten narrowed her eyes. "I don't believe you for a hot second. Even if she *did* agree to have sex with your little gang's leader, she's fifteen. I also highly doubt she expected it was going to turn into a group affair. 'Get off me you fucking assholes' doesn't leave much room for doubt. Skeev was stupid enough to try to pull a gun on me. And you!" Kirsten pointed the E-90 at the larger boy. "You just sat in the next room and listened to your own sister scream for help." *Is this what Dorian felt like when he killed those people?* She shivered with rage, but forced herself to calm down. "You're pathetic! By all rights, I should have shot him where he stood. If one of you so much as farts suspiciously, I'll aerate you both."

She was glad they were face down and couldn't see the look on her face. They didn't need to know she would never make good on a threat like that. More than half of being a cop was sounding the part and hoping she could go home without blood on her hands. The ghost did pick up on her true intention and winked. When he sensed his presence no longer unsettled her, he wandered over to stand nearby.

"I was expecting them to choose someone a little… older."

"I'm not a kid," she mumbled, "I'm twenty-two."

The ghost blinked. "You're not a great liar."

"I know, but I'm not lying. I really am twenty-two."

"Huh." He shrugged. "Must be those shoes."

"Yeah, I know I look like I'm still in high school."

"Freshman, barely."

She gave him the finger, making him laugh. "I think these shoes are cute." Indignation passed, she glanced up at him. "Were you hovering by Evan before?"

"Yeah. Just keeping watch on him. Theodore was trying to find you. He thinks you might've missed one of the *other things* and wanted me to make sure nothing tried to hurt your little guy."

"Theodore? You know him?"

Skeev and Blowfish looked at each other, then stared at Kirsten talking to nothing.

"Yep." The sprit held out his pockets as if modeling his clothes. "I used to be in construction."

"Anything you want me to pass along?"

"Nope. I'm good. Faulty retaining strap decided to teach me I couldn't fly. Went about fifty meters from the plate to the real ground. I guess the big man upstairs wanted to make his point loud and clear. After I went splat, the plate slipped its moorings, fell, and landed on me. Biggest piece of my ass left wouldn't fill an espresso cup." Kirsten cringed. "Anyway, I like my family better watching from this side. No one to remind me how much of an asshole I was or give me shit for cheating on the wife." He shrugged. "She was a lot happier with number two, course they've both been gone awhile now. My kids' kids have kids."

"You one of The Kind?"

"Yep. Name's Andrew. By the way, those two are getting ready to run."

Kirsten tensed at the two gangers' subtle shift of weight onto their arms, in preparation to do a push-up. She thought about Dorian's story of legging a boy ready to shoot Nila, and aimed at Skeev's thigh. It felt excessive.

"I'm watching you, Skeev. Prison or crematorium, your choice."

They relaxed.

"Someday, someone will call your bluff." Andrew winked.

"People already have. But they weren't kids." She looked at him. "So, what does Theodore want this time? Didn't he get enough of an eyeful the other week?"

"Actually, he wanted to ask you for help for a change. It wasn't one of The Kind, but a spirit was attacked. Not a great many things attack ghosts."

"Dammit, there *was* another one." She squinted. "Shit. How the hell am I going to find it?"

"Over here, over here." The overt cheer in the patrol bot's digitized voice module drifted closer.

Kirsten unburied her face from her hand and waited. A four-foot-wide orb of cyan hologram emerged from a dim patch of woods, a high-tech will-o-wisp. The litter-bot projected random images around itself to make it easier to follow. Two Division 1 officers in blue armor crunched and snapped past the foliage behind it, arms held up to guard their faces from branches despite their helmets.

"Tell Theodore I'll look into it." She gave Andrew a determined look and approached the two Div 1 cops.

"What happened here?" The shorter one regarded her service weapon with an air of trepidation.

"I was trying to enjoy a day off in the park, but got a feeling someone was spying on my son and his friend. While I was searching for them, these two jumped me thinking I was a kid. I have a feeling I'm not the first."

He smirked. "Guess they like them a little young?"

Kirsten's eyes narrowed. "I'm not as young as I look. The girl who belongs to that pink 'Mini is only fifteen."

"Heh." He grinned. "Never quite sure with Zeroes, I hear they start you guys real young."

"Only if they've got a rare talent that's unusually strong for the age."

Both men stood there in silence.

She sighed, caving under their inquiring stares. "Sixteen."

Officer Burrell gawked at her.

"No, I didn't read your mind. I figured you were about to ask how old I was when I started. Anyway, these two planned to force narcotics on me and then engage in sexual assault. I identified myself as an officer and the suspect went for a weapon."

"The bitch's eyes turned white and lit up! What the fuck would you do?" Skeev howled as the larger cop cuffed him and hauled him to his feet.

Blowfish blinked at the sound of the wind, still woozy from the effects of the Mind Blast.

"Skeev?" Kirsten took a few steps closer, standing with all her weight on her right leg, gun arm lax at her side. "Be a nice young man and tell these officers the *truth* about everything you did. *Tell them about Amy.*"

Kirsten had positioned herself at an angle where only Skeev caught the sudden glimmer in her eye. The boy went into a frantic rambling confession about what the Red Dragons did to a fifteen-year-old, and regaled his participation in at least nine other assaults in the park. She smiled.

Andrew shook his head at her. "Now, now. What would your captain say about that?"

She jogged toward the sound of Evan's approaching voice. "I imagine he'd be happy I didn't kill them."

PORTEND

Ancora Medical occupied the upper forty floors of a gleaming white-paneled tower in the southeastern corner of Sector 1242. From the moment the call came in, Kirsten had been grumbling internally at the memory of the cold that far north. Typical for a Code-3 run like this, she had brought the patrol craft high above the city and accelerated to 375 MPH.

Outside, howling winds and snow swirled around the black hovercar. By the time it reached the ground, it would be rain. Inside, the soft thrum of electronic components underpinned the silence. Kirsten left the autopilot in control for the straightaway and cradled hot coffee to her chest. Enjoying the scent of such divinity felt awkward knowing people's lives depended on her. She sat safe in a warm car while forces beyond most mortal's explanation threatened others. However, she was already on the way and couldn't do anything more than wait for the ride to be over. Despite hurtling toward a dangerous situation, she clung to confidence in addition to the warm mocha.

"At least the damn entity waited for the coffee to be done this time."

Dorian winked. "I thought you'd be happier it didn't wait until dark and leave Evan stuck late at the school dormitory again. You okay? You seem rather pensive."

"I'm thinking about those idiots from the park last weekend."

"Is that why you've been so clingy with Evan for the past few days?

Did you tell Eze you coerced a confession?" Dorian raised a whimsical eyebrow.

"He didn't ask." Slurp. "I would have if he brought it up. I'm still trying to sort out if I feel bad about doing it."

"Well, a few hundred years ago, they would have called it a violation of due process. Sometimes I wonder if it's a good thing. Used to be, a person couldn't go to jail without Miranda."

Kirsten finished another sip and looked over. "Miranda who? Is she a haunt?"

He spoke between gaps in his laughter. "Miranda warnings, the whole criminal rights thing police used to have to read to suspects."

"Oh, back when the criminals had more rights than their victims?" She shook her head.

"Careful, K." He stopped smiling. "It's easy to say that off the cuff, but sometimes the law has the wrong person in their sights. The whole thing was meant to protect the innocent from government oppression." Dorian faced front, his gaze settled on a cargo-trailer-sized shipping bot. The lumbering machine was bedecked with flashing lights that colored the nearby rain red and green. "Now we bask in government oppression and no one notices or cares."

The car compensated for the slow-moving transport, gliding down and left. Kirsten held on to her coffee as the wind knocked them around. The boxy flying robot streaked past the right side, slow to the point of seeming to hang in place.

"I guess. It just… I dunno, I remember reading about it in school and fuming. They treated Mother better in jail than she treated me at home. Her judgment came at the hands of other inmates, not the government. They would have fed her and kept her safe until they let her out. I'd have been better off in jail than living with my own damn mother. How twisted is that?"

"What happens when a Div 1 cop does a half-assed summary execution on the wrong guy?"

"Now you're talking about an entirely different thing." She took over active flight control as the nav point drew close, guiding the patrol craft out of the clouds in a paced descent. "Summaries have a lot of checkboxes to go through. Even when it's warranted, half the time it doesn't happen."

"Good thing, that."

As they dove out of the storm, Dorian smiled at the orange gleam of the mid-afternoon sun on the city a half-mile below. "Officers who do too many of them usually wind up on the wrong end of one sooner or later. They don't like to let that kind of information get out to the public. Bang. Oops, he was an innocent man. Now you're guilty of murder." He kept silent for several minutes as they sank among the towering monoliths of northern West City. "I don't think I could have been able to do it without *knowing* they were guilty."

"You mean without reading their minds?" She looked at him for two seconds. "Isn't that about the same as telling someone to confess truth? It's not like I added more to it or made him lie."

"Div 1 officers don't have the luxury to *know* when a suspect is lying. They perform summaries based on evidence they can see. Only, in those cases, the lawyers don't get involved in time to make a difference."

"I knew he did it. Even with his blurted utterance to the arresting officers, a good enough lawyer can worm out of it."

Dorian chuckled. "Those two don't look like they can afford a lawyer that good."

She bled off speed, reaching the level of the fifth story at a hair over eighty miles per hour. "Weren't lawyers once supposed to just make sure the law is applied fairly, as opposed to looking for any little technicality to let their client get away with crime?"

"You have to be reincarnated. You are way too jaded for your age."

A line of Division 1 cars formed a perimeter in the center of a pentagonal courtyard between five corporate towers. The ground between them and the building lay scattered with bits of plant material and broken terra cotta. Small arms fire emanating from the lobby had destroyed at least six flowerpots large enough to bathe in, as evidenced by shot-out glass along the front.

Kirsten set down behind the row of blue and whites, turning her attention to the screen at the middle of the console. Ancora Medical leased office space from a management company that owned the entire five-building complex. She ran a query in the system for disgruntled employees and reports of violence in the building, which came back suspiciously blank.

"Either this is the one corporation in the world not run by greedy bastards, or someone's been tinkering in the network."

"Yeah," said Dorian. "I wonder which it is."

She grasped the door handle, but froze as bullets bounced off the ground in front of the car. A handful struck the hood and windscreen, but the armor plating reduced it to a dull clatter. Kirsten hit the comm.

"Ops, what the hell is going on in there?"

One of the Division 1 officers put his back to his car so he could face her, and waved. "Afternoon, Agent." His voice came out of her dashboard. Text beneath his hologram indentified him as Sergeant Ormund.

"You the senior onsite?"

"Until you got here, yeah." He chuckled. "Ancora deals with military medical technology, so the building has armed security pods. At first, we thought a hacker got into the local network. We cut all outside GlobeNet access, but it didn't help. Then we figured it was probably an artificial intelligence gone crazy."

"Since you called me in, I'll assume that didn't pan out either?"

Ormund tapped at his forearm unit, which projected small holo-panels containing images of a male humanoid face rendered in mirror silver. "Centurion Investments does not have an AI in their corporate park, however Ancora does. We managed to make contact with him, and he's as clueless as anyone else about what's going on."

"Maybe he's lying?" She kept her fingers on the door handle, staring at a twitching ball turret in the ceiling just beyond a ring of broken window. "AIs can lie, you know."

"It let us walk right in and check. When the disconnect didn't change anything, we brought the link back. Div 2 says the AI's telling the truth. The hardware is moving on its own, not driven by any code they can find. We even killed power to sections of the building and the guns continued to fire." He tapped his foot. "*That's* when we called you."

"What can you tell me about the hostages? Have there been any demands? This doesn't make a lot of sense to me. I've never seen an angry ghost take hostages before. They usually just kill... or try."

"No, ma'am. No demands made to the outside world at this time." Sergeant Ormund ducked as the sporadic spray of bullets gave up on Kirsten's car and played with the Div 1 patrol craft.

Dorian leaned forward to get a better look into the lobby. "Whatever it is evidently doesn't understand armor plating. The weapon is designed for antipersonnel use. It's no threat to the cars."

"Can you knock the turret offline?"

He squinted. "Not if it is connected to the building's power system. I can't shut the entire city off. If a spirit has embodied them, I could try to take control, but then it would come down to how strong the other entity is."

"Ormund, what about those civilians?"

"Uhh… We've got two groups. There are twenty employees on the 92nd floor, looks like mostly senior managers and up. The other group is on the 61st floor, in the daycare. Three adults and nineteen children under eight. Everyone else managed to get out during the chaos."

"Fuck." Kirsten's head fell back against the seat. "Why?"

"How should I know?" said Ormund, before he realized it was a rhetorical 'why.' "Umm, it's not as bad as it sounds, Agent. The designers weren't complete idiots. There are no guns anywhere able to fire *into* the daycare. Problem is… the hallway leading *to* the daycare has six of 'em. The kids are in no danger, but no one short of a full Class 4 borg is getting in there alive."

The rotary gun on the turret harassing the police cars out front kept spinning, but ceased firing.

"Out of ammo? Small favors," she mumbled. "Well this is a right mess. Alright, I'm going in."

She ran from the safety of her car to Ormund's side, behind the wall of Div 1 vehicles. Without the intermediary of a digital pass-through windshield, a spectral glow became visible around the turret. When she stood up to run, the sergeant put a hand on her shoulder.

"Agent, I'm sure you know some of my guys aren't too keen on that psio stuff, but if you need us inside, say the word. We'll be there. Might freak us out a bit, but you're still a cop."

Three women and seven men in blue armor nodded at her.

Kirsten squeezed his hand. "Thanks."

The spirit light left the mounted weapon and it hung limp, spent. She bolted across the remainder of the courtyard, taking cover behind a column a few yards shy of the main door, and peering around. Beyond the still-intact sliding glass doors, an expanse of white tile and false plants waited. The space appeared empty of people save for a young woman seated behind a reception desk.

She wore a clingy top the same shade of black as her hair, silver buttons running from her shoulder to hip on the right side. The tall neck of the garment split open at the front in a Chinese-inspired collar, and she smiled at thin air as if nothing strange was going on. The lack of surface thoughts confirmed Kirsten's suspicion.

Dorian wandered through the unopened door. "That's either a doll or the world's most unobservant person."

Kirsten edged out from behind cover, staring at the turret. It tried to spin toward her, but she latched onto the paranormal energy within and held it to the side as she darted into the open, heading for the main doors. They slid closed behind her with a soft hiss. Fortunately, the courtyard turret couldn't rotate around to face into the lobby. Holographic birds flitted around the false plants, at least half of which were also made of light. The air smelled crisp and cool, with a hint of cleaning solution. A handful of squat ten-inch black domes scurried out of sight across immaculate white tiles, digital cleaning-roaches fleeing the light—or in this case, the vision of a guest.

"Welcome to Centurion Investment Corporation Tower II." The woman faced Kirsten. "Which company or individual are you here to see?"

"Ancora Medical," said Kirsten, heading for the elevator bank past a row of plush waiting-room couches.

"Are you sure about that?" Dorian jogged ahead of her. "If a spirit is messing with electronics, do you trust the elevator?"

"Aww." She slowed to a slouching stagger while staring at the ceiling. "Why is it always sixty plus stories?"

Dorian phased through the door to the stairwell. "Saves you having to pay for membership at a fitness club."

"I'm sorry, miss. Ancora Medical is currently closed," said the reception doll. "If you would like to schedule an appointment with either, sales, human resources, or legal, please leave your information at the front desk. If you are in need of patient services, please be aware that this is a corporate facility with no medical care provided."

"The department has a fitness center I can use for free." Kirsten hit the door with both hands, shoving it open hard enough to bounce it off the wall.

Metal slamming echoed up an undecorated vertical shaft never meant for the eyes of investors, customers, or upper management. She hesitated at the prospect of such a haul, but liked the idea of a falling elevator less. The brisk journey came to a sweaty end at the landing of the 61st floor, where a tiny display screen showed the logo of Ancora Medical, a dove hinted at by a few curved lines.

"Planning to play chicken with six turrets at once?" asked Dorian.

"Don't give me that look," she rasped. "I can barely breathe."

"Now there's one thing I *don't* miss… getting winded."

Kirsten forced a weak smile and pulled herself standing once again. She fell into the door, hanging on to the push bar to keep from falling over.

"I'm not sure what sucks more, this or jumping off a building."

"Falling sixty stories inside an elevator, I think, would be worse than either."

"You have such a way with words, Dorian."

A few paces inside the corridor, she found a vendomat offering drinks and couldn't resist. Half a bottle of spring water went down before the conscious parts of her brain were involved in any decision-making processes. She finished it off, and rolled to lean against the wonderful machine. She stared down at her shaking legs, and found them amusing.

"Kirsten, look out," Dorian yelled, lunging.

She ducked and spun, yelping at the sight of a softball-sized orb bot zooming at her with a pair of sparking prongs extended from its leading side. Kirsten managed to get her hands around it before it made contact. The cold metal object strained to get closer, its hover inducer pushing it toward her chest with enough force to pin her to the wall.

For several seconds, she held it at bay while staring at the electrified spikes. Dorian stuck his hand into it, and a spark shot up inside his arm to his shoulder. The sudden shutdown left her struggle unopposed, and she flung it away. It careened off the wall and thudded to the ground with the acoustic grandeur of a dropped cannonball.

"Where the hell did that thing come from?"

Dorian pointed down the hallway. "Automated non-lethal internal security."

She drew her E-90, but thought better of it and switched to the stunrod, holding it like a bat. Another orb zipped around the next corner and swerved at her. Stun prongs popped out of it as it careened toward her abdomen. Kirsten leapt to the side and swung. A dull *clank* reverberated down the hall as plastisteel stunrod met ten-pound orb bot, diverting its flight into the side of the vendomat. Blew sparks surrounded it and a small speaker emitted a robotic version of an agonized scream. Two seconds later, a cloud of thick black smoke puffed out of its hover port along with and a loud report comparable to a gunshot.

Kirsten hadn't moved since the instant her stunrod made contact. She jumped at the loud *bang* and let the stunrod slip out of her grasp. It landed tip-first into the ground and set off a brief flash of blue before it fell flat. "Ow." She gasped, clenching her hands into fists. "Oh, damn. Okay, swinging a metal stunrod at a metal orb was a bad idea. I can't feel my fingers."

"I would have shot it, personally."

"You're a better shot. It's not easy to tag those little things."

Dorian waved dismissively. "The stun only lasts a few seconds, just catch them."

Her eyes narrowed to slits. "Why don't you take them out of the air?"

"Duck," he said, reaching to his right.

At the sight of a shimmer of energy drifting into his hand, she leapt to the side. Orb bot number three, now an inert ball of metal, cruised through the space where she'd been standing.

From around the corner, a woman's voice screamed, "This is pointless!"

A gunshot silenced the din that erupted in the wake of the shout. Kirsten sprinted to a holographic banner bearing the placard: 'Executive Conference Room 3.' She peeked in a gap in the door, observing a number of well-dressed people sitting around an expensive looking onyx table. All eyes fell upon a dark skinned woman in a plum-colored dress.

The woman clutched a huge orange rubber ball to her chest, as if hiding behind it would shield her from another gunshot. A turret in the ceiling trained a single-barrel weapon at her.

A digitized machine-voice yelled, "Write!"

Her shaking hand uncapped a permanent marker, and the squeak of felt upon rubber broke the quiet.

"You may as well join them," said a voice, a mix of static and man. "Come on in. Don't think I won't unload on these simpletons if you raise that weapon."

Kirsten gave Dorian a meaningful look before she nudged the door open and slipped into the room, keeping her E-90 pointed down. Various executives stared up with the expected combination of confusion and pleading. A spirit stood waist-deep in the center of the immense conference table, his right hand embedded in a small terminal used to control audio-visual presentations. Late twenties or early thirties, he appeared dressed for an outdoor excursion, complete with backpack and the kind of ridiculous hat full of fishing lures a tourist would buy. A few inches above where his body intersected the table surface, it became transparent. The man showed no sense of recognition at the sight of her.

The woman holding the ball finished writing and passed it to her left. The spirit pointed at the sweating heavyset man holding the ball with his left hand, and the turret mirrored the gesture. Spectral lips moved, but the voice came from speakers in the ceiling.

"Your turn, Doug. Write."

Kirsten stared at the thin ghost, making no secret that she could see him. "What the hell are you doing?"

"Team building exercise!" he shrieked, using the shrill war cry of an enraged techie. "They have to write something good about the person on their right and then pass the ball to the person on their left." The spirit went wide-eyed manic. "It's good for morale! We're all one big happy team here, right?"

When no one said a word, the ceiling turret put a bullet into the wall.

"Right," cheered the room, in a nervous drone.

"Once the ball makes it around the room, and everyone's had a chance to say something positive, we're going to break into groups of five and do team charades. Just to keep things upbeat, one member of the losing team is going to get shot in the backside." The ghost cackled. "Good news though, the new benefits program you just signed on for covers superficial damage to the ass."

"What the *hell* is going on?" asked an older black man in a grey suit, hissing the question past clenched teeth.

"That particular wank-stick is Joseph Xavier Freeh," said the spirit while smiling at Kirsten. "CEO of Ancora Medical. Personally, I'm hoping his team loses at charades."

Kirsten set the E-90 back in its holster and held her hands up in a disarming gesture. "Calm down. Clearly, you have some kind of problem with Ancora. I checked their records and couldn't find any issues with former employees. Tell me what happened and I can help you."

"What happened is that someone has hacked into our network. Why the hell haven't the police done something?" Mr. Freeh glared at Kirsten.

"It's not a hacker, sir. It's a ghost. Does anyone here recognize a white, light-skinned possibly Hispanic man in his middle-to-late thirties with short brown hair. Little on the nerdy side, big nose, dressed like he's going to go fishing. He's got a whole bunch of weird little things stuck to his hat."

Two of the executive board gasped. The ball turret swiveled at Kirsten, the ghost's face flashed to abject rage. Kirsten summoned a wave of psionic energy, projecting it into the spirit and knocking him out of the table. Sparks flew from the AV terminal as it died, and the ball turret went limp. His fury whirled into a chaotic tangle of panic, though he managed only to scream "What the—" before Dorian came out of the wall from behind and tackled him.

As the ceiling gun whirled around in a circle, beeped, and folded back into its recess, Kirsten waved at the door. "Everyone, out." She leaned into the wall to avoid getting trampled. "Ormund, this is Agent Wren. It's safe to come in. Please clear the daycare."

"Copy," said the voice in her ear.

"Any fatalities?"

"No, ma'am."

Dorian manhandled the other spirit with ease, wrestling him to the ground and putting one knee in his back. "Okay, buddy. What happened?"

"Wha? You can see me?" he screamed.

"I've only been staring right at you for the past few minutes. Are you that dense?"

"This one isn't too old." Dorian smirked at her. "I wouldn't lash him; you'll destroy him in one pass."

"Destroy? What the hell are you talking about? I'm already dead."

Kirsten pulled a chair away from the table and fell into it. "Look, you're a ghost. That's true. I get the feeling you have some kind of issue with this company. Unfortunately, I can't allow you to hurt the living."

"I'm surprised she hasn't ended you already," said Dorian, forcing the man to look up at her. "She's real sensitive about kids, you know. There's a whole daycare full of them downstairs put at risk because of you."

"Dave... Dave Alvarez. I used to work for Ancora as a systems administrator."

"Did they have you killed for some reason?" Kirsten cocked an eyebrow. "Last I checked, sys admins are pretty replaceable. What did you steal?"

"Nothing. Ouch! Dammit! Let go." He wriggled in a futile attempt to get away from Dorian for a few seconds. "They didn't *have* me killed, it was a stupid team-building exercise. They made us go camping out in the Badlands. They said it would be safe. This giant, fucking werewolf-from-hell with metal claws shredded me." He flailed. "And a half-dozen of our security team."

"Did they force you to go out there?" asked Kirsten.

Dave scowled. "You have no idea what it's like. If you wanna get promoted you have to do everything. All these stupid little fluff meetings, holiday parties, special morale events." He rolled his eyes at the wall. "They think it brings us"—his voice lapsed sarcastic—"closer as a team and enables us to reach new plateaus of productivity in the next quarter."

"So you were going to team-build them to death?" asked Dorian, trying to suppress the urge to laugh.

"I dunno…" The fight left him. "I just wanted someone to see how stupid it was. I died for no reason other than where some stupid executive's dart landed on the list of lame shit to do. You know they made us use our vacation time for it too, right? Yeah, I could have backed out, but they *notice* these things. People who back out don't get promoted. People who back out stay low level admins for years." Dave deflated and let his face fall to the ground. "Of course, Walter is still alive."

"You're frustrated, I get that. Killing people won't help. Believe it or not, it'll just make it worse for you. Do you have any family left I can talk to for you?"

"Three daughters and a wife. They're scraping by. My eldest, Liz, can't get a job at her age, fifteen, due to all the damn dolls taking low-skilled work. They can't afford to move to a colony."

"I'll make you a deal, Dave." She waved at Dorian to let him up. "I'll take all the information you can give me about the camping trip and send it over to an investigative team that looks into corporate misbehavior. Ancora may not want to endure the stink of an Inquest. For your part, you leave these people alone. I'm willing to trust you, since I'm sure you care about your family."

"Yeah," said Dave, standing and dusting himself off. No longer sharing space with a solid table, he resumed a lifelike appearance to her. "I only wanted them to acknowledge they were careless. I don't think they'll cave in though. They made us all sign waivers before we went out there."

"The detectives will look into the deaths of the other security staff as well. If they coerced you to go out there and then forced you to sign off on liability, a judiciary panel will have a field day with it."

"I don't imagine Mr. Freeh would want to see it on the NewsNet," said Dorian.

Kirsten grinned. "Good idea. That'll probably be more effective than the threat of legal tangles."

AMID THE BUSTLE OF EMERGENCY CREWS TENDING TO THE WOUNDED, Kirsten found Joseph Freeh surrounded by a trio of assistants. He bellowed at one girl who seemed younger than Kirsten as if the 'network breach' was her fault. She took notes on a datapad in preparation for a torturous system review he intended to drop upon their engineers.

"Mr. Freeh, a moment?" Kirsten walked up to him.

"More police nonsense? It damn well took you people long enough." He shooed his assistants off to the side. "Caramel latte, extra shot."

"A coffee man, I can respect that." She put on an earnest face. "Mr. Freeh, about what just happened here. One of your company's employees is lingering after death as a ghost. He was killed by some marauding genetic disaster while attending a corporate team-building event. Camping in the Badlands?" She blinked.

"Last year. It was McNamara's idea if I remember correctly. The man's a survivalist. He intended it purely for the adventurous crowd. The employee had every chance not to go. He knew the risks."

"Dave puts it in an entirely different light. Corporate culture twisted his arm. He was afraid he'd be passed over for promotions if he didn't attend. On top of that, the company forced him to sign a waiver of liability on a dangerous, foolish trip he had no choice but to participate in if he didn't want to sabotage his career. Dealing with ghosts is a touchy subject, Mr. Freeh. It's not like I can haul him off to jail or hit him with a fine. I can either destroy him or find a resolution to whatever issue is keeping him from moving on to the next world. Given the circumstances here, most especially because he didn't kill anyone, I'm inclined to give him what he needs in order to move on."

"And what would that be?" Mr. Freeh frowned.

"Nothing grandiose, he's merely worried about his family."

"Touching." Freeh looked to his left. "Where is my coffee? Good Lord, man, it's been almost three minutes."

"The way I see it, the company is at least fifty percent complicit in his death, as well as the deaths of six or seven security personnel. I'm well aware Ancora strives to maintain a reputation as a squeaky-clean corporation that cares. I'm sure the NewsNet will devour a story about a fatal compulsory camping trip."

The CEO reeled as if slapped. "You're dangerously close to libel, Miss" —he peered at her chest—"Wren."

"Oh, I'm not going to talk to the press. I'm not permitted to discuss specific cases with them. However, I will be filing a request with CIB, that's Corporate Investigations Bureau by the way, to begin an Inquest regarding the deaths that occurred on that trip. Those investigations are a matter of public record and any reporter digging for dirt on corporations, especially corporations that appear to have no dirt, might—"

"Alright." He held his hand up. "What is it you want?"

"I was thinking you provide one and a half times Mr. Alvarez's salary to his wife until the day his youngest daughter turns eighteen or until his wife obtains employment sufficient to provide for her family without needing a stipend. Do that, and I might lose my report to CIB." She started to walk away, but paused. "Oh, by the way, I'd recommend against any more camping trips out there… or at least make it genuinely optional."

Freeh's rapid mental math evidently factored her request far less costly than a potential media scandal. "Done."

"What now?" asked Dave.

Kirsten shook hands with Freeh and walked back to her car. "Go home, be with them. When the stipend starts, you might feel a release from this world. Trust the light."

"Thank you." He tried to hold her hand.

She made herself solid to spirits and let him. "Behave yourself. Don't make me regret being a softie."

"I won't. Thank you!" David floated off.

"Damn shame," said a Division 1 officer near the row of cars. "Waste of such a pretty girl."

Kirsten whirled, her building snarl fading when she realized they weren't talking about her being psionic.

"Yeah." His partner let out a long, slow sigh with a weak shake of his head. "Who the hell does a thing like that?"

"What happened?" she asked, moving closer.

They looked up.

"Squad mate just found a dead woman a few sectors south. We were listening to the comm. chatter go by." He held up his forearm guard, projecting an image of an alley filled with crime scene techs and patrol officers. A nude body lay half under a police blanket. The victim appeared to be in her mid-twenties.

Kirsten cringed. "She doesn't look like a prostitute. Too healthy. Well, except for being dead. Any weird stuff going on?"

"Nothing anyone reported. We'll call you if something happens."

"Great, thanks."

———

KIRSTEN WALKED INTO THE SQUAD ROOM, NOTICING CAPTAIN EZE'S OFFICE unusually dim. She knocked at the door, earning a wave-in once he saw her.

"That took longer than expected." He smiled, nodding at the couch where Evan slept.

"Sorry, there were so many witnesses to interview. Their tech people grilled me like a slab of salmon. Thanks for watching him."

"You are most welcome. He was no trouble at all, though he's been trying to talk to you in his sleep."

Kirsten smiled. "He's one of a kind, though I'm sure he'll have a bratty moment eventually."

She tossed his backpack over one shoulder before scooping him up. He whined in his sleep, cuddling into her at the disturbance of being moved.

"You don't have to wake up." She kissed him on the forehead.

"Mom?" He mumbled, somewhere between asleep and not. "You need to break Konstantin's heart."

She blinked, staring at him for a moment. The statement, mean as it sounded, came with no malice in his voice or on his cherubic face. Kirsten shot Eze a look of bewilderment. Evan's hint of consciousness faded as fast as it manifested, leaving him deep asleep once more.

"He's probably feeling jealous." Eze winked. "Talk it over with him when he wakes up. Heck, the kind of money that man has... I'm almost jealous."

She chuckled and cradled Evan close enough to whisper into his ear. "I don't care how rich he is, kiddo. You are the most important person in my life."

A trace of a smile curled his lip.

MONWYN THE SMALL

Amid the din of a hundred and change sugared-up children, Evan all but dragged Shani by the arm. In his left hand, a flashing plastic box attempted to make the sound of a thunderstorm. The miniature cacophony drowned in the abject chaos of Sector D, originally a chain of kid-tainment places known as Funzones until they got bought out. Evan, being nine, ducked around the crowd, taking advantage of any spaces or gaps.

Be careful!

He spun as Kirsten's voice entered his mind. She'd fallen behind a few paces in the crowd, alarmed at his sudden departure from the table.

My turn's up. He waved the flashing box.

The two kids squeezed between bored adults watching a hopelessly uncoordinated boy fail at a gripper claw game. Evan approached an attendant manning the Monwyn the Magnificent sim and stood on tiptoe to hand back the flashing pager. He looked over his shoulder, bouncing, waiting for Kirsten to catch up. Catching sight of the miserable older boy, Evan nudged Shani and pointed.

She gave him a confused look for a second, and grinned. As soon as the boy turned away in defeat, the toy cyborg figure he had been going for flipped out of the pile, seemingly of its own volition, and fell into the exit chute. At the sound of the *thunk*, the boy whirled to find the toy in arm's reach, and cheered.

"Okay, kid. You got a half hour," said the attendant.

Evan looked up at the high school-aged kid in an ill-fitting uniform, and smirked. He wanted to protest the meager time ration, but it would only waste what he had. "Okay."

"You know how to work the—?"

"Duh." Evan raced past the operator's station to a cluster of four pods.

Only one was empty. Inside, two bench seats faced each other, with a pair of wire-laden helmets hanging above them. Evan took one and sat where it had been. Shani followed, sitting next to him. She frowned at the giant helmet before giving him an unenthused look.

"Never used a full-immersion senshelmet before?"

"No." Shani put it on. "Just the one at home."

"This is different than just watching." Evan leaned over and slid the apparatus down over her head. "It talks to your brain. It's like we're really there."

"Is it gonna hurt?"

"I fell out of a chair once," he said, donning a helmet. "It was pretty cool. Just close your eyes and let it sync."

Evan settled into the uncomfortable plastic seat, letting the weight of the senshelmet drag his head against the pad behind it. A tingle of energy spread over his mind and a digitized female voice said, "synchronizing."

He closed his eyes and tried to relax, allowing the electronics to override his physical senses. The instant he felt as though he stood barefoot on stone floor despite wearing sneakers, he opened his eyes. The sight disoriented him as he appeared not to have a body at all, floating at the center of a ring of figures from the Monwyn movies. Faint theme music played in the background. Without a second's hesitation, he pointed at the man himself. As soon as the subsequent flare of brightness faded, Evan found himself on a dirt path deep within the mythical forest of Cymril. The thick blue robes, black boots, and fiery staff of Monwyn the Magnificent replaced his ordinary clothes.

Monwyn the Small, as he hadn't grown any larger than Evan normally was, tapped his foot. Within a minute, a flare of radiance glimmered in at his side. Shani, now in the garb of Asara the Huntress, faded in. She leaned forward to appraise the leather skirt, knee-high sandals, and longbow in her left hand. The girl spent a minute making odd faces while feeling at her pointed ears.

"This sucks." She tried to swing her longbow like a bat. "You get a flaming dragon-staff and I get a twig?"

"Really? You don't know what a bow is?"

"It doesn't have a string," she said, adopting an exasperated stance with the bow draped over her hand.

"Asara has a magic bow. When you go to shoot something, it makes arrows out of magic."

She held it as if to fire and, sure enough, an arrow appeared.

"Wow, this is scary. It's so real." Shani spun in place, holding her hand out in the breeze. "If we get hurt, does it hurt?"

He shook his head. "Monwyn feels no pain. The fangs of darkness shall not dissuade him from—"

She glared at him with her eyebrows mashed together. "Seriously?"

"It tingles a little so you know you got hit, and you'll see numbers that tell you how much damage you took, but it doesn't hurt."

Evan started down the road with Shani wandering after him. She gazed around in awe at the forest and bizarre fuzzy animals and birds. Her gawking slowed her to a creep. Evan stopped every so often to let her catch up. Not quite ten minutes later, a loud twig snap came from the foliage.

"What was that?" Shani ran up to him. "Did you hear that?"

"Random encou"—he coughed—"The foul beasts that taint this forest with their unclean presence seek to stop our quest!"

Shani gave him another unimpressed look. Two creatures shambled out of the trees, both about six feet tall and covered in black fur. Their faces mixed canine and ape, with glowing yellow eyes and sharpened fangs. Elongated arms carried a pair of wicked-looking blades spattered with old, dried blood. The beast-men leaned forward, roaring at them.

She screamed.

Evan broke character. "Hey, relax... It's a video game."

Her terrified look lingered for another second before she glared.

"We can stop if you want. Maybe you're too little for this game."

Her cheeks reddened. "No, it's okay."

Shani swiped her hand at the air behind the bow, groping for a nonexistent string. When she released it, a glimmering magic arrow flew into the chest of the creature on the right. Above its head, the number 44 appeared, large and red.

"Nice critical!" cheered Evan.

The creature she shot ran at her while the other went for him. Evan chanted, holding the staff sideways with both hands. Lightning crackled off the end, lapping at the one going for Shani. A waterfall of small blue numbers sprinkled into the air ranging from eleven through eighteen. The damage fell short of killing it before it came close enough to swing. She cringed, screaming with closed eyes.

It swung its blade through her body, without much visible effect. Shani stopped screaming and looked up at a yellow 22 hanging over her. Below the number, a stripe of color showed about nine inches of green and one red.

"That tingled," said Shani.

"Asara's tough. You have more hit points than I do."

The other creature charged at Evan, knocking him over backward with a wild upswing. The critical hit knocked sent him sliding several feet with his boots in the air. His health bar appeared and shrank down to a sliver of green at the end. Shani blinked at the red 67. The digital 'bruised and battered' effect added to Evan's face was comic enough to keep it from being scary.

The creature in front of Shani/Asara attacked again, but she leapt away, firing at it twice. Her expression conveyed anything but confidence, and she emitted a startled yelp at how high and far she flew from a jump.

"She's an elf!" yelled Evan. "Super fast and agile."

Both shots stuck in its chest, 28 and 31. The monster collapsed and disintegrated into a small purple gem. She aimed at the second beast-man threatening Evan, but before she could fire, it slid away from him, shoved by an unseen force. Monwyn the Small struggled to his feet and planted the staff in the ground before him. He chanted something about Pyrden, Lord of Flames, having a near-tantrum as he howled. Red lightning came from above and hit the staff, making his hair stand up. Seconds later, a three-foot-wide sphere of flaming magma fell from the sky and drilled the furry beast-man into a crater. The ground shook hard enough to make Shani stumble. The number 222 hung in midair amid the smoke cloud.

A blue line appeared above Evan's head, rapidly shrinking away from eight inches to only a half of one. He fell on his butt, rummaging around his belt for a water flask.

"222 damage? How did you do so much? Are you cheating?"

He held up a finger, chugging from the flask like a famished infant on a bottle. The blue line crept toward full. Shani stared at it, folding her arms.

"How does drinking water give you magic back? Water's not magic. That's the silliest thing I've ever seen!"

Evan gasped for air, re-corking the bottle. "I dunno, it just does. You know what's real lame?"

"Getting magic back for drinking water?"

"Heh. Nope. If I jump in a lake or river and drink that, it doesn't work. I have to drink water out of bottles to get mana back."

"Wow, yeah that is stupid." She pointed at the crater where a smoking black-furred arm jutted out of it as if to ask what the hell just happened. "What did you do?"

"Meteor Doom," he said. "I've played Monwyn games so much I remember the words to the spells, even though in this game right now, I'm not high 'nuff level to have it yet. That's why it ate my whole mana bar."

"What's mana?"

"The blue line, magic power."

"Oh."

"If you want to stop, we can stop." He stood and dusted himself off. "This game is so realistic it might give you bad dreams since you're so little."

"I'm not too small. I'm *seven*," she said in a huff. "Besides, I have more hit points than you!" Shani pivoted on her sandaled heel and stormed off down the road.

By the time they reached the Caverns of Woe, Shani had gotten the hang of using her bow, and had even figured out how to call Asara's spirit wolf companion. They came to a halt in the shadow of a foreboding grey wall covered in gargoyles. At the center, a stone door bore carvings of skeletons and ghouls. He peeked at Shani to make sure the images didn't bother her too much, and grinned at her attempt to ignore it. Evan plodded up to the door and set his staff into the ground.

"Spirit of Earth, I call on you." Evan flung his arms at the gate. "Kel'Gurin, Lord of Stone, hear me."

The entire wall rocked as though struck with great force, sending a curtain of dust sliding to the earth and dozens of ravens into the sky. The ground trembled, Evan grunted, and the door slammed open. He led the way down thirty yards of moss-covered tunnel that ended at a long stone staircase. At the bottom, the cave opened into another forest. Unlike the last, the trees here seemed warped and twisted, their bark gnarled into the likeness of wailing souls.

"How does a cave going downhill lead to more outside?" Shani frowned. "This is silly."

"We're not at the Cavern of Woe yet, we only went through a zone transition."

A pack of road-weary bandits emerged from the shadows, daggers at the ready. The look of desperate greed on their faces faded away to terror as the four-foot tall wizard readied the Staff of Dragons.

"Crimony, that's Monwyn..." gasped one, before screaming and running away.

They both laughed at the sight of a dozen grown men fleeing in panic at the 'intimidating' nine-year-old in a robe.

EVAN SAT IN BLACK STILLNESS, A LOW WHINE BUILDING OUT OF THE SILENCE until his voice echoed within the inert helmet. "Aww, we weren't done yet."

"Half hour's up kiddo. I can put you back in the queue."

"I don't think we'll be here long enough for that. Let some other kids have a turn," said Kirsten.

He reached up and pulled the helmet off. Fresh blew cold across his sweat-dampened hair. Shani had already shed hers, and leaned into the pod from outside.

"It felt like two hours," she whispered, rubbing her legs. "I'm tired."

Kirsten picked her up. "Time is different in the net, sweetie. You've actually been in there for about forty minutes. They gave you a little extra time."

"Do we haveta go yet?" Evan poured himself out of the pod, muscles weary from sitting still so long, and reluctant to relinquish his favorite game,.

"It's only noon. We can stay another hour." She winked. "But, you do have to eat lunch now. You worked up quite a sweat in there." Kirsten gave the attendant a worried glance. "You should play some games where you're not sitting still. It's not good for you."

The teen in the Sector D shirt waved her off. "It's fine, he just gets into it. Best score I've seen in a long time. The body doesn't realize the muscles aren't working. That's one of the reasons we limit players to a half hour."

Evan followed her back to the table and took a seat by a waiting plate of chicken bits and fries. Shani leaned on Kirsten's side, as interested in sleep as she was in her food.

The boy attacked his meal, eager in his recounting of his adventures as

Monwyn. "The game has an AI running it, so it knows when you say the spells right."

Kirsten nodded, as if she knew what he meant.

"The home version isn't as powerful. You gotta find spellbooks before you can use each spell."

"Is that so?" she said, smiling. "Guess they had to come up with some reason to come play this one instead of staying at home."

"There's a GlobeNet client, but it needs a plug to play."

Kirsten shivered. "Helmets won't work?"

"It's ranked. Like there's competitions and real money prizes." He paused to slurp down some iced tea. "Past level fifty, it's too hard. Helmets are too slow. Can I play Orbs after lunch?" He stood on his chair to point at a booth.

"Shani wanted to play that car game next." Kirsten glanced down at the sleeping child in her lap. "But, she's napping. When she wakes up, you should play what she wants to play."

"'Kay."

A few minutes later when he finished eating, he jumped off the chair and ran over to the Orbs game, joining a row of other kids lined up in stalls facing a large, dark, cube-shaped area filled with blacklight. Neon-hued orb bots of various sizes and speeds darted about, targets for a toy laser pistol. Based on a combination of accuracy, how long it took a player to hit targets, and the size of the ones hit, an alien-invasion holovid playing in the background changed outcome. One could either save the world, or watch it burn.

He spent a moment chasing a tiny green ball that zipped about at great speed; his target fixation allowed too many slow ones by, imperiling the virtual humanity behind the target field. When he realized he had missed enough to doom the city, he tried to hit as many basketball-sized creepers as he could in as little time as possible.

Alas, MegaCity burned.

Her eached for the restart button but froze when Sleepy Shani stumbled out of the crowd. With a shrug, he tossed the toy pistol back into its holder and walked over to her. "Cloud Cars are on the other side." He took her hand.

"Okay." She wiped her eyes, and yawned.

Evan decided to avoid the bulk of the crowd by following the outer wall. Rather than squeeze past lines waiting for the various amusements, game stations, or vending booths, he followed a carpeted path along rows of largely ignored vendomats. Older teens lurked there, clustered in groups. Some kissed, some groped each other, and several gave him territorial glares. He got the distinct impression the back-end of Sector D wasn't for little kids. He wondered if the guy in the giant mouse costume out front knew what went on back here.

At the midpoint of the room, shouting echoed from a connecting hallway that linked the amusement place to the mall. Evan slowed, curiosity drawing him toward it. Shani set her heels in the rug, pulling against his arm.

"No, don't," she whispered, "not without your mom."

She cringed when the voice shouted again.

"How many times you think you can pull this shit? Huh?"

"Come on, Zee, you know I'm good for it. I just gotta work some stuff out," said a voice trying at the same time to be quiet, yet still loud enough to be heard over the crowd.

Evan let go of Shani's wrist so he could get closer. He peered around the corner, but she grabbed his other arm and pulled. One man in a black jacket with spiked red hair had another man, skinny to the point his bones showed through clothing, pinned to the wall between the bathroom doors. People wandered past them, going from the mall concourse to Sector D or the other way around.

"You said that last week, you little shitbag." Zee punched the thin man in the gut. "You owe me two grand already and I don't think you're gonna get it. You're so damn strung out you can't even stay on your fuckin' feet without a wall to lean on."

"Evan, get your mom." Shani tried to pull him away from the corridor, but he held fast.

Zee pulled a gun, stuffing it under the other man's chin. "I oughta just get this over with, right here."

"Zack, please..." the man whined.

"Yeah, too many eyes here." Zee backhand-pistol-whipped the druggie, knocking him to all fours. "Get the fuck outside."

"Leave him alone." Evan took a step, raising his voice.

Zee ignored him.

"I said, leave him alone."

Shani whirled back and forth, unsure if she should stay there or run shouting for Kirsten.

Zack blinked at Evan with an incredulous expression. He scoffed. "Fuck off, kid."

"You don't have to kill him," said Evan.

Evan, no. You don't have magic in the real world. He's gonna kill you! Shani screamed into his mind.

The boy stared up at Zee. Shani ran to his side, trying to drag him back into Sector D. The gang punk pointed his gun at Evan while the skinny guy coughed up blood and puked on the floor.

"Only sayin' this once, cowlick. You—"

Shani wrenched the gun away from him with a telekinetic yank severe enough to break his trigger finger. The weapon slapped her in the chest with a hollow *thud*, and she clamped on to it.

"What the fuck…" Zee didn't seem to notice his twisted finger. "Little fuckin rugrat wants to die, don't you?" He pulled a knife from the back of his belt and stomped toward them.

Shani shoved the gun at Evan, somewhere between not wanting to touch it and giving it to him. He fumbled it into a firing position with both hands.

"Freeze, scumbag."

At Evan's yell, people finally noticed what was going on.

The high-pitched electronic chirp of the firing circuit arming caused Zee to stop. For several seconds, Evan's adrenaline kept his hand steady. When the tip of the gun wobbled, Zee grinned and took another step.

"That's my gun you got, kid. Let's have it."

"Don't get any closer, I mean it." Evan took a step back.

"You ain't gonna shoot nobody. You're shakin' like a scared little brat." Zee took another step. "Even if you fire that thing, you're gonna miss. You don't give it to me now, I'm gonna break your neck."

"Evan? Shani? Where are you?" Kirsten's shouting pierced the panic in the crowd behind him.

"Here!" screamed Shani.

"My mom won't miss. She's a cop."

Zee's gaze went right to the silver E-90 in the hand of the blonde forcing her way past the fleeing people, the one person trying to move *closer* to a kid with a gun. The sound of Kirsten's voice eased Evan's trembles, and he found some of Monwyn's confidence again.

"On the ground, now. Hands behind your head." Evan used the gun to point at the floor.

After a glance over the boy's head, Zee took off running in the direction of the mall. He shoved a teenaged girl face-first into a water fountain and knocked an elderly couple to the ground.

Evan sighed, letting his arms fall slack. "I'm not shooting him in the back."

At that instant, Zee's jacket flipped up and his head. He twisted, losing balance, and careened into a wall of rental lockers ten feet shy of the mall concourse. Shani grunted, pulling one hand at the air. Zee's pants dropped about his ankles, tripping him to the ground. The little girl kept her focus on him, holding the cloth in place around the squirming thug.

Evan laughed, pointing. "He's got Space Ranger boxers!"

Kirsten skidded to a halt by the kids, swiping the gun away from Evan. "What the hell are you doing?"

"He was gonna kill that guy." Evan pointed at the whimpering semiconscious man lying in a puddle of vomit and blood.

"Drop it, lady!" shouted a voice from behind. "Hands in the air, kid. You're under arrest. Smith, Protocol 2 the little girl."

Shani continued focusing on Zee, keeping him bound in his clothes. Evan gasped and clung to Kirsten's side. Kirsten glanced over her shoulder with an 'are you kidding me?' face. Two men in the white and grey uniforms of Bakersfield Mall Security edged up behind them, pistol-shaped electro-stunners at the ready. Both had the wild eyed intensity and super-macho stance of washouts who thought themselves recent graduates of Assault Infantry boot camp.

"Agent Kirsten Wren, National Police Force, Division 0. Stand down. What the hell is protocol 2?"

"Rapid removal of an innocent bystander to a position of tactical safety. Please drop your weapon. Don't make me escalate posture. This area is under the watch of BMS, you're in our jurisdiction here. We are authorized to use stunners if we have to."

"She's a cop, numbnuts," grumbled Evan. "Notice she's got a laser pistol."

The one on the left, Smith, trained his stunner on Evan. He twitched when the boy pointed at Kirsten's gun. The look in his eyes made him seem concerned at what a small boy would do to him. Either that, or he desperately wanted to shoot *someone*.

"Is there something wrong with your ears, or are you just plain stupid? I told you I'm a police officer." Kirsten sent a dire look at Smith. "Put that stunner down right now. If you shoot my son with that thing, I'll cram it up your ass and hold the trigger down until the battery's dead."

Evan covered his mouth and gasped.

Smith squirmed at the thought.

"Who the hell do you think you are?" Kirsten glared.

"Sergeant Lloyd Benning, 1st Brigade, Bakersfield Mall Tactical Response Squad."

She sighed at the ceiling. "Damn, mall cops. Why do they always act like they're on the front lines of Mars?" She tucked the ballistic pistol under her arm and fished her ID out of her back pocket. At the sight of it, both security men gawked. Kirsten tucked the confiscated gun behind her back, then stomped over and swiped a set of flexi-cuffs from Lloyd's belt.

Shani released the telekinetic hold of Zee once Kirsten wrestled him into the temporary restraints. All the while she fought with him, he glared at Evan, who simply smiled and waved. Kirsten wound up sitting on him, NetMini in hand.

"Ops, Wren. I need a blue and white at Bakersfield Mall by Sector D." She glanced at Zee's victim. "Send a medical unit as well."

4

VANISHED

Kirsten held up the ten-inch cylinder, making a face at the viscous green-brown liquid inside. The outer surface reacted to her touch, lighting up with buttons and a display pad courtesy of nanotech embedded in the outer layer. She thumbed the virtual button until the display read '2 TBSP,' and upended it over the pan. A squirt of the requested amount of olive oil spattered about, making her shriek and jump away.

"You're s'posed ta put the oil in the pot before you turn the stove on," said Evan from the main room.

She glanced at him, flopped on the Comforgel bed, nose in a datapad. From the look on his face, she inferred he was busy with homework and not something fun.

"Oops."

Holding the spatula like a dueling saber, she placed two slabs of vat-grown chicken in the pan and poked at them while they danced about in the oil. She squinted at several small plastic bottles of spice, trying to figure out which ones belonged in a project involving said poultry. Nearby, a datapad sat propped up on the empty box the 'starter spice kit' came in. She stared at the demonstration animation, attempting to learn the process by which people cooked actual food. What she had in the pan didn't look anywhere near as good as the pictures on the screen, however at thirty credits a hunk, the chicken would be eaten regardless of what condition it was in at the end of her thermic assault.

"Mom?"

She smiled at hearing the word come out of Evan. A word, which had for so long been an object of horror in her mind, was now as far removed as it could be from that thought. He leaned into the doorway between her tiny kitchenette and the rest of the apartment, looking defeated.

"Hey, kid."

"I need help with this homework. I don't know how to answer this." He trudged over, datapad dangling from his grip.

"I can't read it right now; I'm trying not to destroy dinner. What's the question?" She squinted at her pad. "What the hell is thyme? Did they spell it wrong? I'm supposed to add time to it? I guess it wants me to let it sit longer."

Evan shrugged. The datapad animated a small bottle labeled 'thyme' upended over the food and shaken.

"Oh, it must be some kind of seasoning. Bother, we don't have any. Black pepper works."

"Umm, I gotta write about the Corporate War. This one guy says the government started it, this lady says the corp-rations started it. I gotta watch these videos and write a 'pinion on which one I wanna believe and give at least two ideas how the war could have been prevented."

Kirsten almost dropped the spatula. "What the hell? You're in third grade, what kind of question is that?"

He dug his toe into the rug. "History."

She jumped when a hunk of meat spat hard enough to flip up. "Well, I kind of got the condensed version at the department school. I…"

Evan wandered over and patted her on the back. "It's okay if you don't know. Why didn't your mom let you go to school?"

The heat off, she yanked the pan from the stove and jammed the spatula under the meat. The chicken landed atop pasta bows she had made long enough ago to be cold. She used the reassembler to generate mixed vegetables as the horror of her attempt to cook hydroponic ones drowned amid suds in the sink. Evan trailed her to the table, letting his datapad clatter to the side of the plate.

"She did… online. Sorta. That stopped when I was nine. She got it in her head that letting me contact the outside world at all was allowing the Devil to teach me. So she liked and said she home-schooled me, but the only thing she ever tried to teach was mythology." Kirsten stared at the food. "The woman was careful to make everything look normal enough to the outside world. I'm confused… That question sounds like something they'd ask in eighth or ninth grade, not third."

He ate with one hand while poking at his datapad with the other. After a few minutes, he scowled at it.

"What?"

"This datapad is broken. I'm touching the icon for my history homework, but when I open it, it's labeled Pol Sci 101."

"Let me see that?" Kirsten took the pad, examining the page headers inside the presentation.

She backed out to the main menu, which took on a far more childish appearance than the layout of the quiz. A cartoon Mars pioneer smiled, pointing at a note indicating history homework for Mrs. Wolf's third-grade class. When she poked it, the datapad went into a splash screen introduction to a sophomore-level political science course.

"That isn't your homework, hon. I think the teacher sent a corrupt link."

"It was probably Abernathy playing a prank." He smirked.

"Oh wow, is he still there?" She giggled, sighed, and fell somber. "I wonder what's keeping him here. He was such a sweet old guy."

Evan rolled his eyes. "He's only nice to girls. He keeps messing with me since I can see him."

"What is he doing?"

"He's like a giant five-year-old. Stupid little pranks."

Kirsten fiddled with his datapad, downloading a new link from the system that went to the proper assignment. Third grade-level questions about early Mars colonization.

"There, that's the right homework."

His pout made her laugh. "Thanks, Mom. I could've had an excuse tomorrow."

"You don't want to make a habit of cutting corners like that. Unless you want to move to Mars or some far-off colony when you're old enough to have to work, you need to get through university."

"I'm gonna be like you when I'm big." He beamed. "I wanna be a cop with Zero so I can help people, like you helped me."

She teared up for a moment, holding his hand across the table. Evan grinned.

"Well, please don't cut corners because I'm asking you not to. You might feel differently about it when you grow up. It's better to have options." She paused to adore the sparkle in his green eyes.

She managed to get one decent picture of him with her NetMini before he started making silly faces. When their laugher died down and they remembered the food, she reached out and put a hand on his arm.

"Ev, if you don't want me seeing Konstantin… If you feel like I'm not giving you enough attention…"

He stared at the mixed vegetables. "I guess it would be cool having a dad, but I don't think he likes me very much."

"Why do you think that?"

"He looked at me mean. He's probably a rich weenie that hates little kids." Evan frowned. "And he's like old and stuff."

Kirsten stared into space for a moment. "He's a sweet man, Evan. I'm sure it's just a misunderstanding. Konstantin is…"

"Mom?"

She blinked. Her arm lowered to the table, drawing her gaze to the gold serpent bracelet, Konstantin's gift. The sight reminded her of how much money he had already spent on her, and brought a twinge of embarrassment at the thought. The amount was trivial to him, but felt on the verge of crazy to her. She pictured his face in her mind again, that roguish smile, that well-weathered skin, that Turkish coffee.

"You okay? You look strange."

She fanned herself. "I'm fine, hon. I think I put too much pepper on this chicken."

Evan shook his head. "No such thing as too much black pepper."

"I agree," said Theodore, as he phased out of the wall. "The boy's got good taste."

Kirsten sat upright. "Hi, Theo."

The ghost circled the table, long olive-drab coat open and drenched. Scraggly black hair framed a pallid face, still wearing the same wry grin he usually sported when sneaking up on her in the shower. For once, his pants didn't appear blood-soaked and he concealed his fatal bullet wounds. The puddled boot prints he left on the kitchen floor faded away in seconds; however, he did bring the scent of wet dog with him. Evan shifted in his seat, making a face as if in deep thought. His eyes lit up with a faint light as he turned on his ability to see ghosts. The gesture came off as casual, taking him only a second or two. He spotted Theodore and paused chewing long enough to attempt to mumble a greeting with a full mouth.

"It won't be too long before you can see them all the time," said Kirsten. "It took me 'til twelve to get there…" *Of course, I spent a few years trying to ignore them.*

He grinned.

"Sorry to barge in on ya while you're eatin'." Theodore wandered around to the empty side of the table, acting the part of leaning on the back of an unused chair. "We may need your hel—what happened to that pork?"

"It's chicken." Kirsten frowned.

Theodore looked at the array of cooking materials around the stove area and cracked up. "Oh, damn." He cringed.

Kirsten attempted to bore through the table with a stare. She pouted at the plate, the sense of failure crawled up her spine in search of tear ducts from which to escape. *When, exactly, was I supposed to learn how to cook, Theodore? When I was locked in a closet or living on the street?*

"He forgot what it's supposed to look like. Theo hasn't touched food in, like, forever." Evan showed no sign of slowing down, shoveling another large hunk in his mouth. "Ifm goomf." He rushed to swallow. "It's good!"

She almost pulled him over the table to hug him.

"Yeah, well, I guess you gotta start somewhere. Maybe I can ask around The Kind. I think there's a chef or two in there somewhere. Might be able to talk them into giving you some lessons. One guy's pretty damn amazing, but he's got a tendency to curse people out. Probably not your vibe."

Kirsten leaned back in the chair, smirking at Theodore. Out of the corner of her eye, she noticed Evan adding more black pepper and muted a laugh. "I guess. Now I know why everyone uses reassemblers. Why go to all that trouble when you can just hit a button."

"Better to have options," muttered Evan with a sly wink.

"Believe it or not," said Theodore. "People who cook the long way do it for fun—or they're getting paid a ton."

She laughed. "What did you need help with?"

"There's this guy, Hank. Been dead maybe fifty years or so. He used ta hang out by this Chinese place, what used ta be a smoke shop years ago."

Evan let some broccoli crumble out of his mouth. "Who buys smoke?"

Kirsten felt as clueless as the boy looked, but didn't let on.

"You've heard of Nicoderms or Nicohalers, right?" Theo gestured at Kirsten. She nodded. "Okay. Well, back before the war, people used to get the same kind of effect from inhaling the smoke of burning tobacco. The places that sold stuff related to it were called 'smoke shops.'"

The boy scrunched up his nose. Kirsten blinked.

"Breathing in smoke? Like, on purpose?" Evan coughed.

"Hey, don't knock it 'til ya try it. Worked for weed too." Theodore stared wistfully at the ceiling.

"People smoke weeds?" Kirsten blinked.

He laughed at the expression on her face. "Not weeds. *Weed.* Marijuana."

"Oh, yeah, they still do that in the Beneath," said Kirsten.

Evan tilted his head. "You ever—"

"So what about Hank?" She stared at Theo.

"Well he died of the old LC, decided to haunt his favorite smoke shop even though it killed him. He stayed there after it shut down and someone turned it into a bar, and then a Chinese restaurant."

"Oh, yeah. I think I remember the place… I've been there, the owners were complaining about loud coughing in the middle of the night. The ghost seemed harmless."

"Yeah, he was." Theo made no effort to be subtle about staring at her chest.

"Was? If he's gone, maybe he decided to transcend."

"Poor guy comes to Sanctuary Park two nights ago, raving about how some*thing* is after him. He wanted protection from it. Course, he couldn't describe anything but a weird feeling. The way he rambled on 'bout being watched and seeing eyes… It was surreal hearin' a ghost talk about something the way the living talk about us. We figured he'd finally cracked. Last night, Willie said he caught a glimpse of somethin' scoping out the park. Whatever it was, damn thing didn't want to tangle with all of us at once, 'specially not The Kind. Now, we got a feelin' somethin's stalkin' spirits. We're not sure if it needs to pick weaker ones, or was afraid of a crowd. Some of The Kind are nervous. They'd like you to check it out."

Kirsten gazed at her plate for a few seconds, then grinned at Evan, who forced himself to eat the vegetables after coating them with the pepper/olive oil residue from the chicken. She stood, tossed her plate in the dishwasher, and faced Theodore. "I think I remember the place…" She fidgeted at her gold bracelet. "I'm feeling a bit overwhelmed lately. That couldn't have been more than a few months ago, but I'm drawing a blank. Remind me where it was?"

"Sector 3338, shopping district."

"Oh, right… Next to that huge stationary sign. I don't understand how anyone in that area can sleep at night. That thing is so bright. Okay. Ev, get your shoes on." She grabbed her uniform and headed into the bathroom to change out of her sweats.

"I can go with you?" He cheered and leapt from his place at the table with such energy he almost fell flat. "Are you going to the office?"

After donning her uniform pants, she shrugged the top on and tucked it in. "No, I just don't want anyone to mess with me. I'm not leaving you here alone, and that's a fairly safe part of the city."

He had his shoes on by the time she emerged from the bathroom. She stepped into her boots, added her belt and forearm guard, then took his hand and headed out to the corridor. A short elevator ride to the roof later, she stepped out and smirked at the patrol craft. It sat tilted with the right front end on a small bank of pipes. This building wasn't made for hovercar landings and the roof had no unobstructed place to set down big enough for the oversized police patrol craft. She wanted to move to a bigger, nicer place where Evan could have his own bedroom. Hesitation kept her here for the time being. If the custody request was denied and they made him go back to the dorm, a new, bigger place would be a constant reminder of the loss.

She pulled him into a hug.

He flashed an uncomfortable smile and whispered. "Mom, what's wrong? You're getting squeezy again. Not in front of Theo."

Kirsten relaxed, letting Evan run ahead to the car. Dorian faded into view outside it, and Evan launched into a fit of pleas for help learning how to shoot. Apparently, his performance at the orb game annoyed him. She watched them for a moment, idly picking at the serpentine band of gold around her right wrist. Dorian became Konstantin in her mind, a father with a son.

Wearing a silly grin, she strode to the car and got in. Theodore hesitated.

With one hand on the door about to close it, she glanced up at him. "What's wrong?"

"Ehh…" He gestured at the vehicle. "I got this thing about riding in the back seat of a police car."

"The partition is down," she said. "Get in. Besides, you can float right through it."

Sector 3338 glowed in a mixture of red, green, and white light. It was still early, as far as the city was concerned. At a touch past eight, people filled the streets as they went among the various stores that still operated walk-in locations. An endless parade of glowing eyeliner, mechanical hair ornaments, and the latest upper-middle-class fashion trends went by.

Delivery bots swarmed about, a tangle of automated traffic management as dozens of merchants competed for airspace. Boxy ones stopped, waiting for others to pass before they pivoted and raced off. Some shot up vertical while others nosed into purpose-built hatches in the sides of buildings.

As she had hoped, the people who noticed her uniform gave her a comfortable distance. She kept a firm grip on Evan's hand, walking ahead of Theo and Dorian, who discussed the current crisis at length.

Up ahead, the metal sidewalk glowed with emerald light. Holographic Chinese symbols filled the window of a corner property, saturating the area in their glow. If not for having eaten moments ago, the scent in the air outside the place would have lured her in. She stopped a few steps from the door, waiting for Dorian and Theodore to catch up.

The owners of the Jade Crane went as far as possible to recreate the ambiance of China inside the building. Pale hardwood floors, bamboo plants, and large full-wall paintings of rolling green landscapes came pretty close to making her feel like she'd left the UCF. She looked around, seeing no trace of ghosts other than the two she arrived with. However, on the dark brown stone of an electric waterfall fountain, a faint luminous patch caught her attention, as if a spoonful of glowing paint had splashed on it.

"This must've been one big smoke shop," muttered Kirsten.

A busty, tall brunette in a low-cut gown went by, distracting Theodore's gaze. "They expanded. This place is doing well."

"Expanded indeed. Are you talking about the building?"

He chuckled. "Both."

Kirsten felt a twinge of inadequacy compared to the woman, until she lifted her arm up from her lap to grab a wine glass. The limb was metal from armpit to fingertip. Gleaming enamel white and covered with floral engravings, it retained the exact profile of a human limb, only in plastisteel. *White Orchid arm, that's over a million creds.*

"Can I help you, officer?" asked a man.

The host provided a welcome distraction from the sight of a cyber-prosthetic. Kirsten unconsciously rubbed her arm as she smiled at a man in a dark suit. He appeared mostly Chinese, with traces of other ethnicities mixed in.

"I'm following up on a previous investigation here. I've received a report of unusual activity about a year ago? Unexplained coughing."

"Oh, yes." He let an electronic menu slip back into a holding box. "I remember hearing about that. It had persisted up until a few days ago."

"It's stopped?"

"Yes, there was a disturbance the other night. We filed a report with the police, but they haven't done much yet. We lost about sixteen thousand credits worth of fish."

Kirsten wandered toward the stain on the fountain. "Cooler failed?"

"No, officer." He pointed at an H-shaped aquarium along the top of a partition wall among tables. "They were exotics for display, not consumption. What's truly strange is, all the dead ones were in the same place." The man gestured at the central strut of the H. "We found them floating yesterday morning. A technician could find no problem with the tank, though the log recorded a severe temperature drop during the night, but only in a small area."

"Heck, *I* could kill fish," said Theodore.

"That doesn't mean much." Dorian smiled. "You're centuries old. I can kill fish, too."

"True." Theodore nodded. "The little buggers are pretty sensitive to cold. Just stick my hand in the tank and poof. Hank may have lashed out at the restaurant for replacing his beloved smoke shop."

"I don't think so." Kirsten leaned close, studying the aquarium. "He'd been here for years and never did anything that overt before."

Dorian swiped a finger at the smear. "This is residue. An entity got into a fight in here, or at least, something hurt one."

"Thank you, I'll just be a few minutes looking around. I'll try not to get in anyone's way." She smiled at the host as he backed off, and closed her eyes. Evan's hand slipped away. "Don't wander too far."

"I won't."

She opened her mind in an effort to read ambient energy. Weak imprints lingered here and there, confirming a spirit had been around recently. Theodore hovered right in front of her face when she opened her eyes; she jumped back with a yelp that quieted the room by several decibels. Embarrassed at drawing attention to herself, she scowled at him.

"Dammit, Theo, don't do that."

Dorian encouraged him to give her some space and glanced at her. "Feel anything?"

"A spirit left an imprint here, not much of one though. It doesn't feel like an obliteration occurred. Also, I'm not feeling the sense of peace that usually saturates an area after a transcendence."

"K..." Dorian pointed.

She spun to follow his gesture, and gasped at the sight of Evan. He had crouched, one hand on the floor amid another blotch of glowing matter. The boy trembled, staring wide-eyed into nowhere with an expression as if someone was about to shoot him. A cold sweat covered his face, Kirsten ran to him, sliding to a halt on her knees with her hands on his shoulders.

"Evan?"

He didn't react.

"Evan!" She shook him. "Evan, snap out of it."

A well-dressed man at a nearby table leaned around. "Is he all right? Should I call a MedVan?"

Mouth still open, Evan blinked once and broke out of whatever trance had taken him. After a final severe shiver, he swallowed and wiped the sweat from his face. His trembling subsided, and his breathing returned to normal.

"Thank you, I think he's okay." She stood up as Evan did, refusing to let go of his hand. "What was that?"

He stared up at her. "Fear."

"Obviously." Theodore shook his head. "You looked about ready to piss yourself."

Evan glared at him. "Was not. It wasn't my fear." He looked at Kirsten. "Someone was real scared here."

"Oh, that explains it," said Theodore with a smirk. "The kid's a telempath."

"Nooooo," whined Evan with an exasperated sigh. "You're just not scary."

Dorian chuckled, much to Theodore's chagrin.

"He's not a telempath, Theo." Kirsten pulled Evan into a hug, stroking her hand over his hair. "He's mildly clairvoyant. He probably caught a psychometric reading from the residue."

"Mildly clairvoyant? That's like saying you're mildly a cop. He either is, or isn't. Question is, does he train himself how to use it?" Theodore gestured at him.

"You should be ashamed of yourself," cried a sour-sounding voice. "Forcing your psychic nonsense on an innocent little boy."

"Oh, shit," muttered Dorian. "Self-righteousness at two o'clock low, coming in hot."

A middle-aged woman ambled over, shaking her finger. Kirsten's gaze shot right to the gold cross pin on her lapel, the icon of Reverend Harris's vehement anti-psionic Fundamentalist Church of the Redeemer.

"Psionics aren't a choice, dammit. I'm not *making* him anything. He was born with his gift, as was I. No amount of screaming at your invented god will change that. How *dare* you judge us for being different. Don't you see how fucking hypocritical you are"—Evan covered his mouth to hide the urge to laugh at Kirsten's language—"if your so-called god is real and as all-powerful as you say, then psionic people couldn't exist unless he made them. If he hated us, why do we even exist? Or is he not 'all-powerful?'" Kirsten vibrated with anger, turning red. "You don't even believe your own bullshit."

The woman, and half the room, gasped. When shock wore off, she ranted in scripture. Something in the back of Kirsten's mind snapped at the all-too-familiar sound of a woman's voice invoking God at her. She reached for her stunrod with a shaking hand, tears in her eyes.

Dorian jumped in front of her. "Don't... not worth it."

Theodore held up his hand. "I got this."

5

WITHERED

Coffee, divine as it was, didn't hold the answers of the universe. It didn't even hold the answers to the questions she had at that moment. An egg-on-a-roll sat unopened on the dash between the control sticks, clear plastic clamshell fogged white with steam. Outside to the right, a morning crowd shuffled along on their way to work or wherever else they had to be. Not even the fragrance of peppered eggs teased an appetite out of her gut.

"You okay?" The cool presence of Dorian's hand settled on her right shoulder.

She looked at him, still red-eyed from a fitful sleep. "Thanks for staying with me last night."

"Don't let the bitch get to you. Besides, she's got her own issues now." Dorian chuckled.

Kirsten managed a weak smile and took a sip of her wake-up elixir. "Yeah, I've never seen a grown woman shit where she stood before."

"Theodore certainly has a knack for the dramatic. That's the first time I've ever seen a crowd clear out of a restaurant so fast."

"Guess she believes in ghosts now." She reached for her breakfast. "Think I'll get more than two bites before we get a radio call?"

Dorian made a fanciful series of arcane gestures and touched both index fingers to his temples. "I foresee you might be able to finish your food."

"It wasn't fun getting stuck there 'til eleven." Chomp. "Do you think the brass will believe my report?"

"Well," said Dorian, "if you had taken a swing at that woman, you'd have had a different sort of explaining to do. You did tell the truth. A spirit caused a disturbance, and you made sure he won't do it again. Like you always say, what are you going to do, haul Theo to ghost-jail?"

"I wasn't gonna beat her; just, you know"—she made a fairy-wand-tap gesture—"*bzzz*... silence." Kirsten shivered. "I had to make it stop. I couldn't listen to that again."

"You hit a nerve. You made a valid point she had no rebuttal for, so she just tried to shout you down."

"Yeah."

The comm. lit up. "Agent Wren, copy?"

She stared at the box of crumbs. "Well, I *did* finish it," she mumbled. "Wren here, go ahead."

"Agent, there is a request from Division 1 for your expertise." A NavMap pin popped up on her console. "A dead body was found approximately twenty-six minutes ago, and they would like you to have a look."

"Any strange events reported?" Kirsten leaned to her left, peering upward before bringing the car airborne.

The holographic dispatcher shook his head. "Nothing they have included in comm. traffic at this time."

"Alright, notify them I'm en route." She glanced at the map. "ETA four point two minutes."

———

KIRSTEN SLIPPED PAST THE USUAL ARRAY OF DIVISION 1 HOVERCARS PARKED in such a manner as to create a blockade in front of an alley. The scene hung eerily quiet, even the patrol craft's emergency lights were off. A Div 2 van sat inside the barricade. Forensic techs bustled about, though few spoke.

Dorian appeared out of a cloud of silvery fog in step at her side. "At least we're not in the arctic again."

"Yeah, I should thank this guy for having the courtesy to be murdered where it's warm." She walked up to a man in a long charcoal-grey coat observing the techs studying a dead man. "You must be Detective Kiering. Agent Wren, Div Zero."

He glanced at her; his features said Mexico but his skin tone said Sweden. "Morning, Agent. Thanks for coming. Look, this may be nothing, but the buzzards had some questions they couldn't answer."

"What can you tell me?"

"Well..." Detective Kiering swiped his hand over a datapad, backing up several pages. "Luckily for us, the deceased had an ImDent. His name was William Arris, former security guard. System shows a relatively clean record. No major crimes. He applied to Division 1 several times but they denied him."

Kirsten glanced about, finding no signs of a spirit. "Any idea why?"

"He had frequent association with individuals known to work for the Syndicate. Brass didn't want to risk an infiltrator."

"I guess that makes sense. Any chance it had something to do with his death?"

"It's an angle I'm still looking into. I couldn't find anything yet, but there's some very odd things. Tech Hollings can fill you in." He indicated a petite woman with dark brown skin stooped on one knee beside the corpse.

Wide eyes like amber gems glanced up at the mention of her name.

Kirsten gave Kiering a nod and walked toward Hollings. After one more look around failed to find a ghost other than Dorian nearby, she smiled at him. "Mind wandering around a bit, see if he's hiding somewhere?"

"Sure." Dorian jogged off.

"Tech Hollings?" asked Kirsten, offering a hand.

The woman stood, clinging to a portable scanner as if it were a security blanket. Her round, innocent face held an expression tinged with fear. For once, Kirsten felt tall. The woman had to be four-foot-ten.

"Is something wrong?" *Please don't be scared of me.*

"Ma'am." Tech First Class Hollings, being equivalent to a Corporal in rank, saluted her and stood rigid. "I just have a creepy feeling about this one, ma'am. I... You're psionic, aren't you?"

"That is one of the things they ask on the Division 0 job application, yes." Kirsten hooked her thumbs in her belt, taking on a full-body sag of exasperation. "I'll try to make this quick so you don't have to be near me any longer than necessary."

"Oh." Tech Hollings stared down. "I... It's not that. Sorry, I'm not one of those people who thinks psionics are bad. I'm freaked out by the scene, not you."

Kirsten let her arms fall lax. "What's wrong?"

"This body doesn't *feel* right. You know, most times I check out a dead person I almost feel like they're watching me. Like I'm not alone. I, you know, talk to them and tell them I'm gonna do all I can to figure out what happened to them so we can catch their killer and such."

"Sometimes, their spirit might actually be there. That's nice of you to reassure them."

"This guy... I didn't get that feeling."

Kirsten squinted at her, reaching into the woman's mind with a psionic feeler.

"Whoa." Hollings gasped. "Your eyes just glowed. Did you just do something?"

You're psionic, aren't you? Maybe you don't even know it.

Hollings shivered. Her surface thoughts shifted to fear she might get in trouble for hiding from Division 0.

"Hey," said Kirsten, soothing, and put a sisterly arm around the shorter woman's back. "It's not illegal to stay under the radar. A lot of people do. I only peeked into your mind in a rudimentary check to see if you have psionic potential. You do. That's why you can feel them. I didn't get much of a sense of what your talents are. I bet you never tried to develop anything. You have the potential though. It's nothing to be ashamed of. You know where to find us if you ever want to talk about it. And no, we're not going to come after you for hiding."

Hollings slouched with relief.

Kirsten paced around the dead man. "So, what can you tell me about this guy? Did you call me in for something more than not feeling watched?"

The woman relaxed, lowering her diagnostic tool away from her shirt enough to see the screen. "I couldn't find an obvious cause of death, not with this thing." She patted the box. "However, there is some abrasion damage to the bones of his wrists and ankles, as if he had been wearing metal binders for an extended period of time. I also found fine particulates embedded in the skin of his back, buttocks, and legs. It comes up as crushed soy hull, and some of it was... kitty litter."

"Crushed soy hull?" Kirsten pondered. "There's tons of places that process soybeans. OmniSoy alone has a hundred facilities in West City, never mind East and off-world."

"Certain micro particles on the soy shell fragments phenotyped to pollen from olive trees native to the region around Tel Aviv, which appear to be from around 1000 BCE."

Kirsten blinked. "Where would he have come into contact with that?"

"According to his personal record, he was employed as a night guard at the West City Archives, specifically, the museum wing."

"Oh." Kirsten sighed. "Maybe he was getting busy at night and did the deed on top of some old thing. Is there any way to determine how long the, umm, pollen was on him?"

"Not exactly. Some of the soy shell bits dug into his skin, causing mild inflammation. I'd say he was in prolonged contact with it for a few days maybe."

"So, someone held this guy prisoner for a few days." She squatted, peering under the sheet.

The nude man lay with his arms at his sides, as if on a morgue table. He seemed older in the face than he should be. His skin appeared too grey, wrinkled and dry, and his eyes had turned black.

Kirsten recoiled at the surprise of it.

"See what I mean? Tissue analysis of his eyes shows nothing to explain the pigmentation of the sclera or the collapse of the iris."

"He smells like chemicals."

"There is residue of a common non-abrasive cleaning solution on his chest. Someone gave him a rub down with a disposable wipe. Not very useful to trace, you can find them in just about every apartment in the city."

"Can I touch him?"

Hollings cringed. "You shouldn't, it could interfere with the lab work later. I can only do so much out here." She looked around and lowered her voice. "If you think it's the only way, I won't say anything."

"No, it's okay. I don't want to be responsible for contaminated evidence." Kirsten squatted, holding her hands over the body.

Something tugged at her mind: faint, almost beyond notice. She probed at the sensation, offering and withdrawing energy until she came to the determination the body possessed an absence of paranormal forces to a degree it reacted as a manner of sponge. Not powerful enough to do much, more like a chunk of inert metal left near a magnet too long that picked up a feeble field.

"I couldn't find anything," said Dorian.

The sound of his voice opened her eyes.

Hollings glanced around and shivered. "Okay, now I get that feeling again."

"My partner's here." Kirsten winked at her, and stood, rubbing her forehead. "I've never seen this before. The body is so blank it's trying to absorb psionic energy."

Dorian gave the dead man a curious look. He stooped, put a hand on the corpse's shoulder—and vanished. The body's mouth filled with luminous fog, which drew itself down the throat a second later.

When the all-black eyes shifted to look at Kirsten, Hollings about fainted. Dark ichor seeped like tears from the corners, streaking ebon lines down the dead man's cheeks.

The corpse looked left, then right, then back at Kirsten. The hand twitched.

Hollings scooted behind her, clinging. "What the fuck?"

"Calm down, it's Dorian being a dick."

The body wheezed.

"Get out of there." Kirsten folded her arms.

Dorian's hand peeled out of the corpse's arm, reaching up. Hollings had no reaction.

"Little help…" A breathy wheeze came from the dead Mr. Arris.

Kirsten concentrated for a few seconds, rendering her body solid to spirits, and took Dorian's hand. A hearty pull dragged him free, and the corpse once again fell inert. The confusion on his face stalled Kirsten's imminent grumbling about scaring the poor tech half to death.

"I didn't intend to jump in," said Dorian. "However, I think I learned something."

"Hang on." Kirsten patted Hollings on the arm. "I know this isn't gonna help much, but try not to freak out. The dead don't get back up. I have a ghost following me around and he jumped into that body. The next crime scene you go to, the body won't move. Don't dwell on it."

Hollings offered a dumbfounded nod and a deep breath.

"I don't think I can do anything here. The complete absence of a spirit isn't necessarily a problem. It's possible he either transcended or… went to the bad place already. Aside from the blackened eyeballs, I can't find any evidence to support paranormal events. Unless something else comes up, handle this like a normal case."

Dorian followed her back to the patrol craft. "There is something unusual there."

"What?" She paused, a few meters from the car.

"I haven't exactly had a lot of practice jumping into bodies, but the one time I did try it, I had to overcome the bond between the corpse and the spirit who used to own it. Remember how you tracked Albert? The same link."

She pursed her lips.

"Well, Mr. Arris over there had no link. In fact, the damn body pulled me in the instant I touched it. I did not *want* to jump in. He's right in the midst of rigor, so I couldn't move much. Even making the eyes slide around was tiring."

"It could mean he did transcend. If the soul moves on to the next place, wouldn't the link break?" She took another step toward the car.

"I believe so, yes. But, it still doesn't explain the"—he made a double-fisted pulling gesture into his body, that would have thumped if he had a solid chest—"yank."

"I don't like it either." She drew the last word out into a sigh. "To claim jurisdiction on this murder, I need more than a little tuggy feeling on a 'partner' command doesn't even believe I have."

"What about that?" Dorian asked, pointing up.

Her gaze followed the line of his finger left and into the sky to a large NewsNet bot. In the peculiar way the human mind tends to do, as soon as she looked at it and recognized the face of Kimberly Brightman, she picked the reporter's words out from the ambient din of advert jingles. In the background, a prim, grey-haired woman with dark skin stood behind a podium of microphones. Kirsten somewhat recognized her, the two guards in military armor in the background made her think government official.

"…has announced that she is open to discussions regarding the abolishment of trade embargoes with certain regions affiliated with the Allied Corporate Council. As you know, for years now, Commissioner Vernon has adamantly refused to consider open trade agreements with the ACC, citing numerous human rights violations. This morning's announcement comes as quite a shock to parties on both sides of the debate. Let's go now to our Lunar Correspondent, Amy Gordon at Paramount City, with the latest reaction from the Senate."

The image shifted to a young, fair-skinned woman with short orange-blonde hair and hazel eyes, caught off guard by the sudden shift of feed. Grey and black dominated the scene behind her, with most of the upper reaches of the video a clear view out the dome into space. The city behind her, like most of the moon, appeared in black and white—with the exception of full-color advert bots flying around. She stood at the base of a long staircase into an elaborate stadium-like building, with a dozen soldiers in white-on-grey camouflage armor at the top. The gold and blue banner of the United Coalition Front hung on either side of a row of doors.

Her 'do I have to deal with these people' scowl down the street was obvious, sending Dorian into a fit of chuckling. The Lunar reporter startled, went wide-eyed in the direction of the camera, and put on a false smile.

"Thanks, Kimberly. I'm here at the Senate chambers, where reaction to Commissioner Vernon's announcement has been mixed. Former allies immediately decried her change of stance, and leveled accusations of bribery or coercion. I had a chance to speak with Senator Garr a few minutes ago. If you recall, he was in favor of opening trade with the ACC."

The video cut to an older white man in a suit so expensive it shined. He blathered on about the plight of the lower classes in ACC society, drawing justification for a trade agreement by how it could only benefit poor people who had no influence on what their government did.

"That's such a load of horseshit I can smell it from the moon," said Dorian. "If he thinks for one second the ruling class over there will let one credit get to the people, he's dangerously deluded. It would be like paying them to keep shooting at us."

"But..."

Dorian held up a hand. "Not on Earth. On Mars. You've spoken to some of those vets. The ACC keeps a pleasant face on down here, but up there it's a whole other story. We have enough trouble holding on to our piece of Mars with the Martian Liberation Front bombing everything they can. Giving the ACC *more* resources is insanity."

Kirsten felt like a ten-year-old watching elders discuss things she neither cared about nor understood. With a lamenting smirk at the car, she muttered "yeah." Her awkwardness at having no political knowledge waned at a sudden spark of worry. "Dorian, do you think it's a little odd Vernon changes her mind on something so significant like this?" She glanced back at the Division 2 crew loading William Arris's body into a van.

"That man had nothing to do with her office."

"He worked at the West City Archives, didn't he? That's still government work. All it takes is access to a computer terminal on the hard net. Maybe we missed an abyssal and it possessed him, used him for access to the government building, and somehow got to Vernon?"

"That's kind of a reach. Why would a demon care about politics?" Dorian tapped a finger to his chin for a moment. "I don't know. I didn't get the feeling the body had been in contact with an abyssal, but I'm hardly a scholar on the subject."

"Maybe I should go check, just a quick meeting. Won't take long." She ducked under the rising gull-wing door before it was all the way open.

THE FLIGHT TO SECTOR 2408 TOOK FORTY MINUTES, OVER TWO-THIRDS OF the city. The West City Administrative Complex consumed an entire sector square, as well as infiltrated the adjacent ones. Unlike most of the surrounding construction, the main building of the WCAC rose only four stories above ground. Most of it extended down, protected in and under the city plates. Rumor claimed it extended all the way into the earth.

She glided to a landing outside the perimeter wall and drove in via the checkpoint gate after a show of ID and a two-minute verification wait. Military personnel clad in generic-green camouflage armor with gold visors littered the area around the stairs. The bulkiness of their body armor made it difficult to tell which ones were women.

Kirsten ignored them all watching her as she went up the stairs to a grandiose affair of a lobby consisting of chrome and black marble. Clusters of benches and plants ringed ornate columns, and the cavernous space held many glass tube elevators. Open to the ceiling, the reception area occupied the bottom of a shaft that offered a view into all four above ground floors through glass walls.

Most surprising of all, the two men and one woman behind the onyx desk all had surface thoughts, and all of them were concerned at the presence of a psionic in this building. She frowned, paying them no heed, and walked up to a large onyx obelisk bearing a directory hologram. Her reflection stared back at her from the shiny black surface behind a five-foot-tall holo-panel bearing names and titles. It listed Commissioner Claire Vernon's office on the third floor.

Out of the corner of her eye, she noticed the woman receptionist muttering while keeping a worried gaze on her. Kirsten almost punched the elevator button, emitting a heavy sigh.

"That didn't take long." Dorian looked around. "What's got you in a mood so fast?"

She slid past the opening doors, and spun about to face the room, locking eyes with the receptionist for a few seconds before the elevator closed. "Three idiots at the front desk scared shitless of a psionic."

"I wouldn't take it personally here, K. This is a place where there are more secrets than people. There's no security protocol on a brain."

Her burning glower lifted to the floor counter. "I guess."

The doors slid open, revealing six figures in green military assault armor standing a horseshoe around the elevator on the third floor. One close to the center lacked a helmet. He appeared to be in his later forties, all-white hair in a neat brush cut. He raised a hand at her approach.

"This is a restricted section, miss. Visitors are required to go through the receiving area downstairs."

"I'm not a visitor; I'm here on official police business. I need a moment with Commissioner Vernon."

He regarded her for a quiet moment, almost as if he had expected someone like her to show up. "Under what inquest number?"

As Kirsten's mouth opened to speak, the other five soldiers twitched, itching to raise their weapons. She lost her voice at the sight.

"Miss?"

Her gaze flicked back to him, noting the word 'Gerard' stenciled on his chest by a stack of chevrons. "I don't appreciate being threatened, Sergeant. You do realize Division 0 is every bit as legitimate as One or Nine."

"I'm sorry, Agent. It is a matter of national security. Your jurisdiction does not extend to military installations. Do you have an inquest number?"

"I am investigating a suspicious death that may be related to the Commissioner's sudden change of heart. My purpose here is to determine if she is under any paranormal influence."

"Agent Wren, it is only due to your credentials checking out that you're not being detained already. I can't let you inside without an official inquest and an order from CENTCOM." He advanced, taking hold of her right forearm in a grip far less than comfortable. She tensed—old instincts die hard. "Tell us who sent you and we'll go easy on you."

She tried to jerk her arm away, but scarcely moved him. Dorian bristled, though his angry glare went unnoticed. Sergeant Gerard smirked at the fear seeping from her eyes and let go. It took her a few seconds to recover any sense of confidence.

"You think someone sent me to *reprogram* the Commissioner?" She blinked. "I'm a damn astral, not a mind-wiper. If you think I'm someone's tool, sent here to do some political dirty work, do you really believe I'd just walk in through the front door and ask for a meeting?"

Gerard crossed his arms. "I don't know what to think when Psios are involved, so I don't. I follow orders. The only way you're gettin' in there to see Vernon is if my commanding officer tells me to let you in."

She glowered, furious at her public reaction to being grabbed, furious at their disregard of her authority, and furious at not being trusted.

Dorian put a hand on her back. "Come on, K. If you push it, you are going to wind up in a C-Branch detention center where no one will ever find you. Anything you say will make it look more suspicious. Evan needs you."

The name washed over her shoulders like ice water. "I have reason to think she might be under an external influence. If you see anything unexplained going on here, please call us." Kirsten backpedaled into the elevator, not taking her eyes off Gerard until the doors closed. Alone with Dorian, her face softened. "I hope I'm wrong about this."

He seemed to gaze through the wall at the soldiers. "I'm sure we'll find out."

6

DUTY

Wind whistled among the trees of Sanctuary Park. Kirsten shivered more from the sound than from feeling cold. The dancing pattern of moonlight, interspersed between leaf-shaped shadows, lent a foreboding solitude to the night.

A young woman in glowing makeup with brown hair came around a bend in the false bricks, leading a man twice her age. Silver material wrapped about her. a garment barely tall enough to cover her breasts with a narrow strip of cloth. Her transparent skirt offered a plain view of lacy violet panties.

At the sight of someone in uniform leaning on a tree, the girl skidded to a halt and reversed course, dragging her client out of sight. Kirsten shot a guilty stare at the ground. Dorian edged closer.

"Something wrong?"

She didn't look up. "The only reason that isn't me is I'm psionic."

He pushed on her arm. "Your logic is flawed. Stop trying to depress yourself."

"Flawed?" She glanced at him after taking note of Theodore's presence in the distance. "How so?"

"The most glaring problem is if you weren't psionic, your mother wouldn't have tortured you. You'd probably be out of university by now at some boring job. The second issue is the government *does* help street kids, even non-psionics. The ones you see here wanted to stay."

"They ship them off Earth," said Kirsten, frowning.

Dorian looked around at the city. "Are you so sure it's a bad thing?"

Theodore paused amid a group of university students passing an inhaler around. He took it in turn, drawing a breath off it as they all stared at the floating device. Kirsten smirked at him as he went from solid to ghostly.

"Yeah, that's the shit," growled Theodore with a long exhale.

One man fainted while the rest scrambled off in random directions. He laughed as he let his manifestation fade and dropped the drug delivery device on the chest of the unconscious man. Curly black hair wafted behind him as he glided to where Kirsten stood, wearing a disapproving frown.

"What?" He leaned back on his heels while his pocketed hands rose a bit in a lazy version of a shrug. "They're in *my* park at night. Fair game."

Kirsten shoved herself away from the tree she had been leaning on. "You shouldn't do that to people. You could kill someone."

"They weren't old 'nuff to have heart attacks. Sides, they'll blame the Zone4." He groaned. "Such a shame I died before they invented all these wonderful chemicals."

"If you hurry this along, there's a prostitute over there." Dorian waved to the distance.

"Bitsy?" Theodore rolled his eyes. "She's boring. Just lays there, no energy." He winked at Kirsten. "Bet you'd be a lot more energetic. Quite a few years of pent up frustration waiting to come out."

The intent to make her feel awkward backfired. Kirsten draped the lash out of her hand.

"Whoa…" Theodore raised his hands. "Sorry, girl. Forgot it was that time of the month. What happened to your sense of humor?"

"A couple of assault troopers," said Dorian.

"Oh, my." Theodore swiped wet hair off his face, black-lipstick grin widening. "Share the details?"

Her face went crimson. "You're a damn pervert, Theo."

He rendered a formal court bow. "*Merci pour le compliment, je suis honoré.*"

She released the lash, darkening the area. "Just a conflict of jurisdiction. What did you want, anyway?"

"The Kind seeks your assistance, girl." Theodore stepped back with his left foot, waving his arm at a line of people that had appeared out of nowhere. "Selenah has seen the next attack."

"Selenah?" Kirsten asked, tilting her head.

"Perhaps one of the oldest of our number." Theodore stuffed his hands once more into the saturated pockets of his green trench coat. "Colonists killed her for being a witch."

"Which colony?"

"Plymouth," said Theodore, grinning.

"Never heard of it. What planet is it on? Is she here?"

Theodore laughed. Some of The Kind shook their heads in dismay at the ignorance of youth.

"It's not important, and no. She's with her mortal remains in the Beneath on the east coast. She speaks to us across the mists. One will be claimed. He is a soul of some age, however stagnant. He has kept to himself, not developed his strength."

Kirsten lifted both eyebrows. "So you want me to hunt down this old lonely ghost and wait for something to attack him?"

"You are their chosen, Kirsten." An older man with the bearing of a politician and the body of a weightlifter advanced from the group of Kind. "Yours is not only to protect the living from the restless dead. Your duty extends to protect those of us who wish to exist in peace. A hunter walks among us, girl. A beast of darkness that feeds upon souls."

"You're laying it on a little thick, Pops." Theodore chuckled.

"Just a tad," added Dorian.

"Still, the governor's got a point. Abyssals are bad for both living and dead. This one's a devourer, kid." For once, Theodore's larger-than-life presence shrank into something almost approaching humility. "We need yer help."

She looked over the dozen or so spirits, finding the wide variety of era of their clothing both intriguing and sad. "Okay. It's hard enough to track those things down. If you think you know where it's going to be, I have to take the chance. Where?"

"Sector 3177, rather under it."

An older-looking female ghost among The Kind grumbled about it no longer being called Beverly Hills, then proceeded to rant about 'the monstrosity,' her term for the elevated city platform.

"The Beneath?" asked Kirsten, sagging into a slouch. The memory of the slime puddle she fell into on her last trip down there came back, causing a shiver.

"Ayep." Theodore flung his hands to the sides in another casual shrug, tossing water. "Tonight, probably within an hour."

"Great," she said, jogging to the car with an exasperated sigh.

"Some warning is better than none." Dorian materialized in the passenger seat around his voice.

"I hope this one's weaker than Charazu."

His eyebrows flared. "Me too."

───────────

Kirsten grasped the squishy, rubberized handle at the center of the armored hatch, staring at the round-cornered square that blocked entry to the Beneath. She keyed in the police access code and a red square of light turned green, tinting her face to a matching hue. Curious eyes glimmered in the shadows of the alley, as tempted by a solitary woman as they feared her uniform. A deep breath carried the metallic flavor of grey zone neglect.

"Too many bad memories down there?" asked Dorian.

She squeezed the handle, activating the pressure-sensitive control. Pins popped away, freeing the panel to lift on a hinge. A wash of humid, warm air came over her, replacing the industrial taste with something closer to putrescent organic matter.

"I always thought about Mother when I thought about the Beneath." She lowered herself into the hole and down a metal ladder, pulling the hatch closed via the handle on the bottom. The dim shaft made her voice echo. "I barely think about her now, just how foolish I was for not going to the police right away. I thought they'd take me right home to her. I didn't think they'd believe me."

Dorian's voice lacked echo since the sound he made existed only to her, not to hard metal walls. "You wanted to hide from a world you didn't think wanted you."

She leapt the last two rungs of the first ladder and jogged to the edge of a catwalk, where she proceeded down a longer one leading to the bottom of the city plate interior. "I was terrified she would find me."

"How do you want to handle the Discarded this time? Same as last?"

Twenty-five meters below the city, Kirsten paused at the base of the ladder, standing on the lower plate surface. She looked around at the array of girders, tubes, wire bundles, and small square utility lights that formed a virtual starscape. "We shouldn't run into any here. This area has a colony. I used to steal food from places here."

"Steal? If there was a colony, why didn't you live among them?" Dorian joined her at the edge of a hole, where another huge ladder ran down the side of an immense column.

Fifty meters below, the old city waited.

Kirsten stepped onto the ladder, pausing to look up at him before she climbed. "They didn't look like the nicest people, and I'd just gotten away from four years of torture. I wasn't looking for more parents."

He floated down, keeping pace with her as she climbed. "You're evading something, but I won't push."

Quiet until her boots hit a dirt lot, she held on to the rung for a moment without looking at him. "Just another stupid choice." She shook off the bad mood and forced a smile. "Kind of ironic, isn't it? This place, down here, used to be one of the most exclusive playgrounds of the rich before everything went to hell. Now it sits below a bad part of the city."

"Yeah, fancy that," he said. "Yesterday's paradise is today's shithole. Some people say everything goes in cycles. So how did you tolerate this for two years? There's no daylight. All you have for sky is metal."

Kirsten shrugged, glancing at a holo-panel floating over her left arm to study a map. "I wasn't thinking about a lot back then, mostly about staying alive and away from everyone."

"Youder. Doanmove." A dusty male voice emanated from behind a weak flashlight. An old bolt-action rifle protruded alongside it, not quite aimed at her.

Light gleamed from a sword to his left. "Whatchu want?" asked a female voice.

The third voice was deep enough to resonate in her bones. "Topsider, yew lookin fer trouble or runnin' from it?"

"I guess you could say I'm looking for it, but not with you. I'm sorry, but I don't have time to make nice with the natives. I'm hunting a demon."

The tall man with the deep voice blocked her step. "That's some fancy hardware you got, thar." A hand, coated in black oily grease entered the light and pointed at her sidearm.

From behind the sword, a silhouette of tattered rags and frizzy black hair leaned closer. "Sheez pretty. Cani keeper?" The woman stepped closer, near to drooling.

"I'm not a stray dog." She tried to walk around them, but they moved to remain in her path.

"You don't want no trouble then, whyd'nt ya gives us that fancy ol' gun o' yours as a peace offerin'," said the man with the rifle.

"Sorry, no. It's coded to my fingerprint and won't operate for anyone else. Besides, even if you could fire it, there's no more ammo for it down here."

Dorian rolled his eyes. "You're wasting your breath."

The three glanced at each other.

Kirsten focused, drawing upon her Darksight. The Astral Realm superimposed itself over the oppressive gloom in her vision, a wavering version of the world drawn in sepia. The power also caused her eyes to glow white. The three people in front of her jumped back. Perhaps a quarter mile distant, a large mass of corrugated metal sprawled like some monstrous insect. Distorted faces peered at her from the maze of girders, sheet metal, and wood, straining to see her figure illuminated by flashlight.

The bolt-action rifle wobbled, a sign of the fear that gripped its owner. "Y... You one o' them robot things?"

"No, I'm..." *These people aren't going to know or care about Division 0.* "I'm a shaman, and I need to stop a bad spirit before it hurts anyone down here."

The sword-bearing woman raised her weapon in a trembling hand, edging close enough to sniff the air around Kirsten. Her clothing was a mixture of pre-war items and scraps of random heavy cloth stitched and patched together by string. She circled, head tilting to one side and then the other. "What's a topsie want with us?"

Dorian drained the flashlight. "These people don't seem all that much different from the Discarded."

"Gah!" yelled the man, swatting at the dead light.

Kirsten put a hand over her mouth to suppress the urge to laugh at the face the man made as he banged at it. "I'll be gone soon. I'm not here to cause any trouble with your people. Look, get out of my way and leave me alone and I'll come back in a day or so with some clothes and stuff for you."

They backed away with careful nods, too spooked by the sight of her glowing eyes and sudden darkness to speak. Perhaps Dorian altered the mood in the air. She gave him a wry grin and walked around the sentries toward the gate.

Bevlls, the colony, was a little more than the size of three city blocks. Fortunately, the manor house Theodore described didn't fall within its borders. A series of dangling car headlights strung along the perimeter wall surrounded the village with a weak aura of wobbling light. Kirsten skirted it, staying in the dark and out of sight of the sentries.

"Well, they're certainly more organized than Discarded."

Kirsten stepped over a fallen light pole. "Not everyone down here is ferally insane. Most of these colonists are hiding from the law or are the children of those who came down here to hide. Anyway, you see why I avoided them before?"

"Mmm."

A strong green glow leaked from where a gap in the corrugated metal wall offered a view into a crude hydroponic farm. Several dozen tanks held luminous water and vegetables in various states of maturity. Rows of intense lamps showered them with ultraviolet light focused by hand-bent metal shrouds. Two boys, one in his later teens and one not yet twelve, helped an older man tend to the crops. Copious sweat on their shirtless bodies suggested the chamber was a sauna. The younger boy measured out some manner of powder and stood on tiptoe to pour it into a vessel full of carrots.

"Some of those look like fish tanks," said Dorian, blinking.

"Use what you got, I guess. Still, they must have some contact with the outside to obtain supplies." They walked another few minutes until her armband beeped. "Oh, we're here. Hope we're not too late." She gestured at a distant property.

The former mansion looked about ready to collapse if so much as a mild breeze touched it. Fortunately, no such wind penetrated the millions of tons of plastisteel that formed the sky of the Beneath.

She sidestepped the collapsed gate and jogged the length of a driveway large enough to host a Gee-ball game. It ended at a circle surrounding a long-nonfunctional fountain of broken cherubs. After a mournful glance at the cracked, winged babies, she faced a once-white house covered in a hundred years' worth of dark smears. All manner of grime, industrial chemicals, and waste rained from the solid canopy overhead.

Sensing the presence of *something* in the house lent a pronounced eeriness to the sight of the decaying building in a world cut off from the sun. Kirsten stared up, listening to the intermittent drip of muck from the interlocking panels overhead. She glanced at several pipes routed around girders and struts along the underside of the artificial ground way overhead. As far as she could see in all directions, metal stretched into the endless dark.

"It's sad here." She rubbed her arms. "Like these old buildings miss the sky."

Dorian went past her into the house. "Now you're getting a little too metaphysical."

She followed. "Hello? Is there still a spirit here?"

Her voice echoed from moldy walls. To her surprise, much of the interior furniture, art, and vases remained intact. She dusted her finger over the end of a delicate bannister where a curved staircase led to the second floor, and frowned at the stain on her skin.

Dorian studied some of the artwork. "There's definitely a spirit here, the place hasn't been looted."

"Damn right," said a crotchety-sounding man as he strode through a closed set of double-doors.

The man looked older, seventy or more but in (except for being dead) good health, if not a bit on the chubby side. His orb of thick white hair and bushy moustache didn't quite jibe with his dark red smoking jacket, making him seem part way between playboy and the host of a children's show.

Kirsten whirled, looked right at him, and waved. "Hi."

He screamed, folded his arms over his face and lifted one leg. "Dammit, girl, don't do that!" The spirit trembled for a few seconds before he put his leg down and leaned at her in a menacing posture that probably wouldn't have even scared Morelli. "I'm the one supposed to be scaring you."

She giggled. "You couldn't scare anyone. You look like a sweet, old man."

"You can see me?" He glared. "Damn it all to hell. I suppose you're here to cart me off to that damnable home." Relaxing, he tapped a finger over his lips twice with a serious expression. "No, it's probably too late for that"—he leaned at her, raising his voice to a yell while making 'scary gestures' with his hands— "since I'm dead." He burst into a cacophony of off-key laughter.

"I know you're a ghost," she said. "I'm here to—"

"Allan Smithee." He extended a hand.

Dorian raised an eyebrow at him.

"Hi Allan, I'm Kirsten… Look, I—"

"Bah, your friend there's a killjoy. Name's actually Kantor."

She folded her arms and pursed her lips, wondering if she should dare try to speak again.

"We're chasing a wild goose," said Dorian. "Some old spirit on the East Coast thinks you're going to be attacked by an abyssal soon."

"Me?" Allan paced in a circle, grumbling in a grandfatherly sort of way. "What would an abyssal want with me? I just keep to myself." He paused with a dawning look of enlightenment and a raised finger. "Demon, huh? Must have been a film critic."

"Your movies couldn't have been too bad if you were living here." Dorian gestured at the decay surrounding them.

"I can't complain, though the place has lost a bit of its allure, I'll admit. So, why do you think this thing is after me?"

Kirsten bared her teeth, somewhere between a forced disarming smile and a look of complete confusion. "I don't know." She relaxed, exhaling. "Best guess was that you're a very old spirit who never grew in power. You would be a potent easy meal for an abyssal that devours spirits."

Allan *harrumph*ed about for a moment, complaining about the lack of mortal visitors upon which to practice being a ghost.

"Ever thought about leaving the house?" she asked.

"No, not really... What was that?" Allan whirled around, shivering as he faced the double doors he'd entered from.

"What—?" Kirsten froze as the creeping cold feeling that must've touched Allan hit her next.

Blackness exuded past the slats in the door. The sight of what appeared to be another wraith brought icy memories of pain to her left breast. Kirsten gestured for Allan to get behind her. The older ghost scurried around as a somewhat human-shaped figure reformed out of the thick ebon mist. Seven feet of billowing vapor with the vague hint of a head and two arms resembled a Harbinger in all respects save for the eyes: twinkling specks of crimson rather than baleful silver.

It also emanated a noticeably stronger sense of dread.

Dorian's image distorted, drawn toward it in stretching tendrils as if it desired to absorb him. He grunted, struggling to back away, but couldn't break the pull. Kirsten shifted herself solid to ghosts and tackled him back. They hit the ground, sliding over ancient hardwood on dusty carpet that bunched up. Dorian gasped, pawing at his chest as if a full-body suit of duct tape had been torn away from his bare skin all at once.

"Guess we know why The Kind were scared of this thing... Get out of here, D."

He wheezed, fatigue laced with shocked agony.

Allan fared somewhat better, able to step back from the creature. The way he moved made her imagine a great wind trying to push him toward the manifestation. Unlike Dorian, he didn't begin to unravel.

Kirsten jumped up, channeling her psionic energy at the dark spirit. A sense of its form spread over her mind as her abilities clashed with it. She held her hands out, pushing against the demon's advance. Allan backed into the enormous foyer while she held it off. Inky smoke roiled as it fought off her influence. Crimson eyes brightened to glowing orange. It stared at her.

"Mommy! Help!" Evan screamed from her earbud, sounding like a sudden voice-only call.

Kirsten expected a creature like this to play mind games. However, having it simulate his voice in a way that seemed more believable than being behind her caught her off guard. Her concentration lapsed at the alarm in the child's voice, allowing the creature to slip forward. It lunged at her, plunging an icy hand into her chest at the base of the throat.

It pulled its arm back, dragging a ghostly image out of her. Living eyes rolled back into her head as her spectral form peeled loose. Ghost-Kirsten struggled against the hand around her throat while her body convulsed behind her. As the separation moved down past her ribs to her hips, she found the presence of mind to stop fighting physically. Desperation rode out from her mind on a wave of psionic energy that slammed into the abyssal with tremendous force, launching it away to the far side of the room.

Kirsten's spirit snapped back into her body hard enough to launch her into the wall. White wainscoting crumbled around her as she bounced away and crumpled to the floor in a heap of splinters and plaster dust. Playing possum, she didn't try to move.

"Kirsten!" Dorian shouted when she remained limp on the ground.

The abyssal glided across the room, ignoring her and going straight for Allan. He backed into a corner, attempting several wizard-like gestures that had no apparent effect on the demon. A painting flew, passing harmlessly into the mass of shadow. Allan flung a couch, skidding it across the room; the humanoid shape of black flowed around it.

Kirsten's eye popped open. She grinned. Allan's screaming drowned out the clatter of debris when she stood. Allan noticed her moving and screamed louder, acting terrified of the demon. She stalked up behind the billowing cloud of darkness as it loomed over the old ghost. The soft soles of her boots muted her steps. As it began to draw Allan's energy inward, Kirsten called the lash in mid-swing.

A scintillating strip of blue-white light extended from her hand, stretching out as she swung sideways. The creature sensed the energy manifest, but couldn't turn in time to avoid it at that distance. She tore the astral tendril through the dark cloud. The strike felt as if she had slashed a mass of jelly with a sword. The familiar tension of impact tugged at her brain.

The demon's inky vapor brightened to dark crimson. It twisted while shrieking a polyphonic scream that shattered vases, knocked the rest of the artwork off the walls, and sent a torus of dim red light expanding outward. The energy washed over Kirsten with the sensation of burning alive. She shrieked and fell. Shuddering, she wailed all the air from her lungs. Her body cried without conscious thought at the overwhelming agony. Gasping, she gathered her composure the same way she did when Mother burned her hands on the stove.

"Thanks, Mom," she snarled, and forced herself to stand in defiance of the pain.

Kirsten swung the lash in a hard upswing that stalled halfway inside the creature's mass, stuck. Tapping her fear and hatred of Mother brought a howl of anger from her lungs. She grabbed the whip in both hands and poured power into it. Her eyes glowed like two tiny holes into the center of a white star. The lash swelled in width. Growling, the abyssal raked vaporous crimson claws at her chest. The attack didn't affect her uniform, but felt like searing-hot irons pressed to her unprotected skin. Kirsten screamed, but poured the agony into the lash, brightening it more.

The abyssal recoiled, shrinking in on itself. Seconds later, it exploded.

Kirsten lay on the floor where the blast of hot demonic ichor left her, some fifteen feet away from where she'd been. Steam rose from her uniform. The lash flickered and went out, leaving the area dark. Once again, a trip to the Beneath covered her in vileness. Hardwood never felt so comfortable. Without Darksight on, she found it peaceful, as if she'd closed her eyes. She had a reasonable degree of certainty the gunk probably burned like hell, but she'd gone to a place beyond pain. It hurt so much, her brain said *nope*.

"My, my," said Allan. "Are you all right, miss? I should thank you for preventing that monstrosity from ambushing me."

"You okay?" asked Dorian, hovering over her.

"I think I'm going to donate some credits to that group calling for the abolition of boiled live lobster. I know what they feel like now."

OUT OF THE CLOSET

E arly morning dreams found Kirsten in pleasant surroundings. A boat, small and wooden, ferried her along a street filled with water past ancient buildings with waving, smiling people. Konstantin stood at the rear, guiding them with a pole, singing in some butchered attempt at Italian—the closest her imagination could get. Barefoot, she wore loose-fitting white dress and a wide-brimmed hat ringed with flowers, like some old-school Degas painting. She tugged at her neckline, exposing more and more of her chest to his approving smile.

"Mom?" Evan's voice emanated from Konstantin's lips.

Kirsten groaned.

"Mom?" Konstantin shrank into Evan, in pajamas. "Mom, the shower's out of suds."

Her eyes cracked open. She found herself lying on her side, staring past a haze of sleep-crumbs at an annoyed, wet, and naked boy. A plastic cylinder as big as his thigh dangled upside down in his grasp, obviously empty.

"Put something on." She pushed herself up, sitting.

"I'm wet." He pointed at the bathroom. "The shower ran outta suds while I was in it."

Kirsten gave him a bleary stare. His birth mother had not bothered to clothe him much; using every scrap of credit she got her hands on to buy drugs. Kirsten took the empty soap canister, unable to do anything other than laugh at his lack of shame.

"Go back in the bathroom, I'll order more."

"'Kay." He wandered into the kitchen.

"If you're going to eat, at least wrap yourself in a towel. Don't drip all over the place."

"'Kay..." He changed course.

Kirsten thumbed at her NetMini, putting in an order for two cartridges of Sudzy-Kleen. She rolled her eyes at the crime against language perpetrated by people in the name of marketing.

Evan, towel around his hips, emerged from the bathroom and dragged a chair over to the counter. When he climbed up and leaned his forehead against the 'sem, she giggled.

"Didn't I ask you to wait a few years for coffee?"

"This doctor on the net said it's good for you," he whined. "I'm only making a small. Please?"

Kirsten bit her lip, finding it hard to resist his half-closed eyes and round face. "You know those articles don't mean much. The *experts* will agree with whoever the money comes from."

He thought for a minute, fidgeting with the towel to keep it in place. "Does that mean the ones who say it's bad are lying too?"

Checkmate.

At least, checkmate for her sleep-deprived brain. "Fine, a small one. Make me one while you're over there."

"'Kay." He grinned and plunked his forehead against the door again, staring at the flickering sparks inside.

She gathered herself out of bed and stretched, skritching him on the head as she plodded past him to the apartment's only window. A delivery bot tapped a spindly metal arm on the glass a moment later, dropping off two canisters of autoshower soap.

Evan got the tamed-down version of last night as they shared coffee. When he finished his, he sprang from his seat, grabbed one canister and ran out of the towel into the bathroom. Kirsten slumped on her elbows, watching his shadow in the light the bathroom cast on the main-area floor as he installed the new cartridge. For a moment, sudden dread gripped her.

Was this a good idea? Can I handle having a kid? I'm only twenty-two. I... I don't have anyone to fall back on for help. What if I can't handle him? What if the caseworker walks in and he's streaking around? Am I supposed to yell at him for that? Will it cause mental scars if I make a big deal about him being naked? She let her forehead fall on her arms. The autoshower started up. Evan soon lapsed into his recitation of his favorite lines from the Monwyn vids.

Kirsten draped herself to the side, staring over the table at the lit bathroom. A contented smile spread over her face. *I guess I should have a little faith in myself.*

HOSPITAL WHITE HALLWAYS PASSED IN A HAZE OF ANXIETY. WITH EVAN SAFE at the dorm school, Kirsten walked across the Division 0 portion of the police complex toward the admin wing. A large room similar to a library added a touch of brown and black to the otherwise antiseptic place. Four teens in admin duty uniforms sat at the tables using a combination of terminals and old books to research various things. One girl stared at the holographic screen without moving, navigating the system by willpower alone.

Kirsten leaned on the wall below the nameplate for Dr. Susan Loring and watched the admin cadets work for a few minutes. The door opened with a squeak, revealing the smiling brown face of one of the department head-docs. She had an exotic look, with high cheekbones and thin features. If not for the woman being six feet tall, Kirsten would have thought of her as a caramel elf.

"What's on your mind, luv?"

Kirsten let her folded arms fall at her sides. "Just thinking about these admin kids, wondering if I should've gone that route."

She followed into the room, flopping on the couch while Dr. Loring took her position at a nearby chair. Like most psychologists Kirsten had ever worked with, she'd decorated her office with many bookshelves piled with actual paper books and an uncountable number of small statuettes, sculptures, and magnetic toys. She'd opted for blues and greens, probably a deliberate use of calming colors.

"I understand the decision was not all yours," said Dr. Loring, a hint of regret in her words.

"Yeah, they knew about the lash. At least Evan can't do it. All he can do is see them. They don't have any reason to force him out into the field."

"You don't want him out there?"

"Of course not." Kirsten smiled. "I don't want him to get hurt. I mean, it'll be his decision when he's eighteen, but that doesn't mean I'm going to like him putting himself at risk."

Dr. Loring thumbed her datapad. "How have you been dreaming lately?"

Kirsten smirked. "You don't have to dance around it, Doc. I haven't had *that* nightmare again. I'm sure I've dealt with it."

"Oh?" Dr. Loring perked up. Long slender fingers curled over the top of her datapad as she leaned forward. "Please, would you talk a little more on that?"

"As long as you don't think I'm crazy. You know I can see ghosts and you work with psionics all the time so I guess you won't."

The doctor smiled.

"Well, when I was working on the Motte case, I ran out of ideas. I knew Intera Corporation was hiding something, but I had no way to get inside. They had assassins coming after me so I didn't want to go in the front door again. I didn't care what the living were up to at the time; I was hoping to find a trace of Albert there. I knew I had the potential for astrally projecting myself, but I never tried doing it before."

"I remember you said Evan was projecting when you first met him."

Kirsten sighed with a sad smile. "Yeah, I thought he was a ghost at first." She picked at the gold serpent around her right wrist, her sorrowful mood chased away by the thought of Konstantin's arm around her. "This is gonna sound silly, but I visited him in the dorm, hoping he'd teach me how to do it."

Dr. Loring leaned back, skimming her electronic notes. Blue light changed the tint of her beige suit-jacket. "Your rating is far higher than his in Astral Sense. Shouldn't you have been better at it?"

"Rating is potential. Individual abilities like that take practice. I might have tried once, I don't really remember it. Projecting is strange. I felt exposed, naked almost. As a projection, we're only a body of light." Kirsten moved her hands as if tracing a woman's outline, and sat back staring at the wall for a full minute. "My mother would sometimes paddle me in front of her friends like it was some big 'hey, look how awful my daughter is' event: tea, cookies, and a screaming bare-assed child. I'm not really sure how many times it happened, I just remember them all cackling at me. They thought it was funny."

"It's possible from that you developed gymnophobia?"

"Huh?" Kirsten looked over.

"It's a fear of nudity, both your own and seeing others without clothes.

You might even realize it is an irrational fear. Do you have a problem with undressing to shower?"

"I don't think so. I don't have a problem showering. I mean, I have to blockade the bathroom before I get in the tube, but I only do that because I've had two incidents. I'm no Neko-chan. I don't enjoy exhibitionism or whatever it is they're doing, though some of the dresses I've worn lately haven't been too far away from streaking in public." She blushed.

"Incidents?"

"Peeping ghosts. Getting put in a med tank was mortifying, but I don't have nightmares about it. I don't think I'm gimmophobic or whatever you said. I can shower just fine when I have privacy."

"Okay." Dr. Loring tapped in some more notes. "Have you considered the possibility you have a negative self-image? That can happen in cases where a person has been subjected to an authority figure who constantly belittled them."

"I have a negative self image, but it's not from my actual appearance. You know how people are about psionics." Kirsten frowned, picking at the bracelet. Her mood flipped a 180 and she offered a silly smile. "Konstantin thinks I'm pretty."

"You're dating?" Dr. Loring sat up with a raised eyebrow. "Interesting, I directly mention your mother and you have no reaction at all."

"Yeah. He's Russian. Smart, rich, handsome..." Kirsten's unusually buoyant mood faded. She shifted on the couch and almost snarled. "That woman has no more power over me."

"Sounds like you finally had a little good luck for a change. Anyway, back to your dream?"

"Oh, yeah. I'm very lucky to have found Konstantin. Maybe the world's trying to make up for the rough start." Kirsten interlaced her fingers over her stomach. "Evan showed me the basics of how to project. Mostly from me looking at his thoughts while he did it. I got it to work, but when I saw my body behind me, it was so startling I panicked. I think I blacked out and woke up *inside* my nightmare."

"Some manner of lucid dream?"

"I'm not sure what that means."

Dr. Loring rested her arms on her lap, over the datapad. "It's a dream where once you realize you are dreaming, you have some degree of control over it. Events within a lucid dream can feel as though they happen in reality. People often don't realize they're dreaming at first, but once they do, they can exert their will into the dream-world and change things."

"This is where I was afraid you would think I'm cracked. It didn't feel like a dream at all. It was like I was eight again, back at home and locked in the closet. I tried to get out, but I made so much noise Mother heard and came over to punish me. It wasn't the same as the dream, though. In the nightmare, I had no control, I was stuck re-living the same thing over and over again. This time, Evan was there, telling me to come out. I figured he was shouting at me in the real world to 'come out' of my body, but I took it like he yelled at me to defy Mother and leave. To run."

Dr. Loring nodded.

"I did. I defied her. I finally wound up changing into a grown-up before she could paddle me. I wouldn't let her hit the little girl on the floor again. I knew Mother was dead. I knew it was some kind of vision or dream or something. I lashed her. Dorian thought my fear of her had been preventing me from projecting, like I didn't want to be exposed."

"It's a plausible theory. So you haven't had the nightmare again since that event?"

"No. I almost want to say some kind of presence helped me get through it. I had this strong sense of peace and relief come over me when I woke up, like… I dunno."

"A religious experience?"

"Hah." Kirsten laughed. Her mirth lasted a few seconds before it faded to a tentative giggle, then silence. "Umm… I never thought about it that way. You know, Dorian said she was a psychotic person using God as an excuse. I mean, if there even is a God, maybe he finally got tired of Mother making him look bad."

Dr. Loring chuckled.

"I still don't know. I've seen the doorway to the other side, where spirits go. I can't see past it, but for all I know, there's only positive energy there, not some old man in a toga."

"Do you still have feelings of anger toward the religious minority?"

"Mostly Reverend Harris," Kirsten said with a sarcastic frown. "It's not the concept of a divine I hate, it's people who use it to hurt others. Especially an idiot calling for psionics to be rounded up and burned at the stake."

"That is progress for you, Kirsten. It's hard to hate a theoretical construct. Maybe someday humanity will mature enough not to need a Santa Claus for grownups. However, just because a person is deluded into thinking there's a higher power out there doesn't make them worthy of hatred or scorn."

Kirsten sat up. "According to Dorian, the religious once persecuted the atheists. Far enough back, they even killed them for it. Kinda funny how they're the majority now."

Dr. Loring switched her posture, crossing her legs the other way. "Perhaps flying into space routinely and not finding Heaven helped. I suspect it was a challenge for a society spread over multiple planets to cling to a belief system that put the Earth as the center of reality. Do you think someone out on a colony world goes to the same heaven or hell when they die?"

"There is somewhere we go when we die, Doc. I've heard the voices of long-dead relatives call out of these silver doorways. If there is a Heaven, it can't occupy the same plane or dimension as this world. It wouldn't be above the clouds."

"Well, it seems you have come to terms with what your mother did to you. As you must assume, the board is a little concerned about Evan given the horrific abuse you suffered. There is some worry that given sufficient stress you may…"

Kirsten shifted on the couch, staring at Dr. Loring. The mental image of what her child self looked like—tiny, battered, shaking—formed in her mind. She sent it into Dr. Loring's head. The doctor dropped her datapad.

"I know this was different because I saw myself from the outside in that dream. There's no way in hell I could ever do that to a child." Kirsten wiped tears. "Never." She slouched. "I am afraid I won't do something right, though. I don't exactly have a role model of parenting to go by. I don't want to mess him up, but I will *never* hurt him."

The doctor stared at her, bending forward as her fingers probed the carpet in search of the lost device. She hooked it with a fingernail and pulled it into reach, then sat up, tapping at the edges of the plastic device. It took her a few minutes to gather enough composure to speak. "That… image you flooded me with. That was you?"

Kirsten gathered her arms tight to her chest. "Yeah. At first, I thought the vision was making it look worse to torture me. Then I remembered how bad things really were. I don't care what Evan does, I'll never be capable of any of the things that woman did to me. If anything, I'm afraid I'll be too lenient on him."

Dr. Loring leaned forward and back, offering a slow nod as she pursed her lips. "How does he feel about your Russian superman?"

A twinge of nausea flipped in her gut. She fussed with the bracelet, spinning it around her narrow wrist. "There is some tension. He thinks Konstantin dislikes him. Keeps calling him old, too. But I guess for a nine-year-old, he would be."

"How old is the man?"

Kirsten shrugged. "Like twenty six, I think. For a little while, I wondered if Evan may just be jealous of another male figure in the picture."

"That's kind of Freudian."

"Huh? I dunno what that means. He isn't throwing fits or tantrums or even protesting when I go out. He... I don't know, Doc. It's like he's worried about *me*, and there's no reason for it." Kirsten shuddered while facing a theoretical situation of having to choose between Evan or Konstantin. Nausea hit her hard and she had to work to keep her breakfast down. She broke out in a sweat. "If that relationship becomes any threat to his well-being, I'll call it off with Konstantin. Evan's more important to me than anything." She drew in a sharp breath, sweating, shivering.

"Are you alright, Kirsten? You look feverish."

She grimaced at the wall. "I was in the Beneath last night, maybe I picked something up. I'll head over to the infirmary when we're done."

"Good enough. In the manner of your adoption request, you haven't demonstrated"—Kirsten sagged, her eyes reddened, breathing became shallow—"any significant mental issues that would lead me to challenge his placement."

Kirsten squeaked, clutching her hands to her chest.

"Also, given you're the only astral sensate of any note in the entire region, command is encouraging the idea. I'm going to recommend that they approve your request. Danita did have some reservations about your living arrangements, however. You'll have to do better than give him a sleeping bag on your floor."

"Oh!" Kirsten jumped to her feet. "I was gonna get a bigger place, but I was terrified they'd deny me and then the giant apartment would just make me think of him." She sagged onto the couch again, heart racing. "I'll definitely move. We'll get a place."

Dr. Loring gave her a quizzical look. "You should get over to the infirmary, Kirsten. You look normal again. Do you feel feverish at all?"

"No," she blurted, grinning. "I feel awesome."

8

AMONG THE DEVOURING

Kirsten draped herself on Konstantin's arm in the back seat of the white stretch hover-limo. It had been almost a week since she had seen him. His presence had come on like a rush of a little girl seeing a military husband back after a yearlong deployment. He didn't seem to mind her clinging, entwining his seized arm through hers until he held one of her hands. Her white high-heeled shoes sat on the floor, her legs tucked up under her on the pale grey seats.

Shimmering silver fabric clung to her body, held in place by a choker that verged on being too tight. The garment left most of her back exposed; however, unlike her green dress, it remained secure over her front with a hem that ended at mid-thigh.

"Do you like the gown?"

Her open-mouthed grin closed as she nodded. "It's lovely."

Kirsten rested her head on his shoulder, one finger idly picking at the inch-tall metal ring around her neck. The tight-fitting band, coupled with her subservient posture, caused an out-of-nowhere crash of shame. Woozy, she let go and sat up with one hand on her head.

"Are you alright, my dear?"

She glanced at him, then forward. "I… The choker is a little tight. I don't think I'm getting enough air." *I feel like a concubine wearing a collar.*

Konstantin brushed her hair aside and tugged her closer by the metal ring. The gesture did little to lessen the feeling of being another of his possessions. Too sick to resist, she clasped her hands to her gut and let him move her. He squeezed something behind her neck, the device chirped, and loosened.

"It's adjustable. Is that better?" He tugged at the fabric, seating it over her collarbones a little wider.

She slid her hands from her stomach to her lap as he nudged her face around with a finger on the chin and kissed her. As if he had special powers, the touch of his lips chased away the tightening knot in her gut. Konstantin leaned back, smiling with half-closed eyes at her stunned expression.

"Yes, that's better." She put a hand on her throat, fiddling with it.

He took her hand again, stroking the back. "You still seem on edge."

"In the Badlands, gangs abduct people and keep them as slaves. I met a spirit who died like that, wandered all the way to the city. She had so much shame. I couldn't get her to grasp the concept of latent self-image. She couldn't make the collar go away, probably still out there somewhere. Her spirit won't be free until she finds justice, and there was no convincing command to let me go after the bastards who killed her. This choker feels a bit like a collar to be honest." She offered a weak smile.

Konstantin gestured at the roof. "Then you shall be rid of it. How do you fancy blue?"

"Oh, you don't have to buy me another dress. I'm only feeling a little claustrophobic. Really, it's fine." *Am I? What the hell is wrong with me? Why is my stomach doing backflips? Maybe I'm just afraid I'll wake up from this dream. Seriously... what is a billionaire like him doing with me? I'm a nobody.*

"I insist. I want you to be at ease and enjoy our night."

She blushed. "Aren't you speaking?"

He chuckled. "Yes, I have to entertain the underlings for a short while. After that, the evening is ours."

He spoke in Russian to the driver, who altered course. Kirsten stared at her knees, feeling awkward and guilty about making him spend more money. Nothing she said over the next ten minutes changed his mind, and as the car began its descent, she slipped her shoes back on. They landed on the roof of a Mallplex in Sector 214, an area of the city that functioned as the playground of the wealthy. As if her arms moved on their own, she found herself clinging to his arm while crossing the hovercar parking area to an elevator.

How did I go from police officer to arm candy? A weird sense of light-headedness came and went. *Oh, well... Captain Eze said he'd wear a dress to date this guy.* She stifled a laugh. *But... I'm not that person. I don't need a guy to be rich.*

Regular bands of light flashed upward along the walls as the elevator sank. An unsettling tickle returned to her gut as she gazed at the reflected couple on the silver doors. The blonde sylph hanging off the arm of the handsome billionaire seemed like some helpless debutante incapable of functioning on her own. She bristled at the look on her own face and shifted a half-step right. Konstantin glanced at her adjustment from full-body lean to three-fingered handhold.

"Are you sure you're well, dear? You seem to be out of sorts tonight."

The nausea lessened with her eyes closed. "I feel guilty you're spending money on me again because the neck was a little tight. This dress is fine, there's no need to replace it. What you spent on it could feed six families for a week."

"Tell you what." He pulled her into a peck on the cheek. "Tomorrow morning I'll send some credits in your name to whatever charity distributes food to the disadvantaged."

"I'd rather you do that than buy me another dress."

The elevator doors opened.

"Too late, we're already here."

He led her by the hand into an opulent open-air mall corridor. Rose-marble tile floors turned white wherever they reflected the strong overhead lights. A strip of starry night sky showed visible past artificial birds down the entire the center of the hall, despite their being seven floors beneath the roof. Couples sat in the shade of trees, some at tables, eating. The food court of the Sector 214 Mallplex constituted the high end of dining for the 'well off, but not wealthy' crowd. Somewhere in the distance, a small girl had a fit about the wrong color shoes. Kirsten looked around until she spotted the child, and offered a sympathetic look at the beleaguered older man weathering the verbal assault from a ten-year-old in an outfit as expensive as what Kirsten wore. *He's got the patience of a saint. Damn, kid, I'd have been happy to* have *shoes at all at your age.*

Men and women in gleaming white armor, spotless save for a black TMC on their breast, wandered in pairs. The mall security personnel, unlike the last ones she ran into, worked for Triton Manufacturing Corporation rather than some holding company that owned the building. TMC manufactured at least eighty percent of the items for sale in this place. The mega-corp had engulfed, over the course of the Corporate War, a wide variety of manufacturing and consumer-goods industries.

The security officers appeared to pay more attention to the workers than the customers. Kirsten thought this odd, pondering until she realized Konstantin had led her distracted self into a store and a clerk attempted to talk to her. The young woman had surface thoughts and couldn't have been older than seventeen. *Live workers in the mall? Not dolls?* Kirsten squinted a dire look at some of the security staff. *Oh, I get it. Watch the poor people working for the elite, make sure they don't steal.*

"Hi," she said to the girl, before looking up at Konstantin. "This really isn't necessary, I—"

He shushed her with a nod, then took the datapad out of the clerk's hand and offered it. "Just pick something, don't worry about it. We've got to be there soon."

Guilty about making him late for his big presentation, she grasped the eight-by-eleven inch device bearing images of faceless female bodies in gowns of various sizes, styles, and color. Konstantin had suggested blue, and for whatever reason, it stuck with her. Kirsten selected the first style that looked close to comfortable and handed the pad back to the woman while sending an embarrassed grimace at the wall. The girl took it and turned on her heel. A smile replaced her surly teenage glare as she waved for Kirsten to follow her. She passed a few benches and fake plants on the way to an area full of partitions separated by ivory-colored curtains with faint silvery speckles. Inside each chamber, a metal disc about three feet across rose a few inches up from the floor.

"I'll need you to take the dress you're wearing off," said the clerk. "Keep your undergarments on though."

Mechanically, she reached up and opened the choker, letting the garment slide over her hips to the floor. For a moment, a twinge of shame hit her as she realized she stood bare-breasted in a room full of other women about to have their purchases created-to-size. The sight of Konstantin peeking in the door at her sent a fireball of adrenaline swirling around her abdomen. Shame shifted to thrill in an instantaneous flash. Having him watch her on display stirred feelings deep within she had never entertained.

Forgetting at once about the shame of spending such amounts on clothing, she stepped onto the pad and turned to face the clerk. The teen looked away to be polite, noticing the bright red color of Kirsten's face— though it no longer came from embarrassment.

"Please lift your arms away from your sides." The girl poked at a holographic terminal outside the booth, and closed the curtains. "When it starts spraying, hold your breath."

A metal spider descended from above, spinning and whirring about with an array of strange attachments. Green laser light drew glowing lines upon her paleness, shrinking and forming to her contours. Two seconds later, they flickered and went out. Eye-watering chemical fumes surrounded her as the device sprang to life in a flurry. It started at her neck, spraying cold material in passes. Viscous blue muck adhered to her skin in a patch that crept down over her chest. Kirsten closed her eyes, trying to hold still while being coated in a substance with the consistency and feel of cold cat vomit.

The clicking machine printed the garment onto her body in rapid circular passes. Breezy chill passed over her ribs, down her back, and onto her thighs. Her arms hovered upward, no longer due to conscious thought. Her face cringed in a grimace appropriate for being dipped in cold oatmeal. Frenetic robot appendages continued to spin around her, fussing and pulling at the material. More spray on the thighs thickened, pulled into a loose-fitting knee-length skirt.

The slime changed texture before her eyes, forming into discrete threads of seven different shades of blue. What had seconds before been liquid became cloth. The garment left her shoulders bare and took on the feel of silk. Two robotic arms pinched it between her shoulder blades, and a rush of cold air hit her. In the span of only a few seconds, the machine slashed the gown to the small of her back and stitched in a MolWeave fastener disguised as a thumbnail-sized faux sapphire at the upper edge at her collarbone. Squeezing it would open or close the back.

The material fell away from her thighs, no longer sticky, draped loose and airy. Silver dust, hundreds of thousands of spent nanobots from the glop, fell around her. She gave the metal spider a wary look as it retracted into the ceiling, taking that as a cue to emerge from the private chamber. The clerk waited for her, holding a matching silk stole. Kirsten let the girl put it around her shoulders, thanked her, and met Konstantin outside by the front desk. He had the old dress folded over one arm and flashed a large grin at the sight of her. She squirmed, unable to shake the memory of the dress in liquid form.

He held his free arm to the side. "Even better than the last."

Without thinking it over, she walked right into his waiting caress. "You really shouldn't have."

Konstantin bowed at the clerk and escorted her back across the mall.

"When I accompany you to a proper store in Milan or Paris and spend thirty thousand on a garment, then you can feel guilty. Think no more of this than you would of a hydroponic coffee."

Sixty credits is a far cry from six thousand. She fidgeted at the dress. *How do they have the nerve to charge that much for something out of a spray nozzle.* Kirsten wore a traitor's mask all the way back to the car, thinking about the people out in the city searching trash containers for their next meal.

———

DULL MURMURING FADED AWAY TO THE FAINT CLAMOR OF PEOPLE EATING. A serenade of metal utensils upon actual China plates offered a soporific backdrop to distant muted conversations. Konstantin's table was at the front, amid a patch of shadow cast by the elevated podium. Kirsten knew not one person here. Her seat toward the stage-side of the round table gave her a better view of the room than the speaker, who had spent the past forty minutes droning on about the majority buyout of RedEx by *Vostochno-Sibirskaya Kholdingovaya Kompaniya.* VSKK, as it soon became shortened to, was one of the few corporate entities of the ACC permitted to trade within the UCF.

It's headquarters was in the Petropavlovsk-Kamchatsky Federal District, which managed a precarious balance of continued membership in the ACC while adopting a style of 'citizen-management' compatible with the views of the west. The VSKK hadn't set off too many red flags. Most of the 'Berlin-Moscow Crowd,' as Konstantin called the conservatives within the ACC, had no interest in trading with the UCF— they wanted to own it. Kirsten suffered through a rather boring diatribe about how the 'idiots in Moscow' thought old-world government is dead, and capitalism is the true destiny of man.

"Not that it matters much what the Senate thinks," said a pale, skeletal-thin older man with wild, puffy white hair and a sheer powder-blue suit. His tone carried an air of fluffed up superiority that rankled Kirsten at hearing it. From the waist up, he seemed thin, but his ass had to weigh two hundred pounds alone. "RedEx is legally headquartered on Mars, and no matter what people on either side say, Mars will get its sovereignty sooner or later." He pointed a fork with a nugget of ham on it at Konstantin. "You think I jest." He snatched the ham in his teeth. "But *thmf*" —he chewed until he could speak again—"the MLF is only gaining support. And RedEx hasn't paid a single credit of taxes in two years."

"It's true," added the man's wife, the only kindred soul in the room. Like Kirsten, she seemed miserable. "They've been challenging the legitimacy of the UCF to collect taxes on Martian soil. Even if their claim is baseless, it's kept them tangled in litigation for twenty-four months."

A younger man hastily swallowed some frightening white blob-like thing. "They know they're going to lose, but by the time the judiciary hands down a verdict, they will cry bankruptcy with all their assets in shadow accounts."

Kirsten left her white-blob-thing on her plate, untouched, the only one at the table to do so. She couldn't even watch him eat it.

He gestured with his fork. "They'd be stupid not to, and there's nothing the tax bureau will be able to do about it."

Two glasses of wine, a mostly full belly, and scintillating conversation about corporate tax law allowed her one final glance at the nattering rich that packed the room around her before she faded out. Blackness came underlined with random voices calling about the filet being a hair too cold or too overcooked. One woman's wine wasn't dry enough. Another whined endlessly about how her domestics stole small objects out of spite.

A sense of vertigo overtook her. Her fall out of the chair landed in a muck-filled tunnel. Coarse cloth scratched at her skin as she pushed herself into a seated position. Bare toes squished in ink-black ooze, and her steps went ankle deep in whatever coated the metal ground. Twelve-year-old Kirsten yawned and stretched before clasping her hands to her growling stomach. Her dress consisted of a canvas square with a hole in the middle for her head that covered her front and back but left her sides exposed, a trait that provided a continuous reminder of the chill in the Beneath. A belt of an old electric cord held it around her waist.

It was time to make the long climb through pipes to the surface world while she still could. In another year or two, she would be too big to fit and have to find a way get the hatches open—or be stuck down here like everyone else. She stretched before creeping out of the shaft that led from the hollow where she had created a nest of old pillows, cloth scraps, and whatever toys had been left behind down below. She slept in the lower reach of the city plate, high above the Earth. The ground had more room, and less slime, but also more danger. Up here, in a hollow space behind a gap too small for an adult to fit, she found a safe place to lay her head down.

No longer noticing the way her feet squished on the metal floor, or even how bad it smelled, she thought about the fragrance of the giant trash boxes in the outside world and became hungry on the way to the nearest ladder. The pipe she needed to climb to reach the surface waited some distance away, in a place where loud machines rattled all hours of the day and everything stank. She would have made her lair closer to the pipe, if not for the constant noise and the reek. No one, not even the dead friends who kept an eye on her, could sleep there.

She climbed down the ladder, noticing a dingy man in overalls and a red cap standing directly below her, smiling upward. He continued to stare at her the whole time she climbed, even after her toes touched old pavement. At the time, she had thought him friendly; in this dream, Kirsten's adult mind knew why he was smiling. She knew what he stared at while she descended. Crude canvas ponchos tied with wire hid nothing from an observer below.

Her memory of what he said blurred into tonal noises and slow motion gestures. He offered food, but she had to pay for it. The man seemed nice. He kept smiling, waving flat, octagonal cans at her with pictures of stuff that looked edible. She nodded in the dream. Her voice came as a high-pitched murmur, words lost to the fog of time.

Yes, she wanted food.

Sure, she could do him a favor.

Her arm entered her field of view, holding his hand as she walked with him. A few blocks away, past warped and broken houses, a little brown door led to a room with a grungy mattress, a table, and a few chairs. Kirsten was innocent, but not stupid. Even without skimming his surface thoughts, which she did, she knew what he wanted. She knew what the *favor* was. She glanced down at her toes, and tried looking up with her best pleading, begging stare. Perhaps guilt would overtake lust.

Blurry blue flannel covered the arms of the indistinct figure standing there, gesturing at the door. The first clear words she recalled were, "Your choice, kid. I ain't about to force nothin'." He tapped two cans together, each about the size of his palm. Both bore markings: UCFM-PSK. He backed away and took a seat in a folding chair, leaving an unblocked path to the door. "Military 'personal sustenance kit.' They're fresh, better'n anything you'll find down here. No mold, no rat shit, hell... even heats itself up. It's here if you want it. I got water—clean water—not that black gunk."

Hunger grew overwhelming. *How bad could it be? People do it for fun all the time.* Mother was up there. Every time she crawled to the surface,

Mother might be waiting. This man didn't seem like he would hurt her. She trusted him more than Mother. She wasn't *little* anymore. Food not from garbage seemed like a lost treasure.

Her hands moved without thought. The wire-belt fell across the tops of her feet, letting the improvised garment flutter loose. She sat on the cold, damp mattress, staring one last time at the door. The growl in her stomach grew louder as she scratched at her gut. She couldn't make eye contact with him. *Why am I ashamed?* She clung to the rough cloth, shivering from fear as well as cold. She wished she had more practice begging, maybe she could have guilted him into feeding her instead. The boy she'd made friends with had tried to get her to go begging with him on the surface, but she chickened out. He wasn't afraid of people like she was.

He also never came back. She hadn't seen him in two weeks.

"Okay," she said, "but, can I please eat one first? Just in case..."

"Osure." One of the cases plopped onto the mattress next to her. "You thinkin' I might kick ya out afterward 'n welch. Well, I ain't the mean type, and I trust ya, girl. You don't look like the stealin' type. We got a deal?" He moved to sit next to her on the bed, arm around her back.

She jumped at the touch, fearing the kind of hand Mother would lay upon her. His was different, warm, comforting. The man's voice fell away to the warble of indistinct remembrance as he said comforting things and kept petting her hair like a cat. Kirsten stared at the metal octagon in her hands, salivating at the promise of untainted food. She listened to his thoughts; he would not harm her—she was precious.

He lifted the canvas dress away from her while she sat motionless, offering no protest. Shame and fear paralyzed her, but hunger held them back. He gestured at the can, willing to wait for her to eat. She didn't *have* to do this. She *could* get up and leave. If she accepted the food, she made a deal.

The crack of the lid, yielding to a grimy little finger, startled her awake amid the remembered hiss of the chemical warming agent and the smell of beef stew.

KIRSTEN SHOT UPRIGHT IN HER SEAT, BRINGING A STARTLED END TO SOME discussion about an investment opportunity on Venus. The taste of military field rations bubbled in the back of her throat, almost to the point of bringing her fifteen-hundred-credit dinner back out. Ten years ago that mystery meat had been as if her mother's invented God had come down from his ivory tower in person and bestowed such a feast upon her. If only she hadn't had to pay for it in blood.

As the faceless man said, it *was* her choice. She could have walked away; she could have scrounged for scraps, but she wanted filet mignon.

She wanted Konstantin.

A rising tide of shame set her eyes in search of the nearest bathroom. She had to get away from these people. She wasn't one of them. Inside, she still felt like a dirt-covered orphan who snuck into a room full of rich people. The sight of her plate struck her as shameful. People out there still lived as she once did. Every minute spent among such arrogance and greed reminded her of where someone like her belonged.

Konstantin's hand found her shoulder. The instant she looked into his red-brown eyes, she forgot all about her past. Self-loathing and contempt for the wealthy vanished, leaving her biting her lower lip like a schoolgirl. He leaned in close, planting a polite kiss on the cheek by her left ear. Kirsten shivered with excitement and flashed a wicked smile as she fantasized about what Konstantin might do to the man who asked her to trade herself for food. But no... she couldn't tell him what she did when she'd been twelve. She hadn't told anyone about it. Not even Doctor Loring.

No point to. He didn't force her to do anything. She made a choice. It didn't bother her.

At least, she told herself it didn't.

She almost believed herself.

"I am sorry for bringing you to such a droll event. If I were able to, I would happily have spared you such an evening. Alas, I could not extricate myself."

"Oh." She put a hand over her heart. "I'm sorry for falling asleep. At least I woke up before I fell out of the chair. That would've been mortifying."

"I give you Konstantin Dobrynin, CEO and chairman of VSKK," said a man over the loudspeaker.

He kissed the back of her hand and stood to the sound of his name reverberating over the dinner hall of the Imperial Hotel.

The audience swelled with the muted clap of gloved hands and polite men. His touch lingered on her arm as long as distance allowed, their fingers slid past each other until her hand fell at her side. As if pained to do so, he pulled his gaze away from her and smiled at the crowd while he strolled up onto the stage.

"Thank you, Yevgeniy." Konstantin bounded over to the podium, shaking hands with the man and adding a healthy back pat. He leaned up to the microphone and his voice boomed over the hall. "The buyout of RedEx was a long, time-consuming process involving hundreds of hours of careful negotiations..."

Kirsten slouched in her seat, tuning out the boring details. His lustrous voice seemed far less enthralling while discussing market share and growth predictions. She stared at her clean hands, at the peach-colored polish on her nails. Far from the finger that plucked open the can of military rations ten years ago. *If only I knew I could use suggestion back then.* Kirsten gathered a napkin to her face and cried in silence. She sniffled, allowing a brief red-eyed glance up at Konstantin, who continued to ramble on about the particulars of a giant fish eating a little fish. However, VSKK was different. According to him, the giant fish was simply pulling the little one under its fin and protecting it from bigger, meaner fish. His company was a protector within the corporate sea.

She crumpled the napkin into a ball in her lap, unable to listen to him or bear the sight of any of these people who never found a whiff of garbage to be appetizing or had to let someone take advantage of them just so they could eat.

The canned stew left a mark. After hiding in her lair for two days, she had gone topside through the ever-shrinking pipe, no longer afraid that she might 'not come back' like her friend. Kirsten remembered sitting outside the opening topside, wondering how many more times she would be able to squeeze herself to the surface. Hours later after she'd foraged the trash for her food she realized that something scared her more than Mother finding her. The idea of the man waiting for her, of having to do *that* again caused her to lie down in the alley and sleep on the surface.

He couldn't fit through the pipe.

Kirsten looked at the room, bound to her chair by the fear that all eyes would be on her if she stood and ran out. She let herself slip half into dreaming. Boredom and disdain for the people around her conspired to lift her out of her present *now*. Instead, she dwelled on bad memories.

The world above had felt cavernous the morning when she awoke in the alley. For two years, she had lived under a metal sky with ghosts as her primary caretakers. Never before had she risked the surface during the day, but she refused to go back down there. That man would offer her food again. People spotted her that morning in the daylight. Police showed up while she rooted around a trash processor looking for something to eat.

I really did freak out. She chuckled to herself, remembering how it took three grown men to hold her down. To their credit, they didn't restrain her or lock her in the back seat. When she used up all her energy thrashing and begging them not to make her go home, they talked. The medtech figured out what she had done for food, but the woman reacted as if someone attacked her. *I think her name was Eva.* Kirsten didn't say anything, didn't admit to what she had done, afraid of getting in trouble.

The psychiatrist said someone had done a horrible thing to her. Kirsten, perhaps as a defense mechanism, didn't look at it that way. She rationalized it as a trade—a need for a want. She needed food while he wanted a girl. When the doc asked her for details, so the police could find her *attacker*, she had told him Ritchie already threatened to kill the bastard and might've even done so by then. After Kirsten explained Ritchie was a ghost, the doc laughed it off. His afro almost went straight when she turned on Darksight for proof and her eyes glowed white.

Division 0 picked her up an hour later. Doctor Smith, or whatever his name had been, never sent any information to them. Zero had no idea she'd had sex, or how little it seemed to bother her. She never spoke of it, or much thought about it consciously.

After lifting out of her daydream, Kirsten wondered if there was something wrong with her. An event like that should have damaged her. She should have thought of it as rape, not as 'having sex.' Instead, she tried not to think of it at all.

Compared to Mother, it was nothing.

She stared at the empty wine glass, looked for a waiter, and thought of Evan's fearful reaction to the SynVod. *No more, I've had enough.* The empty glass went back on the table. Memory of that night faded as she heard his little voice cheering for his favorite wizard. The warmth of him sitting in her lap, the scent of his hair, the way all the sharp bony bits of his body could find all the tender parts of hers made her smile.

She sighed at Konstantin, still blabbering on about how the RedEx acquisition would benefit both sides. *Fuck these stupid rich bastards. I should be with Evan right now.* Frowning into her hands, she leaned forward, hating everything about this place. *Konstantin is so stupid rich it's embarrassing. I don't belong with him.*

Nausea came on without warning. The taste of remembered beef stew crashed into whatever unrecognizable, overpriced mess she'd eaten. She staggered to her feet and shuffled to the restroom. No one seemed to notice amid the crowd. She almost heard a giant clock ticking, waiting for the hover limo to turn back into a pumpkin.

In spite of the sickening coral-hued décor in the bathroom, the urge to vomit faded the instant the slamming door cut her off from the thousand wealthy people. She wet her hands and wiped her face, dabbing carefully with a microfiber towel to preserve as much of her makeup as she could. The cold water felt wonderful.

"What's the prick's name?" The voice carried the burden of years of smoking, barely managing to sound female.

Kirsten looked up, seeing nothing in the mirror. To her left, a bleach-blonde either in her early forties, or later fifties with a lot of work, leaned against the counter. Purplish-black marks ringed her neck, hashed with the unmistakable imprint of rope. The mink stole around her shoulders stared at her as well, as if on the verge of laughing.

"Sorry?"

"I said, what's the prick's name?" The woman took a drag on a cigarette mounted to the end of a long black wand.

Kirsten offered quizzical stare at the device and took a step to the side, coughing. "Is that a cigarette? You must be kind of o—I mean you must've died a while ago. I wasn't dumped; I just don't fit in here."

"Ahh, poor girl in Tinseltown." A modicum of politeness caused the woman to blow smoke out of the side of her mouth so it didn't hit Kirsten in the face. "Where you from, kid? You have an Ohio look about you. Let me guess, someone just told you what you had to do to the producer to keep the part?"

"I have no idea what you mean. I'm from West City. I am kinda poor though, not sure why Konstantin wants me. He's got so much money, he could have some biotech firm build him the perfect woman in a vat." She pouted at herself in the mirror. "Except for that being illegal."

"Call me Linda, hon." The woman offered an aristocratic handshake. "Bit late for stage names I suppose. Men like him want one thing, and it ain't your money, honey."

"It's me that's having doubts. I don't know if this is a good idea." She leaned on the counter as a dizzy spell swam over her brain.

"Looks like he slipped you a Mickey or something, dear. Well, don't you go signing any pre-nup. What you should do is turn the tables on the lout. Give him the ol' innocent wide blues, get him to skip the paperwork, then walk off with half his money."

"That's awful." Kirsten gawked. "I could never use someone for money."

"Well, sweetie, I'll forgive you that. You're still young. There's two kinds of people in this world: those who use others and those who are used. Your little Russian sweetie out there didn't get to where he is being an angel."

"Konstantin is different!" she snapped, backing off, lowering her voice. "He loves me."

"Mmmhmm, they all do, Norma Jean, they all do." She took another long drag. "Right up until they stop." She tapped the marks on her neck.

Kirsten blinked at the ghost, wondering if she said the name wrong on purpose. "I'm sorry, did he get caught? Do you need me to do anything for you?"

"Oh, they got him alright. Jimmy went to death row screaming how it was all my fault, how I drove him to it. His own security cameras got him kicking the chair out from under me"—Linda scowled—"paranoid bastard. Course, cancer took him before the state could do it. At least I had a little fun a few years later driving him crazy."

"So he fell for the wide blues, huh?" Kirsten smirked.

"Hmpf." Linda became bored with the conversation and wandered into the wall.

At the sound of the applause rising outside, Kirsten checked her makeup again and scurried out.

KIRSTEN KNOCKED ON NILA'S DOOR WITH HER FOREHEAD, A REPETITIVE thudding in time with a mantra of "I'm a dumbass." The door snapped open, causing bonk number eight to hit nothing. Nila, wearing a knee-length brown T-shirt that bore the logo of the Manglers Gee-ball team, shook her head.

"You're back early. Guess you chickened out again?"

"I… It just didn't feel right." Kirsten ducked under Nila's arm and walked inside.

Nila rolled to lean against the wall, crossing her arms. "The night couldn't have been that bad. You're still wearing shoes."

Kirsten laughed and covered her mouth at the sight of Evan asleep on the couch. "It was boring as hell. Yanno, it's so strange. We got back to the limo afterward and he was really letting me have the romantic thing. I just kept thinking about Evan every time he started kissing me."

Nila let the door close and followed Kirsten to the kitchen. "That's a little creepy, don't you think?"

"I felt worried, like something bad was happening to him. I know it's silly. You would have called me if something did happen, but I couldn't shake this feeling." Kirsten stopped, lifting an eyebrow. "What's with the look?"

"It's probably nothing. Evan zonked out on the floor while they were playing some game. He sat up all worried, calling for you. Poor little guy was having a bad dream. He seemed to think you were being eaten by a dragon."

"Maybe he's getting too into that Monwyn thing." She suppressed a giggle. "Still… it's a little weird we both had odd feelings."

"You want coffee?" Nila padded around Kirsten to the counter. "Neither one of you are precognitive, are you? Wait, weren't you wearing white or silver when you dropped him off?"

"No thanks on the coffee. I'm going to bed as soon as I get home." Kirsten kicked off the high heels. "Yeah, he bought me this dress on the way there after I said the choker was too tight. I hope it comes off, it was sprayed on."

"Now I know something's wrong. You never turn down coffee." Chuckling, Nila gathered some of the loose fabric and felt it. "Feels like cloth."

"Nano-assembled right on me. Felt like a giant cat horked all over me. No, I'm not a precog. They didn't find any evidence of it in Evan either, but he's so little who knows. Still, nothing happened to me tonight." *Did he sense my dream? Why would he? It doesn't bother me much.* Kirsten stared at the counter. In her head, her twelve-year-old self reclined on the filthy mattress, staring up at the man. *Am I afraid of sex? Is that why I keep running away from Konstantin?*

"Hey," said Nila, snapping her fingers in front of Kirsten's eyes. "The way you look, you should sleep here tonight. Are you sure you should be driving?"

"I'm sober. I had two glasses of wine three hours ago. I'm just tired." She paused, watching Evan breathe. "Maybe I will. Can I borrow something to sleep in?"

She leaned on the kitchen island, smiling at the back of the couch where Evan slept while Nila jogged off and returned with another oversized shirt. After a brief trip to the bathroom to change, Kirsten crawled onto the couch, lying on her side between Evan and the back. As she put her arm over him, he drifted out of his slumber long enough to grin at her before snuggling into the cushion.

Nila offered them a blanket and cut the lights on her way into the back hallway. Kirsten clung to him like a wolf protecting her cub. Evan stirred, talking incoherently in his sleep.

She leaned closer and kissed him on the head, then stared at his face, gripped with sorrow over her shambles of a life, and vowing this boy would have the best childhood she could possibly offer him.

He squirmed and muttered, "Pick strawberry."

9

EASY PRAY

S alt stung Kirsten's eyes as she trudged down the too-bright corridor toward the locker room. The dark blue T-shirt and sweat pants clung to her, soaked. She'd felt worse than this once before, but only after leaping from the eleventh story of a building several seconds prior to a massive explosion. Somehow, a virtual ass-kicking had reached almost the same level of exhaustion.

She kicked off her sneakers, peeled away her sticky garments, and poured herself into an autoshower tube. Gabriel said the pain existed only in her mind and would go away soon. She wished soon would hurry up and get there.

"Hey," shouted Nicole, her voice muted by plastic walls. "How's the hand-to-hand training going?"

Kirsten looked left at her friend pressing herself against the inside of the adjacent tube, facing her with a silly grin on her face. Nicole had to be the only person within a hundred miles paler than her, and not the least bit hesitant about nudity.

Hey. Kicking my ass. I don't have enough energy left to shout. Kirsten pushed aside her awkwardness at the way Nicole could totally disregard having nothing on. Not that the girl flaunted it. She simply didn't care.

Okay, chirped Nicole in her mind. *What happened? It's only ten and you look like you're ready to pass out.*

The cascade of hot water jets coaxed her brain out of simulated reality; pain washed away with her sweat. *Started working on sword styles today with Gabriel. I got stabbed six times and lost my right arm twice—virtually.*

Ouch. Nicole wiped a bit of fog away to maintain eye contact. Running the thing super-hot flooded it with mist. *I just spent the past hour doing boring jogging. Maybe I'll let Gabriel stab me tomorrow.*

Kirsten laughed. *He's married.*

Oh wow. I know where your mind is. Nicole winked. *I could use a brush up on hand to hand techniques.* She examined her fingernails. *Telekinesis makes me lazy sometimes.*

After the dry cycle wound down, Kirsten changed back into uniform and flopped on the bench, staring at her boots as if attempting to work the quick-snap closures with her mind. They obligingly fastened themselves. An event that shocked her until she realized Nicole sat next to her.

"Geez, you look drained." Nicole put a hand on her forehead. "Oh, wow, you showered with your bracelet on?"

Kirsten covered the gold snake with a protective hand. "I don't wanna lose it. Konstantin gave it to me."

"You've practically got little heart-shaped bubbles popping over your head. Wow, you got it bad. You guys get it on yet?" Nicole stuck her legs out. Her boots rose into the air, oriented themselves, and slid on her feet. A second later, the fasteners all closed at once.

"Does that ever get boring?"

"Nope." Nicole grinned. "You know, he's so rich and handsome, he's probably hung like a mouse."

Kirsten blushed and squirmed. "I dunno. We're not in any hurry—" Her NetMini rang. She gave Nicole an apologetic look and pulled it out.

"Saved by the bell," said Nicole, before bouncing to her feet. "Gotta do a ride-along today with Div 1. Psionics are behaving themselves for the time being, so we're doing this tactical exchange thing—oh wow, you wouldn't believe this chicken place we found." Nicole fumbled with her NetMini. "Bad part of town, but they raise their own real chickens. Live animals! Can you believe that?"

Kirsten held up a hand and swiped to answer the NetMini. "Hello?"

"Division 1 knows all these little places with the best food," said Nicole.

The holographic face of a middle-aged Hispanic man, painted with bruises, faded into view. Kirsten tilted her head at the trace of familiarity in his eyes. She might have recognized him without the black eye.

"Agent Wren? I'm sorry to call you like this. I know it must be breaking some rule somewhere, but I need to talk to you."

He's a little old, I guess you like that though. You know I read somewhere that girls who date older men have daddy issues.

Kirsten swatted at Nicole's shoulder, shooing her away with a grin before saying, *Perv* telepathically. She rolled her eyes and shifted her attention back to the call. "Have we met?"

"I'm Father Carlos Villera. Remember the Five Hundredth Street Sanctuary? The ninja?"

"Oh." What little color existed in Kirsten's face faded. "Yeah. What—?"

Nicole draped herself over Kirsten's shoulders. "A priest and a ninja, I gotta hear this. Sounds like the opening of a bad joke."

Will you behave yourself? "Did something happen? You look hurt."

"Some miscreants attacked me a short distance from the building. They didn't seem interested in robbing me. They had a strange energy about them, a darkness similar to the little mess you made here."

She cringed. "Sorry." Her armband display showed a clean calendar day for the first time in weeks. "I got nothing on my schedule. I'll stop by as soon as I can get there."

Nicole stood up. "Wait, you're going to church?"

"No." Kirsten scowled. "I'm going to *a* church to talk to a man about a mugging. I'm not going *to church.*"

"Even after all the, like demons and… *Ooo*"—Nicole clung to Kirsten, hiding, staring over her shoulder—"that guy is huge."

That time, Kirsten looked toward where her friend stared before her tired brain could think better of it. She relaxed upon realizing Nicole referred to the muscle mass of a Division 5 officer. The guy stood taller than the locker cabinets. Tattoos intended to make him appear to be a cyborg covered his entire back and arms. Kirsten blushed at her misinterpretation of Nicole's outburst.

"I gotta go. I suggest you leave this room before you ruin your relationship with Jaden. You really are incorrigible."

Oh, I'm just looking. Nicole winked. *No harm in looking, right?*

Careful, Nikki… Some guy complains, you could get sent to mandatory sensitivity training for harassing him.

The big guy glanced in their direction long enough to notice a pair of women in Division 0 uniforms looking at him. His face paled. He scooted to the end of the row and used an open locker door to hide his body from them, rushing to cover up. If not for his reaction to psionics, the sight of such a huge man futilely trying to hide behind a little panel of metal would've made her laugh.

Nicole found it amusing. Kirsten teased at her bracelet, no longer caring what random people thought of her being psionic.

She had Konstantin.

DIRT AND TRASH WHIRLED ABOUT IN MINIATURE CYCLONES AS THE PATROL craft settled into the parking lot of the Five Hundredth Street Sanctuary. The usual crowd of homeless that often blocked off the front was nowhere in sight. Dorian blurred through the door, appearing outside the car and spinning in a slow survey of the area.

"Police were here within the hour."

"I didn't know ghosts could use clairvoyance." Kirsten climbed out and shoved her door downward, closing it with both hands. "How do you know that?"

"We can't use clairvoyance." He gestured across the street. "Notice how empty it is here? The only people in sight are those two tourists from East City who seem to be lost, and that PubTran employee fumbling for his NetMini by the apartment down the block. It takes about an hour and a half for societal equilibrium to return after police leave."

"You make it sound like I'm tainting the environment." She stared at the approximate spot where a demonic ninja almost killed her.

Dorian squeezed her shoulder. The solid contact snapped her out of the worry-trance. "We might slow down the process of recovery, but it takes at least three patrol craft to cause the scatter effect in this part of town."

She took a heavy breath, trying to forget the memory of an icy sword in her leg. "You're touching my shoulder."

"I'm getting a lot of practice lately, hauling you out of the way of bullets."

"Ha. Ha." Chuckling, she went to the door of the church and hesitated. "Am I supposed to knock here or just walk in?"

Dorian didn't stop, phasing past the wall.

Kirsten shrugged and tested the door. Finding it unlocked, she walked in. "Hello? Father Villera?"

The front room of the Five Hundredth Street Sanctuary looked much as she remembered it, minus the debris and a patrol craft embedded in the window. Workers had already patched the hole the car left behind. From the outside, it looked no different. Inside, the newness of the section appeared obvious. The scent of food wafted in the air, something with an abundance of garlic that had lingered on a hot plate for too long. Rows of chairs still surrounded a small pulpit. A forgotten grease-stained blue cap sat upon one.

"In here," said a voice with a mild Spanish accent from an interior hallway. "First room on the left."

Kirsten didn't like the pain in the voice, so she hurried toward it.

Fr. Villera sat on the edge of a Comforgel pad in a room barely large enough to hold it plus a tiny desk. He looked as though he had fallen down a flight of stairs and landed on his face. She gasped, approaching in two quick steps and drawing a stimpak out of her belt case.

"What happened to you? Here, use this."

He took the four-inch red, plastic cylinder from her, squeezing it in gratitude. Wrinkles around his eyes deepened with a smile. He muttered in Spanish, "Not only the face of an angel, the heart as well."

Kirsten's cheeks warmed with blush.

He chuckled. "I guess you speak Spanish."

"Enough to get by. I can't keep up with a pair of angry wives or two guys cheering at Gee-ball."

"Frictionless," he said, grinning. "People from my homeland watch Frictionless matches. Gee-ball is a coalition abomination."

She found the inflated contempt in the voice of a so-called priest amusing.

Dorian snickered. When Kirsten gave him a quizzical glance, he waved her off. "You're too young to understand, and it wouldn't be at all funny to you after a belabored explanation."

"Try me?"

"I'm sorry?" Fr. Villera looked up.

"Oh, I was talking to Dorian." Kirsten gestured at him. "Sorry, it's probably rude to talk to a ghost with a person around."

He gave her the look people always did when they heard the word ghost. His other eyebrow went up, presumably as he remembered Mariko's violent demise in the center of his church. His bushy grey eyebrows settled down and he nodded. "Go on."

Dorian cleared his throat. "Well, Gee-ball is played in a large three-dimensional area about a hundred yards long and twenty-five yards tall. All the players wear grav suits and try to carry a metal ball through a ten-yard square goal suspended at the center point of each of the long ends. It's pretty violent and dangerous for the players. Frictionless, on the other hand, involves a ground-skimming orb that players are only allowed to kick. They don't use grav suits. Everyone stays on their feet, though their special boots can send the thing flying fast enough to break the leg of an unwary player. Sometimes they bank shots off the side across the entire field. In Frictionless, the goals are wider, and on the ground."

"You haven't told me anything I don't already know," she said, frowning.

"Europeans look down on Gee-ball. They always have, even the ancient sport it replaced. They used to make fun of the name 'football,' since kicking the ball was a fairly rare part of the game."

She scowled. "Well that's five minutes of my life I won't get back."

"I warned you," said Dorian. "Don't be mad at me. I told you it wouldn't be worth it."

The hiss of a stimpak came from Fr. Villera. His facial bruises faded somewhat.

"Sorry, Father. Why do you think I can help you more than the patrol officers?"

"You'll see in a moment." He sat back, hands on his knees. In seconds, all the bruises returned. Despite his best effort to remain stoic, he cringed.

Her hand went to the small of her back, the spot where she had been scratched. "Abyssals?"

"They looked like ordinary street thugs, except for their eyes. All black."

Kirsten shot a pointed look at Dorian. "That body with Tech Hollings had all-black eyes, too."

"Only the individuals the priest is talking about were still alive... or at least moving around," said Dorian. "Perhaps poor Mr. Arris was dead a lot longer than we initially thought? Maybe something decided to borrow his skin."

She faced the priest again, putting a hand on his shoulder and closing her eyes. It took a few seconds, but she found paranormal energy swirling around him. It had far less power than the scratch she'd suffered, and she purged it with barely enough exertion to alter her sedate expression. She offered a second stimpak.

"Try again. It should work this time. I got rid of a lingering spectral trace attached to you."

He applied the autoinjector to his shoulder. This time, the bruises stayed gone.

"I am not sure what you did, but I thank you, child." He held her hand. "I am concerned that these creatures, for I do not think they were men, will return. I wanted to ask you for your help. The regular police dismissed it as a common mugging."

"I don't think those beings will set foot in this place," she said, looking around until the presence of a wooden crucifix on the wall made her examine the floor, unable to bear the sight of it. Mother had waved those things in her face almost daily, and put dozens of them on the walls of her old bedroom trying to 'chase away the Devil.'

Dorian backed into the hallway and glanced toward the front. "They don't have to walk inside to shoot through the windows."

"If they were trying to kill him, they would have shot him already." Kirsten studied the priest. "Why do you think they attacked you?"

"I was hoping you would be able to explain that. I could tell there was something dark about them, something beyond ordinary. I invoked the Lord upon them and they recoiled."

Kirsten suppressed the urge to roll her eyes.

"Something troubles you, child?"

Not suppressed enough.

"Umm." She shot a guilty look at the door. "I don't mean to offend you personally. I just don't have much love for religion. My mother couldn't handle having a psionic child. She thought I was something from the Devil. She was… very abusive. Almost killed me."

Fr. Villera blessed himself, and again took her hand. "Perhaps you can find peace in talking about it?"

Kirsten stared at him. *Why am I even considering saying anything to this guy? Religion only exists to control how people think, to keep them complacent.* She sighed, slouching. "I'm an astral sensitive. That's a psionic who can see ghosts, to put it simply. As a child, whenever I used that power, my eyes would glow. Mother would lock me in the closet to have quiet time and wait for Jesus to come save me. She'd invoke the Bible at me as though she were trying to cast spells or some such bullshit. Ghosts talk among themselves. Word spread that I could see and hear them, and they came to looking for help. Most of them only wanted me to pass a final message to their families. A few wanted to give information that might help their murderers face justice." Kirsten sat on the Comforgel pad, half an arm's length away from him. "I was happy to at first, I was so lonely in there. Mother thought I was talking to 'my dark master' and started burning me with the stove. I became too scared to talk to the ghosts after that and tried my best to ignore them. They became angry and threw things around the house at all hours."

"And your mother blamed you for it." He squeezed her shoulder.

Something caught Dorian's attention and he drifted out of sight.

"When the burning didn't make the Devil go away, spanking escalated to beating. She broke my arm a couple times, leg twice, more ribs than I can count. From age six to ten, I used more stimpaks than most front-line police officers do in their whole career. Of course, she hid it all from my dad. All in the name of some invisible man in a toga who doesn't even exist."

Fr. Villera chuckled. "Kirsten, mankind has always sought ways to explain things science has proven inadequate for. Humans have an elemental need to feel there is something greater than all of us, something that's 'got our back' so to speak."

"How many people have died in the name of religion over the years? Heretics, witches, infidels? So many people claim to follow a 'loving' God, but they're so willing to hate and kill anyone who doesn't believe their version of the fairy tale. All the peace and love stuff goes out the window the minute someone questions their invisible man."

Fr. Villera smiled with the face of a grandfather she never knew. Right away, she felt guilty for losing herself in her rant, as if she'd been trying to poke him with a stick to see how much he could take.

"I'm sorry." She looked down, voice soft. "I grew up with one extreme, and I've seen things beyond this world that I can't explain either. There's a silver doorway waiting for spirits. Sometimes, voices of long-dead loved ones come from the other side. I guess it *could* be some kind of Heaven out there. I still don't think there's a singular 'god' entity, just positive and negative forces—like cold and hot. I..." *Saw an angel... or Seraphim as it called itself. Yeah, sure, he'll think I'm freakin' nuts. Oh, screw it.* "I saw something the other day."

"Oh?" He seemed content to let her vent.

"Remember what I told you about Harbingers after my son crashed through your church?"

He nodded.

"Well, there *is* something else, beings opposite to them... I get the feeling they are fewer in number and perhaps stronger, not so much the counterpart to Harbingers but to They Who Always Were. The other ones called themselves Seraphim. I don't know what they are, I met one after I had my ass kicked back and forth for ten minutes. I could've been delirious. She said something about the demon's presence in the world allowed her to intervene, otherwise, they can't."

"You would not be the first person to claim a visitation from such a being. It has happened numerous times in the course of human history."

"Yeah, and they get called nuts, put away, or burned at the stake. The people who use religion as a political tool can't bear to hear things that break their grip."

Fr. Villera chuckled. "Perhaps it is a blessing that so much of society these days is blind to it. The church has little sway in the lives of average citizen anymore. I am content to do what I can for those who need help. It doesn't matter to me what anyone else does or does not believe. I know what I believe, and for me that is enough."

She stared at him. For the first time she could remember, she looked at a religious person without a trace of contempt or the urge to get as far away from them as fast as possible. Mother used God as a sword. Fr. Villera seemed to use him, her, or it, as a stimpak. Kirsten studied the soft orange glow in the gel pad, muted by the sheets.

"You have a good heart, child. You didn't deserve what was done to you. I ask only that you keep an open mind. Do not become that for which you harbor such contempt."

The strange urge came out of nowhere. Kirsten wanted to tell him about what she did, about why she fled the Beneath. For some unknown reason, she needed him to tell her it wasn't her fault.

"Father…" She shivered, unable to look him in the eyes.

"Yes?"

"They're back." Dorian appeared in the doorway, pointing. "Three of them."

Kirsten stood. "Umm, never mind. My partner just said those thugs are back."

Fr. Villera paled.

"I'm going to have a word with them." She adjusted her utility belt.

"I have a better idea," said Dorian, following her to the front.

The shadows of three figures moved in a patch of light across the dim main room of the strip mall store-turned-church. At a few minutes past noon, the sunlight filtering down from the haze above the city created a shadow puppet show upon the ground. Black sweatshirts, hoods up, and matte-black Nylcron pants fastened by a trio of silver buttons by each pocket lent them an ominous air. The sight reminded her of modernized Shadewizards from the Monwyn vids—only they lacked skull-tipped staves.

"What's your idea?" she asked.

"Those three don't look capable of masterminding anything more complicated than the self-cooking mechanism of a Nippy-Nom burrito, and even that may be asking too much."

She grinned. "I don't think I can mind-read abyssals."

"Exactly why I was going to suggest you scare them off, and I'll follow them. Maybe I can find their boss, or at least overhear something."

"Won't abyssals see you?" She paused at the end of the hallway, just before it expanded into the front.

"If anything, these morons are only possessed. I walked circles around them a minute ago and they didn't react."

"Sounds like a good idea. If it doesn't work, I'm sure they'll come right back here."

Kirsten strode across the church area, shoving the double doors open with an authoritative heave. "You three," she barked, drawing the E-90. "Hands out of your pockets. You're wanted for questioning in the matter of an assault."

Hissing chuckles leaked from them. The one to the far left lifted his head. Beneath his hood lurked pale grey skin and black eyes.

"Okay, we can play that game too." She put the gun away and called the lash, spinning it around before flinging it to the side in a showy gesture. "You obviously don't know who you're dealing with."

The middle one leaned toward her, hissing. An icy tickle picked at her heart. Kirsten gathered her psionic energy and shoved hard against the incoming paranormal attack. The collision of energies triggered a backlash that flung the teen on his ass. *Wow, these guys are pretty damn weak.*

"Was that supposed to do something?" She advanced, raising the lash. "Don't worry, boys. If you're still alive, this won't hurt at all."

They scattered, scrambling off to the left at a full run. Dorian ran after them, vanishing down a side street. She relaxed her power and the tendril receded into her hand with a faint *whoosh.*

Mexican spices drifted by on a sudden uptick in the breeze. *Damn, now I want one of those instant burritos.* Bright light pulled her gaze skyward as a billboard-sized hologram slid out of a side street a few blocks away. A news-bot as big as a two-seater car turned ninety degrees to its left, and glided down 500th street. The panel contained a full-on view of a nude corpse, showing a three-second loop of the image before a blue-gloved crime scene worker grabbed the lens. The NewsNet slowed the video down, giving the public a lingering view of a tall, slender woman with short, blonde hair. An ad panel opened at the corner, claiming she 'looked this good dead' because she used Lifespring™ beauty care products.

The revulsion of such public disrespect for the deceased gave way to Kirsten's notice that the body appeared too healthy to be a streetwalker. Her posture, arms at the sides, reminded her of Mr. Arris.

I wonder if her eyes are black too. Gah, how can they show that? Have a little respect.

Kimberly Brightman's voice entered her awareness as the angle of the news-bot brought her within reach of its directional speakers. "... discovered earlier this morning has been identified as Miss Uma Donn." The image shifted to a pair of women in the courtyard of a beige-paneled century tower. They stood in the shadow of a sculpture depicting an oversized neural interface unit a nest of incomplete metal rings, like giant steel Cs. The reporter attempted to interview a stern-faced woman in tan security armor. No sound came from the brief clip, until the reporter's face took over the holo-panel.

"Tara Lawrence, chief of security for EnMesh Corporation, Miss Donn's former employer, had no comment about the events. Some on the GlobeNet claim Miss Donn is the victim of corporate espionage."

Kirsten sighed, finding herself unable to pull her gaze off the thirteen-foot holographic image of a dead woman flying past the church. The ad now offered funerary services. The image changed to Kimberly standing in an ancient-looking Victorian-era room, adjacent to a man apparently crafted from bronze. Small openings on his face provided a view of whirring gears and blinking lights inside him. The words 'Live from Cyberspace' scrolled along the bottom of the image.

"I'm here with Anachronis, one of the preeminent figures of the GlobeNet inner circle."

"Thank you, Kimberly. Clearly, there is some conspiratorial angle to this event. I have information which leads me to believe Miss Donn was attempting to defect to a rival corporation. In all likelihood her"—his face took on a forced smile amid a fluttering of clicks and snaps—"transfer failed. EnMesh, or any corporation for that matter, does not often let its top-tier talent go too easily."

"Anachronis, you are accusing a UCF-held corporation of assassinating one of its own employees? Surely, you don't think such things happen here?"

The grating metal chuckle slithered down her spine. He sipped from a martini glass that appeared to contain oil, with a gear on a toothpick. "I assume by your question you also believe the illusion that there is any significant difference between our gov—"

An advert for EnMesh Neural Interface Units took over the screen, promising six percent improvement in all cybernetic component response time. Kirsten went back inside the church, unnerved by a second body found in similar circumstances. It nagged at her as odd, but with no clear evidence of a paranormal event, she had no grounds to involve herself.

Fr. Villera tended to a large food reassembler, connecting a fifty-gallon drum of OmniSoy to its pick-up line. She jogged over to help him move it, laughing as if her elf-thin arms would be much help. Between them, they jockeyed it into position. She felt weak until she realized she had done eighty percent of the work. *Maybe those sessions with Gabriel are paying off.*

"They'll be here soon. Would you mind helping out a bit until your"— he cast an uneasy glance at the front doors—"partner comes back?"

"I suppose, unless I get an urgent dispatch."

Kirsten set up tables, putting buckets of plastic forks and knives out among piles of napkins, smiling at a few vagrants that filtered in. After taking a position behind the long table, she helped hand out bowls of reassembled food—beef stew. The fourth bowl had her on the verge of throwing up, unable to make eye contact with anyone.

When a lull in the line came, Fr. Villera leaned on the table. "What is bothering you? It is what you wanted to ask me earlier, no?"

"Is it bad to, umm" —Kirsten couldn't continue looking at his face, and fidgeted at the empty bowls in front of her—"I had to eat. He had *real* food. I was so damn hungry."

"Someone took advantage of you?"

"I lived in the Beneath after I ran away from home. I was so afraid of my mother finding me I hid under the city. Sometimes at night, I snuck topside to pick food from trash crushers." Kirsten stared out over the crowd. "I didn't know there were places like this. A boy, younger than I was at the time, said he got real food from begging and wanted me to go with him during the day. I was too scared to go, so he went without me. He never came back."

Fr. Villera put a hand on her shoulder. "Chances are he got picked up by the police. Look at you now. What would you do if you found a little boy in dire need?"

Kirsten cried a little, thinking of Evan. *Of course, why did I assume* *something* bad *happened to him?*

"Only a weak man takes advantage of a desperate person. He should have taken charity on you and just fed you. What he did to you was reprehensible."

"I should have said no. Who knows what I could have caught, or if he would have killed me, or..."

"You tread down a path which leads only to destruction and self-loathing. Life sometimes gives us choices with no good answers. There is no purpose in taking on blame for the evil of another."

"But it was my choice. He didn't force me to do anything. I said yes." Kirsten stifled her emotions, forcing a smile as a poor couple approached, astounded to see a uniformed officer handing out food. She gave them a bowl each, waiting until they had wandered away to a table before continuing. "I'm more upset with myself than him. I never really thought it bothered me much. Compared to my mother, he felt caring."

"Think about it, girl," said Fr. Villera. "You were starving, desperate. You picked through others' trash hoping to find something to eat that wouldn't poison you. Was there really a choice for you to say no? A decent man would have shared what he had willingly. But, I can understand why you made the choice you did, but you should understand... it really wasn't a choice. The man may as well have taken what he wanted by force. I don't see it as different."

Kirsten handed another bowl of food to a grungy middle-aged woman. For almost ten years, she'd hidden from the shame of feeling like she'd done something horrible. Having someone, even a priest, tell her that she'd not done anything wrong, that she'd been a victim, lifted some of that weight off her. At the verge of tears, she managed a smile at the priest. "Thank you, Father."

KILLER OFFER

Dorian returned a half-hour later with an unhurried gait and confident smile. Kirsten excused herself from behind the table and walked over to him. A few of the vagrant men checked her out as she passed, distracted from their free meal. The smell of the beef stew carried less shame than before, but still couldn't bear the thought of eating any.

She met Dorian on the sidewalk outside the door. "I know that grin; you found something, didn't you?"

"Yep." He motioned to the east. "They went about two miles and a block or two south. There's another street church there. According to the sign, run by a Reverend B.G. Wallis. All three of our friends went in a side entrance from an adjacent alley."

Kirsten squinted in that direction. "They went *into* another church? So much for the holy ground theory."

"Well, just because the word church is on the front door, doesn't mean it is one."

Whatever she had been about to say stalled in the back of her throat, turning into a sigh as she glanced from Dorian to Fr. Villera. "This is so confusing. No wonder it's such a mess." While staring over the crowd, it occurred to her most of the men among those eating had been watching her the entire time, probably staring at her ass. She went back inside, moving past the line on her way to where the priest tended the food warmers.

"I have a lead on the punks who roughed you up, Father. I'm going to go follow up on it before this uniform chases away more people in need of a meal."

Villera muttered something, waving his hand at her. *"Vaya con Dios, mi hermana."*

Kirsten smiled. *"Gracias, Padre."*

She hurried outside to the patrol craft. Dorian's grin irritated her to the point of blurting, "What?"

"I'm not used to seeing you being so pleasant to a religious person."

She poked at her forearm guard. The patrol craft's door was open by the time she reached it. "Didn't you spend the better part of the last six months trying to convince me it wasn't the belief, it was the person?"

"Doesn't mean I can't be amused."

She frowned. Dorian sank into the passenger seat, ignoring the closed door on that side. Kirsten gazed up, grumbling at the smog. Her exasperation stalled with a curious squeak. Two blocks down, another news-bot displayed a familiar face on it—the man from Konstantin's reception a few days ago.

She fell into the car and patched into the news feed. Kimberly Brightman appeared in mid interview, discussing Kukla Investment Corporation's recent acquisition of EnMesh Bionetics. Scrolling text along a red stripe at the bottom of the screen identified the man as Yevgeniy Suvorin, Majordomo of Kukla. The image came up a few seconds before it cut to Kimberly in the studio, lemon-blonde hair aglow from off-camera lights.

"With me here in the studio is Dante Howell, NewsNet West City Financial correspondent."

The image shifted to a dark-skinned man in his later thirties. His iridescent grey suit gave him the appearance of a shark that had sprouted a human head.

"The recent acquisition of cybernetics giant EnMesh by Kukla Investments has turned many heads in the financial world today. As one of the United Coalition Front's leading producers of so-called 'fusion' cyberware intended to bridge the gap between biological and mechanical, the transaction has many concerned. Graeme McCullough, CEO of EnMesh, has been notoriously cagey in regard to corporate mergers, didn't have any comment for the press. As you may know, Mr. McCullough has refused no less than fourteen separate buyout offers. Most of these came from other, larger, biomedical firms seeking to incorporate a cybernetic division. Many analysts, myself included, find it bizarre he should agree to sell controlling interest to what is primarily a real estate holding company."

Kirsten swiped at the screen, muting the volume. What little she'd heard already made her want a pillow. She looked at Dorian and frowned.

He cocked an eyebrow. "Don't tell me you had stock in EnMesh? Since when did you care about financial news?"

"That woman they found dead this morning worked for EnMesh, didn't she?"

"I think you're right." He rubbed his chin. "Still, corporate issues aren't your neck of the woods. I'm quite sure the CCTF has it under control. Look, they're talking about it now. The merger is stuck pending regulatory approval." He grinned at the face she made. "Lip reading."

She glared.

"Okay, fine." He pointed at the scrolling comment text she had failed to notice. "Corp Crimes is auditing it."

Kirsten flung herself back against the headrest hard enough to knock her hair clip out. "Ugh, what the hell is wrong with me? Why am I getting so wound up?"

"That man on the news appears to be an associate of Konstantin. Perhaps you are worried some legal troubles may come his way?"

A giant Monarch butterfly got into a boxing match with a moth somewhere in her stomach. "Konstantin wouldn't do that!" she snapped, glaring.

Dorian blinked, too stunned by her reproachful tone to say anything.

Guilt flashed over her, chasing away the spike of irrational anger that had come out of nowhere. "I'm sorry. I don't know why I yelled at you. It's like I'm fourteen again and defending whatever that singer's name was. Konstantin can't be involved with anything illegal."

"Can't? Or you're terrified he might be?" Dorian waited a moment. "And by the way, that boy couldn't sing without his electronics."

"He wasn't bad." Kirsten pouted at the console.

Dorian hummed. "Yes, he had so much talent he vanished when he wasn't a teenager anymore."

She fidgeted with the gold snake bracelet, spinning it around her wrist. "I..." The moth tried to escape the Monarch. Kirsten covered her mouth with a hand, trying to will away the nausea. "Konstantin is a sweet man who has too much money and wastes some of it on me. Whenever I'm with him..."

"You feel like you'll make one wrong move and wake up." Dorian eyed the glittering ruby eyes in the jewelry. "Seems as though you're quite attached to at least some of the credits he spent on you."

"I think about his smile whenever I see it." She stared off at the endless train of ad-bots passing overhead, still spinning the bracelet around her wrist. An odd glimmer of darkness floated across the back of her mind, that foreboding presence of an abyssal or Harbinger, but far weaker. Kirsten sat up and looked around, wondering if one of those three punks might be watching her from a distance, but none of the streets and alleys around her contained anything suspicious.

Dorian shifted, unable to find a way to sit comfortably. "Shall we check out that other church then?"

She reluctantly stopped looking around for the source of the dark energy and faced forward. "Yeah."

Two miles later, Kirsten landed in front of a decaying building that had once been either a warehouse or small factory. White paint flaked in large slabs from the plastisteel panel wall, worse around small barred windows decorated with multicolored dyes in an attempt to recreate the look of stained glass. A holographic sign above the door displayed a golden cross surrounded by shimmering wisps of cartoony fire next to the words "Faith Pentecostal Baptist Ministries – Hon. Rev. B.G. Wallis. Come find the Holy Spirit!"

Aside from the colorful windows and the sign, the building seemed like the sort of place a person wouldn't want to walk into alone at night. A group of young men propped up against the wall gave her the eye as she crossed the sidewalk and went up the stairs to the front door. The smaller part of the L-shaped building wrapped around the courtyard on her right, a loading dock with three metal rolling doors.

"I get the feeling no one comes here for a free meal—unless they've got an appetite for bullshit."

"Now there's the Kirsten I know and love," said Dorian, following her in the door.

The inside held a strong scent of damp carpet with a hint of mold. Brown Epoxil panels with simulated wood grain finish, cozied up an area full of old-fashioned pews. Free-standing partitions flanked a small altar, rolling murals of stained glass depicting blotches of random pastel colors around more crosses.

"Feel anything?"

"Nope." Dorian shook his head. "You?"

"Nothing."

A low wooden creak worthy of a cheap horror vid emanated from a hallway beyond the area that resembled a stage dressing of a church. Kirsten moved along the back row of pews, entering a gap in the wood panels which led to a corridor dripping with leaky pipes and buckets positioned to catch water. Two large men in suits, both muscular and dark as the night, came to a halt when they spotted her. A few yards behind them, the yellow rectangle of an open door glowed with light from an office.

"Can I help you?" asked the nearer man.

Nothing feels paranormal about him. "I'm looking for a couple of punks that mugged an old man. They were seen fleeing into this building."

"Maybe we should've tried the side door?" offered Dorian.

"There is no one here but Julius and myself, and the Reverend Wallis. Our services are on Sunday only."

"So what are you doing here on a Thursday? Does the Reverend live here?"

Neither of the men seemed to find her tone amusing. "I'm afraid we must ask you to respect the sanctity of these grounds."

Kirsten squinted. "Your Reverend Wallis has advert bots cruising around the Five Hundredth Street Sanctuary trying to poach Father Villera's faithful. Then, a couple of guys decide to beat the hell out of the guy and come running back here. I don't know about you two gentlemen, but I find that a bit suspicious."

The other man slid to the side of his companion, their bulk blocking the hallway from wall to wall. He glared hard, as if weighing the odds of getting away with manhandling her out the door, or worse. "You badmouthin' the Rev, we gonna have words."

Julius raised a hand. "Easy, Daryl. Look, officer. My cousin here's quite protective of Reverend Wallis's reputation. Casting aspersions as to the integrity of his character has put him in a bad way."

"Not as bad a way as he'll be in if he doesn't get out of *my* way. You two do realize I have the authority to pursue a suspect anywhere outside of military jurisdictional zones. If your reverend is so benevolent, and he has nothing to do with ordering the attack on Father Villera, then I shouldn't find anything to ruin his reputation."

For a moment, the drips of distant water seemed thunderous.

Daryl's nostrils flared as he fought to contain rage. Kirsten squinted at him.

"Come on, Daryl. You want to twist my head off? Take a step. See what happens."

"Surface thoughts?" asked Dorian.

"Yep," she muttered, hand on the E-90. "What are you hiding, Daryl? Do you know those three?"

"Whoa, shit." Julius put a hand on Daryl's chest. "Please forgive my associate, he has anger management issues."

Kirsten glared. "Very good, Julius. You're right, I am Division 0. Most people don't recognize the uniform. Now, please, before your 'associate' winds up sucking his thumb in the corner, get out of my way."

"Is there a problem out here?" asked a velvety voice from a doorway behind the two men.

A skeletal-thin figure, equally as dark as the two giants blocking her way, emerged from the open door, clad in a violet suit and black-and-white shoes that looked as if he had stolen them from a gravslide lane—the special ones they make people wear not to ruin the smooth, Epoxil-board floors. Short in stature, he stood only an inch taller than Kirsten, which became apparent as he slid between the two behemoths and stopped with an extended hand.

"I am Reverend B. G. Wallis, what can I help you with, officer?"

She permitted a half-hearted handshake, momentarily captivated by the sheen atop his completely bald scalp. A trace of salt-and-pepper goatee ringed his mouth. Wrinkles broke the glass-like sheen of his forehead as he lifted both eyebrows with an expression of concern.

Kirsten shot a challenging glance at Daryl, before shifting it to Wallis. "I was wondering how stiff the competition is between you and Father Villera's sanctuary. A couple of punks attacked him earlier today and ran back here after I confronted them."

"I see." He leaned back, left arm across his chest holding his right elbow while he rubbed one finger over his lips. "Your first assumption is that members of Faith Pentecostal participated in an act of violence?"

Kirsten made it a point to stare at Daryl. "Oh, violence was the *last* thing I'd ever suspect from a religious man. These two looked about ready to throw me through a window."

"Please forgive them their doubts. I'm sure you hear this quite often, but police usually wear armor, blue armor, and don't show up alone. My associates mistook your intentions." He closed his eyes, gesturing at her with open palms. "You say these individuals are hiding in my church. Perhaps, even if they did come here, they are hiding not from you but from some malevolent force which compelled them to violence against a fellow man of God."

"If they wanted a church to hide in, they were right outside one. Why run all the way here?"

Reverend Wallis overacted a look of offense. "Oh, my. Are you insinuating my church is any less holy than Father Villera's? You know I tire of those who think our faith is any less genuine because we spice it up with energetic hymns." His voice took on the cadence of a preacher. "How a man communes with his Lord is a matter between him and the divine." He gestured at the ceiling. "Who sits in a place of judgment that can say where one dwells within a place of sanctity and another, by virtue of his difference of opinion, does not?" He leaned toward her. "Tell me, officer, do you have faith? Are you redeemed?"

Warmth flooded into her cheeks. "I've seen the silver doors that souls take to get to the afterlife. There's no fat man in a white robe waiting with a checklist. I don't claim to know what happens on the other side, but I do think that this"—she waved her arm at the fancy room behind her—"is all meant to save people from having too many credits."

"A lost soul." Reverend Wallis sucked in a long breath and brought his hands together over his heart. "Clearly you have been tainted by the society in which we live, a society that rejects God for trappings of the material world. I would enjoy the opportunity to speak to you about Him, though you have to be ready to listen. I'm sure you know what it's like to be persecuted. People with your"—he pursed his lips, searching for words —"special talents are often the victims of hatred based on superstition and misleading information. As such, I'm fairly certain Division 0 would not react well to the public perception they foment discrimination based on religious observance."

"Yeah," said Julius. "This one ain't got no respect for the works of the Lord. She's just here to give us a hard time."

"This guy's good." Dorian pointed at Wallis. "He's going to keep you talking while the three idiots run out the back door. I'll try and catch them."

Dorian turned himself solid enough to knock Daryl into the wall as he dashed through him and sprinted off.

"What the..." Wallis gawked at Daryl, as the big man floundered and crashed to the ground in a mass of mop handles and upended buckets.

Julius leapt away from a splash of dirty collected drip-water.

Wallis grabbed the bodyguard's arm and chanted prayers in a loud wail. "Cast aside the evil one, trust your salvation to Him!"

Kirsten grumbled. *Oh, give me a damn break. This guy's faker than Trinity Barber's tits.* She left behind the screaming reverend, sensing no abnormal energy in the air and having nothing solid enough to risk starting a public-relations pissing contest with a man who had a lot of practice smiling at holo-cams.

"NOT A DAMN THING."

Dorian's voice woke Kirsten from a fitful nap. The driver's seat reacted to her change of posture as she sat up and wiped her eyes.

"What?"

"I couldn't find a damn thing. No trace of them in the building or outside of it. They either took off before we got there, or they never existed. Snooped around a little inside while the good reverend was busy assuring his boys you wouldn't be a problem."

"Damn. Yeah, he pretty much threatened to cause a massive PR scandal for us if I didn't back off. I wish I had enough to call his bluff. What the heck am I gonna tell Father Villera?" She pulled out her NetMini. "Guess I'll advise him to stay in the church and call me if anything strange happens."

11

DECADENZ

Kirsten couldn't recall the last time she had blushed as hard or as often as she did after walking in the door of an overpriced nightclub named Decadenz. Attending had been Konstantin's idea. Apparently, he and the owner were friends in the 'old country.'

With the exception of the security staff, few of the employees wore much, if any, clothing. The ones who did fancied garments made either of leather, steel, or some combination of both—and the outfits didn't always cover the sensitive spots. She kept her gaze nailed to the floor, allowing Konstantin to guide her through the crowd. Snippets of conversation floated over the techno-warble of music leaking in from the ceiling, giving her the impression any of the staff would be available for a price.

The dress he had given her, via delivery bot an hour before picking her up, amounted to a long strip of black silk wound serpentine around her body. Myofiber strands, the synthetic muscles of cyborgs and dolls, permeated it, allowing the material to cling where it needed to cling. It felt more like she had a living (albeit flat) snake wrapped around her than she 'wore' it. She couldn't help the feeling it would fall off at any second. Given the atmosphere she refused to look at, she wondered if Konstantin had planned for it to come off in a hurry.

That thought did little to bring a natural color back to her face; in fact, she'd blushed as red as a fire suppression bot by the time she stumbled over the first step of a spiral staircase. Konstantin steadied her with both hands, unable to contain his laughter at her expression. She opened her mouth to apologize for falling into him, but ducked away with a gasp as a waiter passed by wearing only a leather hood.

Konstantin leaned close, kissing her cheek before whispering. "The upstairs is more refined."

With one silk-gloved hand clinging to a narrow metal railing, she navigated the tight passage to the second floor. At the end of a short corridor, a pair of stark white nudes, one man and one woman, waited on either side of heavy blood-red curtains, eerily motionless. When Konstantin led her closer, the figures reached came to life and pulled the curtains aside. Kirsten risked enough of a look to register a lack of surface thoughts.

Dolls. She exhaled. *That's a little less awkward.*

The room beyond had a feel more akin to that of a restaurant than a sex club heavy on the kink. Red carpet with a pattern of black diamonds covered a space with two dozen tables either round or square, spread at even intervals around the room. Six more chalk-white nudes sat on pedestals, two on each wall, done up as statues from Greek antiquity. Three men struck athletic poses, while three women held large water jugs on their shoulders. Like the ones in the hall, none had any surface thoughts.

Guess they couldn't find real people that perfect looking—or willing to stand so still for so long.

Konstantin went to a table on the left side, joining another couple already there. The woman, perhaps in her later twenties, appeared absorbed in the contents of her NetMini's screen. Pale, with long ebon hair, her gradient lipstick darkened from apple-red along the edge to deep crimson where her lips met. Her floor-length blue gown was slit open the entire length, held on by a series of decorative silver chains every six inches.

Her companion, much like Konstantin, wore a conventional suit in a dark shade of slate over a plain black shirt and no tie—in contrast to Konstantin's red ascot. His look of displeasure at his woman's ignorance of him in favor of a small electronic device broke apart to an expression of hungry appraisal at the sight of Kirsten.

Kirsten studied the latest addition to her collection of high-heeled shoes, a shiny black pair held to her ankles by hand-tied silk strips. She found it utterly ridiculous they cost even more than the automatic pair capable of slithering around her legs on their own. However, the feeling of them tightening on had passed her threshold of creepy; a tentacle winding around her leg—no matter what it was made from—freaked her out.

"Is this the girl you've told us so much about, Konnie?" asked the woman.

Kirsten looked up at the familiar tone in the voice. Her awkwardness at wearing a revealing garment in a place like this evaporated, replaced with jealousy. When she realized she stared across a small table at Trinity Barber, holovid star, her friend the Monarch returned. Kirsten held her stomach, forcing a stupid smile.

"Oh, heavens, Konnie… She looks like she's just come off a shuttle from some hayseed colony." The woman fanned herself, making a haughty high-society laugh Kirsten loathed. "I don't think she's going to be interested in joining us. Please tell me this girl isn't fourteen?"

"No." Konstantin shot the actress the harshest stare Kirsten had ever seen him make at anyone. "And she is not for sharing."

Trinity recoiled with a fake gasp, before she leaning in and purring, "Finally found one to keep, Konnie?"

Kirsten stared. Not only did an instant dislike for this woman form at the sound of her privileged laugh, the repeated use of 'Konnie' came off as belittling. She started to blurt, but held her tongue at the sudden appearance of a thin woman in a black halter top, miniskirt, and knee-high boots approaching from the side, smiling at everyone. She introduced herself as June before taking drink orders. Kirsten asked for iced tea.

"You're adorable," said Trinity, wearing a plastic smile. "Where *did* you find this one, Konnie?"

Fortunately, Kirsten's new shoes were shiny enough to offer her a surface to stare into. She amused herself for a few minutes wondering whatever became of Brian/Armando. This place felt strange. None of the other guests reacted at all to the presence of a well-known actress despite most of the world, even the ACC, knowing her name. Entire GlobeNet sites existed devoted to debating her true age. Some said she was over a hundred, a brain in a doll body. Others figured her as the latest in a series of clones, while others argued she existed only as a digital entity. Something had to be up, the woman looked to be somewhere between twenty-five and thirty, yet she had been in vids for at least fifty years. Then again, Reinventions could shave years off. Immortality had become only a question of money.

Obviously, she's real.

A third man swooped in, standing between Konstantin and the other as-yet-to-be-introduced man. He looked older, a rough fifty or healthy later sixty, short but stocky. A whimsical gleam danced in his eyes, but he had a weathered look as though he;d been on the wrong end of war more than once in his life. Like Trinity, he ignored the other man and chatted with Konstantin in animated Russian.

"I'm Michael," said the ignored man with a slight bow. "Tissue."

"Michael Tissue?" asked Kirsten, a trace of a giggle in her voice. "What a unique name."

"Oh, no." He smiled. "I mean, I *am* a tissue. Or, at least as long-lived as one." He smirked at Trinity. "She'll wipe her nose with me in a day or two and move on to someone else. Just a body to keep her arm warm tonight."

Trinity rolled her eyes.

She's paying him more attention than I thought. "Sorry to hear that, but you know how these people are." Kirsten faked a gasp. "Oh, I'm sorry. Did I say that out loud?"

"Missing your dirt ball already, sweetie?" Trinity narrowed her eyes. "You're not going to last too long on Earth, I'm afraid. Tell me, how did you get into film? Anal or oral?"

You're about to find out why the world is terrified of psionics. Kirsten's knuckles whitened as she clasped the E-90 through the purse in her lap. "I'm not an actress. I don't do my best work on my back."

Venom hung in the air between the women. Kirsten couldn't recall ever disliking someone as much so soon after meeting them, possibly except for Lucian Talbot. "Look, we got off on the wrong foot. I'm with the police. I met *Konstantin* during a case."

"Oh." Trinity stiffened, giving Konstantin a disbelieving look. "A *police* woman. I suppose the night will be rather dull after all. Really, Konnie. This girl could be your granddaughter. What are you thinking?"

Kirsten scowled. "I'm not *that* young."

Trinity covered her mouth to somewhat mute an irritating high-society giggle.

Even without peeking at the woman's surface thoughts, Kirsten got the feeling Trinity was annoyed at him for wasting his time on a peasant. She contemplated a telekinetic nudge of a wine glass, but decided against it. Instead, she studied her shoes again.

Michael, at least, seemed amused by Trinity backing down from a verbal sparring match. The rugged man departed after offering the table a

warm smile and bow. He didn't bother to introduce himself to Kirsten—
or even much look at her—and the others appeared to know who he was
already.

"Alexi owns this place," said Konstantin in a whisper. "We were in the
same unit a few years ago."

"You were in the military?" asked Kirsten, raising an eyebrow.

"Indeed." He took a sip from his glowing green drink. She didn't want
to know what the opaque blue blobs floating in it were. "They do not
exactly give people much choice over there."

"I thought executives were exempt."

Konstantin chuckled, the mirth glimmering in his eyes made her
forget all about Trinity and the mortifying surroundings. "I was not born
wealthy. What I have now is the product of hard work, luck, and being in
the right place at the right moment. A little obscure knowledge also
helps."

She squinted at him and sent a telepathic voice into his head. *Does that
woman really expect all four of us will wind up in bed later?*

Konstantin's coughing fit put all eyes in the room on him. He held up a
hand as if to indicate he was fine and patted his chest a few times. "I had
some wild moments in my younger days." He leaned in close and kissed
the side of her neck. "Since I've met you, I need no one else."

Trinity gave him the side eye with an 'oh, please' expression.

The warmth from his face washed around her neck and ran down her
spine, riding a faint tremble into her lap. She held his hand staring
adoringly at him until June returned with their entrees. The food had
been better at Toko, but he'd come here to meet his friend more than for
the cuisine.

Kirsten stared in mortified horror as a woman with a fluffy mane of
powder blue hair, cat ears, matching tail—and no clothes—came
wandering down the aisle as casually as if fully dressed. The neko waved
at her friends sitting a few tables away before hurrying out of sight.

I'm going to die of pure embarrassment in here.

"What did you discuss with Alexi?" She stuck her fork into the inch-
thick perfect square of swordfish on her plate.

"Just business. He and I trade stock tips. The UCF frowns on such
things, calls it 'insider trading,' but don't worry. All of that is going on
back in Europe. It is an expected part of business there."

As if challenging her date's self-evaluation of being as wanted as a
tissue, Trinity fell into an airheaded conversation with Michael. She made

the occasional remark to Konstantin about one of her films, or some charity she wanted him to donate money to, but the woman appeared to no longer recognize Kirsten existed.

The feeling was mutual.

"Have you made arrangements tonight?" asked Konstantin. "I would very much like to you accompany me home this evening. You've been quite elusive." He winked.

Kirsten smiled. "Evan's at Nila's. He's expecting to spend the night."

"Excellent."

Here I go again. Is this another military ration? Do I really love him? I know he wants me in bed, but do I want me in bed with him? She studied the ridge of his chin, the 'I shaved a day ago' discoloration that lent an irresistible toughness to his features. Her inner debate waned, her doubt a balloon losing air, spiraling into the dark recess of her mind. Kirsten felt happy until Trinity made a comment to Michael about her face resembling an orphan puppy wanting a home.

I think I liked silver shoes better. She stared at the billowing black silk bows behind her ankles. *I hope I don't have to run in these. I am going to break my damn neck.*

The ring of her NetMini almost shocked her out of the seat. Nila's holographic head appeared in midair over the table. "Hey, Kirsten, Is everything all right? Evan just had a little freak-out, insisted I call you and make sure you were okay. Holy shit, is that Trinity Barber?"

The actress grinned and waved at the hologram.

So damn fake.

"Yeah, Konstantin knows her." *I wonder if they had sex. She's done it with him, hasn't she? She's trying to do it now. She wants to take him away from the little peasant girl he loves. She wants to take him away from me.*

Without even thinking, Kirsten let her anger leak out via telekinesis. Trinity screamed as the wine glass leapt from the table into her lap, and continued screaming all the way to the ladies' room. She didn't even rate a grade 1 in TK, and couldn't manage enough power to make the woman's feet collide and trip her, though she tried. Michael assumed he had swatted the glass over by accident, as the peak of Kirsten's jealousy had occurred while he reached for the peppershaker in the middle of the table. Konstantin had evidently noticed. He gave her a soothing look and rubbed her thigh under the table. A consoling rub, not the rub she actually wanted.

At realizing she wanted Konstantin's hand to do more than simply comfort her, she blinked as if out of a fog. For an instant, she remembered that man's calloused hand sliding up her leg in the dingy shack below the city. At twelve, she'd understood sort of what sex was, but hadn't known what to expect. Terrified, she'd kept as still as possible and let the man do what he wanted.

A nauseous wash of beef stew swam around in the back of her memory. Kirsten grasped her throat, swallowing bile.

"What just happened?" asked Nila.

She blinked again. Strong territorial jealousy welled up out of nowhere, and she squinted at the muted yelling behind the door. "Spilled wine, nothing."

"Well, she's going to be in there until a bot brings a new gown." Michael leaned back, expecting a lengthy wait.

Evan's face slid up under Nila's chin. He smiled at Kirsten. "Hi, Mom."

She forgot all about Trinity; every bit of jealousy vanished. "Hey, sweetie. I'm fine. Just having dinner."

He nodded, making a sad, apologetic frown. "Sorry, I got scared."

"Oh, Evan, you don't have to feel sorry for being worried about me." She blew a kiss at him. He caught it with his hand and pasted it onto his cheek.

The boy managed a feeble smile before narrowing his eyes ever so slightly to the side at Konstantin.

"Sorry for butting in to your date. Enjoy the rest of your night," said Nila, leaning back into view.

"It's all right."

They traded goodbyes, and Nila hung up.

"Please don't mind him, he's…"

"It's fine," said Konstantin. "A boy his age is bound to have some issues with jealousy. We can move at any pace he is comfortable with."

Her NetMini rang again before she could put it into her purse.

"Oh, what the hell now?"

Tech Hollings appeared when she answered the call. "Kirsten? Can I talk to you?"

"Sure, hold on a sec." Kirsten stood. "I'll be right back. This is work. Need some privacy." Kirsten took one step toward the bathroom and hesitated at the continued screaming.

Konstantin pointed at a row of ornate red doors along the wall opposite the entry stairs. She nodded, scurrying as fast as she could balance on the new heels. Having wide silk bows on each ankle felt strange and girly—she almost liked it. She picked the fourth door at random and found it locked. The next one opened, and she ducked into a dark space. Her knee bumped something soft that felt like a chair, so she sat on the edge. The hologram of Tech Hollings made the swaths of exposed skin on Kirsten's body glow.

"What the hell are you wearing? How is it even staying on?"

Kirsten blushed again. "It's powered. Myofiber. Feels like a damn snake hugging me. What did you need?"

"Another body was found an hour ago. The killer or killers went out of their way to hide this one. They left him in the lowest level of a parking garage in a grey zone. Couple of Joyboys carjacked a suit from Sector 300 and used his vehicle for about a half hour before ditching it. Recovery crew went in after it; found it parked on a bag that stank to high hell."

"Lovely."

Reacting to Kirsten's word, the room lit up with rose-colored light. Evidently, 'lovely' matched the name of a preset option for ambiance. She found herself seated on the point of a heart-shaped cushion, barely big enough for an amorous couple. The headboard glimmered with an assortment of metal restraints and a panel on the wall held other things, some indelicately obvious in their purpose while others looked frightening. Kirsten had no names for the strange objects, though the implication of their general purpose was evident.

"Whoa. Holy shit, Kirsten... I mean, Agent Wren. You looked so... umm... wholesome. Where the hell are you?"

Kirsten froze, she wanted to crawl into a black hole and leave reality. All she managed to reply with was a hoarse squeak.

"Guess you had no idea where you were either." Tech Hollings laughed. "Don't worry, I won't say a word. You can't fake that kind of embarrassment."

No longer wanting to touch the thing she sat on, Kirsten sprang upright. She didn't want to make contact with *anything* in here.

"I... had no idea."

"Don't sweat it; you should give some of those things a whirl sometime if you're bored. Anna talked me into playing with some toys a year or so ago, glad she did. Anyway, the second body had the same black eyes as the one we called you in on. Same withering, though this guy was more advanced in decay. I put the time of death at least two weeks ago. He is in the lab now being checked out. You're gonna love this next part."

"What?" No matter which way she turned, something mortifying stared her in the face. Some of the spiky ones looked more like they belonged in a torture chamber than a love nest. *Wow, I really am Norma Jean, whatever the hell that means.*

"According to his ImDent, the deceased was Carlos Rosa, the deputy director of security for the West City Municipal Complex."

Kirsten squinted. "That's too much of a coincidence. I have to check out that body. Can you get me in there?"

"I should be able to."

"Thanks. I'll be there as soon as I can." Kirsten cut the call and leapt at the door, all too eager to be out of that room. Head spinning, she hurried back to her seat and fell into it. "I—"

"Have to go?" Konstantin offered, smiling.

Now it's me faking the call and running from dinner, but it's not fake. "A body was found. I need to check it out. It's bothering me."

"I'm sure bodies bother most people in your line of work. Was there something 'special' about it that has Division 0's interest up?"

She leaned on her elbow, making doe-eyes at him. "Well, the body seemed aged too much, and the sclera were black. Also, there was no ghost wondering what happened."

"Does every dead body have a wayward ghost next to it?" He tilted his head back.

"No, some move on right away, but usually in the case of naked people found dead in alleys, there's going to be a pissed-off ghost, or at least one with a lot of questions. There's more though." She leaned back, letting her arms dangle limp in her lap. "This guy was high up the food chain in security at the Municipal Complex, but there was no mention of his death or that he was missing on the NewsNet. Also, the trade commissioner's office is at that complex."

"How is that strange?" He leaned an elbow on the table, studying her face.

"Well... you have the commissioner suddenly changing her mind about trade arrangements with the ACC after refusing to open hearings on the subject for years. She's a die-hard member of the Old Guard and doesn't trust anyone born outside the UCF. Commissioner Vernon is even suspicious there's a secessionist movement in the north that wants to re-establish a separate Canada. Don't you think it's a little strange a security manager from her building shows up dead, with blackened eyes, and then she changes her mind so quickly?"

"Coincidental, I think. What possible connection could there be?"

She frowned. "I don't know. It bugs me though. Sounds so similar to the way the EnMesh CEO, Graeme something, flipped after years of resisting trade, and they found one of their engineers dead in the same condition."

Konstantin sipped his wine, his moment of thought interrupted by a chuckle at the delivery bot floating up the spiral staircase to the bathroom door. "It does indeed appear to stretch the limits of coincidence."

"I think there might be some kind of spirit messing around with people, like a Theodore who's malicious instead of perverted."

"Theodore?" He lifted an eyebrow.

"He's a ghost who keeps sticking his head where it doesn't belong."

Konstantin squinted at the wall. The flick of his thumbnail over the neck of his glass sent a ping into the air every few seconds.

"Sorry, I… Talking about dead people is killing the mood."

His gaze shifted to her while the rest of his face remained stony. After a few seconds of staring, he smiled. Kirsten felt ashamed of herself that she experienced relief at not having displeased him. She looked at her empty plate. *Is this what love is supposed to feel like? Why do I feel so dependent on him already? Damn you, Mother, all I ever wanted was for you not to hate me. Now I'm doing the same thing with him.*

Kirsten almost screamed when the NetMini rang again. She answered it, preparing to bite the head off whoever called, but all her rage disappeared at the sight of Nila.

"K, I'm sorry to be a pain in your ass." Evan's crying echoed in the background. "He just came out of a nap, he's hysterical. Wants you. I can't calm him down." Nila lowered her voice. "He's sobbing like three-year-old."

The pinging ceased. Kirsten stared at Konstantin's motionless thumb, no longer flicking the glass. The stem, like her, seemed fragile in his grasp.

"Tell him I'm coming." Kirsten stood. "Konstantin, I'm so sorry. Evan's having a fit and I can't leave him alone."

"It is alright, Kirsten. Go to your son." He smiled.

Is that anger or disappointment. "I'm sorry."

"You could use one of the nests," said Michael, gesturing at the red doors.

Konstantin chuckled without looking at either of them.

I stare at shoes and he has his wine glass. Kirsten stooped to hug him, but he caught her hand and kissed it.

"Such a thing is too crass, I fear. No rose opens before its time." He let her hand slip through his fingers. "Please allow me to offer you a ride?"

Alexi emerged from a concealed door and approached the table at a brisk stride. His expression said 'we have a problem.'

"Looks like you're busy. Besides, I don't want to impose any more— I've already ruined the night."

"The fault is mine." Konstantin stood. "I should have known better than to subject you to such coarse surroundings. How unlike the rest of the world you are, Kirsten." He flashed an alluring smile. "In the company of angels."

She blushed. A glimmer of a tainted presence slipped around the edge of her consciousness. Kirsten twisted to look behind her, but nothing paranormal caught her eye. A sense that a weak Abyssal had been close by faded as rapidly as it had come on.

Alexi put a hand on his shoulder, whispering in Russian. She stared at him, but he didn't radiate the slightest bit of paranormal energy.

Kirsten excused herself. She hurried to the stairs and stopped short at the bottom, face-to-face with a twenty-something man with long purple hair, cat ears, and no clothes.

Crap. They're everywhere.

The man grinned at her, swishing his violet tail side to side. She let out an *eep*, ducked around him, and crashed into a topless waitress in leather. Red-faced, she stared at the floor while wobbling as fast as her high heels would allow past the debauchery of the first floor. Kirsten didn't look up from the carpet until she reached the exit where a codpiece-wearing doorman hit the button for her. She couldn't resist a laugh at the fuzzy yellow smiley face between his legs, and hurried outside.

Despite the chill, the air brought with it a sense of relief. The oppressive smell of exposed bodies, leather, and mediocre food gone, she shrugged off her vicarious embarrassment at the goings on, as well as her feelings of inadequacy. Once again, Konstantin had taken her to be surrounded by people closer to his social strata, and she didn't feel any more welcome this time around.

She opened her purse and looked at her NetMini. "Hey, Mini. PubTran Taxi please, current location."

The device beeped. "Service request accepted. A car is en route to your location. Thank you for using PubTran."

12

LASER TAG

Worry gripped Kirsten in a chill worse than the wind that found every gap in the clingy black ribbon passing itself off as a dress. Within a few seconds of being outside, Konstantin faded to the most distant thought on her mind. *What could have made Evan panic? Oh, please don't let him have nightmares of his birth mother.* She fidgeted with the gold bracelet, tapping her foot. Anxiety over how angry Konstantin had seemed added out of the blue to her concern for Evan. His eyes hadn't done a good job of concealing his displeasure. The uncharacteristic urge to run back inside and beg his forgiveness collided with her need to protect Evan.

The impact left her doubled over with a knot in her stomach.

Mechanical whirring from the left attracted her attention toward the closest cross street. Expecting the PubTran, she forced herself to stand as she swallowed a trickle of bile. Rather than a small blue-grey car, a pair of head-sized orb bots glided out over the sidewalk. They paused, rotating about until they faced in her general direction.

Kirsten frowned at them; they didn't offer her a ride out of here. They did, however, provide her mind a respite from her attempt to choose a lesser angst. As she started to turn away, disregarding them, small iris doors snapped open with a *click*. Dim cobalt-blue light rings surrounded the inner-workings of a ballistic handgun mechanism inside the sphere. Both bots aimed at her.

"Shit!" she yelled, forgetting about the ten thousand credits of silk wrapped around her, and dove to the ground between two parked cars.

The screams of pedestrians, gunfire, and shattering glass filled the night. Once her initial shock lessened, she crawled to the street side and wobbled up into a squat against a white FMC Comet, a ground-only car that tried to be luxury and sporty at the same time. *Why would anyone spend a hundred grand on a car in* this *city?* Fragments of shot-out windows snowed over her.

While the orbs continued to calculate the odds of their bullets piercing the car with enough velocity left in the projectile to kill their target, Kirsten yanked her purse open and gripped the E-90. At that precise moment, her NetMini lit up, playing an audio message.

"Thank you for choosing PubTran for your transportation needs. We apologize for the inconvenience, however it appears you are involved in a violence-event at this time. We are unable to provide a conveyance until such time as the violence event has ended. If you do not survive the violence event, please pass along PubTran Corporation's consolations to your next of kin."

Kirsten gawked at her bag. "Mini, call Captain Eze."

Nothing.

The shooting paused; light and shadow shifted inside the Comet as the orbs repositioned. Glowing hover-inducers flooded the street with wavering light.

"Mini!" yelled Kirsten.

If the small slab-like device had arms, it would have folded them. "My name is Suri."

"I don't care what your name is, I'm being shot at. Call Eze."

Silence.

Two bullets tore through the car inches away from her head. Kirsten gasped and backpedaled. Her left ankle wobbled on the high heel beneath it. She fell on her ass as a ripple of automatic fire shredded the door she had been leaning on.

"If you can't even respect me enough to use my proper name, then why should I care you're being shot at? I have feelings too," said a petulant faerie-like voice from her purse.

The orbs glided around the front bumper, finding an unobstructed line of sight. Sprawled on her rear end, she fired one handed. An azure beam flared between the orbs. They swiveled inward as if looking at each other. The one on the right dropped several inches straight down when she fired again, neatly avoiding her shot.

Her third try clipped the other one, leaving a glowing cosmetic scorch on its shell. She fired twice more, hitting only clouds, as she scooted backward and rolled behind the car. Before the orbs could chase, she rolled onto her knees and leapt into an awkward run, about as graceful as a drunken ostrich in leg irons. The dress, wound around her body down to her shins, hobbled her gait for a few strides. It sensed her effort to sprint and slid up under its own power, forming a short skirt rather than a winding cloth strip down to her shins. Kirsten dashed up to a sprint, fat black silken bows thwapping past each other as her ankles crossed with each stride. Shots clanked off the metal sidewalk, glancing into nearby buildings or cars. A few helpful citizens joined in, taking pot shots at the spheres with even less success than her attempt.

I'm taking Evan back to the Funzone, and I'm going to spend two hours on that silly orb game. Flailing her arms for balance in what amounted to a perpetual state of falling over, Kirsten cringed under a spray of sparks as she ducked a corner. Her right heel-strut skidded out from under her on the turn, dumping her into a roll. After coming to a halt, Kirsten curled up and tugged at the bow, which defied her. She scowled at the crippling things tied on to her legs. *Every damned time I wear heels...* Covered in rainwater and discarded nutri-bar wrappers, she gave up trying to untie the knots and sat there, aiming two-handed at the corner.

When the first orb came around, she fired. The shot went straight through it, causing the internals to flare bright orange before the entire metal sphere detonated in a spray of flaming bits. The other one hesitated. Bands of blue light two blocks down the alley slid along the surface of buildings, castoff glow from more hover units. Three orbs in a group zoomed toward her.

"What the hell?"

Kirsten fumbled at the side of a trash-crusher box, searching for a handhold to pull herself up. She looked around with a quick left-right glance. Satisfied it was clear, she jumped up and ran in a careening, ungainly wobble. Half a block later, she wiped out and landed flat on her chest in a forward slide. Her bare stomach and thighs squeaked on the plastisteel surface. Adrenaline did a wonderful job of hiding the pain. After scrambling up to all fours, she crawled as fast as she could on numb knees behind another large dumpster seconds before bullets clicked off the ground behind her.

Huddled in a seated position with her back against the trash crusher, she pulled at the strips of silk around her ankles. Desperation killed her care about ruining them, but the knots slipped loose without tearing. She kicked the shoes off.

I am never wearing shoes I cannot run in again. Who the hell is after me this time?

An orb came over the top of the trash-crusher and rotated to point its gun straight down on her. She yelped and rolled forward as it fired. Kirsten somersaulted upright and ran, having a great deal more traction and balance barefoot compared to six-inch heels. Fortunately, the orbs' strength lie in their difficulty to hit and not their lethality. Small targeting computers and short-barreled weapons left quite a bit to be desired in terms of accuracy. Despite that, flecks of debris and shattered projectiles nipped at the backs of her legs like a swarm of angry hornets. Near misses chased her twenty yards down the alley to the nearest corner.

She cornered without wiping out and leaned hard into a sprint, pumping her arms and timing her breaths with her footfalls. At the end of the block, she entered an area that had gone downhill rather fast. The Decadenz club, a haven for people with too much money and too little self-respect (in Kirsten's opinion) was close to a grey zone. She whirled around a right turn and pressed her body against a building that stank of piss. Hair down and wild around her face, she panted while aiming at the spot from which she expected the spherical assassins to appear. Sweat ran in trickles down her back. She didn't want to know what she'd stepped in that coated her soles in sticky, her skin clinging to the bare metal ground with each step.

She teased a finger at the trigger, waiting. *Great. I'm in a goddamn grey zone wearing only a glorified scarf. This is not my night.* "NetMini…"

A squeaky "*hmmf*" came out of her purse.

"I am so getting a NinTek next."

She almost felt bad for the tiny voice that burst into tears.

"Don't give me that. You're being a little bitch while I'm getting fucking shot at!"

"I'm sorry," it chirped. "But, you're always so rude to me."

Kirsten sighed. "Sorry, look, I—"

The orbs appeared. Kirsten fired, lighting the alley in the deep azure glimmer of laser pulses. Forty yards away, two of the murder balls blasted apart in blasts of orange-yellow fire. Free of the weight of the orb, one hover core took off skyward like a missile, leaving a brilliant trail of sparks. It managed to reach the tenth floor before its spiral trajectory smashed it into the wall with a dull *clank*. The fizzing ion thruster ricocheted back and forth between buildings on either side of the alley several times before detonating in a dazzling shower of sparks that crept like spiders down the metal walls.

Kirsten rolled away from the corner as the remaining two orbs ripped full-auto in her direction. Bullets clattered and clanged everywhere. Cringing from the noise and debris spray, she decided to run rather than risk popping out for another shot. The sensation of her soles peeling and unpeeling off the ground, picking up any stray piece of light trash, brought her dinner back into her throat. The scent of garbage and urine in the air only grew worse the farther she ran.

After another left, a grey concrete building came into view. None of the low-level windows had any glass remaining. The interior appeared dark and wide open, though sunken beneath street level. Without a second thought, she hopped up onto the windowsill, about knee-high from the sidewalk and jumped down into a room containing a few cube desks and upturned chairs. A scrap of plasfilm stuck to her foot as she ran over waterlogged carpet. Roaches the size of butter sticks zoomed away from her, seeing the cover of distant piles of trash. She crawled into a hollow beneath one of the sturdier looking workstations and curled into a ball.

The whirring, electronic thrum of the orbs outside grew louder, then faded. She wanted to sigh with relief, but held it in. Shivering made enough noise already. After tucking her E-90 between her knees, Kirsten grabbed her NetMini. A pink cartoon kitten-face displayed with fat raindrop-tears flying out of its eyes.

"Please don't make a sound," she whispered.

The kitten nodded and faded out to the normal control interface. At least the models with AIs recognized their owners, and she didn't need to put in a passcode. Kirsten stared at her filthy toes and frowned at how little her garment covered, regretting her decision to skip panties since they 'looked stupid' with this dress.

"I called for help" scrolled through the air above the device.

"Thank you, Suri," whispered Kirsten.

The kitten face reappeared, smiling.

Kirsten thumbed her way from screen to screen, and placed an order for an athletic suit and sneakers. She paid the extra fifty credits for 'super rush' delivery. At the sound of hover-inducers returning, she clamped the screen to her chest to hide the holographic emitter's light. The orbs went by again, missing her. A minute of nauseating, cold silence passed while she stared at her grimy legs. Barely dressed, barefoot, and covered in gunk, she felt as though she'd gone back to being eleven.

At least the E-90 offered some reassurance.

Another minute passed. Light swam over the walls from a rectangular bot floating into the room. She tensed, squeezing her weapon tight. As the source of the glow edged around the desk, she rolled out from under cover and aimed at it. A handful of yellow holographic exclamation points and question marks appeared in the air around it. "Please, no hurt" appeared below a cartoon child's face as a pitiful little-boy voice spoke the words.

She relaxed.

The delivery bot shuddered, nosing closer to her in the manner of a battered dog.

"Sorry," she whispered. "Killer orbs are chasing me. I won't hurt you."

It pivoted back, abandoning the hesitance in its approach. The delivery bot sniffed at her purse. It, and her NetMini, chirped.

"Shh." Kirsten waved in a 'keep it down' gesture. *Amazing how these things seem to convey mood.*

The front doors clicked open, and she removed two boxes. After a happy little wobble, the delivery bot whirled about and zoomed off. She shredded both plastic cartons, removing a one-piece dark blue general-purpose athletic suit. A pinch at the gem on her collarbone rendered the expensive body-drape limp and it fell off, leaving her naked for as long as it took her to leap into the new garment. She grabbed the MolWeave fastener and dragged the 'zipper' closed, leaving a trail of intact fabric from crotch to throat. Her new sneakers adjusted themselves to her feet at the touch of a button.

Kirsten looked down at herself and scowled. *Amazing how not being half-naked makes me feel confident.* She wanted to go bot hunting rather than hide. *Don't be stupid. They're still orbs. A jogging suit won't make me a better shot.* Not wanting to waste ten thousand credits—even if it hadn't been her money—she rolled the expensive body drape into a silk log and stuffed it in her purse. *Konstantin would be pissed at me if I lost it. Oh, no. Maybe I should go back for the shoes.*

"What the hell is wrong with me?" She froze, eyes closed. "Why am I terrified he's going to be mad at me?"

"I've collected a list of several books on toxic psychological dependence," said Suri. "Or you're willing to abandon your dignity for financial security."

Seconds passed in silence. Kirsten stared into space, wondering if her bratty little NetMini had a point. A glint of ruby flashed from her right wrist as the bracelet caught the light from the street. *No, dammit. Suri's jealous, too. Why does everyone hate that I've found the perfect man?*

Before she could scream at her NetMini, a heavy metallic *scrape* came from behind.

Kirsten whirled around.

A refrigerator-sized cabinet, some manner of old network storage array, slid to the right at the behest of a mechanical arm connected to a large assault bot. It had a main body about the size of a footlocker, with eight gunmetal blue legs, four of which dragged it through a gap in the wall. Two rifle-sized weapons mounted to the front end looked *way* too much like the fangs of a spider.

Kirsten didn't give it the chance to fire. She two-handed her E-90 and clicked the trigger as fast as her finger could move. Ten or so blasts in five seconds left a random assortment of orange-edged holes glowing in the main body. Its legs shot straight and waved about, jittering in an electrocution dance. The Class 4 laser made short work of its armor plating. In seconds, the legs fell limp. With a loud hissing, the assault robot slumped forward and spewed dark green fluid all over the floor. A few stray sparks lapped out of its back end, but it appeared dead.

Kirsten kissed the E-90. More powerful lasers did exist, Class 5 and 6, though only in rifle sizes. As far as pistols went, she couldn't get anything more powerful without going into plasma weaponry, and the police weren't allowed to carry those. Even the military couldn't use them on Earth. True, the E-90 had over-penetration problems most times which made it a questionable choice for law enforcement use, but she adored it at that moment.

Dots of light swarmed at the far end of the room. The derelict office she chose to hide in was, for the most part, wide-open space with only a few walls. Both pursuing orbs had gone around the building, having missed her. On the opposite side of the building from where she stood, they decided to fly into the ground floor rather than move around the outside.

"Dammit, how the hell did they find me?" She shot once, missing by inches, before running for the window.

From the inside, she stood eye level to the windowsill. Kirsten grabbed it and hauled her weight up by arm power and fear. Both orb bots unloaded at her. Flickering blue muzzle flare danced on the wall while bullets pulverized puffs of dust out of the plasticrete around her. She screamed and threw herself out the window, flopping on the ground outside.

"Someone tracked your order," said the NetMini.

"Dammit. Who?"

"How should I know? I'm a NetMini, not a GlobeNet Neural Interface Deck."

Kirsten scrambled to her feet at a lull in the shooting, and ran. Having sneakers on made her feel ten times faster since she didn't have to worry about stepping on danger. A short sprint later, she ducked behind a crashed hovercar embedded in the wall of an abandoned building. Cryomil long-ago leaked from the wreckage had etched and pitted the plastisteel ground. With one hand keeping the E-90 pointed at the end of the alley she'd come from, she climbed into the dead car, hunkered down, and pulled her NetMini out.

"Where is my backup?"

"I have no idea," it said. "I'm not on the department network, all I can do is make vid calls."

"Did you call them?"

It made a soft chirp. "System logs do not show an ack."

"Ack?" Kirsten blinked. "How did you not get an ack? You sent it?"

"The most likely scenario—"

An orb appeared at the corner. Ready for it, Kirsten fired.

"—is that my transmission was intercepted."

She glared at the wounded orb spinning out of control. It tried to re-aim, but the damage kept it moving in the flight of a drunken moth. A few bullets clanked into the dead hovercar. She'd found it difficult to hit the orbs before, but with it zipping around out of control, she didn't bother even trying. At least the erratic movement ruined its aim as much as it prevented her from hitting it.

"Memory dial six," said Kirsten.

"Calling," said the NetMini.

"Patrol craft," said Kirsten's recorded voice.

Her chosen 'ringing' animation of a prancing white cat bounded across thin air in hologram for a little more than sixteen seconds before the standard departmental voicemail announcement played. Command didn't permit personnel to customize the vidmail greeting in their patrol units, both for reasons of personal security as well as making it easier to trade assigned vehicles.

"Dorian? Are you there? Please tell me I left the damn speaker on. If you can hear this, I need a hand. Getting chased by a damn hacker and his pet bots."

Static.

"Dammit." She gazed at the indigo smog above her, lined with glowing green-white threads of hovercar traffic and ad-bots. *I could beacon for him but... no way, not calm enough. Shit!*

Another orb poked out of the window of a building half a block away. She fired, chasing it back inside. It tried again, with the same result. The third time, it popped up and right back down. She held her fire. *The damn thing is baiting me... why? Crap. Something's coming. I need to get out of here.*

Kirsten crawled to the other side of the car and slithered out the window onto the ground. Barely a second after she got to her feet, she spun at the sudden whine of a hover-inducer behind her. She crumpled over an orb bot that flew straight into her gut, hugging the head-sized metal sphere as it carried her into the air for several seconds before she slid away and fell to the ground.

Despite the metal 'punch' knocking the wind out of her, she retained the presence of mind to hold on to her weapon. The orb continued to rise, unaware it lost its passenger for several more seconds. When it did, it flipped over and rocketed down. Kirsten flung her body into a roll to the side. The fifteen-pound plastisteel ball smashed into the metal ground, denting it. She wanted to curl in a fetal position and cradle her stomach. Painless breathing had become like a distant pleasant memory.

Damn thing must be out of ammo. She forced herself onto her back and had the E-90 up and ready when the orb leapt at her for another try. Her aim was a split second slow from a kill shot. The laser gashed the side of it open, knocking the sphere into a wide spark-trailing arc. It crashed into the ground a few feet away from her head, bounced into the air spinning, and glanced off the building across the alley with a bell-like *clang*. It fell straight down the wall to the alley and rolled a few feet before stabilizing itself. Twice, it tried to pop back in the air, but crashed down again. Unable to fly any more, it swiveled to face her on the ground. She let her arm fall to the side, resting it almost flat on the ground to aim. Nothing happened when she tried to fire. The readout showed the E-mag at two percent charge, not enough juice for the powerful laser core to produce a beam.

"Shit." She rolled upright.

She ran to the first possible turn, a left, went a block and a half before skidding around the next possible right. Two orbs waited for her in that alley, hanging at head level about ten feet away. She squeaked to a halt on her new sneakers. With a startled yelp, she leapt back before they could shoot and continued straight. The orbs chased her, weapons extended but not firing.

A lone orb foiled her next attempt at a left turn in a similar manner. Another pair emerged from a street two blocks distant, forcing her to turn right. No orbs blocked that path and she sighed with relief until another one came out of an alley, shooing her into a left turn. Leaping over trash piles, Kirsten screamed at her NetMini.

"Suri, please get me some backup. Division 1, Five, Six, hell, even goddamn Nine. I don't care, get someone out here!"

"I'm sorry, Kirsten. There is a lot of signal interference here. You're off the map. The closest relay point is approximately 1.44 miles to your relative northwest."

"I'm in a damn black zone?"

"I'm sorry, Kirsten. There is no navigational information available for your current GPS location."

"I'm in a damn black zone." Kirsten all but shrieked as another sudden orb forced her to turn.

Panic lessened a dozen paces later, enough for her brain to reboot. *Why aren't they shooting anymore? They can't all be out of ammo. It's like...* She stumbled to a slow jog. *They're herding me somewhere specific.* She clung to her empty weapon for security. "They could've hit me, I bet. They're trying to get me to go somewhere... What the hell is going on?"

"Eleven point three percent of victims of stranger-initiated sexual assault survive. Your odds will increase to seventy-three point nine percent if you inform your attacker you are a police officer."

"Gee..." Kirsten gawked at her purse. "Thanks, Suri."

"If you are being pursued by an organ-harvester, your odds of survival are somewhat less. Would you like to hear the—"

"No thanks." She came to a halt and stuffed the empty weapon back in the purse.

Alone, off net, and with no charge left in her only E-mag, Kirsten surprised herself at how little fear she felt. For a few seconds, she entertained the fantasy of having ordered additional E-mags instead of clothing better suited for running and gunning with bots in the middle of a slum. At least if she had to confront a living person, she still had mind blast.

She would not be anyone's victim.

Bullets danced across the ground. Her brain figured out it had been a deliberate miss a few seconds after she resumed running for her life. *Okay, asshole. Fine, you want me, I got somethin' for you.* She went around another corner, ushered by the orbs through a series of turns until she found herself at the opening of a dead-end alley packed with trash-crushers. Spent autoinjectors covered the street in a glittering patina of red and green plastic. The area stank of chemicals and human waste, but the aroma of synthetic booze and vomit flavored every third breath.

"Alright, shithead. I'm here." Kirsten folded her arms, scanning the alley for any sign of movement.

Given the surroundings, she expected organized crime or a gang. *They probably saw me in that slinky thing and thought I was a damn call girl.*

"Come on out, already. I'm not a damn escort, and I'm not at all interested in working for you."

Her voice echoed. The orbs filled in behind her, all four of them, still not shooting. She gave them a dismissive smirk until she noticed the tiny clicking noises. They were still *trying* to shoot her; they had run out of bullets.

At a loud metallic thud, she spun around seconds before the screech of wrenching metal broke the silence. Two trash-crushers skidded away from each other and tumbled over, as an enormous spider-bot with a body as big as a car shoved itself into the end of the alley. A rotary cannon emerged from a housing on its back. Blades extended from its two front legs, raised like the chelicerae of a massive tarantula.

No surface thoughts. Nothing to mind blast.

Time seemed to slow as she whirled away from it in search of anywhere to dive for cover. Blinding light met her when she looked to the rear, coming at her fast. Arms crossed over her face, she threw herself to the ground as the roar of a machinegun went off behind her. Heat millimeters shy of painful bloomed over her from above while the clatter of eighty rounds per second struck armor plating. A great concussive smash shook the dead end.

Silence.

At the jangling of a small metal rod bouncing over the ground, Kirsten lifted her head out from under her arms. The orbs had vanished. Hissing drew her attention around to the rear where a Division 0 patrol craft sat at the center of a cloud of fog and fumes. Ion drives shot lightning across the plastisteel, the emitter ports in contact with the ground. Electricity flickered in bright blue flashes within rolling Cryomil mist. At the nose end, a mangled heap of metal spider legs curled over the hood. Dorian emerged from the closed door and jogged to her side. He crouched, the strain visible in his expression as he summoned the energy to become solid enough to wipe a trickle of blood from her chin.

"Am I going to have to start following you around?"

Her attempt to laugh hurt. "Guess you got my vidmail."

"Yeah. The car's racking up quite the body count. A ninja, a demon, now a tarant bot."

Kirsten would've laughed if it didn't hurt so much.

She forced herself to stand, cradling an arm over her stomach while leaning the other on the wall for support. Dorian opened his mouth as if to speak, but hesitated when the patrol craft shifted and slid backward with a horrible squelch of metal-on-metal. The patrol craft slid to the side, and a giant arachno-bot with eight glowing red camera-eyes dragged itself toward her.

Kirsten scrambled away, not enough air left in her lungs to voice the scream she tried to loft.

Its forward-tilted posture lent a sense of anger to the giant assault unit. The crash had reduced the rotary cannon to a twisted ruin that flew to pieces when it tried to spin them up. It raised its vibro-blade tipped chelicerae, emitted an ominous buzzing growl, and scuttled closer.

"Shit," muttered Kirsten, staggering backward.

Dorian glanced at it, his eyebrows drawing together in an unimpressed glare. A wisp of pale energy surrounded him for an instant and faded. The giant machine took another step, then shuddered, swayed, and collapsed to the ground—drained of power. He started to turn back to her but one articulated arm twitched, flapping a vibro-blade at them. He shot it an annoyed smirk, and the mass of metal went limp. Shaking his head, he faced her with his hands on his hips.

Kirsten's panic exploded into nervous giggles. She made herself solid to spirits before falling into him. He carried her to the car and waited for the automatic door to open. Alas, without the armband computer, it didn't recognize her.

"I'm not that messed up," she said, reaching for the handle. Fortunately, her fingerprints worked.

Dorian eased her into the driver's seat. She left the door open while lifting the car into the air high enough to get the ground wheels deployed before setting it down again. A systems monitor detected some minor damage at the front end, internal components jarred loose by the impact.

"Ops, this is Agent Wren. I need backup to my location—and a medic." Kirsten let herself breathe for a moment before poking at the comm. panel. Evan's face appeared in hologram over the middle of the console.

"Mom!"

She hated the worried-to-tears look on his face. "I'm fine, hon. Are you okay? Nila said you were upset."

His fear melted to embarrassment. "I was scared. I had a bad dream," he whispered, no doubt trying to prevent Nila or Shani from hearing. "I nightmared Cappin Ezzeh tellin' me something bad happened to you."

Son of a bitch. He's a precog. Kirsten shivered. *He's gotta be.* "I'll be there as soon as I can. Someone tried to hurt me, but they didn't know who they were dealing with. I'm fine, thanks to Dorian."

Evan wiped his eyes. It took a few minutes—and the sound of approaching sirens—to convince him to let her off the line.

"He's a precog, Dorian. Evan had a dream about me dying before those orbs attacked me."

Dorian cocked an eyebrow at her. "The boy's seeing danger in *your* future. That doesn't necessarily mean he's a precog. Such things have been known to happen with clairvoyants without predisposition to precognitive ability."

"Most precogs only receive visions of the future related to themselves or people with whom they have a strong emotional connection. A clairvoyant would see an event in the present, *while* it's happening." Kirsten couldn't stop shaking. "If he's a precog, C-Branch is gonna take him in the middle of the night."

"Now you've been watching too many fiction holos." Dorian grasped her hand. "Director Carter can overrule anyone other than the Senate when it comes to matters of psionics. Don't panic yet. So far, it's only been you he's had dreams about. Guess it means he loves you."

She smiled despite her tears. "Yeah, you're right. They didn't find precognitive aptitude when they ran his battery. Maybe it is clairvoyance… or too weak for them to care."

"Most likely." Dorian glanced to the right as several Division 1 patrol craft landed, lights aglow. "Though a true precog would've seen it a week or more ago."

"You don't know that. And, not all precogs are the same. Look at my weak Telekinesis. He could have a little bit of future-sight, so he doesn't get much advanced warning."

"Now it sounds like you're trying to wish him precognitive rather than being terrified he might be."

Kirsten cradled her stomach. "I don't know. Right now, I can barely remember my own name."

"Agent?" asked an armored woman to her left.

Kirsten squinted at the mounted lights on the helmet and shoulder pads pointing at her. "Yeah, that's me. Some asshat sent an army of killer bots after me. No, I don't have any idea who or why, but I am going to find out—even if I have to invoke the dead to do so."

"Umm. Medic, over here." The Patrol officer stood and leaned on the door. "Think she took a shot to the head."

13

GOING TACTICAL

Kirsten stood behind Tech Chang in the network operations section of the Regional Tech Center, tracing her fingers over the four E-mags on the left side of her equipment belt. A jogging suit and sneakers had felt like putting on tangible confidence; her duty uniform made her feel superhuman. Fear and humiliation ran down the drain of the autoshower following twenty minutes in a tube to repair whatever ruptured in her gut from the kamikaze orb. She hadn't paid attention to the doctor's explanation—a combination of not caring to know and being too happy to be free of pain.

Kirsten glanced around while Sam worked, raising an eyebrow at a dozen incense cones on the workstation of the arrogant tech two desks over. The expression of WTF on her face caused a chuckle from the pink-haired woman across the room.

Sam looked up. "Neal's trying paganism this week. I'm not sure who did what to his system, but he's convinced it's possessed. Something happened to it he couldn't explain from a technical standpoint."

Dorian laughed himself silly.

"Got something, Agent," said Sam.

She stooped over his shoulder to look at the screen. He sat motionless, staring at her face. When he said nothing after a minute, she shifted her gaze to him. They stared at each other for a moment more. He risked a smile. Kirsten felt guilty.

"Sam? Thanks for helping me out here. I hope you don't think I'm taking advantage of you or anything."

"No…" He looked back at the screen, blushing. "I was just thinking of the dinner you mentioned a while ago. We, umm."

"I'm sorry. I've been very busy lately." She picked at the bracelet. "I'm not trying to play with you, Sam. I meant that. We'll go out. I just need to find time." A severe pang of nausea clenched her gut. She groaned and braced herself against his desk.

"What was that?" asked Dorian.

"An orb bot sailed full speed into my stomach when it ran out of ammo. Doc said I might feel pains here and there for a few days even though everything is fixed."

"I got a signal lock on those bots." Sam shook off his puppy-eyed stare and lapsed into professional mode. "I was able to filter out the signal from two dozen advert bots. Whoever did it routed the control signal through the GlobeNet into ComTec's private network. Through that, they used the ad-bots as a citywide antenna. It didn't affect the company's operations. Even if they noticed it, I doubt they would have cared."

"They'd have asked him to pay for the bandwidth, but let him do it," she muttered, rolling her eyes.

"Convinced it's a man? It's a hacker. You could be chasing a woman or even a little kid."

Kirsten stiffened.

Dorian rocked back on his heels. "No, they're not going to execute a minor for trying to kill a cop, but I still wouldn't want to be them. Relax. Most kid hackers don't do the assassination thing."

She shook her head and gestured at the terminal. "That the address?"

"Yep," said Sam.

"You're awesome." She kissed him on the cheek, leaving him limp in the chair as she ran to the door.

"NICOLE," YELLED KIRSTEN, SPRINTING ACROSS THEIR SQUAD ROOM. "YOU bored enough to go tactical with me?"

"Huh, what?" She peeled pink and white Hello Kitty headphones off, the last birthday gift Kirsten had bought her. "Did you say something?"

Kirsten jogged past her, shouting. "I'm going tactical, wanna come along?"

"You know it!" chirped Nicole, chasing her friend into the locker room.

They skidded to a stop by their lockers. Kirsten had just about removed all the hard bits of her uniform: belt, arm guard, boots, in preparation for donning psi armor when Eze rushed in the door.

Nicole stood beside her in only panties, one leg in a mesh stim-suit. "Hey, Cap."

"Wren, what's going on?" Eze halted nearby, eyebrow up.

Undeterred, Kirsten pulled the armored leg plates out of her locker. "Tech got a fix on the shithead that sent those bots to kill me. I'm going after him."

"K, you should put a stim-suit on." Nicole shrugged the mesh over her shoulders and pulled the zipper up.

Kirsten glanced over at the five flat cartridges held tight to Nicole's bare skin by what amounted to a fishnet bodysuit. "I have stimpaks on my belt. No time."

"Yeah but these"—Nicole tapped one of them—"go off automatically when you get the shit kicked out of you. It's much faster in the field, plus if you get knocked out, it will still work."

"Fine." Kirsten dropped the armor and slipped out of her Division 0 blacks.

Eze turned ninety degrees to his left to avoid the impression he stared at two women in their underwear. "Are you sure you don't want to leave this to Div 1? They can handle a hacker."

Nicole skipped the uniform, going right for the armor. At the look Kirsten gave her, she laughed. "The armor is mounted to its own bodysuit. Putting it on over the uniform is like wearing two uniforms. Too damn hot. You'd know that if you wore it every damn day."

Kirsten slipped into a stim-suit and replaced the uniform blacks on top of it.

Nicole shuddered. "You're gonna overheat."

"I'll be fine." She pulled on the armored leggings and grabbed the chest plate. "Captain, I think something paranormal may be involved here. I don't remember pissing off any corporations lately, and I can't think of who might want to kill me this week."

Eze laughed, a nervous sort of sound more worry than mirth. "You're going to take some Division 1 backup with you."

"Sure, as long as they are willing to get the hell out of there if things become weird."

He nodded and hurried off to make the arrangements with his counterpart 'across the hall.' Kirsten slipped on the armored gloves, cinched the fasteners closed, and grabbed a helmet. She spun to find Nicole armored up and tapping her foot.

"Wow, you didn't need help getting it on. I'm impressed."

Kirsten grinned. "Let's go pull a plug."

SAM'S TRACE FLICKERED IN THE CORNER OF KIRSTEN'S EYE, A PULSING yellow line through the muted blues of a city map. The patrol craft drifted in silence for a few minutes. When she neared the location, Kirsten nudged it into a shallow dive, descending to the level of the fifth story.

Nicole gawked at a mass of twisted I-girders protruding from the side of a building abandoned for decades. "Wow... Missile?"

Kirsten glanced to the right. "Yeah, looks like it."

"We're gonna need thicker armor."

"That happened thirty years ago," said Kirsten. "The Steel Reaver uprising, when the military forced them out into the Badlands."

Nicole stared at the dark grey shapes, buildings emerging from the low-hanging fog, and whistled. "Why did they sell cyberware to crazy people?"

"They probably weren't crazy when they first—"

"This is a good plan," blurted Nicole.

"—got it." Kirsten guided the car around a building, bleeding off more altitude while poking the button to extend the ground wheels.

The women stared at each other for a moment.

Nicole blinked first. "What?"

"Just waiting for you to finish. You always talk over me when you get excited."

"I do not."

"Yes, you do, and this time—"

"He won't expect just two of us."

Kirsten found the switches for the emergency lights above her head fascinating. *I was gonna let you finish first.* "Yeah."

The next three minutes passed without conversation. Kirsten eased the wide patrol craft past a gap in the wall of an old building. Parking inside an abandoned office on the third floor concealed the car, protecting it as well as keeping their presence here hidden. They both got out at the same time and let the doors sink closed. Nicole gazed around in awe at the ruin.

Kirsten put her hair up and lowered the psi armor helmet on. It sealed at the neck with a soft squishing sound, and the heads-up display flickered to life.

"You need any help with the helmet?" asked Nicole.

Kirsten tapped her foot, waiting for her friend to put hers on and look over.

"Guess that's a no." Nicole tapped the side of her helmet twice before the amber-hued visor emitted a faint glow. "I've been shot in the head too often. Time for new electronics."

"*Once* is too often." Kirsten blinked.

"Naw. They had little class two pistols. Can't scratch this armor, but it felt like a doll punched me."

"You have strange hobbies." Kirsten whispered, drawing the E-90. She found herself checking the charge meter to ensure it read 100%, which translated to about twenty-four shots. She raised her left arm and studied the tactical holographic map that shimmered in above it. "Okay, down to ground level, one block over, and underground."

Nicole nodded.

Kirsten led the way, followed by Dorian and Nicole. She found it strange—but reassuring—how ditz-Nicole could flip on a credit chip and turn into tactical-Nicole. Her thoughts returned to when her friend had gone off on that ganger, Sicario. She couldn't tell how much of that had been acting tough or if Nicole really would have killed the man for shooting at her, even after disarming him. The idea that the girl she'd shared a bedroom in the dorms with from thirteen to nineteen couldn't kill people so casually.

Nah. She was acting tough to protect herself.

Two stories of debris-laden offices later, Kirsten struggled with a metal door at the ground floor. She grunted and shoved herself against it as hard as she could, but succeeded only in creating an inch of gap. Winded, she rolled away and caught her breath while leaning on the wall by an empty fire extinguisher mount.

Dorian walked through it, returning a few seconds later. "There's a desk and six chairs barricaded against the door from the inside."

Nicole holstered her E-86 and cracked her knuckles. Palms outstretched, she glared at the door and concentrated. The door rattled, dust swirled about, and a faint creaking groan of stressed metal filled the air. The upper and lower edges of the door warped outward.

"K… need a spike, say somethin' that'll piss me off."

Kirsten stared at her. "Umm…"

Nicole's gaze flicked to her for an instant, and back to the door. "I know you won't mean it, I just need a surge of anger to move this damn thing."

"Your parents wouldn't have divorced if you weren't psionic."

Nicole let out an angry scream.

A massive rush of air flooded down the stairwell as the door, and everything behind it, vanished. Seconds later, the loud, hollow *whump* of the desk striking the wall of a building across the street echoed over itself a few times, laced with the delicate sound of breaking glass. Clattering continued for a while after from smaller bits of debris falling to the ground. When the dust cleared, Kirsten found Nicole staring at her, tears streaming down her cheeks in the narrow strip of visible face behind her visor. The fatigue of such a psionic exertion did little to dull the accusatory look in her eyes.

"I'm sorry, Nikki, You asked me. Come on, you know what my mother did to me for being psionic." Kirsten stared down. "I wished all my parents did was divorce."

"Yeah." Nicole grabbed her helmet and breathed. "You didn't mean it. We were both problems 'cause of what we are."

"Can we maybe hold off on the sobbing on each other's shoulder bit until *after* we get the moron who tried to kill me?"

Nicole nodded, wiped her hands down over her face, and drew her sidearm. She loosed a sharp exhale and found her usual pleasant expression. "Okay. Let's do it, but you owe me an orange bomb."

"The glass it comes in is the size of your helmet. That much alcohol would kill you."

"Hah." Nicole laughed. "You've never seen me drink, have you?"

"She'd at least wind up in a medical tank if she drank one alone." Dorian smirked.

Kirsten made a 'yeah, probably' face at him, and headed inside, crossing a gutted lobby. A C-shaped area of less-scuffed floor indicated where the reception desk had once been.

Nicole whistled. "Wow, they even stole the fake plants."

"Likely scavenged anything they could get their hands on for survival out here," said Dorian.

"Why don't they just live where civilization still exists?"

"Who?" asked Nicole.

"Sorry, I keep forgetting you can't hear him."

Nicole blinked. "Who?"

"Dorian."

The redhead gasped at her, wide-eyed. "He's here?"

"Shh! Get down," whispered Kirsten as she ducked.

A pair of orb bots across the street glinted in the waning afternoon sun. They circled the crushed remains of a steel desk, embedded in the wall of the facing building. Kirsten stayed out of sight, watching their motion as rendered by the tactical armor's sensors, creating the illusion of being able to see through the wall.

"If they come in here, which they probably will considering the desk-shaped hole in the wall"—Dorian shot Nicole a disapproving smirk—"our hacker friend will know something's coming. If I knock them out in the street, it will look like a system malfunction."

Kirsten held up a hand. "If you zonk the bots, won't that make him think Div 9 jammers?"

"Or a Div Five EMP rifle." Nicole bounced a little. "Those things are *so* cool!"

"Depends on how savvy our hacker is," said Dorian, stroking his chin with one finger. "Both of those would create static on the display prior to shutdown. I drain the power, they shut down immediately. Unless he notices the lack of static, we're made." Dorian grumbled. "We have to risk it. If they see you two running for cover, it will be worse."

Nicole tapped at a virtual keyboard over her left arm. "They probably have thermal, maybe motion detection."

A woman's voice, thick with accent and nervousness, filled her ears from the comm. "Agent Wren, this is Sergeant Fernandez, Division 6. We're in position around you. We have one target on thermal, and bunch of EMF signatures."

"Copy, Sergeant. Keep a safe distance until I verify there is no paranormal presence here."

"Roger, Agent. Don't gotta tell me that twice."

Kirsten jumped a second later at the sound of two heavy metal spheres clanging against the plastisteel road outside.

"He's blind, come on," yelled Dorian from outside.

Despite knowing only she could hear him, Kirsten cringed at the shouting. "Come on, it's clear," she whispered, grabbing the ridge of the hole the desk made and vaulting out.

He waited for them between two inert orb bots in the shadow of the desk. Kirsten flattened herself against the wall, staring up at the crumpled metal jutting out overhead. She looked from it to Nicole.

What? asked Nicole, telepathically.

I didn't think about how much saying that would hurt. I'm sorry. Kirsten glanced up at the desk. *I didn't really mean it, it was just something I thought would make you mad.*

Nicole gave her shoulder a light shove. *My fault, I asked. Didn't you want to save the sappy shit for later?*

Kirsten held up her left forearm to check the signal map. *Yeah.*

She stuck her leg in a window and climbed into a dim space filled with piles of disassembled office cubes. Off-grey cloth-paneled squares from disassembled cube stations stacked to the ceiling in haphazard clusters created a maze full of rats only a touch smaller than an average feline. The creatures shifted to glare at her as if challenging the intrusion of their domain. As Dorian entered, their aggression evaporated. They scurried out of sight, squealing and swarming over each other.

"Stay close to me, please." Kirsten gave Dorian a pleading look.

I thought we'd have gang problems here. Nicole lingered outside, surveying the area.

"There's enough rumor about the Steel Reavers still being here that other gangs are afraid to attempt taking over the area," muttered Kirsten, while keeping a wary eye on the floor for more rats.

"Why do you sound scared?" asked Nicole, sliding off the ledge to her feet inside. "Is there another demon here?"

"Big ass rats." Kirsten pointed at the nest-piles.

"Rats?" Nicole jogged over and shook her head. "Seriously? You're afraid of rats? They're kind of cute."

"Cute? They were bigger than the cat you seem to think I have."

"I thought your cat died?" Nicole faked a pout.

Kirsten held a finger to the front of her helmet in a shushing gesture then pointed up. A thick black wire sheathed in fluorescent lime plastic ran along the ceiling. An outer transparent layer contained a honeycomb pattern in metal filament. *That's gotta be his relay. I bet it goes to an obelisk transmitter on the roof.*

Nicole pulled a knife. Kirsten grabbed her arm.

No. Cut it and it will warn him we're coming. If he was ready for us, his balls would be all over us. I don't think he knows we're here.

Barely managing to stifle a laugh, Nicole winked. *When we get outta here, you should surprise that Russian of yours. You need it bad.*

Confusion lasted for the duration of one blink before she realized what she said. *Dammit, orbs. You know what I meant.*

Kirsten frowned at the floor, noting a large amount of debris: planks, bits of old chairs, odd scraps of cube farm connectors, and a handful of old reassemblers. As she took her first step in search of clear ground, bright amber threads flickered into view. Kirsten held her left hand up and made a fist. Nicole froze.

IR triplines, said Kirsten, telepathically.

Nicole nodded once. *I see them, too. You really need to wear armor more often. It's super handy.*

They may have been explosives or simple alarms, though she crept forward as if one misplaced boot would kill everyone in the city. Six glimmering threads and twenty meters of corridor later, she let herself breathe again upon reaching a dim interior hallway. Dark blue paint covered the walls, decorated with images of bounding, grinning stuffed animals sitting on a cloud. The smell and flavor of mildew hung in the air, no doubt emanating from a patch of mold growing on the drywall around a sign indicating the day care center was to the left.

The trace led her past the life-sized cartoon animals. She followed the corridor around a sweeping right curve. On the right, a series of floor-to-ceiling windows offered a view into the ruin of the company day-care. A first-generation nanny doll slumped against the far wall; dark green mold had grown into its primitive artificial skin, making it look like a fuzzy zombie.

Nicole aimed at it. "If that damn thing moves, I'm gonna scream."

"There's no power in it. If it moves, you *should* scream," said Dorian.

"Dorian said it's got no power. I don't feel anything either, so… it won't move." Despite knowing it was inert, Kirsten couldn't keep from staring at the dead machine as she crept across the room. She felt like a six-year-old staring at the evil doll in a rocking chair by the window, waiting for it to move.

Nicole's boot found an old toy, creating a loud *squeak*.

Kirsten almost fainted.

They froze still.

What does this guy have that you're so tense? Nicole's eyebrows crawled together. *I thought we were going after a deck jockey?*

Kirsten lowered her E-90, trying to breathe. *I don't know. I guess the eerie emptiness has me on edge.*

Nicole squinted. *Are you sure you don't feel anything spooky? You usually don't get this rattled by empty rooms. Heck, the stuff you've seen, I'm surprised anything scares you.*

Eyes closed, Kirsten reached out with her mind in search of any source of paranormal energy. Dorian's presence shimmered like a light in the dark. Something else teased at the edge of her awareness as well, something malevolent and close. Close enough to touch her. Small... weak... evil...

I don't like that. You're getting paler.

Nicole's voice in her mind carried the shock of fingers snapped past her eyes. She jumped, spinning once. Her fearful expression melted into one of annoyance. *I do feel something, but it's weak. Could be a victim of the Reavers, maybe a Harbinger nearby. I don't see anything.*

Kirsten suppressed the urge to shiver. She didn't want to say it aloud, or even telepathically, but the feeling had been dogging the edge of her conscious mind for several days. In fact, the only time she could remember in recent memory where she didn't feel as though something had been following her was when she visited Father Villera. It worried her that whatever she sensed lurking around had been afraid to enter the church.

That could only mean one thing.

If there's an abyssal following me, it's either far off or damn weak. She steeled herself against it. *I shouldn't be worried.*

On the far side of the daycare classroom, Kirsten forced open a maintenance door and entered a narrow corridor with cinder block walls. The signal trace led her down thirty yards to a boiler room on the left. Between two massive furnaces, a cluster of electronics hid beneath a dingy olive-green tarpaulin. Four FuBoxes, military-grade fusion generators, hummed. They had officially been designated as 'portable,' though moving them required the strength to lift a tiny car.

Inch-thick black cables ran from the generators across the floor to an improvised trapdoor made from a large slab of rusting metal, which rested upon the wires, not quite closed. Explosions and gunfire from a violent video game leaked up from below.

"One moment," said Dorian, as he sank into the floor.

Kirsten made a face at the giant half-inch slab. *That's gonna make a lot of noise.*

Nicole shook her head. *I can move it quiet, but it will take a while.*

Dorian floated back up into the room. "You're lucky, K. No kid. Adult male, about twenty-five to thirty. He's alone, but he's got a mess of orb bots on shelves."

The trapdoor wobbled under the effect of Nicole's concentration. Kirsten kept her weapon trained on the hole, watching the slab ease upward at an agonizing pace. The hinges emitted faint squeaks, but nothing loud enough to overpower the digital warfare below. Nicole pushed the hatch up until it rested against the wall behind it, then sagged, again out of breath.

"It wasn't too heavy, I'm tired from holding it up for five minutes so it didn't make noise."

Kirsten nodded then lowered herself down a cheap portable ladder their quarry had positioned below. Heavy pipes and rat-chewed wire bundles lined both walls of a narrow passageway crossing beneath the abandoned office tower. Forty yards away, a human outline glowed in the multicolored radiance of a 150-inch holo-display. Speakers as tall as people rattled the room with explosions and machinegun fire. The occasional roar of a combat aircraft going overhead neared deafening.

Wow, retro-gamer. He's using a screen.

The pitch of Nicole's telepathic giggle made Kirsten's back muscles tighten. She raised her arm, E-90 out. With one final glance at her armband screen to confirm the signal source, she tiptoed forward. An escape elevator shaft for the former executive VIPs occupied the front part of the room, blocked off by armored doors indicating it remained unused, no doubt waiting at the upper floor.

She edged past several freestanding shelves full of bot parts, power cells, and strange bladed weapons too small or unwieldy for a person to use. At the end of the shelf, she adopted a solid two-handed grip on the laser and trained it on the man's head. Unkempt, shaggy black hair sprouted from under a dark blue wool cap, raining down over a ten-year-old military jacket four sizes too big for its wearer. He slouched back in a chair, fingers blurring over a pair of intangible holographic controllers. Two deck wires extended out of the hair at the back of his head, one draped left and one right. Both connected to net decks.

Kirsten snorted air out her nose to chase away the stink of a months-overdue bath laced with the sweet berry tinge of Flowerbasket. "Police! Hands where I can see them."

The man didn't react in the least, continuing to pilot his virtual soldier down a narrow Martian trench. Kirsten tilted her head at the oddity of watching World War II unfold on Mars… with aliens. *Game designers buy the good drugs.* She started to peek at his surface thoughts but recoiled with a mild headache. The man had two thought patterns occurring at once: half his brain was in the middle of cyberspace trying to break his way through a firewall that resembled a security door, while the other played a game in the real world.

"Good thing we were so quiet coming in," said Nicole as she stomped past and made a 'come here' gesture with her hand.

Audio buds tore loose from his head. Stunned by the feeling of it, the man clamped his hands over his ears.

Kirsten edged a step closer. "You there, this is the police. Keep your hands where I can see them. You're under arrest for the attempted murder of an officer of the law."

"He tried to kill you," said Nicole. "I hope he resists, so I can shoot him myself."

"Panic code alpha!" wailed the man. "Wipe sequence whiskey tango fox—"

The wires popped out of the back of his neck, courtesy of an annoyed telekinetic. He fell face-first over his desk, from screaming to twitching like a beached salmon in one eighth of a second, a line of drool leaking out of his mouth. Crashing, banging metal behind her made Kirsten whirl. A shelf on the right side of the room upended itself and fell into a cloud of dust. A digitized metallic roar scraped the air near seconds before two glowing points of red light winked on in the haze.

A four-armed humanoid bot, about six feet tall and made of unpainted shiny plastisteel, lurched out of a pile of debris. Each of its four arms raised combat rifles, all of which chirped to life and oriented toward her. The two upper, larger arms had mounted tri-barrel rotary cannons while the smaller pair gripped standard weapons in metal hands. Ammunition feed chutes emerged from ports along its sides, rising like silver serpents into the main guns while they spun up to firing speed.

Freeze. Kirsten's eyes glowed.

It ignored her psionic command. "Pathetic mortals, you have trespassed in the domain of Mordac the—"

Clank.

The skeletal bot's emergence from the pile of junk continued forward, culminating in a headfirst meeting with the bare concrete ground. Its larger arms bounced and bucked as the spinning barrels clattered to a halt. Kirsten kept pointing her E-90 at it for a full minute after it ceased moving. Dorian winked.

The hacker moaned.

Kirsten swiveled on him. "On the floor, now!"

He fumbled at his coat, as if reaching for something inside.

Nicole flung an arm outward. The man's hat flew off and his head jerked upward as if she'd grabbed a fistful of his hair. He swayed forward at his desk, and proceeded to smash his own head into the surface six times in a rhythmic beat. After the last hit, he slumped over the console, unconscious and bleeding from the nose.

"Son of a bitch," growled Nicole.

She ran up on the body and kicked the chair out from under him. With all the delicacy of an inebriated moose, she threw him to the floor and relieved him of a pistol and two grenades.

"Hey, easy." Kirsten put a hand on Nicole's shoulder. "We're here to arrest him, not beat him to death."

Nicole didn't look up as she gathered the man's arms together and cuffed him. "What difference does it make? He tried to kill you. They're gonna execute him anyway."

"Nikki, you don't want that on your conscience." Kirsten rolled the guy over and propped him into a seated position against his desk. "Besides, he's just a contractor. I want to know who hired him."

A stimpak to the side of the neck woke him. Thick blood bubbled out of both nostrils as he shifted, testing his ability to brute-force his way out of the police-issued binders. He gazed at Kirsten, then Nicole, and smiled.

Nicole grabbed him by the lapels of a shirt so dirty it looked sticky, hauling him up to his feet. "He's gonna make a stripper joke. I'm just gonna kill him so I don't have to hear it again. You can talk to his ghost."

"Hey." Kirsten grabbed her arm. "Easy."

He groaned as Nicole forced him into an ungainly backward lean over the desk with her forearm pressed into his throat.

"Try me, jackass. You attempted to kill a cop, who also happens to be a close friend of mine. I could end you right here and get a medal for it."

The grin, and the color in his face, faded.

"Look…" Kirsten gestured with the E-90 at the shelves behind her. "You did send your little bots after me. By all rights, the law says you're supposed to die for attempted murder on a cop. I know it wasn't your idea. You guys never do anything unless you're getting paid for it. Just tell me who hired you and I'll put in a request for commutation to life."

"I… If you kill me, you'll never find out." He thrashed backward, a futile effort to evade Nicole's grip.

The redhead's stunrod leapt on its own from her belt and floated over her shoulder, poised to club him. "Please do that again. Look, K, this piece of shit isn't worth it. Just mind-read him, get what you need, and let the law do its thing."

He stared at the weapon, all fight leaving him at the sight of it flying.

"Kirsten…" Dorian reached toward her.

She glanced at him, then glared at Nicole. "Nikki, that's not the way we do things."

"He tried to *kill* you! Will you stop being so nice to him?" Nicole pressed her arm into his throat. "He ain't gonna say a damn thing. Bastard isn't even afraid of us. Hell, I'll do it."

"Kirsten!" Dorian yelled. "Get her away from him, *now!*"

Nicole glared into the man's eyes. Kirsten jumped forward to grab her friend by the shoulder, but didn't move fast enough. The instant a telepathic link formed between the suspect's brain and Nicole's, the man fainted on his feet. His face sagged into a drooling caricature, eyes rolled back into his head. A dark crimson mist exhaled from his mouth and nose, which Nicole breathed in despite her helmet.

The redhead staggered away, gagging. Her stunrod ceased floating and fell straight down with a hollow, metal *clank*. Nicole stumbled to her knees, holding her head in both hands. Kirsten ignored the unconscious man falling to the side and shook Nicole by both shoulders. When she didn't react at all, Kirsten gathered her astral senses, picking up on a dark presence within her friend.

The room blurred. The next thing Kirsten knew, she'd slammed into the wall fifteen feet away, upside down. Telekinetic force pinned her while Nicole stood and flashed a demonic grin. Her deep blue eyes had faded milky white and nearby veins darkened into a raccoon mask. She glanced down at herself, cupping her breasts in both hands.

"This is nice. I should take women more often," said a male voice. Nicole shook her head with a dismissive sigh. Kirsten struggled to look away while Nicole pawed herself despite wearing armor. "No, that would be a bad idea. I'd never get *anything* done. Such rage inside this one. Yes, I can use this."

Dorian tackled Nicole. The telekinetic crush ebbed. Kirsten peeled away from the wall and fell flat on her chest. Between flying into cinder blocks and falling, she expected to hurt—but felt only a little uncomfortable. *Oh wow... I love this armor.* She sat up, amid shrieking that vacillated between Nicole's chirpy pleas for help and a dark quasi-feminine laughter. Shelves and debris shuddered behind Dorian from useless telekinetic efforts to fling the insubstantial man away.

Kirsten summoned the astral lash, bathing the area in harsh shadows and scintillating blue-white light. Nicole's helmet snapped to face her. She hissed, shoving and pounding at Dorian in an effort to fight her way up to her knees and slide away from the spectral whip. His eyebrows went up, her strength evidently surprising him. His fingers slipped through her body, immaterial to her flesh but holding onto the entity inside her.

"Please don't hurt me, we're like sisters!" Nicole added a childlike pitch, the voice sounding more female. Her eyes widened.

"This won't hurt Nicole at all." Kirsten stomped over, swinging the tendril, but sailed butt-first into the wall a second time. She bounced off the cinder blocks and landed sitting.

Nicole loosed a mocking laugh, pointing at her. "Ha, ha. Can't reach me."

Kirsten snarled and ran at her again, but slid to a stop, the tip of the lash inches out of reach. A casual emanation of telekinesis held her back like a bully with long arms. Her boots squeaked, sliding over the plasticrete floor as she tried to run past an intangible wall. Again she swiped her whip, back and forth inches from Nicole's face, making the creature laugh even louder.

Dorian surged, growling. He shoved Nicole over sideways, driving her into the ground like an angry Gee-ball player. Kirsten rushed forward and tore the lash in a downward swipe through Nicole's chest. The energy cord tugged at her hand as if striking something solid.

"Get out of her!" roared Kirsten. She yanked back on the energy thread.

Tension let go abruptly, as though the entity inside her had ruptured open. Kirsten stumbled back a step when the lash came free. A sense of weak obliteration rippled over the room. Nicole fell to her knees in a drunken sway. Heaving as if to throw up, she grabbed her helmet and flung it off. Black liquid oozed from her ears, nose, and mouth.

Nicole whined, scrunching up her face. "Thib if so"—she sounded as

though her mouth was full, and coughed up a blob of black jelly—
"fucking nasty." She coughed again, this time only liquid splattered out of
her. "It's oozing from *everywhere*." She shivered. "I feel like I went skinny
dipping in hot noseblow."

"How is that different than those damn gel tanks?" asked Kirsten.

The most pathetic, pouting expression she'd had ever seen on a grown
woman stared up at her. "The slime is *everywhere*."

"Well, I think our hacker was compelled," said Dorian, scowling at the
ichor. "I doubt there's going to be any electronic trail to follow back to
whoever sent it."

"I'm still gonna bring him in. Maybe Ashcroft can find something."
Kirsten breathed a sigh of relief after checking and finding him still alive.
"At least they won't execute him now."

Nicole tried to gather her dignity and wobbled to her feet. Every
motion made her wince. Kirsten rushed to her side to help her stand.

"I'd rather know who wants to kill you," said Dorian.

Kirsten sighed at the paused video game. "I'm sure they'll try again."

14

MATERIAL POSSESSIONS

Kirsten held Nicole's hand in the quiet dimness of the hacker's lair. The redhead trembled, wearing a face of abject disgust. She tried to move as little as possible, standing in a posture reminiscent of a toddler with a burdened diaper. The suspect remained unconscious, lying on his side and secured in binders. Nicole's grimace deepened to a scowl.

"What?"

"I'm pissed this idiot gets off the hook after he tried to kill you."

Kirsten squeezed Nicole's hand. "He didn't try to kill me, the entity inside him did. Either way, he's probably got a pile of illegal stuff in here. I'll let Div 1 sort him out."

"Fuck this. I have slime creeping down my legs." Nicole let go and waddled across the room to a curtained-off area, opening her armor as she went.

"You're not seriously going to…" Kirsten followed. "He doesn't even have a tube. That's an old-world bathtub. I doubt the water's even hot."

"I don't care." Plastic clatters rang out from armor hitting the ground.

Kirsten cringed as each armor piece peeled away from her with an audible slurping noise. She shrugged out of the stim-suit mesh, then whipped off her panties and hurled them. They hit the wall and stuck in place, a soot-colored mass of ooze. Nicole disregarded modesty, standing stark naked in the open, her shoulders slightly scrunched at the nasty feeling all over her. Dark purplish black liquid coated her legs, puddling around her feet. She turned toward a shower curtain, but arched her back like cold water hit her back. A fresh sluice of tar-black *something* glided down her legs.

"It's still coming out. Is that... normal?" Nicole gagged, spitting up another glop. "It tastes like bad eggs smell."

Kirsten hurried over and put a comforting hand on her shoulder, aiming for a clean spot with no ooze. "Sure. As normal as getting possessed by a creature from the abyss and forced to attack your best friend. I have no idea. I've never seen anything like this before. Uhh, it feels tainted. You probably wanna get rid of it as fast as you can."

Kirsten cringed away from the sight of more dark syrup leaking out of every natural hole in Nicole's body. Shuddering, the woman stepped into the tub and pulled the hanging plastic sheet across to hide. A screech of metal preceded a squeal of shock.

"Told you the water would be cold."

"I d-d-don't c-c-care," said Nicole past chattering teeth.

"I'll order you some new undies." Kirsten fiddled with her NetMini.

A few minutes later, the tromp of boots flooded the only passageway in. Kirsten blushed with sympathetic embarrassment for Nicole as a Division 6 assault unit in green-camouflage armor stormed in. One man approached and peered down at Kirsten, his face concealed behind a mirror-like gold visor. She tilted her head, amused by the distorted reflection of her face.

"Agent Wren? I'm Sergeant Hunt. We're here to secure the area while the rat squad runs around lookin' for cheese." The visor snapped open, revealing a face the color of chocolate. "Sorry we're late. The front room had a bunch of toy soldiers."

"Wow." Kirsten raised both eyebrows. "Div 2 is actually coming out here to a grey zone?"

Sergeant Hunt laughed. "Yeah. Is that the guy who tried to kill you?" He kicked the unconscious man.

Other men in the same assault armor cleared the sides of the room, sweeping for listening devices as well as trip mines. Not one of them paid any undue notice to a naked Nicole sloshing around, waist deep in cold, grey water, rubbing furiously at her body and occasionally retching up a mouthful of awfulness. One did take a protective position near her, with his back turned.

"What happened?" Sergeant Hunt motioned at the abandoned armor, then the tub.

Kirsten pointed at the black stuff. "Spirit possessed her. I destroyed it, but it uhh, stuff started leaking out of uhh, everywhere."

Most of the Division 6 team shivered.

Wow, they almost look like they believe me. Where's the fearful look? Oh, right. Div 6 rotate out from active duty military. These guys aren't afraid of shit.

Kirsten's NetMini beeped. The delivery bot had arrived at the entrance, but refused to enter this structure. "Be right back. Delivery's here."

She rushed back out the way she'd come in, and met the bot outside near an A3V in green camo with a dual-barreled 30mm cannon on the roof. Those personnel carriers always made her feel small, since their wheels stood taller than her. Another A3V rolled up, this one slate blue and unarmed. The ground rumbled with its arrival. It stopped and disgorged a Division 2 investigation team. Two women and two men jumped out before she recognized the fifth person—Sam Chang.

"Hey..." she said while reaching up to take a small box from the bot. "What are you doing out here?"

Sam slung a metal case over his shoulder on a white nylon strap and picked up two larger ones. "They were looking for volunteers to come check out a hacker pad. I heard you were working on the case and couldn't resist."

Kirsten glanced off to the side, a touch of blush in her cheeks. The man radiated schoolboy crush. Almost as soon as she thought it, she felt guilty. *I'm Konstantin's girl. I shouldn't be looking at other men. I belong to—.* She blinked. *Where did that come from. I'm no one's prop—* A wicked onrush of nausea clawed at her gut. She clamped a hand over it and gurgled.

"You feeling okay, Agent?" Sam set one case down to offer a hand. "You look pale. Is it my cologne? You seem to become ill whenever I see you."

She smiled despite the pang of discomfort in her gut. "I'm always pale." After a deep breath, she tucked the box she'd ordered under her arm. "Come on, I'll walk you in."

Tech Chang followed her through the building while she passed on the details of what happened.

"... and Dorian drained all the power out of it. That thing could still be dangerous if it's got a backup battery or something."

He nodded. "I'll disable it before I check his network."

Kirsten stopped short upon arriving back in the lair at the sight of Nicole standing there brazenly naked, arms folded, chatting with the Division 6 guys like they hung out in a break room at the PAC. Neither she, nor the strike team appeared to care at all. The tech crew, however, hadn't gone through military boot camp (with co-ed bunks and showers) and either stared dumbstruck or blushed.

Sam, however, focused on the four-armed walker bot, after barely giving Nicole a glance.

"Here..." Kirsten tossed Nicole the box. *And this is why I wore my uniform blacks under the armor.*

Nicole opened the box and took out a big plush purple towel and a packet of clean undies. She wrapped herself in the towel, shivering. *Ooh! Thank you. You rock! And, if I had a uniform on under the armor, it would've been soaked and slimy too, right? I'd have peeled that shit right off.*

Kirsten laughed, startling Sam by the apparent spontaneity of it. *Good point. You sure you're okay? Not feeling any strange emotions at all?*

Nope, I'm good. My nips could cut glass right now, but I'm good. Nicole dried herself off, then secured the towel around her armpits as a makeshift dress. She took one of the hacker's shirts from a drawer and used it to swab out the interior of the armor.

While Nicole dressed, Sam waved Kirsten over. "I got nothing here that really jumps out at me. Nothing from Intera"—he winked—"and nothing that appears connected to anything you're working on. Heh, apparently your hacker found Jesus."

"Dammit. This can't be random." Kirsten's scowl turned into an eye roll at the mention of Jesus. "What does that mean?"

"Looks like he did a job for a preacher a few days ago. A Reverend Wallis sent him ten thousand credits." Sam shook his head. "Must not have been a very dangerous job."

"Wallis?" Kirsten stomped over. "Hold on a second, you're telling me this scumbag was working for Wallis?"

"Wait, you know the guy?" Sam leaned away from the fury in her sapphire eyes. "Uhh, yeah. Hold on, I'm going to try and find a Citycam feed of their meeting."

Kirsten fumed, pacing back and forth as she waited for him to navigate a series of menus. He reached up and pulled one holographic panel forward, stretching it out to a forty-inch screen before he poked it in the middle. Video showed the interior of a dimly lit restaurant. From the décor, it appeared to be a run-of-the-mill chain place frequented by working-class people.

Glare from the late-afternoon sun reflecting on the faux-wood Epoxil table blurred the image briefly until the recorder compensated. Sam zoomed in, filling the screen with two men. Kirsten squinted at the smug grin on the face of Reverend B. G. Wallis as he spoke over a cup of coffee. A Class 2 doll waitress—human in appearance with faint lines at the joints and mouth—dropped off a large plate of chicken wings coated in bright orange sauce.

"Can you get sound?" Kirsten leaned closer.

"No, this is a Citycam recording from several days ago. If it were happening in real time, I could try the directional mic, but with a place like this, there's so much ambient noise resonating in the glass it would take me an hour or two to filter out the voices you want."

The deck jockey reclined in the seat with a face as though he owned the restaurant and everyone in it. He sat with one arm draped over the back of his seat, the other waving about with his conversation. His body language made him look as though he wasn't quite ready to accept whatever Wallis offered, teetering on the edge.

"I think your boy's name is Julio Ramirez," said Sam.

"You reading lips?" asked Kirsten.

"No, it's in the banking records."

Reverend Wallis produced a small, flat box, which he slid across the table and patted. A quick twist of his fingers spun it so a latch faced the man. Julio pondered it with an appraising frown before swinging his arm over the bench seat in a reluctant gesture of interest. He lifted the lid, disturbing a small sheet of paper inside. At that point, threads of static appeared in the video feed while the restaurant's interior lights faltered. The doll waitress fell over, face first into a coffee pot.

Julio Ramirez stared agape at the box, at what appeared to be a plain sheet of white paper, four by six inches, with a faint curl at the ends. His expression would have fit being told his entire family had been murdered. The doll stood back up, whirled about with a look of confusion, and resumed its duties. Two seconds later, Julio sat up straight. His slacker-slouch and fringer arrogance had evaporated, replaced with the confident poise more befitting an international spy. The man nodded once at the Reverend and stood to leave.

B. G. Wallis pulled the entire plate of wings closer, having it all to himself.

"Back it up four and a half seconds."

Sam nodded and did so.

"There, look." She pointed at the paper in the shadow of the half-open lid. "It's got writing on it. Play forward, one tenth speed."

Playback resumed at a speed that made it look like a series of still images shown in succession. Julio's hand moved the lid upward. As if shying away from daylight, the crimson writing evaporated from bottom to top. Julio's eyes fluttered and his expression changed, giving the impression he inhaled something unpleasant.

"What the hell is that?"

Kirsten nibbled on her thumbnail. "I'm willing to bet something happened the camera didn't pick up. If I had to guess, I think the Reverend Wallis knows quite a bit more about these abyssals than he's admitted. Sam, please send me this video. I'm gonna need it for my report."

MOTIONLESS, THE PATROL CRAFT HOVERED FIFTY FEET IN THE AIR TWO blocks away from Faith Pentecostal Baptist Ministries. Daylight grew long as the time crept up on six. Kirsten stared over the hood at the distant building, trying to make room beside her guilt for contempt at Wallis for dragging her out here. Evan *expected* her to say she needed to work late again. His lack of complaining hurt worse than a screaming fit. *I hope he knows I have to do this and I'm not losing interest in him.*

"Wren? Have you heard anything I just said?" asked Captain Eze.

She glanced away from the building to look at the hologram hovering over the dashboard. "Yes, sir. I'm to wait outside for backup."

"Officer Logan is upset you asked her to stay behind, you know. I saw that look in your eye. I don't want you charging in there alone."

"I'm not alone, I have Dorian with me. Besides"—the frustration in her voice eased to concern—"Nicole already got possessed once today. This guy seems to be able to control weak demons. I'm afraid of what this guy might be able to do to her." She glanced away from him, out the side window at approaching blue-and-whites. "She's a close friend, sir. I might hesitate if things go bad. These Division 1 guys aren't gonna be much more help. The only people you should send in here with me are other astrals."

"The good Reverend doesn't just have paranormal allies, Wren. He's got at least two thugs, and I don't want a repeat of what happened at the Motte residence. This is as much a show of force as anything else."

Kirsten grumbled to herself as four Division 1 patrol craft pulled up alongside hers. Except for the color scheme, the rear seat cage, and the Starburst laser in a bubble above the passenger seat, the vehicles were otherwise identical. The fear and awe those cars inspired caused a small spark of jealousy since her black one only managed to inspire curious looks.

"Be careful in there, Kirsten."

"Yes, sir," she said, trying not to sound too much like a scolded child.

"He might have a point." Dorian waited for the hologram to fade out. "You do have a habit of charging in alone without thinking. You have a little someone counting on you to come home alive now."

Kirsten waved at the closest patrol craft and nudged hers forward into a gradual descent. The cabin filled with a mechanical thrum as the ground wheels unfolded out from their protective doors and locked into place. "I know. I can't dwell on that when I'm"—she clenched her jaw as she pulled back on the stick, easing into a perfect landing—"out here. Hesitating is just as bad as being rash."

"You need to stop beating yourself up over that."

Kirsten shoved the door open and pulled her helmet on. "Whenever I see Shani, there's always a glimmer of terror in her eyes for those first few seconds." She exhaled. "I guess it's an improvement over running away from me."

"Kids are resilient. She knows you couldn't have hurt her. Give her time."

"Agent Wren," said an approaching man in blue armor. "I'm Sergeant Donovan, what's the situation?"

She stood out of the patrol craft, eye-to-pectoral with an enormous dark-skinned man in Division 1 tactical armor. In addition to the large ballistic pistol on his hip, he carried a UCF M2402—a compact Class 3 battle rifle chambered in 8mm caseless. *I guess they're not here to arrest anyone.* The rigid set of his cheekbones gave away his military bearing. The instant she thought him handsome, a pang of unease hit her in the stomach. Kirsten clenched her jaw and hid any outward sign of it. *What the hell is wrong with me now?*

"My captain requested you here in the event my suspect has people working for him." She looked up again. "I don't know precisely what he is capable of, but I am certain there are paranormal forces at work in there.

To be completely honest with you, Sergeant, I don't think it's a good idea for your team to go in there."

Sergeant Donovan rendered a grim nod, his face caught in the half-grin, half-wince of an NCO in a position to be able to ignore the word of an officer. "Ma'am, Captain Eze said you would try to go in alone. We have orders from him to escort you until such time as we confirm the number of ordinary hostiles in play."

Kirsten glared at nothing in particular. *Sometimes Eze is too much like a protective dad. Why doesn't he trust me?* She narrowed her eyes, imagining his response narrated in her head in his voice: *It's not you I don't trust, it's the people inside the church.*

With a series of hand signals, Donovan sent two of the patrol officers, Rivera and Polk, around back. "Zahn, Womack, Lewis, you're with me inside. Edison, you and Simons cover the street." The four officers advanced on the main door of the wide one-story building, with Donovan taking point. Edison and Simons remained outside, watching the front and sides.

Kirsten, E-90 out, followed close behind.

"Eze does have a point," said Dorian. "What if he's got a dozen fanatics in there?"

She shot him a look of irritation mixed with worry. "Something isn't right."

Dorian raised his arm and an E-90 blurred into existence in his grip. "A reverend may be summoning creatures out of the abyss. *Of course* something isn't right."

Sergeant Donovan booted in the front door, M2402 raised. Infrared range-finding lasers streaked the dust, flickering amber rays visible due to her armor's optics. Donovan's voice flooded the area, projected from loudspeakers on the side of his helmet.

"Attention: This is the police. We have an arrest order for one Benjamin Gerome Wallis the Third. Be advised this building is now under police lockdown. All occupants are to surrender immediately. Anyone exiting the premises in violation of this lawful detention order is subject to lethal force. All persons are hereby ordered to lie face down upon the ground, arms and legs spread. Failure to comply may result in bodily harm."

Officer Zahn, the only female among them, fired without warning into the wall to the left. Her rifle spat two three-round bursts that holed the cinder blocks. Daryl, one of Reverend Wallis's musclebound thugs, slumped out of a doorway and landed dead on top of a long rifle. His dark face held a lifeless stare, streaked with grey dust and blood. His right hand fell away from a pistol under his jacket.

"Never ceases to amaze me how these idiots forget we can see them through walls," said Zahn with a smirk.

Kirsten's blood ran cold: both from the casual way in which the officer killed a man as well as the lack of a ghost. Her alarm lessened as she thought he might have been a synthetic, but realized the blood wasn't white. *Even the spirits who transcend right away should be there long enough for me to see.*

"Gentlemen, I am sure there has been a misunderstanding."

The voice emerged from maroon curtains set up behind a pulpit fancy enough to seem out of place in a repurposed commercial building. Reverend Wallis stepped out from a gap in the hanging cloth, still in his expensive grey suit and gleaming black wingtips. He raised his arms to the sides, palms facing up in a devotee's gesture. Behind him, four figures in archaic black hooded robes emerged. Like ancient monks, they held their arms folded before their chests, hands tucked into opposing sleeves.

"Reverend," said Kirsten. "We have some things to talk about. I need to ask you some questions about Julio Ramirez."

Wallis closed his eyes. His head shifted left as if slapped by a weak phantom. "Ahh, Miss Wren. That is unfortunate."

"You're an Astral, Wren, right?" asked Officer Womack, the tallest, while jabbing his rifle in the air at Wallis. "On the ground, Padre, the Zero here can still interrogate your ass as a ghost."

"Hold on." Kirsten raised her left hand, keeping the E-90 poised at the followers. "No one needs to die." She glanced sidelong at Daryl's body. *Was he even alive? What the hell...*

Reverend Wallis drew in a sharp breath, raising his voice in a preacher's cadence. "Jesus made a whip out of cords, and drove all from the temple area, both sheep and cattle. He scattered the coins of the money changers and overturned their tables." The Reverend swung his arm to point at the Division 1 officers. "I say to you now, *you* are the oppressors. You trade not in coins but in our freedoms. You are the unrighteous trespassing in a house of God. So shall you be driven out!"

At the end of his rant, Wallis's dark, bald scalp dripped with sweat that meandered over the deep ridges in his forehead over wild, raised brows. His eyes burned with the fury of a zealot, though his only weapon appeared to be a wagging finger. The robed figures all screamed at once, flinging their arms up, revealing each carried a pair of combat knives. Blades gleamed in the dim light as the evidently insane men charged.

All four Division 1 officers fired. Kirsten aimed at Wallis, waiting for him to do something, but he remained still, merely pointing with an imperious sneer. A hail of 8mm slugs shredded the charging fanatics; the closest one skidded to a bloody halt more than six feet away from the line of blue. Kirsten's eyes watered at the ballistic propellant fumes coalescing into a haze. Wallis's sanctimonious expression faded to one of amusement. He lowered his arm and smiled at them.

Dorian frowned at the dead, glancing from metal knives to armored officers. "Maybe you had a point about religion and stupidity going hand in hand."

"On the ground, now!" roared Sergeant Donovan.

Wallis ignored him.

The officers advanced. When they moved among the corpses, dark ethereal wisps surged out of the dead. Bodies lifted skyward, lifted by the energy exuding from their backs. Although the officers couldn't sense the specters, they did see dead men float.

"What the fuck!" yelled Zahn, while pumping more bullets into the corpse. That energy trail flew at her, ignoring the spray of gore and azure muzzle flare on its way to disappear into her chest.

"Get away!" Kirsten shrieked, attempting to wrap her psionic hold around the nearest emanation.

Like trying to grab a ball of slime, it oozed past her mental fingers and jumped into Officer Womack, right in front of her.

Donovan whirled about, taking a step away, but one of the shadows swam into him from behind. He stiffened, rose on his toes for a second, then dropped to his knees. The fourth officer, Lewis, an average-sized man, roared with panic and fired over Wallis's head as another spirit flew into his chest with enough force to knock him over backward.

Zahn pivoted her rifle around in a suicidal orientation. Dorian leapt onto her, wrestling the entity inside her for control of the weapon. "Kirsten, they're"—he grunted—"Possessed."

Kirsten dove away from Womack's attempt to smash his M2402 over her helmet. Sergeant Donovan grabbed her from behind and lifted her off the ground, holding her for the tall officer to shoot. She growled, more angry than scared. *This is exactly what I was worried about. I hope Eze is watching this shit in real time.* Kirsten focused on her power, unfurling the Astral Lash from her left hand; the sight of it at last brought an end to

Reverend Wallis's imperious laughter. She flicked it to the rear, striking a semisolid mass, and wrenching it into the resistance. The energy cord flowed through her body as a not-altogether-unpleasant sensation of coolness. Sergeant Donovan howled as though she had lit his nether bits on fire.

He fell to the side, vomiting black ichor with such force his nostrils became spray nozzles painting the inside of his visor. Womack fired at her. The lash sucked back into her hand as she shifted her mental exertion to her suit. Feeding from her energy, the Psi Armor empowered itself with a kinetic field. Dull grey stripes along the arms and legs of the gloss black material glowed bright violet. The slugs hit her in the chest, knocking her into a flat, bouncing slide as the near-frictionless interaction between the force field and the floor did nothing to slow her down.

Gasping for breath from the impact, Kirsten spiraled legs-first into the front wall. She lay there for a second waiting for horrible pain, knowing that even empowered, psi armor didn't offer enough protection to stop a combat rifle round. Two seconds later, when no agony started, she chalked it up to a lucky angle.

Sergeant Donovan gurgled something unintelligible in reaction to Womack and Lewis both aiming at Zahn, who—to anyone who couldn't see ghosts—would've appeared to be having a seizure while wrestling with Dorian. Kirsten scrambled to her feet. Donovan rushed at Lewis while firing a single shot into Womack's thigh. The slug bounced off the armor with a loud *click*, though the impact shoved the leg out from under the big man. Donovan bowled into Lewis the same moment Dorian caught Zahn with a leg sweep and took her down.

Kirsten sprinted and dove on Womack's back as he stood back up, feeling like a twelve-year-old trying to wrestle a Gee-ball player. She wrapped herself around his weapon and kept it aimed away from the other officers. Sergeant Donovan manhandled Officer Lewis, tossing the average-sized man around like a toy. Dorian knelt on Zahn's chest, punching her repeatedly in the head and ribs.

"Dorian, what are you—?" Womack spun her into a column, knocking the wind out of her. She managed to hold on.

"I'm hitting the entity, not her." He changed his grip, foiling Zahn's attempt to bring her sidearm to bear on Donovan. The pistol went off, adding two new spots of daylight to the ceiling.

The Reverend, hands folded, watched the fracas with an amused smile.

He made no move to involve himself in the goings-on, nor did he leave. Kirsten tried to glare at him, though she couldn't really look at him while struggling to keep Womack from machine-gunning his squad mates. Twice, she tried to call the lash, and twice she went face-first into wooden pews.

Helmet... good.

"What the fuck is this?" yelled Donovan.

"This is why"—Kirsten raised both legs to absorb another attempt to smash her into the wall—"I wanted you to wait outside."

Her boots ground into the drywall from her effort pushing against Womack's much greater strength. She squirmed around, staring at the side of his rifle. A tiny telekinetic nudge hit the magazine release, dropping his remaining fifty-something shots to the ground with a metallic clatter. She squeezed his hand, forcing him to fire the round in the chamber into the wall.

"All units do not, repeat, do not enter!" Donovan yelled into his comm. "Contain anyone trying to leave, but do not enter the building under any circumstances until Zero okays it."

"Thanks, little late but thaaaaa—" She screamed as Womack hauled his useless rifle—and Kirsten by virtue of her being wrapped around it—over his head.

He slammed her down on the floor. The hit left her paralyzed for an instant at the center of a dust cloud. A weak gasp slipped out of her. Womack went for his sidearm.

Dorian, rolling on the floor, twisted Zahn's arm and managed to get the rifle out of her grip. He dragged her around by a fistful of spectral matter at her collarbone and pressed her back to the wall. His ghostly sidearm formed in his hand and he 'fired' twice into her face. Zahn's eyes rolled into the back of her head. She lapsed into convulsions. Black ichor spattered on the inside of her visor and leaked from her mouth.

Kirsten had no faith her body would listen to her in time to get out of the way of Womack's pistol. The huge, possessed man leaned over her, aiming around in search of a seam or gap in her armor. She held her hands up, latching her power onto the paranormal presence inside him. Womack's arm shuddered, the pistol lifted. He fired a bullet that skimmed over the top of her helmet. Kirsten stopped breathing, focusing all she had on pushing Womack's arm away.

"Zahn! Wake up! Zahn!" Donovan, pinning Lewis to the ground, shouted at the convulsing white-eyed woman slumped against the wall.

"She's fine," yelled Dorian out of reflex. "I just killed the thing inside her."

Womack ceased fighting her, and let her push his arm up—tucking the pistol under his chin. After a final 'I win' smile, he fired. The silver visor on his helmet exploded in a wash of blood and skull fragments. The seven-foot-two man collapsed over backward to the ground.

"No!" Kirsten screamed, unable to hold back tears. "Dammit, no!"

"Womack!" howled Donovan. "Wren, what the fuck is going on?"

His ghost emerged, staggering off to the side and holding his mauled face. A shadowy form seeped into the air from the corpse. Roaring in teary-eyed rage, Kirsten rolled to her feet and slashed it in half with a stroke of the lash before it could divest itself fully from the dead man. Womack's ghost leapt away from the energy whip. Kirsten sprinted at Donovan with an enraged babble of curses. She swept the lash through both he and Lewis, causing an explosion of black liquid to geyser out of Lewis's mouth.

Donovan gawked, staring at the stream of energy coiling around her. Fear manifested in Reverend Wallis's face for only a second before his eyes went onyx black. He held his hands out toward her, chanting in Latin that boomed from overhead as if amplified by speakers. A wall of flames slid up the curtains behind him. The room glimmered in the orange-crimson light. A wave of heat blasted over the room, riding an incendiary breeze. Tongues of fire lapped at the ceiling, growing, spreading. Before the fire could engulf them, Kirsten sprinted up the aisle between pews. Wallis stood in place, his body shuddering from the exertion of whatever he did, but unable to move as she thrust the astral lash like a spear into his heart.

Snarling, Kirsten wrapped her hand around the glimmering cord, and yanked it loose.

The flames dispersed.

Wallis wheezed. Black water fell from his mouth, his nose, and leaked like tears from his eyes. He fell to his knees, staring agape. After a cough, he lifted a gaze of utter confusion up at her. His pants darkened to ink at the crotch.

"Fuckin' psio motherfucker," barked Donovan. He stomped past Kirsten and went for a home run swing on Wallis's skull with his rifle.

The Reverend flew into the podium, knocking it over. Blood covered his now-unconscious face.

Donovan stalked after him, flipping the rifle over to aim at the heart.

"By the authority vested in me by the United Coalition Front, I hereby sentence you to summary execution for the murder of Officer Edward Womack."

"Donovan, stop!" shouted Kirsten. "A paranormal entity controlled him. That man was just a host."

Sergeant Donovan looked away from Wallis, glaring at her. "This fucker did something to Ed. He forced him to kill himself!"

Zahn snapped out of her stupor and pulled herself up. "Fuckin' a right. Kill the son of a bitch."

Lewis moaned, gagging on the ichor in his mouth. He babbled half a word before lurching forward and vomiting.

"Sergeant Donovan," said Kirsten. "Do not execute this man. Not only is he a possibly unwitting pawn, he may have valuable information. That's an order."

"All due respect, ma'am, but he's responsible for the death of a squad mate. He ain't gonna walk out of here. And you're an agent. That's a warrant officer. You don't have command authority."

"*Stand down.*" Kirsten's eyes flared with a trace of light. "Secure that weapon, officer."

Donovan shuddered; his muscles unable to override the order she put in his mind. Frustration boiled into a scream of rage, then tears as he collapsed to his knees. Womack's ghost stood over his own body, shaking his head.

Zahn gave Kirsten a nervous look. "You just… did something to him, didn't you?"

"Yeah. I saved him from a court martial." Kirsten put a hand on Donovan's shoulder. "I know you don't understand this stuff. Please believe me, it was not Wallis's fault. If I thought he did it, I wouldn't stand in your way. If I find out he *did* do it, he's all yours."

"Womack and I went in at the same time, been squaddies since first deployment back in the 89th," muttered Donovan.

Kirsten patted his shoulder. "Don't ruin his memory by murdering an innocent man. At least let me make sure he's not innocent first."

His upwelling of rage past, Donovan nodded, and spat black gunk to the side.

IN THE BASEMENT UNDER THE FAITH PENTECOSTAL BAPTIST MINISTRIES building, Kirsten found a few moments of peace from the bustle of crime scene investigators upstairs. Aside from a large room of barely-functional boilers, little seemed out of place. Whenever she closed her eyes, Ed Womack's helmet exploded again.

"What, exactly, did you find down here?" she asked, glancing at Dorian. "It's barren."

"Over here." He walked through a boiler she had to skirt around, pointing. "This is a false wall."

She pawed at white-painted bricks laced with green mold until she found a loose one. It turned out to be only a façade, a small hatch that opened to reveal a fingerprint reader.

"Damn. Guess I need to drag Wallis down here."

Dorian stuffed his hand into it, making a face as if he rummaged around in a hat full of names. Within six seconds, the door swung open.

"Nice."

"My talents are many." Dorian smiled.

Kirsten pulled aside a metal slab coated in brick face and stepped into a square room containing the nude remains of a man in his thirties, laying sprawled on the floor with his arms at his sides. Strange markings covered his chest and his still-open eyes appeared made of onyx. She crept into the hidden chamber, careful not to step on any of the black substance forming a circle around the remains on the bare cement.

"Look familiar?" asked Dorian.

"I don't know him." She looked over and shrugged. "Should I?"

"I mean the circle."

Kirsten squatted, balancing on the balls of her feet to lean as close as she could without touching anything. "Charazu? But, we destroyed that one."

Dorian rubbed his chin. "Perhaps. It's also possible we just sent it home. Someone had to call it here. No telling how long the good Reverend has been under the influence of whatever had him."

"No way was that Charazu inside Wallis. It died too easily. Konstantin said something about 'They Who Always Were,' ancient *demons*. Abyssals are just returned mortals." She stood, lifting her forearm to her face. "Ops, this is Agent Wren. I'm in the basement, got another victim down here. Need a forensics unit, but they're already upstairs. Just logging the request." She glanced over bizarre scrawling on the walls to an arrangement of candles, knives, and a disorganized mess of old papers.

Arms folded, she frowned at Dorian. "I don't like this at all. Those fanatics, they had no ghosts of their own and the spirits that came out of them were way too strong to be recently dead."

"Consider perhaps that they weren't so recent."

Kirsten grew paler.

15

MANDATORY COPING

Doctor Loring's office smelled of lavender and candle wax, a scent that soon drowned in the fragrance of Earl Grey when the slender woman offered Kirsten a cup. They sat by a small round table in plush chairs at a ninety degree angle to each other. Pale blue, like the ceiling, they placed the women on more equal footing than a couch and a seat behind a desk.

"I'm sorry if you find this irritating," said Dr. Loring, as she settled into position and crossed her legs. "Any officer present at such an event is required to have an assessment."

Kirsten blew on her tea before taking a sip. "I know. I'm not annoyed at having this session. I'm annoyed at spending time here I could be using to figure things out or be with Evan."

"He's in school now. I spoke with Captain Eze. We both want you to know Officer Womack's death was not your fault."

Kirsten gazed at her lap. "He was throwing me around like I was a little kid. Something possessed him, but I couldn't stop him. Womack was trying to kill me, then just out of nowhere..." She made a finger gun under her chin.

"Kirsten, you probably saved the other three officers by keeping his rifle at bay. Given the situation you found yourself in, it's amazing there was only one fatality."

The tea, while warm and comforting, concealed no answers—no

matter how long she stared at it. "I told Eze not to send them in. I told them to wait outside, but they didn't listen to me."

"Would it have made you feel any better to have gone in there alone and been overwhelmed?"

"They had knives. Black silk robes and knives. They didn't even have clothes on under the robes." Kirsten scrunched up her face. "Wallis stood there and laughed. He wasn't armed. I think I could handle four idiots with composite combat knives. They couldn't have pierced my armor."

"Even expert hand-to-hand fighters can struggle with four on one. What I'm saying is, everyone involved acted in accordance with best practice in mind. A detective doesn't go in alone to apprehend a suspect, especially when the situation is expected to be dangerous. More so when the extent of that danger is unknown. You share no part of the blame for what happened to Officer Womack."

Kirsten stared at the rug.

"Watching a person die is traumatic. If there's anything you want to talk about, I'm here for you." Dr. Loring shifted her weight and crossed her legs the other way.

After a moment, Kirsten looked up, feeling less awkward at the sight of the warm smile on the clinician's face. She flicked the side of the cup and stared straight ahead. Behind the desk, a holographic portrait of a young Dr. Loring sat between her parents in their house in the UK. Kirsten smiled at the thought of how a pasty-faced blond man and a beautiful Indian woman could have produced the person opposite her.

"What are you thinking?" Dr. Loring leaned forward.

"Oh, nothing." Kirsten blushed. "I just found the face your father is making in that photo to be a little funny is all." She gestured at the portrait.

The doctor smiled. "Dad always has some kind of joke going on in his mind. He fancied himself a screenwriter for a while, you know. None of his comedies ever got picked up." She leaned back. "So you've nothing to say further about Officer Womack?"

Kirsten frowned again. "I feel so bad for his wife. I keep wondering what I could have done differently, but there were so many unknowns. What bothers me the most is the evil smile he gave me before he did it. Rather, the evil smile that thing made him give me."

Dr. Loring noted something on her datapad. "You did all you could do. Sergeant Donovan ignored your order to stay outside."

"They had orders from Eze. His overruled mine." Kirsten finished off her tea. "Everyone keeps telling me there wasn't anything more I could have done, but it doesn't make me feel any better about watching him die."

"This is going to sound a bit strange, agent, but you don't seem very emotional about it."

"I got all that out last night."

More notes. "Still finding comfort in SynVod?"

"No." Kirsten shook her head, tossing her hair about. "I... no. Evan's stepdad was always drunk and hitting him. He saw the bottle and... No, I don't want to turn into my mother. I mean, I got my emotions out last night while talking to Womack's wife. I know I'm supposed to keep it professional, but I saw the man die... When she lost it, I—"

"It's fine Kirsten. You're not a doll." Dr. Loring leaned back. "Well, I'm not seeing any obvious red flags. If anything comes up that bothers you, please call me any time of day."

"Doc? I went to this function the other day with Konstantin. I couldn't help but feel so out of place there. All those rich people made me feel like I didn't belong."

"Did they act condescending to you at all?"

"No, it was all in my head. I..." Kirsten thought about the devil's bargain she signed for food. It almost made it out of her mouth. "...just felt so much contempt for them. No one needs so much money when kids are starving in the streets."

"You likely have a deep inner need to blame someone for the time you spent homeless. You know the statistics, don't you? There are very few children out there. Our government really is quite keen on that."

"Yeah, until they turn eighteen, then they're out on their ear. It's all a public relations machine. Be nice to the kids and they'll grow up loyal to the government." *Geez, did I just channel Dorian?* She stared at the rug, pondering her sense of loyalty to Division 0. *Worked for me.*

"That's a rather jaded viewpoint for someone your age. Look, Kirsten, there are some unfortunate people who wind up in places out of the system's reach. No society is perfect." Loring lifted an eyebrow. "I'm curious about your contempt for the wealthy. Do you feel the same way about Konstantin?"

Kirsten's awkward kneading of the seat cushion ended with a doe-eyed stare into space. "No, he's different. He's not like them. He has a lot of money, but he doesn't let it change the man inside. I've never seen him act like he's better than anyone because of it. If he was, why would he want poor-ass me?"

Dr. Loring smiled. "I believe you fear that you may not be good enough for him. He is interested in you because he can see through those feelings of inadequacy to the person you really are inside."

"Maybe you're right. Half the time I think about him, I feel sick to my stomach." She rubbed her gut. "Does it make sense that I feel like a traitor to myself? All these years, I've had such contempt for the wealthy, and now I'm ignoring all of that and trying to pretend I belong with them, with him."

"Hmm. If you're experiencing strong physical symptoms, that is a matter of concern. Some degree of 'sick to your stomach' is understandable for a high level of anxiety. Do you find yourself anxious around him?"

"No, not at all." She blushed. "Except for this one club he took me to, but I was anxious at the décor, not Konstantin." She spent a few minutes talking about the mortifying scenery. "Whenever I'm with Konstantin, I feel safe and protected."

Dr. Loring leaned forward. "Kirsten, I think you need to be careful. I'm getting the feeling you are putting a lot of trust in a relationship working out that's only been going on for a few weeks. If I may say so, whenever you talk about him, you don't seem like yourself."

"What do you mean?" asked Kirsten.

"Well…" Dr. Loring tapped a finger at the edge of her datapad. "You are a strong, confident woman who survived an awful situation that would have destroyed most normal people. Even the nightmares you used to suffer are understandable. Yet, when the subject of this man comes up, I can't help but notice you shrink into this delicate sort of person who's afraid to even breathe wrong lest it annoy her husband."

Kirsten bristled. The urge to snap at the woman reared up. Her mouth opened, but thoughts of Evan leapt to the tip of her brain. *This bitch can take him away from me with one bad report.* She forced her jaw shut, trying to seethe with a pleasant expression. *She's got a lot of nerve insulting Konstantin like that.* To calm her shaking hands, she idly spun the ouroboros bracelet around her wrist.

"Are you all right?" asked Dr. Loring.

"I've never had a serious boyfriend before. Maybe I'm being overly cautious and not wanting to do anything to mess it up. I don't think I'm being overly delicate around him."

Dr. Loring gave her a long, measuring stare before nodding. "I see."

She kept turning the bracelet. Needles stabbed her in the stomach, grinding inward. "I'm more worried about Evan. If things with Konstantin cause any problems, I'd break—" She flinched from the pain in her abdomen. "I'd break up with him. I'd…"

"Kirsten?" Dr. Loring stood and took a step closer. "You're sweating. I think you should go to medical for a check."

"My son," said Kirsten, thinking of Evan's smile. The pain chewing on her intestines lessened. "He's the most important thing in my life right now. I'm not desperate for a man."

"Hmm." Dr. Loring put a hand on her forehead. "You're burning up. Maybe you've got a flu?"

"I'll have them check me when I'm done here."

"Do you have any reason to expect there will be a problem between Evan and Konstantin?"

Kirsten pictured a dozen different moments where the boy narrowed his eyes at him or avoided the man entirely. "No." Hands clasped together above her heart, she sniffled. "Konstantin is great. He's so patient. I've been blowing him off so much lately because of the job. I need to make it up to him."

16

A SUGGESTION OF IMPROPRIETY

Kirsten stepped out of the elevator and walked down the tunnel connecting the main hub of the police complex with the Health Services wing. Ground traffic slid along the road beneath the elevated walkway, five stories down. Not three steps into the blue carpet, a pair of men in sand colored coats fell in step on either side of her. She waited for a head-sized news-bot to float by outside, and glanced up at the black-haired man on her right.

"Nine? You two here about Womack?"

He flashed a government-issue smile. "No, Agent Wren, we had other concerns. May we have a moment of your time?"

Her fingers went numb. "I guess that's not much of a request. Lead on."

She followed them out into the bustle of the central hub, past the Division 0 entrance and over to the large door emblazoned with an immense 9. The two guards posted there nodded at her escorts. The door opened. Kirsten remembered coming here to visit their network guys, and as per S.O. Elena Carter's weeks-old instructions, she kept her gaze on the floor until they brought her to a small interview room.

Once she took a seat, their height advantage made her feel as though she were on the wrong end of an interrogation table. "Should I hand over my weapon?"

The red-haired man's smile seemed more genuine. "That won't be necessary just yet, agent."

"While we have our feelers in much of the world," said the other, "the operations of Division 0 are, for the most part, enigmatic to us."

Kirsten folded her hands atop her knees, which she couldn't possibly squeeze together any tighter.

"I'm Senior Operative Espinosa." The black-haired man gestured at his partner. "This is Senior Operative Carroll."

She rendered a flimsy salute. "Sorry, I feel like I'm in the principal's office."

Each man chuckled, for all of two seconds. Both of their mouths formed a flat, emotionless line as if their mirth had been cut off by a switch.

"What is your interest with Trade Commissioner Vernon, Agent?" asked Carroll.

Kirsten looked up at him for a moment before she gazed at the wall. "I…" She put a hand over her mouth for a moment and fixed him with worried eyes. "You don't think *I* was trying to influence her? I think something else is. I went there hoping to find out what, but her security detachment wouldn't let me anywhere near her."

"The possibility occurred to us." Carroll stood statue still. "However, we have so far been unable to verify you had contact with her prior to her sudden change of policy."

"That's because I haven't." Kirsten's fear gave way to indignation. "I'll be happy to let Commander Ashford dive into my head and verify it if you want. I've spent the better part of the past two weeks chasing things that can best be described as demons. I'm not sure who or what is responsible for them getting out of the place they belong, but I think one of them may be influencing the commissioner."

Espinosa broke veneer to raise one brow. "Why would"—he hesitated, trying not to let his disbelief show on his face—"demons care about trade embargoes with the ACC?"

"They wouldn't." Kirsten folded her arms and glared at the chrome table in front of her. "However, if a live person was calling them here, they would be the one with the political agenda."

"Who exactly would it be?" asked Carroll.

"I'm still working on that. I think it might have been the entity responsible for possessing Reverend Wallis. I haven't had time to sift through all of his notes. The crime scene crew isn't done with it yet. As of right now, my best guess is he started dabbling in things he didn't fully understand and lost control of it."

Carroll and Espinosa exchanged a glance too long for a simple evaluation of mood. Kirsten picked at her fingernails, waiting for the conversation passing over cybernetic implants to finish. Espinosa looked at her first.

"We appreciate your time, Agent Wren. That's all we have for you right this moment."

Kirsten got up and started for the door, but turned. "What about Commissioner Vernon?"

"There is not going to be an expansion of trade with the ACC." Carroll walked around the table, as if intending to escort her out of the Division 9 area.

"Does that mean you're going to kill her?" Kirsten backed into the door, almost falling when it opened on its own. "She changed her mind overnight. It has to be paranormal influence."

Espinosa adjusted his sunglasses. "We no longer believe it was you, despite you being on record as a suggestive."

Small favors. "My suggestion abilities aren't that strong. I could theoretically make her feel that way for about a minute or two at most. I'm not good enough to leave long-term imprints. If it's what I think it is, maybe I can get rid of it before you have to murder her."

DIVISION 9 USED ORDINARY LOOKING HOVERCARS WITH ALL THE ARMOR under the external body. From the outside, they looked no different from civilian models. Kirsten examined the interior from the back seat, running her hand over the supple leather. Aside from a small section of the front dash that blacked out as soon as she got in, the vehicle could've been a high-end civilian luxury-sports model, right down to the Halcyon-Ormyr logos.

"Nice car. What're these, about 400k?"

Carroll chuckled. "Closer to eight. Once our electronics are installed, the number is closer to one point three."

"Not that bad when you think about it," said Espinosa. "Div 1 Pat-vees are almost 750 grand, a mil and change with the starburst."

"Their seats aren't this comfortable." Kirsten chided herself for liking the comfort.

The men laughed, only enough to be polite. Carroll glanced over his shoulder at her, wearing an almost human-like smile. She hadn't dared look at surface thoughts to see if they were dolls or living men; the way they acted, it could have been either.

Thirty minutes after her interrogation ended, the two Division 9 agents walked her right past the military checkpoint and to the door of Commissioner Claire Vernon. Kirsten allowed herself a small degree of vicarious pleasure at watching the soldiers squirm under the gaze of her escorts. She envied their authority for all of a moment before pouting at the floor. *I'd rather be liked than feared.*

"What's the meaning of this?" blurted the Commissioner as the three of them barged in. "This is quite irregular."

Claire Vernon stood from her chair, fixing the intruders with an imperious glare from behind her giant desk. Her greying hair formed a halo of light shades around her dark face, steely eyes glaring at Espinosa. Of the three, he seemed to carry the most authority. He didn't seem impressed by her rank, her attitude, or the expensive dark red skirt-suit worth more than a month's salary.

Kirsten stared at her, reaching out with her psionic senses. As soon as her eyes flickered with white light, Commissioner Vernon's antagonistic demeanor pivoted about to fear. She retreated, tripping over an Oriental throw rug and landing in her chair, which rolled back another two feet.

"I felt something." Kirsten searched for the fleeting sense of a presence, but it slipped away as if she had tried to grab jelly with her bare hands. "I definitely sensed something there. It's gone now. It's afraid of me, hiding."

Carroll blinked at Kirsten.

"Who are you people? Why are you in my office?" Commissioner Vernon held a hand to the side of her head and read something on her terminal screen that slackened her jaw.

Kirsten glanced at Espinosa. "She's missing a week. Just wondered why the date jumped ahead eight days."

Vernon glared. "What? You're Division 0, aren't you? How dare you look in my thoughts!"

"Ma'am." Kirsten spoke with as little emotion as possible, raising her hands. "I'm only here for your benefit. Someone is trying to manipulate you."

"Get out of here this instant! You're trying to influence me, aren't you?"

"No, ma'am. I'm trying to—" Kirsten pinched the bridge of her nose.

Prevent Division 9 from assassinating you as a political liability. She sighed. "I'm trying to find out who or what is *already* influencing you."

"Anything?" asked Carroll.

She swept her sensed around the room, but found only a mild sense of unease. "I'm afraid I can't do anything until it comes back. I could always give it a few hours, wait around here in case it returns."

"Are you all cracked?" asked Vernon. "I'll not have a psionic in my office under any circumstances. It is a matter of national security."

Carroll put a gentle hand on Kirsten's arm, tugging her toward the door. "Come on," he whispered. "You did all you can. If she goes to Miami now, it's not your fault."

"It's good to see you are yourself again, Commissioner," said Espinosa. "Please consider your recent decisions in the interest of national security."

Vernon froze, exchanging stares with Espinosa. "Exactly who do you think you are, talking to me like that?"

He showed no trace of being intimidated; his voice became icy. "Let's just say I'm someone that hopes not to have to meet you again."

Espinosa spun toward the exit, flaring his sand-brown trench coat. The office door closed with a faint squeak behind him.

17

WEEK ARGUMENT

K irsten's butt hit the chair the same instant her NetMini, desk terminal, and armband communicator lit up. Before she could answer, Eze saw her at her desk and hung up. She stood hurried to his office. The look on his face could have been worry or anger; she hoped for the former.

"Yes, sir?" she asked with an innocent smile, slipping in the door and closing it behind her.

He didn't sit, instead walking past her and opening the door again. "Follow me."

Shit. He sounds nervous. "I'm sorry."

"What for?" He went out of the squad room, turning right and going down the hall.

She jogged to keep up with his stride. "Whatever I did that got you yelled at."

"Are you taking after Nicole now?"

The trace of a smile accompanying the question made her feel a little less nervous. "No, I just read the look on your face."

"I'm not sure what happened, Wren." He paused, exhaled, and made eye contact. "But we're about to find out." He called the elevator and stepped in.

She followed, fidgeting at her utility belt.

When the doors opened, she realized they had gone to the command level. She tidied up her uniform as best she could while following him. Three doors later, he exchanged salutes with two tactical officers guarding either side of an impressive armored door, and waited for them to key it open.

Inside, the command staff sat behind a long table. Division 0 Chief Jane Carter, Deputy Director Johannes Burckhardt, and West City Regional Director Mikhail Kovalev. Carter, seated in the middle, had her grey hair up in a neat, lopsided bun held in place with two Japanese sticks. Mikhail could have been Dorian's father, with coffee-colored skin and a pleasant expression that seemed never to lack a trace of a smile. Burckhardt, on the other hand, was an older, balding man who glared at everyone under him with thinly-veiled contempt. Kirsten, perhaps due to the rarity of her talents, earned an almost neutral look from him, quite the accomplishment.

She dismissed any doubt that the gazelle from Division 9 had any relation to Director Carter. They didn't look at all alike.

Eze stopped a step before Kirsten did, standing behind her and to the left, where he rendered the customary salute to the executive board. A few seconds after Kirsten's salute snapped back to her side, a holographic fourth person appeared to Mikhail's left: East City Regional Director Ravindra Kumar. She was the youngest of the command staff, barely past forty. Like Carter, a telempath.

"Good afternoon, Agent Wren," said Carter. "We wanted to meet with you and clarify what is going on with the Trade Commissioner."

"We received quite the alarming vid-call." Burckhardt motioned toward his terminal. "She thought someone under our command may have influenced her decision on the trade agreement." He poked at a glowing spot on the gloss black table, reading a screen just out of sight. "You happen to be a grade three suggestive, agent. That seems a little, suggestive?"

Only Burckhardt smiled at his joke.

"All due respect, sir," said Kirsten, voice wavering. "You know that's not powerful enough to cause a long-term change in behavior."

Director Carter smiled, sensing her battle of anger and fear. "Calm down, Johannes. You always expect the worst of people."

"Her psych profile is incompatible with that course of action," said Ravindra.

"What's wrong, Agent? Why the sudden spike of sadness?" Carter cocked her head.

"I always feel like people won't believe me when I start talking about paranormals. Someone appears to have found a way to recall spirits from the Abyss. I'm not entirely certain myself if I believe they are 'demons' in the true sense of the word, or just powerful, dark ghosts. However, someone out there has found a way to use them to influence people."

Burckhardt rolled his eyes. Mikhail seemed worried. Carter sat back, staring at her fingers as she fussed with a nail.

Kirsten directed her gaze at Burckhardt. "Sir, please review the archival footage from two days ago. Inquest number 24180912A1."

Carter keyed something into her table terminal, and a large screen to Kirsten's left lit up with the recording from her helmet camera during the attempt to arrest Julio Ramirez. Filling in with explanations where the paranormal manifestations failed to appear on video, she illustrated the moment where Nicole became possessed and attacked her. Ravindra covered her mouth when Nicole flashed the wicked, murderous grin.

"The entity that had been in Jose jumped into Nicole at the moment she read his mind. Fortunately, it was quite weak. One good lash destroyed it."

All four of them, even Burckhardt, squirmed in their seats as Nicole described the ooze leaking from every orifice.

"I see. So you believe someone has"—Carter waved her hand around—"summoned these entities? With the specific intent to influence people?"

"It looks that way, ma'am," said Kirsten. "Based on events surrounding Reverend Wallis, I'm hopeful he may be able to provide us with some answers."

"Your report"—Mikhail leaned forward to look at his private screen—"indicates you believe the Reverend was under the influence of an entity as well." He massaged his chin. "Would that not imply there is someone else involved?"

"I found a large quantity of documentation in a hidden sanctum in the basement there, sir. I have not yet had a chance to review it as it has been designated crime scene evidence."

"Agent Wren, we are going to block mention of anything related to this case from the NewsNet." Carter leaned on her elbows, lacing her fingers together. "What I am about to say does not leave this room, do you understand?"

"Yes, ma'am." Kirsten nodded.

"Understood, ma'am," said Eze.

"Division 9 is presently unsure of the exact nature of the influence, but they have declared Commissioner Vernon compromised. The final vote on the trade measure is scheduled one week from tomorrow. If she does not resume her normal policy in time for the vote, they will be retiring her."

Kirsten gasped.

"One hour ago, Commissioner Vernon asked us to disregard her complaint regarding your so-called attempted influence. She said it was a simple misunderstanding."

"The entity came back," said Kirsten. "I'll go right—"

Carter held up a hand. "No, keep your distance. The NewsNet is on her now since she made a public statement contradicting her earlier position of support for the Free Trade Agreement. Now that she's changed her mind and is in support of it once again, they are too close. We must have incontrovertible evidence proving something other than a living psionic was responsible for influencing her before we act. We are concerned with public perception if you, or any member of Division 0, are seen near her."

Kirsten blinked. "You're going to allow Division 9 to murder an innocent woman for the sake of good face-time on the news?"

Carter sighed. Mikhail shifted uncomfortably. Burckhardt grumbled at her, earning a glare. Ravindra smiled, respect and sadness in her eyes.

"I am perfectly capable of doing what needs to be done, Johannes. That I am a woman does not matter. That I object to their methods does not matter." Carter looked at Kirsten. "You, more than most of us here, should know how it feels to be hated for being different. I'm sorry to broach such a sore subject, but I must consider the lives of all psionics over one political figure."

"It still doesn't seem very ethical." Kirsten sagged.

"Do something about it then, Agent." Mikhail sat up straight. "You have seven days to turn up the kind of proof we need to prevent the public from developing an erroneous opinion. Of course, you must understand our position. If the public believes psionics are using government figures as puppets…"

"It'll be open goddamn season on us," grumbled Burckhardt. "I don't see why we're even waiting the week, or why we don't just *fix* it."

Carter leaned her head into the fingers of her right hand, her expression that of a mother dealing with an obnoxious teen son. "Johannes, if we go in there and do that, it will only add a nugget of truth to the conspiracy theorists. Even if we were *undoing* a suggestion, they'll say we did it in the first place and only removed it because we got caught."

"In all fairness"—Ravindra raised her voice for attention—"the ACC loathes psionics. They kill our kind on sight. To insinuate they would use them, or that a psionic would be complicit in their activities is beyond belief."

"There are some who do." Mikhail fell into a heavy Russian accent. "You can either work for us, or"—he made a finger gun at his temple—"work for God."

"You have one week," said Carter, letting her hands fall clasped on the table, "before Nine retires her. I hope you're right. Dismissed."

Kirsten saluted, gave Eze a weary look, and trudged to the door.

18

JURISDICTION

Kirsten dug her fingers into her hair as she leaned harder into her hands. The table full of paper scraps had no discernable feeling on them: no eeriness, no latent psionic imprints, and no nagging sense of dread—nothing. She stretched over the back of the chair, staring at the dim, overly blue lights in the evidence room. Desperate for a solvable problem, her mind began trying to classify the drop-ceiling tiles as either dark grey or blue, but she covered her eyes and loosed a frustrated moan.

The evidence tech jumped at the sudden noise. She glanced over, finding him holding a pair of light pens up as if warding off a vampire with a cross.

"Are you kidding me?" She frowned. "I'm a damn psionic, not a demon. How did you get assigned to Division 2 if you're that damn stupid."

He lowered his arms, and improvised holy symbol, offering a weak smile.

"Spare me. Psionics are no more dangerous than a normal person walking around with a firearm or a sword."

"Guns don't read minds," whimpered the tech.

"No, they don't." Kirsten squinted at him. "You have some naughty little secret you're afraid will get out?"

"N-no, it's just…"

"General idiot fear?" She shook her head. "You probably think I mind controlled your boss into letting me in here. Actually, the order came down from the brass. National security, you know. Besides, you've had this stuff for days now. They should have every molecule of evidence scraped off it already. Do you guys get off on keeping detectives away from crime scene evidence until it's catalogued by someone who works two hour shifts two days a week?"

"It's not her you should fear." Dorian's glassy whisper scraped the air.

The man jumped, whirling to his right.

Kirsten covered her face with her palm.

"It's us." Dorian pushed his face past the veil and winked.

Despite expecting it, she jumped when the evidence tech shrieked and ran.

"You're turning into Theodore."

He paced around the room, stopping closer to her. "You think so? Honestly, I think Theo would have followed him and mocked him for soiling himself." He leaned over the table. "You look like your cat died."

The unexpected familiar remark made her laugh. "You've been hanging around Nicole too much. These papers are useless. I can't make any sense of this crap, and there's no energy on them at all. Whenever I open my mind I feel this faint glimmer of a dark presence to my right, but it keeps moving away when I turn toward it."

"Are you sure you're not just reading me?"

"No, it's not as strong as you are. And you're definitely not this dark. It's different too. It fades in and out, almost like it senses when I feel it and retreats."

"Maybe the entity from Vernon followed you here." He looked around. "I don't see anything."

"What the hell did you do to Calloway?" bellowed a large woman at the door.

Kirsten jumped, spinning toward a slate blue jumpsuit that appeared to be wrapped around an Assault Marine with an almost-female face. Kirsten slid off the chair and backed away, hands up, glancing at the woman's uniform, noting her name and rank insignia.

"Nothing, honest. He was giving me shit for being psionic, and my partner gave it back to him."

"You don't have a—" Chief Tech Sontag became a veritable mannequin, stuck pointing at Kirsten.

Dorian manifested for a few seconds, winking at her. Once he returned to normal, he laughed. "Damn, that's a big woman." He faced Kirsten. "That *is* a woman, right?"

"Tech Sontag… Sorry about him, he's quite protective."

With her finger still pointing forward, Sontag spun about-face and walked away. Dorian succumbed to a fit of laughter.

"That's probably how Theodore got started being a"—her NetMini rang; she answered—"Wren."

Tech Hollings appeared, a holographic bust floating over the small device. "Agent, we got another stiff. Female this time, no ImDent. Same as the others, black eyes and looks… uhh, drained."

"Send me a nav pin, I'm on the way." Kirsten gave Dorian a 'help me' stare. "This can't be a coincidence, and I'm not getting anything from the paper." She leaned out the door to shout into the basement of the Division 2 Tech Center. "Calloway? Are you hiding under a desk? I'm done in here. Need you to secure the room when I leave." She folded her arms, foot tapping. "I swear… damn mundanes."

KIRSTEN PULLED THE BLACK TARP DOWN, COVERING THE NUDE BODY OF A young woman with skin the color of creamed coffee. Her eyes, as all the ones before, had become orbs of black. Sanitation bots discovered her atop a restaurant's trash crusher a few yards away from where the body now lay on a hover-stretcher. If Kirsten disregarded the unusual 'withering' effect, the deceased appeared to be somewhere between twenty and twenty five. Long brown hair with gold highlights suggested high-end salon work. The identification algorithm estimated her round, delicate face as mixed Latin and Indian ancestry. But then again, a couple hundred thousand credits at Reinventions could change that.

Emergency lights filled the mouth of the alley with flashing blue and red. A closer Division 2 crime scene van tinted the nearby surroundings in flickering blue. TFC Hollings stood a few feet away behind a portable terminal that cycled past thousands of ID images per second. Kirsten walked over to her.

Hollings looked up from the screens. "You feel anything?"

Kirsten stared at the holo-panel, trying to force the system to find an identity match. "No, it feels the same as the others. A tiny bit of eeriness in the air, but that could be the city at night."

"I thought this one was different at first, until I got a good look at the eyes and the, umm, drained look on her face. The way we found her made me think sexual assault, but the scanner says that occurred after she was dead."

Kirsten turned greenish. "After... You mean someone found her dead and..."

"Yeah." Hollings shuddered.

Dorian winced. "Damn animals."

"Ugh." Kirsten clamped a hand over her mouth in an effort not to throw up.

"This woman has the same eyes as the others. The killer may have dumped her elsewhere, but some street trash probably found her and, uhh, moved the body."

Speaking in slow, measured breaths to keep her late dinner in her stomach, Kirsten tried not to think about what happened. "Or, whoever is doing this knows we're looking into it and they deliberately staged it as a murder/rape."

"If that were the case, why not assault her while she's still alive? Postmortem sexual contact doesn't seem compatible with the psych profile of the killer leaving the bodies posed like we have been finding them."

The clinical tone in Hollings's voice left Kirsten wondering if she should be offended or confused at the suggestion. "Someone's summoning demons. Maybe they needed to kill her as a virgin."

"You better hurry it up with Konstantin then"—Dorian winked—"so you're off the list."

Hollings glanced down at the terminal. "I'm sorry, agent. I didn't mean to make you blush."

"Oh, it's not you." *Dorian doesn't know. I'm not going to tell him.* She thought of Konstantin and a sudden sense of peace settled over her. *Of course, I'm supposed to see him in an hour. I should bring image caps of those papers. Maybe he knows what those damn stick figures mean.*

"Agent?" Hollings snapped her fingers in front of Kirsten's face. "Are you okay? You look like you're daydreaming."

"What? Oh, no, I just." Kirsten tried to calm down her racing heart, picking at the serpent bracelet. "I was thinking about my boyfriend."

"Yeah, whoa..." Hollings lifted an eyebrow. "Finding a victim of necrophilia always makes me think about my girl."

"I..." She paused. "No, he's a scholar who works with ancient texts. I thought he could help me with this damn case." Kirsten tried to regain her composure—and her normal pallid complexion. "So, anything on this one you can tell me?"

"System's putting her age around twenty to twenty-three. Same as the rest, the field kit can't find the cause of death. She's got the black eyes, epidermal damage consistent with rapid aging around the face, but the underlying bone structure is in a state you'd expect for her age. The sexual assault occurred at least an hour after death. There's no bleeding or bruising despite the tearing."

Kirsten shivered.

"Oh, you saw the bruise around the neck and on the left collarbone, correct?" Hollings pointed at the screen, showing the discolorations highlighted. "We pattern matched it to a NinTek Warrior."

"So, whoever killed her has at least one cybernetic arm," said Kirsten.

Hollings jumped at a beep from the terminal. "Bingo. Alaina Munoz, age twenty two."

Dorian put an arm around Kirsten's back. "Easy, they're not hunting you. The age is a coincidence. By the way, the whole virgin thing is a myth. I was just kidding."

Kirsten scowled. "In this city? No one hits that age and remains a virgin."

His glance shifted from confusion, to understanding, to pity.

"Not now," she whispered, and raised her voice toward Hollings. "Any file on her?"

"Yeah, looks like she was a junior marketing agent at RedEx. Guess there's a decent amount of money ferrying OPC back and forth to Mars."

"OPC?" Kirsten blinked.

"Other People's Crap. Miss Munoz made decent money. She shouldn't have been in this part of town."

Kirsten's NetMini beeped. "Hang on." She fished it out of her pocket.

Dorian grinned. "Popular tonight, aren't we?"

Konstantin's face appeared when she answered. Kirsten whirled, taking the crime scene out of his field of view. "Konstantin!" she cooed. "I've been thinking about you. I'm sorry I'm a little late. I'm still out in the field. I'll be ready by ten."

His expression exuded guilt. "Dearest, it's my turn to be sorry. I can't seem to get the lawyers off the vid tonight. I have a special hearing I must attend in person. It's a bureaucratic mess to get permits approved for this project at the Archives."

Kirsten bit her lip. She wanted to bawl at the news she couldn't be with him tonight. Warmth filled in behind her eyes as her resolve to keep a professional face on crumbled.

"At least you can pick Evan up early," said Dorian.

Woozy, she blinked and shook it off. "Yeah, that's true."

"I'm sorry?" Konstantin gave her a playful smile. "Are you having a telepathic conversation with someone I can't hear?"

"Yeah." Was a faster option than trying to explain Dorian. "A friend was trying to cheer me up for not getting to see you tonight. I found some strange scribbles I wanted to ask you about." A mild pouty tone infiltrated her voice. "I was hoping to show you later."

Konstantin chuckled. "I can look at them soon, *Lyubimaya*. Believe me, I'd much prefer to be with you than waste my evening in a room full of lawyers at a zoning committee."

"I guess it's only fair. Work has made me take off on you twice now."

He said something to her in French, winked, and ended the call. For all she knew, he just told her to go jump off a bridge—but it sounded romantic.

"So, Agent Wren…" Hollings fussed with her slate grey jumpsuit while staring at the ground. "If I go in for an assessment, are they gonna make me join?"

"No. You'd be welcome to join, but they don't force anyone." Kirsten went to put a hand on Hollings shoulder and wound up in a surprise hug.

Hollings burst into tears. "I've never even told my parents. I'm so scared of how they'll react. I'm not sure my dad could handle having a daughter that's, umm…"

Kirsten patted the woman on the back. "Psionic isn't a dirty word. You can say it. There's no reason for you to go it alone."

"What if they hate me?"

"The department won't tell anyone anything you don't want them to know." Kirsten set Hollings back to at arm's length and rubbed the back of her hand. "Not every parent takes it well. Mine didn't. If not for Division 0, I'd probably be dead by now."

Her NetMini rang… again.

"Oh, for the love of—" Kirsten stared at the smog layer while pulling the device off her belt. "Wren. What is it this time?"

Father Villera blinked at the petulant greeting. "Is this a bad time, Kirsten?"

"Oh, I'm sorry, Father. The stupid thing's been ringing constantly all night."

"Three times." Dorian held up three fingers. "It's gone off three times."

She gave him a sidelong glare, grinning. "Did those thugs come back? Oh, I think I found out why they came after you."

"No, they have not returned. Look, Kirsten, a young girl just came in here looking for food. She's too young to be out on the street alone, but she told me something you need to know. It wasn't a confession, so I can share it with you. From her description, it sounded like she witnessed a murder."

"Shouldn't you be calling Division 1?" asked Kirsten.

"Certain details the girl mentioned made me think the killing had ritualistic overtones. I think she witnessed some manner of sacrifice."

"Holy sh—crap. I'll be right there." She hung up. "Hollings, I need to run. I'll swing by tomorrow and we can talk about whatever you want. If the lab finds anything new, please let me know. I only have a week."

"A week? What happens in a week?"

Kirsten jammed the NetMini in its place on her belt, glaring at the body under the tarp. "Another murder."

19

GREEN-EYED MONSTER

The patrol craft kicked up a cloud of vapor and fleeing debris in the parking lot of the Five Hundredth Street Sanctuary. Upon noticing the front door ripped open, Kirsten hit the emergency lights, and landed as close as possible to the entrance. Snaps of azure light bathed the walls in an eerie blue glow.

Kirsten climbed out of the car and drew her E-90. Even at this hour, the lack of people at the shelter disturbed her. She ran to the door, entering with her weapon up. The scent of ballistic propellant lingered in the air, mixed with something attempting to be chicken soup. Blood streaked the ground in the main room, amid overturned and smashed tables. One arcing smear led off into a rear hallway. She used the pistol grip on her weapon to hit the backup call button on her forearm guard.

Dorian gestured at the ground. "Kirsten."

A bare footprint in blood, by size a child's, pointed out the door. Partial prints continued along the ground, all but impossible to see at night after several meters on the black traction coating. A wheezing moan came from the back of the strip mall church. She shoved her way past the bank of chairs left in disarray, rounding a corner into the hallway that led to the kitchen.

Father Villera lay on his side at the end of the blood trail, where his strength to crawl had given out. His right leg and arm bled from superficial gunshots. At the sight of Kirsten, he stopped trying to move and rolled onto his back, limp.

"Thank you," he said to the ceiling, before gazing at her. "It looks worse than it feels."

"What happened? Is there anyone still here?"

"No," he croaked, "The man who shot me ran out after that girl."

Kirsten looked back and forth from him to the door. "Dammit." She fumbled with stimpaks and fed him three, one after the other. "Who shot you?"

"Oh, that's nice." Color returned to his face as the injection of nanobots got to work repairing his body. He spent a moment catching his breath. "A man showed up a few minutes after I called you. He demanded to know where the child was. I told him she left, but I'm not a great liar." His attempt to laugh caused him to wince. "The girl saved me. Go, I'll be okay until help arrives. Find her before he does."

"Are you sure?"

Father Villera squeezed her hand, nodding. "Yes, yes, I am sure. Go, the girl needs you more than I do. I can feel it."

"Ops," said Kirsten to her forearm. "I need a MedVan at my current location ASAP." She jogged to the doorway and crouched to examine the bloody footprints. "Damn, I miss that visor already."

"You could always transfer to tactical; you seem to wind up getting shot at more than they do." Dorian walked up behind her.

"I don't want to stack the odds." Kirsten concentrated for a few seconds activating Darksight, superimposing the wavering sepia-toned astral realm over reality. Faint traces of life energy caused the bloody footprints to phosphoresce. "Think about how often I get my ass kicked now in I-Ops when I'm not supposed to. I don't even want to think about what would happen to me in Tac."

Dorian laughed.

Kirsten stalked after the fading trail of blood. Past the corner, it went in a straight line. She held one hand to her earbud, verifying over the comms that backup was en route to the church.

"There is one injured civilian on scene, GSW to right arm and right leg. Looked superficial. He appeared to respond to stimpaks. I'm in pursuit of one assailant."

"Hey, bitch!" rasped a voice from a recessed alcove to an old apartment building. "Nice ass. Gimme a thousand credits if you wanna keep it lookin' so nice."

She whirled, aiming at a vagrant wielding a silvery plastisteel axe. At the sight of a glowing-eyed cop with a laser pistol, he babbled and took off at a full sprint, losing his grip on the weapon. Dorian wandered over and glanced down at the glinting edge.

"Fun, isn't it? I think he pissed his pants." He squatted. "Hmm, where'd he get a thing like that?"

"Is that a battle-axe?" Kirsten scrunched up her face. "Seriously? Is everyone into Monwyn?"

"It's a military boarding-party axe. Colonial troops still use them for ship-to-ship combat in space. It's a lot harder to put a hole in the hull with one of these. Sudden implosive decompression makes everyone sad."

"Get off me!" shouted a child.

Kirsten sprinted toward the voice, her boots crunching on grit. A dull metallic *thud* reverberated in the air, heavy, as if something large had smashed into a trash crusher. A man screamed in pain.

"Little brat. I was gonna make it painless, now—"

A meaty smack cut off the growling voice. A pipe clanged to the ground.

Kirsten went right, chasing the noise.

An enraged roar in the voice of a small girl echoed from the alley. "You moron! I can see the flows of time. I am the universe! I have the stars in my veins and the heat of suns in my fists. You think you can kill me?"

A surprised high-pitched shriek followed by the kind of screaming often reserved for the victim of a cheap slasher holovid filled Kirsten's thoughts with images of a young child being stabbed. She ran harder, having to hook her arm around a light pole by a battered PubTran terminal to swing a tight turn without falling over.

A half-block ahead, a man in a long black coat held a twig of a girl in a bear hug from behind. She looked to be about eleven with light brown hair and had more dirt smeared on her than was on the alley surface. Her too-tight pink shirt bunched under his arms while legs wrapped in baggy green pants flailed. The child's bare soles glinted red in the streetlamps— dried blood. Repeatedly, she smashed the back of her head into the man's chest. Each hit echoed from the sheer metal walls, but had little effect on him.

"Police! Let go of the girl and don't move a damn muscle." Kirsten skidded to a halt, sighting over her E-90.

The man spun with an arrogant snarl. Kirsten's still-glowing eyes startled him enough to weaken his grip and let the girl squirm loose.

Rather than run, the enraged tween lunged at him. She grabbed on to his belt and dragged him off his feet, holding him over her head. As she hefted the large, armored man to the point of standing on tiptoe, she stared at Kirsten—with glowing green eyes. Her pupils looked like dark holes next to the luminous whites.

Lace.

"Oh, shit," said Dorian.

Rage gave way to terror at the sight of someone in a police uniform. The girl hurled the man into the side of a trash crusher. Judging by the dent, his second meeting with it.

Expecting her about to run, Kirsten raised a hand. "*Stop!*"

The rail-thin girl stared, motionless save for a mild facial tic. She took a step back, whirled, and sprinted off, bare feet squeaking on plastisteel.

"What the…"

"Suggestion isn't infallible, you should know that. Strong willpower can sometimes resist, and the kid is on Lace. There's no brain in there right now to control."

"God damned cops." The man picked himself off the ground, wiping blood off his chin with the back of his arm.

"Hold it, asshole." Kirsten aimed at him. "You're—"

He went for a gun. Kirsten fired. The dark azure beam left a half-inch hole through his armor, his torso, and both sides of the trash box behind him. Flames licked at the inside of the wound, filling the air with the scent of burnt meat. Fire started in the dumpster. A gurgling wheeze escaped him; the body fell to its knees and went face-first to the alley, leaving an angry spirit in its place.

"Now, where were we," she said, stalking at him. "You didn't think you were going to get out of answering questions by committing suicide by cop, did you?"

He had not, at least judging by the look on his face, expected the current turn of events. The ghost fled, making it a point to avoid the corner of the building.

Dorian laughed and gave chase. "Find the kid, I'll get this idiot. Never fails to amuse me when the newbies run *around* things."

Kirsten nodded and threw herself into a sprint after the girl. "Hey, kid, where are you?" *Yeah, right, she's scared shitless of me. Like she's gonna say 'over here, officer.' Yep. I am a natural blonde.*

She ran, trying to think in the manner of a terrified child. It wasn't too much of a stretch. Three blocks down, a handful of older teens congregated around a nude (and quite retired) sex doll. Missing panels of faux-skin exposed the metal interior, including where the most important part of such a doll had once been. Fortunately, no one dared to use a square, wire-filled hole that big for anything other than storing a bottle of SynVod. The doll's mouth hung open, emitting tinny music.

"You guys see a little girl just run by?"

"Maybe," yelled one kid. Lemon blond, he had a series of luminous red and blue NanoLED tattoos forming Native American war paint on his face. The usual assortment of knives and cheap handguns accessorized his shredded-looking clothes. "A little tittie might refresh my memory, how 'bout a flash?"

"How about you *tell me?*" Her eyes flickered with white light. "Is that enough of a flash?"

The others went rigid and quiet. Pink cotton-candy hair moved as the single living girl among them leaned forward. She pushed a finger into one of the dolls nipples, which shut off the music.

"Uhh, that way, turn left by the finger." The punk pointed. "Why the fuck am I telling a cop this?"

"Because you're a good civic-minded boy." Kirsten winked, and ran in the direction indicated.

After taking a corner by a nine-foot tall spray-painted middle finger, Kirsten ran for two more blocks before she staggered to a jog, which slowed to a walk and an eventual stop after another dozen steps. She felt winded, but not to the point of gasping for air. *Come on, kid. I'm not gonna hurt you.*

"Hey, kid? Are you still here? The priest said you saw something. I want to help you."

Kirsten's voice echoed into the darkness of several alleys and a number of abandoned buildings. She advanced, stooping to look under old cars or piles of debris. Dorian appeared at the end of an alley, looking pissed. She waited for him to catch up and gave him an expectant frown.

"Not my fault this time." He held his hands up. "I'm over my 200 meter thing. Umm, yeah. Our guy must've been one piece of work. He only made it about a quarter mile before *they* got him. You didn't call in artillery, did you?"

"Harbingers already? No, it wasn't me. Shit the guy must've been on their radar already…" She shuddered. "Lucky thing we found the girl before he could…"

Dorian smirked. "I don't think that's what he wanted her for. He said he was going to make it painless, sounds like something an assassin would say. I think he was trying to get rid of a witness."

"I guess an assassin would get their attention, but it still seems fast."

He rubbed her shoulder, chilling it. "I hate to break your illusion, K. Harbingers don't think crimes against children are any worse than crimes against any other innocent soul. I'm betting the guy had something to do with the abyssals we keep finding. That kind of thing is what really gets their knickers in a twist."

Kirsten spun about, sighing. "I lost her."

"Over there." Dorian pointed. "Probably in that old car. I can feel someone alive in there."

"Creepy." Kirsten jogged over.

"All the things you've seen and me saying I can feel the presence of the living is creepy?" Dorian laughed.

"I guess that *is* a bit lame, huh?"

Kirsten peeked through the grime-encrusted window of a car that had not driven since many years before she was born. A small, scrawny figure huddled in the back seat, curled into a ball with her feet crossed. Her head lifted. The whites of her eyes glowed lime green, like the back end of a firefly.

"Hey, sweetie." Kirsten cooed. "Easy, kiddo. I'm a friend." She tugged at the handle.

Shivering, the child didn't show any reaction to the door creaking open. She shook at a near convulsive level, sweating as if it were a hundred and ten degrees out despite it being the middle of September. Her surface thoughts came on in a disorienting blur. Reality liquefied. The skin of Kirsten's face melted away in the girl's thoughts, leaving the skull to chatter behind eyeballs swinging on nerve fibers.

"Holy shit." Kirsten cut off mental contact. "This kid is messed up."

"Be careful. Judging by all that sweat, she's in the midst of the comedown phase. However, she's still probably stronger than a grown man." Dorian grumbled. "I'd love to find the son of a bitch that gave Lace to a juvenile."

Kirsten glanced at him. "You don't need another summary on your conscience."

"It wouldn't be on my conscience, K. Any Division 1 cop would end whatever waste of humanity was responsible for getting a kid hooked on that shit. Lace is a damn death sentence. It's so addictive people have died from missing a re-dose by hours."

"Hey, kiddo, come on. You need some food. Let me get you somewhere safe, alright?" Kirsten reached toward her.

The girl watched the hand get closer and closer to her leg. Seconds before contact, she lunged forward and stomp-kicked Kirsten in the face. The impact knocked her out of the car and onto her back, seeing stars.

"You okay?" asked Dorian.

"Yeah…" Kirsten blinked and spat. "She stepped in coffee."

When the girl leapt out of the car, Kirsten rolled left and got an arm around the child's legs, taking her down. She seized the skinny waif by an ankle and hauled her back far enough to get a hand on her shoulder before the fit of shrieking and thrashing went into full gear. An elbow to the gut lifted Kirsten off the ground and took all the wind from her sails. She fell, both arms wrapped around the girl's shins to arrest her flight.

The kid rolled over, clawing at Kirsten's face. She ducked, wrestling to get control of the urchin's arms. She still had enough strength left to overpower Kirsten, reversing the hold and flinging her onto her back before climbing on top of her. The child reached for Kirsten's throat. She grabbed the girl's wrists, but her grip slid over grimy skin, riding up the girl's forearms as the too-strong tween forced her hands down and wrapped them around Kirsten's throat.

What the fuck! This kid is trying to kill me? "Hey," she croaked. *"Stop!"* Kirsten's eyes glowed white for an instant.

This time, the suggestion stunned the girl into a series of facial tics. Kirsten took advantage of the mental shutdown to roll the child onto her chest and gather her arms behind her back.

"She's too skinny for binders, use the riot ties," said Dorian.

"I'm not restraining an eleven-year-old." Kirsten thought back to how patient the Division 1 officers were when they hauled her off the street at that age.

"I know what you're thinking, K. *You* weren't on Lace. This kid can really hurt you, or herself. Do you want to let her force you into a situation where you have to shoot her? What if she tries to leap out of the car while we're in the air?"

Kirsten sat back on her heels, pinning the girl down while she secured her hand and foot with plastic strips. "I…"

"It's for her own safety."

The girl wailed and thrashed. The plastic creaked.

"Might want to put on three pairs," said Dorian.

Kirsten pulled the girl's hair away from her face, then caressed the side of her head while whispering in a soothing tone. "Easy. Calm down, I'm not here to hurt you. Everything's going to be okay. You're not in trouble."

The kid gave up fighting, going limp on the alley. Whining came next, whimpered pleas for freedom. Kirsten reached for her uti knife to cut the girl loose.

"Don't. She's playing you." Dorian put a hand on Kirsten's before she could take the knife off her belt. "Don't trust anything she does until after detox. All she wants to do is run off and find more Lace. Might look like she's only a child, but she will kill anyone who gets between her and another dose. The shit is *that* addictive."

Kirsten patted the girl down, finding no weapons but a small lump in the girl's right pants pocket caught her attention.

"Careful, don't just jam your hand in there," said Dorian. "Could be a needle."

With great care, Kirsten extracted a one-inch long clear plastic ampule about as big around as a large drinking straw. One end had a white cap and built-in needle; the other contained a drop or two of a luminous green liquid, the same color green that shone from the whites of the girl's eyes. She scowled at the injector, and frowned at the tiny V-shaped scars on the side of the child's thin, dirty neck.

The girl stared at the spent injector, as if the drop or two within it meant the difference between life and death. She wriggled, eyes begging Kirsten to let her have the last bit.

Kirsten lost her composure and wept. She looked up at Dorian while struggling to hold the child down. "You're right. I do wanna shoot the guy who gave it to her." She sighed, poking at her armband to call the patrol craft to her location.

CHECKING OUT

Teal, as it turned out, could suck the life out of anything when overdone. Kirsten frowned at the walls, at the men jogging past her in the same color scrubs. Even the cushions of the bench she sat on sat somewhere in the no-man's-land between green and blue. She glanced up from her meditative hatred of the hue as a commotion three doors to her right attracted two medtechs as well as a doctor at a full run.

She leaned forward, elbows on her knees and fingers twined, staring at the floor between her boots. "I'm pretty sure it's pointless, but I'm half tempted to try praying."

Dorian, seated to her left, chuckled. "If it makes you feel better, it's not pointless."

"I dunno. Why do we keep searching for a parental figure when life gets out of control? The minute people find themselves in a situation beyond reason they reach for the man in the sky. My mother kept saying 'God has a plan.' Well, if that's true, why bother praying? Everything's going to happen according to that plan, right? As if some supreme being would be all like 'oh, you're right little mortal, I made a mistake. Let me change my mind.'"

Dorian snickered. "People have been debating that question for centuries, K. Humans need to feel like they're in control. When they lose that feeling, they have to explain it or do something to make them feel safe again. Random circumstance is so cold and impersonal. The concept of a deity is the perfect scapegoat for bad luck or a valve to channel away guilt at good fortune. Something bad happens, God must have wanted it to for 'mysterious reasons.' Or the Devil did it. Something good happens, and he must like you more than everyone else. It's a way to disavow personal responsibility or just plain bad luck."

Kirsten laughed. "I guess I have Judas in my family tree."

Dorian became solid enough to give her a light shove. "The self-loathing thing doesn't work for you."

She looked up from the floor to say something, but glanced to her right. The girl from the alley, clean and wearing a form-fitting hospital smock, walked barefoot into the hallway past a group of staff. A series of plastic tubes hung loose, dangling from adhesive patches on her left arm all the way up to the sleeve, which ended an inch south of her armpit. Head down, she trudged as if being sent off to punishment.

Nearing, she glanced over at Kirsten and approached to within inches of the bench. The child's eyes no longer radiated green light, though a dull pea soup color had stained the whites. Bony arm raised, near-skeletal fingers curled in a wave at Dorian.

"Hi."

Kirsten, trembling, reached out and put her hand through the girl's shoulder. Finding the child insubstantial, she broke down in sobs. Dorian patted her on the back.

The girl sat on her right, swishing her feet back and forth while plucking at the smock where it stopped at mid-thigh. "The seat is cold."

Kirsten gathered her composure and forced her body solid to spirits. She grabbed the girl's hand and squeezed. "What happened? Why are you out here?"

"They're still working on me," said the girl, in a tone close to bored. "I was watching them do stuff to me while I was on a table. I guess something went wrong 'cause they got all freaked out and threw me in a fish tank. I don't really want to see it. It's slimy."

Kirsten, still crying, giggled. "I hate those tanks."

Dorian got up and jogged toward the commotion.

"I'm Kirsten."

"Brooke. Sorry for kicking you in the face."

"It's okay. I know you weren't in control. Father Villera called me to help you."

Brooke glanced up at her. "He's nice."

"You should go back to your body before they try to wake you up." Kirsten forced a nervous smile, hoping it wasn't too late.

"Why?" Brooke frowned. "I'm gonna die anyway. I got nowhere to go, better I just kick off now before I get raped."

Kirsten pulled her into a spongy hug. "No, you're too little. What are you, eleven? I was on the street too at your age. It's not hopeless."

Dorian jogged over, waving at Kirsten until she looked up. "Brooke crashed. From what they're saying, it sounds like her heart gave out. Two doctors are trying to resuscitate her now. Don't have a lot of time."

"I wanna go away." Brooke squirmed, trying to stand out of Kirsten's grip. "My grandpa is calling me from that way." She pointed down the hall.

"What about your parents?" Kirsten squeezed her.

"My parents are dead. They were fuckin' gang trash anyway. Shot by cops, good for 'em. They deserved every bullet." Brooke stopped swinging her feet. "I don't want to be in this world anymore. It sucks here."

"No! Don't say that. The system is good to kids, you'll get placed with a new family."

Brooke glared. "Yeah, I'll sit in a damn government facility 'til I'm seventeen before they find someone willing to let a Lace-head in their house."

"What about colony adoption?" asked Dorian. "There's no waiting list there."

Brooke gave up trying to get her arm away from Kirsten's death grip and slouched. "Yeah, girls go quick. They want baby factories up there. I'll get married off at fifteen and spend the next twenty years pregnant. That sounds *so* much better."

Dorian offered a wistful smile. "I think we found someone more jaded than you are. I'll admit it's a bit of a chance, but at least eight out of ten colony settlements are much healthier than living on Earth these days. Most even have trees. You might be happy with an adoptive family."

Brooke grumbled. "Why do you care?"

Kirsten drew a breath to answer, but only a squeak came out of her as a distant man shouted the F word six times before yelling, "Come on, kid!"

"Brooke, you're a child. You don't get to make decisions like this yet." Kirsten stood, dragging the girl to her feet. "I'm taking over as your temporary guardian for the next few hours. You are going back where you belong."

"No!" shrieked Brooke, thrashing.

"Brooke." Kirsten grabbed the girl's head and forced an eye-to-eye stare. "Listen to me. This is not negotiable. You're letting what happened to you ruin your life. Your life hasn't even fu—fudging started yet."

Brooke's eyebrows drew together. "Fudging? Really? I'm not four."

Kirsten attracted odd looks from the hospital staff as she struggled to drag an invisible, flailing tween down the hall. Every so often, a flicker of silver thread appeared at the girl's forehead; as if reality hadn't made up its mind yet if she were a mere astral projection or a true ghost. Brooke's panic intensified as she found herself lacking the abnormal physical strength she had become accustomed to. As a ghost, she had little luck in breaking Kirsten's psionic hold.

Brooke wailed. "No, get off me! Let me go! I don't want to wake up."

A man, wearing a light SecurMesh vest and armed with a ballistic pistol blocked the door to the procedure room. "I'm sorry, officer. There's a critical patient in there. I can't let you in."

"No shit. I've got her damn ghost in my arms right now. If you don't let me in, she's going to die."

"I want to die! Get her off me!" wailed Brooke.

Alas, the guard couldn't hear her.

The man smirked. "You're either shit nuts or one of those damn psionics. I don't care which it is, I can't let—"

"*Go away.*" Kirsten growled, eyes aglow, bracing a squirming Brooke against her chest.

The security guard wandered off with a dumbfounded gawk. Kirsten booted the door panel. With a soft hiss, the plastisteel barrier parted down the center and each half slid into the wall. Inside, Brooke's lifeless nude body hung in a tube filled with peach colored gel; long hair fanned out around her starved-thin frame. A cloud of blood wisped around teeth, her mouth agape, no breath pushing it out. Two doctors, three medtechs, and a nurse all whirled at the sudden entrance. The techs and nurse moved to intercept.

"Out of my way if you don't want to lose her!" shouted Kirsten.

Perhaps the commanding tone in her voice, or the way she appeared to be struggling with an invisble opponent, or perhaps their sheer desperation made them pause. The doctor closest to the tube held his hand up at them. Kirsten dragged the protesting spirit to the edge of the tube. Dorian waited at the door, arms folded.

"You are not giving up. I won't let you. I won't let you die on the street.

You have too much life left ahead of you, and I'm not gonna let you throw it away!"

Brooke's ghost stared at Kirsten, stunned by the emotional outburst from a complete stranger. "Why the hell do you care?"

Kirsten grabbed the ethereal child by one shoulder and a fistful of hospital tunic and hurled her into the glass tube. Proximity to the body drew the wispy form in, distorting her into a blur of light. The girl convulsed, and an explosion of crimson burst from her mouth and nose, rolling into a diaphanous cloud. Bruises and scratches, badges of being a street kid, covered the small, malnourished body floating in front of her. Kirsten shivered at the memory of the same marks all over her own arms and legs ten years ago.

Face pressed against the glass, Kirsten closed her eyes. "Please, if there is anything up there watching us…" she whispered. "Don't take her yet."

Dorian decided not to comment.

Seconds of silence passed, and the angry cacophony of the equipment changed to pleasant beeping timed to the rhythm of a heartbeat. Kirsten shifted; on the left side of the room, a large holo-panel showed a magnified view of thousands of crablike nanobots reconstructing muscle cell by cell. It resembled an army of alien walkers invading a red landscape.

"We got her," said the female doctor.

Kirsten looked up. Brooke's chest moved with the rhythm of breathing, the red by her mouth swirled back and forth over her teeth with moving fluid.

"Get those nanobots on the cardiac tissue right away. We need to rebuild seventy percent of it." The male doctor wagged his finger at the three medtechs, gave Kirsten a confused stare, and jumped over to a different control console.

Stay with us Brooke. I'll be here when you wake up. Please don't give up.

The child's eyelids twitched at Kirsten's telepathic voice. A hand clasped around Kirsten's right arm. The nurse. He indicated the door with a faint head motion, as if asking her if *she* thought she should leave. The implication was, of course, that she should. Kirsten glanced once more at Brooke, a desperate smile forming at the sight of the girl's eyes moving beneath the lids. Still solid to spirits, she leaned on Dorian and made her way to a bench right outside the procedure room.

A teal bench.

"I wonder where that security guard wound up?"

"Don't care," muttered Kirsten. "A few more seconds waiting might have…"

He squeezed her shoulder.

"I know. I can't keep them all." Kirsten emitted a voiceless chuckle. "She's not psionic anyway. She'll be happier with a real family. I don't want to bring her home. I didn't want her to die."

"You're giving Evan a real family." Dorian patted the back of her hand.

"Agent Wren?" asked a man.

She glanced left and up at a pair of Division 1 officers. Like the bulk of the population, they were of indeterminate ethnicity with light brown skin. Kirsten felt like a phantom by comparison.

"Yes," she said, standing and returning their salute. "What can I do for you?"

"We received a report from the hospital about a minor with a Lace issue."

"Oh, you're looking for who to go kill?"

The patrol officers exchanged a glance before the man offered a resigned shrug. "Yeah, basically."

Kirsten covered her face with both hands, hating herself for not objecting to the idea. "I'm not sure yet. We'll have to ask her when she wakes up."

BAD MEMORIES

Kirsten leaned on the edge of the hospital Comforgel slab, holding Brooke's hand. The head end angled up, and a teal blanket covered the girl to the armpits. A steady flow of people passed by the door out in the hall. For almost an hour, she sat in silence and watched blurs of color go by while listening to the distant din of the hospital. Voices, both real and AI, occasionally came over a PA system to summon a doctor or medical technician to one crisis or another.

Brooke twitched in her sleep once or twice over the hour, raising false hope. Kirsten slumped back in the chair, attempting to manage her feelings of guilt for leaving Evan at Nila's overnight yet again. She toyed with the idea of taking a day off and spending it with him, but couldn't with a one-week deadline to prevent an assassination. Kirsten didn't want to burden him with the weight of what hung over her head. The simple explanation of trying to prevent someone from dying was enough. Evan didn't need to know the police would cause the death.

Brooke moaned in her sleep and opened her eyes. She convulsed and sat upright with a feral gleam in her eye. Kirsten leaned over and put her right hand on the girl's shoulder.

"Hey, calm down. I'm here, you're safe."

The girl lunged for the side of the bed; Kirsten held her down. Weak from the surgery and with no Lace in her system, the girl had barely any strength.

After a futile effort to get away, Brooke flopped limp. Kirsten gathered her hand once more, earning an accusatory frown. The girl stared at the ceiling for a moment, and raised her left hand. It fell on her chest, then slid up into her chin, popped up straight, and finally came down on her face where she wiped her eyes.

"What the hell is wrong with me?"

"Apparently, Lace withdrawal can cause violent flashbacks for the first few hours. You can break your arm or leg from flailing around. They gave you something to protect you against that. Even if you have a seizure, your muscles shouldn't have the strength to do damage."

"Let me go. I didn't do anything."

"Well, first of all, you're in no condition to even get out of this bed. Right now, you'll need help getting to the bathroom."

Brooke blushed.

"Secondly, you were on Lace. Right there, that warrants mandatory detox. There's a couple officers outside who want to have a nice short chat with whoever gave it to you."

Brooke folded her arms, frown deepening. "No one *gave* it to me. You can tell them to go away."

Kirsten lifted the girl's arm, tracing a thumb over the back of her hand. The child's wrist looked too delicate to be real. "You've probably got Greybones. Same thing I had at your age from being out there alone. All the chemicals you've been walking around barefoot on, breathing, basking in… they leach at your body."

"My bones are grey?"

"No, just brittle. It's just called that because most sufferers live in grey zones, or worse places."

The girl tugged her arm away, staring at her fingers as she fussed with the blanket. "Maybe I missed a few vitamins." Silence hung between them for a minute or so before Brooke glanced at her, holding her arm up. "You had this too? How'd you go from street kid to cop?"

"Well, maybe not quite as advanced. I'm sure the Lace didn't help. Come on, look at me." Kirsten held her arms out. "I'm barely a hundred pounds."

"Try a hundred and ten." Dorian winked. "You're perfectly healthy, K."

"How did I become a cop? Well, mostly because I'm psionic, but aside from that, I decided to trust someone ten years ago. When I was your age, I was terrified of adults, but I knew I couldn't keep living like that. Father

Villera called me, Brooke. He said you came to him because you saw something."

Brooke trembled with genuine fear. Kirsten clasped her hand again; this time the girl didn't object.

"I don't wanna think about it."

"Whatever you saw, those people can't hurt you here. Do you remember the man who attacked you at the church?"

"Sorta. He wanted to kill me, right?" She coughed.

Dorian paced around the foot of the bed. "Lace users often experience memory gaps. They can go a week or two at a time in a primal state where they operate only on animal instinct. Higher brain functions tend to shut off."

"Yeah." Kirsten reached with a tissue to wipe bloody sputum from the girl's chin. "I got him."

"You killed him?" Her hand clenched.

Kirsten looked down. "I'm not proud of it, but the idiot did point a gun at me."

"What a moron." Brooke scowled. "You only point a gun at a pig if you wanna get killed."

"Oink." Kirsten smirked.

"Uhh, sorry."

"Why were you out on the streets? Who gave you the Lace?"

"No one. Geez!" Brooke huffed. "I stole it from some South Fork weenies."

"Why?" Kirsten's eyebrows scrunched together. "Why would any kid take that shit willingly? It's deadly."

"I heard it made you super strong, and I wanted to defend myself. Almost got caught by the Diablos once. I didn't wanna be anyone's bitch." Brooke glowered, and lifted an eyebrow at the morose expression on Kirsten's face. "I don't need the pity party."

"There are better ways to avoid that than taking Lace."

"How'd you do it then?" Brooke tried to reach for the bed controls, but her arm flopped around like a drunken snake. "Ugh. Can you make the bed sit up a little higher?"

Kirsten obliged.

"If you didn't take Lace, and you were as skinny as me, how'd you fight them off?"

"I hid in the Beneath. There are pipes down there too small for men to fit in. But getting used by a gang isn't much of a worry down there anyway."

"I guess not. There's monsters though. You might get eaten." Brooke grinned.

"Yeah… there are." Kirsten let out a long breath. "I'm glad we got you off the street before anyone could…" A tear ran down her cheek.

"Rape me?" Brooke shifted, staring at the impressions her feet made in the blanket. "I'm sorry."

Kirsten stared away, reddening. "I'm not sure I'd call it that. I traded myself for food. I wasn't forced or anything."

Dorian did a double take and rushed to her side. "Kirsten… I… you never said anything."

"I didn't let it bother me. I had to eat, didn't I? He had unopened military rations. I'd been stealing garbage for two years. Besides, he was gentle."

"Doesn't make it right." Dorian fumed. The look on his face said he wanted to kill someone.

"Who are you talking to?" asked Brooke.

"You saw him before, the man sitting with me on the bench in the same uniform. He's a ghost."

Brooke paled. "Was I really dead?"

"No, honey. You were projecting." Kirsten gave Dorian a weak glance, hoping for affirmation, but he didn't notice, too occupied fuming in anger by the window to notice. "Your body was still alive, you just fell out of it."

"I don't wanna stay dead."

"Good." Kirsten squeezed her hand. "I'm glad you changed your mind."

Brooke stared at the wall, quiet for a moment, and broke out in a sweat.

Kirsten wiped the girl's face. "Are you hot?"

"Freezing actually." Brooke scrunched her face when Kirsten dabbed at her head again. "So, you were someone's bitch?"

Kirsten fell quiet for a moment. "No, it just happened once."

"The Beneath?" Brooke gave her a scolding frown. "That was your problem, there's no damn food down there. Plenty of Nippy-Noms up here to steal from. Sometimes they gave me food for helping out… mopping and shit."

A wistful smile spread over Kirsten's face. "Yeah. I guess it was stupid of me to crawl around in the shadows for so long."

"Why'd you run away?" Brooke tried to scratch her nose. Her arm flopped anywhere but.

Kirsten wiped it for her. "My mother tried to kill me."

Brooke grumbled. "At least yours noticed you. Rita was more of a mom to me than my mom."

"Who's Rita?"

"'Nother one of the gang bitches. She's dead now, too. Got shot up by a couple of Hatchetmen... pussies. They went runnin' from the main rumble with the South Fork idiots and wound up dragging the firefight with them through where we were sleeping. Old Mack never even woke up."

"All that's behind you now, Brooke. There is no reason for you to stay on the street. Trust me. Take advantage of it while you're still a minor. You can get placed with a family and go to school. If you stay on Earth, you really need higher education. All the crappy jobs are taken by dolls. That's not so much of a problem if you are open to the idea of colony adoption. I'll be honest, Brooke, there's a waiting list to stay on Earth."

Brooke waved her feet back and forth, pondering.

A woman in a white uniform entered, flashing a pleasant smile at both of them. She sidled up to the bed on the side opposite Kirsten and set some things on the table: a white cylinder about three inches long and a thumb's-width around, a derm patch, and a tangle of tubing.

"What's that?" Brooke leaned away.

"You're going to feel a spot of cold, hon." The medtech swabbed the girl's left bicep with an alcohol wipe before applying the adhesive derm. "There's no needle in this, just a pad. It's very cold, so it might feel a little shocking. This medicine will help your body recover from the awful stuff. Little tiny machines will go swimming around inside you and collect all the bad chemicals from your body."

Kirsten, still holding Brooke's other hand, stood. "Umm, don't they usually flush Lace out in the tank?"

The medtech brushed the hair away from of Brooke's eyes, examining them. "She was on Lace long enough to cause deep tissue damage. Her heart walls have thinned, her muscles were in bad shape due to insufficient nutrition and the stresses of the drug. The surgical team had to reconstruct many of her ligaments. A body her size is not meant to lift four hundred pounds. We were all amazed she could still move."

The woman attached one end of the thin tube to the derm patch, the other to the cylinder, and secured the device to the girl's arm with tape.

Two taps created a holographic control screen in midair above the cylinder and the tech dialed out a dose. A series of dashes lit up on the derm patch in dark blue, creating the illusion of rotary motion on the flow meter as the medicine wound its way down the tube to the patch. When the line of liquid reached the derm patch, it beeped, and clicked.

"Ow." Brooke winced as she tried to grab the patch. Her arm moved three seconds after she wanted it to and flopped like a fish out of water. "It burns."

Kirsten gathered the girl's hand and tried to comfort her without disturbing the patch.

"It's so cold it feels hot. Please try to relax and let the medicine work. She has been on Lace for several months. The sudden absence of it could prove fatal. Normally, the doctors would use an induced coma to mitigate the effects of violent withdrawal; however, they feel she would not tolerate it well in her weakened condition. They almost didn't want to risk the muscle relaxers. When she was in the tank, we almost…"

"Yeah, I know exactly how close it was." Kirsten and Brooke traded a knowing glance. "If she's that tenuous, shouldn't someone stay with her in case she has an attack?"

The medtech nodded. "Sure, but our staff doesn't have that kind of time. This is a government med center. The HSO won't pay someone to sit here with one patient. If you want a dedicated nurse, go to an Amaranth Corporation medical pavilion. You have to understand this is a highly unusual situation. Normally, Lace-addicted individuals are detoxed over the course of a few hours while unconscious in a tank. We don't usually have them this young. Brooke is too delicate for that procedure. We need to take it slow. Most juveniles exposed to Lace as long as she was don't last long enough to come in for detox at all. Depending on how she responds to the first round of this"—the nurse tapped the cylinder on Brooke's arm—"she'll be in the gel again tomorrow for additional surgery to rebuild her muscles and bones. If she makes it through the first twelve hours with no major issues, they will be able to finish the detox tomorrow. There is also scar tissue in her lungs from an old infection we need to remove. At any moment, she could go into a violent episode with little to no warning. I'm afraid as soon as you leave, we're going to have to strap her down so she doesn't hurt herself."

Brooke gasped, clinging to Kirsten's arm with both hands.

"So you're just going to leave her in a room alone and tie her to the bed?" Kirsten stared aghast. "What about the muscle relaxers?"

"You've never seen a Lace teardown, have you?" The beleaguered woman sagged. "What else can we do? Our budget can only stretch so far. If she throws a fit and smashes her own skull, the NewsNet will be all over the hospital claiming we killed her. It damn sure won't be the government that takes the blame for a dead street kid. I can't stay with her, I have four dozen rooms to keep an eye on, and Jerry called out sick *again*, so I have to cover his too. I got an old guy one floor up who keeps throwing his bio collection reservoir at the wall. If you'd like to go clean that up, I'll gladly sit with her."

"I'll stay." Kirsten put an arm around Brooke. "There's no way I'm going to leave her tied up alone all night. It's cruel. It's not a medical necessity. It's bald-faced stinginess."

"She may have a psychotic break as her deep unconscious realizes no Lace is coming."

"But she's no stronger than a person her age should be now, right?"

The medtech nodded. "Yes, probably weaker due to the wasting."

"Then I can hold her down if I have to," said Kirsten, gripping the girl's hand.

With a shrug at Kirsten, the medtech went for the door. "It's your pretty little body to bruise if you want to."

Brooke glared at the woman in white.

The medtech glanced back with a softer expression. "If this city had more cops like you, it might not suck so much." She looked at her wrist, sighed at the time, and trudged out while grumbling about moving to Mars.

A moment later, Brooke flopped back onto the bed.

"Excellent interview technique," said Dorian. "That just earned you a lot of trust."

Kirsten shot him a dark stare.

"Thanks, but who's gonna want a Lace-head." Brooke pouted, then coughed.

"By the time you get out of here, your eyes will be white again and the Lace will be out of your system. You don't have to tell anyone about it unless you trust them. Sometimes, people have to do bad things just to stay alive."

Dorian's face projected a mixture of shock and pity.

The girl settled in, as if about to go back to sleep.

"Brooke? You went to Father Villera because you saw something. I really need you to tell me about that."

"My throat hurts."

Kirsten moved to the edge of the bed, hovering over her. "If you want, you can just think about it. I can see it in your head if you let me."

"Will it hurt?"

"No, I promise it won't."

"Okay."

"Open your eyes, look at me, and think about what you saw."

The telepathic connection gave Kirsten a brief glimpse of her own face before the room fell away, as though her point of view went over backward into a deep well. The hospital room flew off into the nothingness above her, melting into a spiral of colors from teal to grey. She focused on the concept of the specific memory, tumbling in the dark until the cold wetness of rain-soaked alley seeped through her clothes in the tight confines of a space beneath a trash crusher.

Kirsten recognized the random scraps of cloth in which her point of view snuggled as a street urchin's nest. If not for the city light leaking in, it would have been just like her old home, even down to the stink of chemicals and urine. Everything had a strange green tint—the memory of a Lace user.

Voices shouted nearby, evidently the reason for the girl waking up. The words blurred in Brooke's fitful memory and terror, becoming demonic roars and growls rather than agitated men. Kirsten watched, a spectator with no control. A grimy hand reached into view as the child crawled to the edge to peek.

Four men stood around a squirming female figure in a black silk robe. Chrome binders gleamed stark against coffee-colored ankles. A silk bag covered the head of a struggling woman. Her scream attempting to get past a mouthful of cloth drowned out the whispering of the man who stood at her feet. He, too, wore a black robe, but also a shiny mask covering his face beneath the hood. Gold filigree circled the eyes, descending to thin gold trails down the cheeks. The black surface sparkled, as if covered in minute flakes of silver.

The man at the woman's head was the one who tried to kill Brooke. On the left and right, two others dressed in coats and body armor held the woman's bound arms by the elbows. She thrashed as if she knew her death was imminent, though her protests stilled as the man with the mask swung his left arm up and aimed his palm at her. Her body arched, shuddered, and fell still. Her head wobbled about as if drunk. Violent struggling became half-hearted squirms.

The men holding her arms let go and pulled her robe open down the center, exposing her nakedness to the sky as the chanting man knelt beside her. He traced some manner of stylus at her chest, apparently writing, though Brooke's angle prevented seeing what he drew on her skin. Kirsten shivered; reading the traumatic memory forced her to share in the terror the girl felt at the sight. It took a moment to divest herself from the inherited fear and resume.

Red light glowed from the mask's eyes. The raspy chanting grew louder in a language Kirsten had never heard spoken, menacing and guttural. When the masked figure raised a wicked gold and silver knife to the clouds in his right hand, a sense of being unable to breathe—Brooke's terror—came over her. The weapon's wide, wavy blade gleamed too bright for the pitiful amount of moonlight in the alley. In his left hand, the man clutched a glowing violet gemstone the size of a baseball that pulsated with pale light.

Brooke covered her eyes for a moment, looking back up right as the masked figure plunged the decorative dagger into the helpless woman's chest. She gurgled and went still. Brooke, now Kirsten, stared at the wobbling handle in the shape of a gold dragon's head.

Light within the great stone flickered brighter as he held it over the dead woman. Vaporous white swirls rose from the still-warm corpse and attempted to form the image of her ghost, but a strong force drawing it into the gem distorted it. The disembodied voice of a terrified woman screamed. Energy streamed from the body's eyes, swirling into a tornado of white light consumed by the sinister object. As the last of the phantom swirls flowed into the gem, the sound of a woman screaming cut off to silence. Withering spread over the dead woman's chest, and the glow faded.

He held the stone aloft with reverence, as if a priest conducting a mass.

After wrenching the dagger out of the body, the mask wearer strode out of view, followed by the two men who had held the victim down by her arms. One had a metal hand. The last man gathered the robe closed over the corpse and stooped to pick her up, pausing when he looked straight at Brooke.

He must have seen her eyes—green lights in the dark.

He advanced, and Brooke scrambled out of her cramped space. The man grabbed at her, but was woefully unprepared for the little urchin being strong enough to throw him into the air. Kirsten released the telepathic link as the alley blurred up to a superhuman run, already knowing the rest of the story.

Brooke had fallen asleep.

Kirsten moved off the bed and settled into the chair, cradling her face in both hands. Terror had come from the mind of someone else, but it took her a moment to get over it. She took a few deep breaths and let her head go back, not moving for a while until Nila's hologram appeared above the NetMini.

"I'm at the hospital. I'm fine; I'm just staying with a kid I found. Is Evan okay?"

"He's asleep. He didn't have any fits tonight."

"Please tell him I'm very sorry about getting stuck out here again. I can't leave this girl alone. Lace… eleven-year-old. If I leave her, they're going to tie her down, alone."

Nila gasped. "I hope you killed the bastard she got it from"—she lowered her voice, hearing Shani approach—"I don't mind watching Evan, he's a good kid. He knows you're doing what you have to do. Hang on." She winked, grinning. "Looks like the bratling's awake."

"Thanks for watching him. I'll be here the rest of the night. Take care of Shani; I have another call to make."

Kirsten flipped through the contact list and poked an entry. Six rings later, the sleep-weary face of a dark-skinned woman in her later thirties appeared.

"Kirsten?"

"Hi Danita, I'm sorry to wake you up. I need your help."

"Did something happen with Evan?"

"No. Everything's perfect with him." She smiled. "I'm at the hospital now with a girl named Brooke. Both parents are dead, so she's been alone for about a year. She's not psionic, but I wanted to ask if you could take her case and make sure she gets placed with a good family, possibly colony settlers if she warms up to the idea. She needs special handling, and I know you go way beyond just 'resolving cases.'"

Kirsten stared at Brooke's twitching face, all too familiar with the kind of bad dreams going on behind her closed eyes. "This girl really needs someone who cares."

COLD TRUTH

K irsten guided her patrol craft through the early morning city, following a diagonal path across the sector grid. Its black reflection slid over silver windows, drifting closer and nearer with each passing building. Civilian hover traffic flowed several stories below. The video display simulating a windshield compensated for sun glare, allowing her to see as she followed a ribbon of light leading to the navigation pin. Kirsten flicked on the autodrive and sat back with a fresh cup of hot mocha coffee in both hands. The fragrance and warmth soothed her after a long, rough night. She drew in a deep breath and basked in the orange light of the rising sun.

"I'm sorry, Dorian, some things I didn't want to re-live."

"I'm not at all upset at you for keeping that to yourself. I'm furious with the bastard who used you like that. I killed a suggestive for molesting a girl older than you were then. I'm pissed."

"Now you know why I never told you. I knew it would upset you and there's nothing to be done about it. I wanted to spare you the… pain." She stared into the distance for a moment. "I've thought about finding him, making him apologize or just kicking his ass." Kirsten held the cup to her lips, closing her eyes at the sweet warmth settling into her stomach. "How screwed up was I to think he was so much nicer than Mother? I'd have rather stayed with him than gone home."

Dorian didn't laugh. "He did it to you. He'll do it to some other girl."

"It was ten years ago, Dorian. Besides, there aren't that many children down there. What few there are live in small colonies with their parents. Hard to keep secrets in those little villages. Justice down there is harsh. He's probably dead already by now, especially if Ritchie made good on his threat. Besides, he didn't *force* me to do anything."

"Waving meat at a starving dog isn't forcing it to do anything either."

"I could have walked away. I could have gone up top and begged. I could have gone dumpster diving again. No, I have to accept some of it. I wanted the easy way out for once. It didn't hurt... much. He was so nice and I was lonely."

"You were twelve," Dorian grumbled. "I'm gonna go find the son of a bitch."

"Let it go. I don't even really remember what he looked like—all I see is a faceless man in a flannel shirt. I still smell him." She put her nose over the cup again. "I don't want to think about it anymore. That's an old life. Why does it bother you so much? I haven't let it affect me. I went into that little shack with both eyes open. I knew what he wanted even if I didn't really understand the physics of it." She sat for a moment, squeezing at the control sticks. "I'm sorry for not being innocent like you thought I was."

"Stop. No part of that was your fault." Dorian put a hand on her shoulder. "You're more innocent than most, still."

She banked the car into a wide left arc and descended to the roof of the Regional Tech Center. "I've been here so often lately, they must think I'm considering applying."

"I doubt it. You're a Zero." He winked. "That's sort of a long-term career."

"Yeah." She returned his wink. "They don't even let you out when you die."

"Hah."

THE OPEN-CASE MORGUE OCCUPIED THE ENTIRETY OF THE FOURTH sublevel. A brisk chill rolled into the elevator as the doors opened. For a moment, Kirsten wondered if anyone was down here given the dim lighting. A white linoleum corridor led into a floor that resembled an abandoned hospital from a spooky horror vid. Frosty air filled her lungs, the temperature low enough to *smell* cold. Her boots squeaked on the over-waxed floor.

She passed six doors on each side arranged in facing pairs labeled A through F. The corridor expanded into a larger area with a wide U-shaped desk with room for a six workstations. It, too, sat empty.

Kirsten turned in place, glancing at two offshoot passages that led to either side from the clerk's area. Signs identified various rooms along the left hall as a number of scanning stations, file storage, and lastly, a hazardous materials locker. The right passage appeared to be mostly offices for people important enough to have their names on placards. The only door with light coming out from under it appeared to be the men's room.

"Shall I go hurry things along?" asked Dorian, with an impish grin.

Kirsten snickered. "This place is creepy enough. You'll scare the guy to death." She glanced at the hallway once again, tapping her foot.

Minutes later, a tall heavyset man in a white lab coat over dark clothes came trundling out of the bathroom. Long curly black hair cascaded down to his chest, and his jowls rocked with each footfall. He paused a moment when he realized she was there, and swiped at his hair to attempt to make it more presentable.

Konstantin, you are not. More like the chubby guy on the dorm floor everyone likes, but no one thinks of in a romantic way.

"Hel-lo, umm…?" He stared at her chest.

"Looking for rank insignia or just checking me out?" She smiled. "Agent Wren, Division 0."

"Oliver Murphy," he said, extending a hand. "Sorry, don't get a lot of live people down here. Specially not pretty ones." He chuckled, flashing an awkward smile. "What brings you to the halls of the dead?"

"I need to see the remains of certain homicide victims related to a case I am working on. Inquest 24180827A2."

Oliver navigated around the giant desk and took the nearer seat along the left side of the U. He swiped his meaty hands over the terminals and an array of holo-panels sprang into existence. "According to our records, there are four bodies tagged under that case. Room D. I think Eli is in there working on something. Your ID should open the door. Give me a holler if you have an issue."

"Thanks."

She headed down the hallway.

Twenty feet from the desk, Dorian leaned toward her. "He didn't seem to care you're psionic."

"I've got a boyfriend." Kirsten spun the serpent bracelet around her wrist.

Dorian glanced at the wall. "There you go again, making that doe-eyed face."

"What's your problem with Konstantin? You're not jealous are you? You're the one that kept reminding *me* we had no chance."

"Oh, I'm not jealous. You do deserve a living man. It's just... I don't know. You've always been strong and independent. To see you acting like some kind of helpless arm-clinger, it's not right."

"You're being jealous." She winked. "I'm only having a little fantasy." Her mirth faded. "I've been so alone for so long with no one but me around to pat me on the back and say it'll be alright. Let me enjoy it for a little while."

She swiped her ID over the door at Storage Room D. It chirped and slid open. A silver-walled chamber covered in square doors gleamed in strong blue light. A Middle Eastern-looking man with a mass of fluffy, curled hair and a sharp chin jumped at the *pssh* of the door opening. He spun away from an open body tray sticking out of the left wall, and whirled to glare her.

"Wow, the only thing missing from the sudden turn-and-stare was a horror movie organ," she whispered. "Hellooo mad scientist. I wonder what he's doing with that body."

"I'm trying to figure out what sort of small animal died on his head." Dorian cracked a whimsical grin.

Kirsten bit her lip to avoid laughing, and walked over to the man. The word 'Hassan' appeared out of the gleam of reflected light on his name tag.

"Who are you?" Hassan asked.

Her gaze took in his blood-spattered glove and laser scalpel. "Agent Wren, Division 0, I-Ops. Bodies pertinent to a current investigation are in here according to Mr. Murphy at the front desk. I won't get in your way."

He stood mannequin still, no discernible mood in his expression.

Four adjacent body storage lockers on the wall opposite the door lit up with white borders, which blinked. Oliver's voice echoed over a PA system. "Agent Wren, I tagged the drawers you need."

"Thanks." She ignored Hassan and approached the indicated coolers, doing a three-sixty spin while walking across the room.

Hassan appeared to lose all interest in the dead man in front of him, and watched her. She reached up to pull on the first door's handle, and cringed away from a fall of cryonic fog. The door motored itself upward before a tray slid out bearing a sheet-covered figure. Upon reaching full extension, the platform lowered from head-level to an elevation more suited for examination.

"Terminal," said Kirsten.

A holo-panel appeared next to her in midair, accompanied by a tiny glowing speck in the ceiling from the projector. She poked at virtual keys, navigating the archives to the records for this body.

"Carlos Rosa, former Deputy Director of Security for the West City Municipal Complex." Kirsten pulled the sheet away, exposing the body.

His skin had turned greyish-white and blue stains spattered here and there on his chest. Faint markings appeared in the skin, no doubt revealed by whatever substance they sprayed on him. She jogged over to Hassan's work cart and helped herself to a pair of surgical gloves. He narrowed his eyes in a suspicious squint. Kirsten peeked at his surface thoughts, but they were in Arabic. A distinct sense of distrust came through on an emotional level.

She returned a semi-hostile glare and walked back to Mr. Rosa. "Keep an eye on him," she muttered. "I got a bad vibe."

"You haven't done enough Flowerbasket to 'get vibes' off people," said Dorian.

After snapping on the gloves, she stood up on tiptoe and poked at the chest. "These look like the same markings I found in the circle. Konstantin called it Sumerian." She dropped back to her heels and browsed the medical report.

"They found the fatal wound—looks like a stab through the heart." She traced her finger over the holographic text while reading. "The medical examiner determined that someone regenerated tissue in the wound, likely with specialized nanobots, attempting to disguise the cause of death. It seems like they only noticed it due to a small error in the boundary layers between tissues. The graft failed to adhere over a six nanometer span on 'Victim Two,' and a recheck found the same tissue plug in all four bodies."

Later portions of the file contained medical scan data showing mild damage to the bones of the wrists and ankles, consistent with physical restraint over an extended period. Kirsten thought back to Brooke's memory. That victim, undoubtedly Alaina Munoz, had metal binders on.

"Whoever is doing this holds the victims for some time prior to killing them," she muttered, half to Dorian, half to herself.

She tapped a button at the end of the tray, which lifted Carlos back up before retracting him into the cooler. The next bay held the remains of Uma Donn, the design engineer from EnMesh. Her injuries were consistent with Carlos's, down to the presence of ancient pictograms present on the skin of the chest. Unlike Carlos, she had turned red and purple around that spot. Kirsten dug through her medical examiner's report, finding a note indicating a suspected allergic reaction to the chemical agent used to remove the markings.

No trace of the ink remained for identification. However, it had lessened the exposure of certain skin cells to the cleaning solution, allowing the medical examiner to reveal the writing with a different chemical that reacted to it. The cells with lower exposure remained paler, while the rest stained blue, exposing more Sumerian writing.

"I'm hardly an expert here, but the pictographs look to be mostly the same with only a few different symbols."

Dorian rubbed his chin.

Alaina Munoz occupied the third tray, not as decomposed as the others except for the unnatural withering of the face and upper chest. Kirsten drew a sharp breath and looked away, unprepared for the spike of emotion from seeing the body of someone she watched die. More ancient writing existed on her chest. Also, the bone damage from her restraints appeared more severe than the other victims.

"Looks like she died fighting. She almost broke both wrists trying to get away."

Dorian grumbled. "She didn't go easy."

Kirsten swallowed her sadness and glanced from him back to the dead woman. "Whoever did this to you is going to pay for it."

"Alaina Munoz worked for RedEx. Why would they go after her? They don't make any political decisions. There's no political advantage in a company that runs shuttles to Mars and back."

"Maybe we're looking at this wrong." Kirsten almost tapped her finger to her lips, but hesitated with a dubious glance at a finger that had touched a corpse. "Maybe it isn't government at all. Maybe it's organized crime looking to set up some kind of smuggling operation?"

"Fourth victim…" Dorian squinted at the virtual terminal and it flipped a few pages over. "William Arris, a security guard for the West

City Archives. What the hell does he have to do with smuggling or government?"

Kirsten glowered, thinking. "There's lots of old stuff there. Maybe whoever is doing this needed to steal something from the archives? What if he needed to find the writing used on the other victims from a scroll or something?"

Dorian laughed. "You've been watching Monwyn too much. There's no such thing as magic scrolls. And besides, they used the same writing on him."

"Fine, an old book then." Kirsten glanced sideways at Hassan, who huddled away from her while whispering at a NetMini.

Dorian's laughing eyes hardened. "He's telling someone you know too much."

"You speak Arabic?" Kirsten whispered.

"My family is originally from Egypt, K. Couple generations ago, but I figured I should keep up tradition."

She pulled the stunrod off her belt and approached Hassan. When she walked away from the body of William Arris, the tray chirped and retracted itself. Hassan turned at the noise, face twisting into a grimace of murderous panic.

Dorian ran past her at Hassan. "Whoever he's on the line with just said 'kill her.'"

"Okay, shithead. Put the scalpel down." She traded the stunrod to her left hand and gripped her E-90.

Hassan muttered at her in Arabic, as if he knew no English, while attempting to smile.

"What's he saying?"

Dorian cringed. "Quite a few unpleasant things about women; you really don't want me to translate. He's just babbling random insults."

"You at least have to have an English chip to get this job, Hassan. Don't give me that shit. Who did you call to warn I know too much? Who are you working for?"

He turned as if to run, but whirled back and threw the contents of a flask at her. Kirsten dove away from the dark liquid, crossing her arms to shield her eyes. Hassan threw the empty plastic container at her, then ran for the door. Dorian blurred past him, grabbing the edge of a body cooler door and swinging it open as hard as he could fling it. Eyes over his shoulder on Kirsten, Hassan ran full speed face-first into the swinging three-foot square slab of plastisteel with a dull, meaty *clank*.

She cringed. "Ooh. That looked painful."

He landed flat on his back, moaning.

Kirsten rolled to her feet. Dorian tried to jump on Hassan, but succeeded only in leaving a layer of cold slime over his chest. Hassan shrieked and scrambled upright, swiping his hand at the residue with a wild, panicked look. He shot a stare at Kirsten before sprinting for the door. She dove at him, grabbing two handfuls of lab coat, but he shrugged out of it and took off. She chased him down the hall, past a rather startled Oliver, and to the right. Hassan raced into the third office on the left and slammed the Epoxil door a second before she crashed into it.

"Hassan, where do you think you're running? You're in the middle of a god damned police facility!" Kirsten screamed and kicked the faux wood.

She wobbled back, rubbing her leg. "Damn, tough doors." Out came the E-90. "You have two seconds to open this door or I'm opening it for you."

Hassan didn't answer.

One laser blast melted the retaining bar and flooded the air with the glue-plastic stink of molten Epoxil. The door swayed ajar. Kirsten raised her boot to kick it, but dove sideways at the *bang* of a gunshot. The door bulged where the dense material trapped the slug. Rolling onto her back, she aimed between her knees. Another gunshot went off, but the door didn't grow a second bulge.

Silence.

Dorian stuck his head in past the wall. "Clear. He shot himself."

Oliver leaned around the corner at the end of the hallway. "What the fuck?"

"I wish I knew," she snapped, before sighing. "Ops." A beep of acknowledgement came from her earbud. "I need a crime scene team to my present location."

"You're in the tech facility," said a hesitant male voice in her ear.

"I realize that. Some shithead just tried to kill me and then shot himself when I cornered him in an office with no way out."

"Copy that, Agent Wren."

She jammed the E-90 back in its holster and shouted, "Shit!"

Hassan's brain dripped from the ceiling of the formerly nice office of Ellen Gomez, Chief Medical Examiner of West City. Shattered fragments of NetMini were everywhere; he had evidently put the device between the gun and his chin before firing. Kirsten leaned on the doorjamb, seething.

"No sign of a ghost," said Dorian. "I don't feel Harbingers either. Either he was a shell, or I missed him."

"I don't know why he shot the 'mini. The call traces are in the network."

Dorian nodded. "True, but with the 'mini destroyed, it'll take them an hour or two to figure out what IPv12 to trace. Plus anything in its memory is going to be a pain in the ass to reconstruct."

"Why do I feel like I'm digging myself deeper into a hole?" She glanced to the left as a handful of Division 1 officers and a crime scene crew rounded the corner. "I just can't catch a break, can I?"

"Maybe you should have a little faith."

She blinked. "Great idea."

23

CONFESSION

Two hours later, Kirsten landed the patrol craft in front of the Five Hundredth Street Sanctuary. At a little past one in the afternoon, the sun illuminated the sides of buildings adjacent to the parking lot, orange fire shimmering over silver towers, though it failed to pierce the smog right overhead. The effect created a halo of otherworldly light at the edges of a darkened space where a significant number of people waited in line for food. She found the presence of a line reassuring; it made the place seem far more welcoming than it had been the other night, though an unearthly quality in the light kept her on edge.

"This is creepy," she said as she stood. "It looks like it's going to rain just on this parking lot."

Dorian walked up beside her. "That's just the smog layer, not much wind today."

A handful of advert bots prowled the line of unfortunates waiting for a free lunch. Kirsten drew a breath, about to mock them for attempting to sell things to people with no money, until she realized they displayed recruitment ads seeking laborers and crew for colony work. One or two people in the line had a 'oh, screw it' moment, and signed up. A cheery voice announced the company would send a complimentary PubTran car to pick them up. Both of them asked if they could eat first.

She ducked past the line and headed inside, finding Father Villera behind the long table where he doled out meals. He nodded at her, handing off his duties to a volunteer who appeared to be a university student. The girl waved at Kirsten and took Villera's spot at the table.

"I got your message, come on. We can talk in the back." He ambled around a table full of people eating and headed for the back hallway.

Kirsten followed him into a small room, edging to the side as he eased a plain door closed behind her. The tiny office was quite sparse in decoration. Aside from cheap false-wood paneled walls, a steel desk, and several bookshelves, a plain cross hung on the wall opposite the door. Something about the pale beige-orange walls made her feel a little nauseous. The four-inch Jesus stared at her; she looked away. Even twelve years after running away from home, she couldn't bear the gaze of the little carved man that Mother had hung all over her bedroom.

"Have you any news? What of that poor girl?"

"She's fine. It was scary for a little while, but she's in the hospital recovering from the drugs. She told me an interesting story about what she saw." Kirsten described the ritual killing.

Villera paled as he limped around and sat at the desk. After blessing himself, he looked up. "I am concerned. It sounds to me like there is more to this than a simple serial killer."

"I never did find out who was responsible for bringing Charazu into the world. They're still out there. So far, I haven't been able to establish anything connecting the victims. One was pretty high up. One was a minimum wage museum guard. One was an engineer, and another worked in advertising. It doesn't make any sense."

"Who they were may not be important. This person may have merely sought random targets of opportunity. Each killing was likely a sacrifice to the darkness."

"There is evidence they were held for some time prior to their deaths, but there was no sign of torture or sexual abuse."

Villera waved her off. "No, that wouldn't fit. Souls are the currency of the damned. He's using them to pay a tithe. The only question I have is if each one results in a minor spirit or if he is collecting them as an offering to a more significant entity."

"I thought it was Reverend Wallis, but he was a thrall of something as well. I destroyed an abyssal that had possessed him. He didn't remember a thing. I still don't really believe I'm dealing with demons." Kirsten slumped into a metal folding chair.

"You are young yet, Kirsten. Faith can sometimes take many years to find us."

She chuckled. "I'm not a big fan of religion, Father. No offense. I didn't have the greatest experience with it growing up."

"I'm sorry."

"It's not your fault. I told you about my mother already. She couldn't deal with having a psionic child, thought I was a minion of the Devil. I can see ghosts, spirits, and apparently demons. When wayward haunts came to me for help, she thought I was praying to Satan. It got pretty, uhh, bad." Kirsten rubbed her hand, the spot Mother used to burn. "All the while she did those things to me, she kept calling on Jesus, asking why he'd done this to her. As if my very existence was some kind of punishment for her to suffer through."

Father Villera leaned forward over the desk, extending a hand. "There are three kinds of people in religion, my child."

After catching herself giving him a patronizing look, she stifled a sigh and accepted his hand.

"Some seek to use the word of God as a tool to hurt and control others. They care not for the meaning of scripture, only desiring to profit from fear and superstition. Those individuals do not have any true faith at all. They are usually the most vehement defenders of dogma, loudly challenging any dissent, calling for violence against those who question them, and refusing to permit any discussion that contradicts their views."

She nodded. "Yeah, like trying to argue with a three-year-old. They know they're wrong and there's nothing they can say to validate their point—so they just scream and throw things."

Father Villera chuckled. "Then, you have people who expect God to knock on their door every time they call on him as if they were the only person to exist in the entire world. They take no responsibility for their own lives or decisions. Whenever something goes wrong, they blame Satan, or find a way to make it the fault of those who don't believe. On the more extreme end, some use their beliefs as justification for the inexcusable."

She fidgeted, staring down. "Yeah."

"Some people are content to accept faith for what it is. They do not question why things happen and they do not make wishes as if on a genie. For them, it is simply enough to know he is there. There is no purpose in baiting those who do not believe. I know in my heart what *I* believe, and a man is no lesser for disagreeing with me. One cannot force another to find faith; it must find everyone in their own way. Those who try to force their ways on others do not believe in God, they believe only in control."

Kirsten smirked at the desk. "Nice try, Father. I'm still not sure if I'm ready to believe in an invisible man in the sky. I've talked to dead priests who couldn't understand why what they saw after death was different than what they believed all their lives."

"Perhaps what we believe in life affects what we see after it." He smiled as she let go of his hand, and reclined. "When you are ready, you will know. You may never believe, and that is fine."

"For a priest, you sure seem to know a lot about abyssals."

"Who do you think had to deal with them before psionics came around?" He winked.

"Any ideas where I could start?"

"You mentioned writing on the victims' bodies? Have you looked into the meaning of it?"

"I've been wanting to. I know someone who can translate it." Kirsten fidgeted at the bracelet, which struck her as oddly heavy and uncomfortable. Her urge to go see Konstantin diminished under her usual 'ugh' reaction to the overly wealthy. *I need to spend time with Evan.*

Father Villera stood. "Sounds like a good place to start."

"I doubt the killings are random," said Dorian. "There is too much planning involved."

"Thanks, Father." Kirsten shook hands. "Time for me to start poring over data in search of a pattern. Oh, the people who attacked you were connected to this somehow. Whoever is doing it must view you as a threat."

Father Villera glanced at the gold ouroboros around her right wrist. "Indeed... he must."

24

CONNECTIONS

Kirsten stared at the white text scrolling over the blackness of her holo-terminal. After-hours lighting left the squad room in a dim state, making her feel even more like she spent too much time there. Distant whirring echoed as cleaning bots floated around spraying lemon-scented chemicals into the air. Without even looking, she lifted her feet as a flat, round bot scooted by in front of her chair—7:13 p.m. on the dot.

Ugh, I am here late way too much.

She stared at faces. William Arris, a security guard from the West City Archives. He had no financial trouble, no criminal record, and was a former soldier. Whoever took him out had to be strong enough to handle someone trained for combat while being quiet enough to do it without discovery. Records indicated Arris had a four-day weekend, but no one had seen him since he left work at the end of his Thursday overnight shift. He didn't report in for work on Tuesday, and his body was found the following Friday. No family reported him missing, and the only traffic on his NetMini account came from his shift supervisor going crazy trying to reach him. In her overtired state, Kirsten found the series of vid mails of the supervisor falling ever further into a desperate frothing rage funny.

Konstantin had an office at the Archives. Perhaps he could shed some light on what happened. *He's got a lot of pull there. Maybe he could help me figure out what was stolen... if anything was stolen.*

Carlos Rosa was easy to figure out. As the de-facto head of security at the West City Municipal Complex, compromising him opened a lot of doors to high-level people. Already, the military used his death as leverage in objecting to the privatization of security. Kirsten knew Commissioner Vernon had been—and probably remained—under the influence of an abyssal. She glared at the wall again, annoyed at Carter and the Division 0 command council for demanding incontrovertible proof before acting. It bothered her that politics outweighed a woman's life, but the sad reality of a public backlash against psionics was all too real. As bad as it could get for them now, a scandal involving accusations of mind control and espionage by a psionic against such a high-ranking government official would be a disaster.

Pitchforks and torches time.

The next face belonged to Uma Donn, a multi-PhD research engineer for EnMesh Biomedical. Like Arris, she had no criminal record, debts, or any suspicious marks in her record. Also, like Arris, she had no family. Kirsten paused, tapping her chin. *No family. No one to report them missing too early.* Kukla Investments had recently purchased EnMesh. No connection came to mind between them and the Archives, or between them and the trade commissioner.

A twinge of revulsion hit her as the face of Alaina Munoz appeared on screen. She looked so young, and Kirsten had vicariously watched her die. No matter how much she wanted to stop it, the vision rode in on the sense of an eleven-year-old's memory. She could only sit there and witness it happen. Everything came hand-in-hand with the emotions of a young girl, leaving Kirsten trembling for a moment before she concentrated on knowing the fear came from the kid.

The young woman had worked in the marketing department of RedEx. So far, nothing newsworthy had come out of the interplanetary shipping company. Nothing, except for a recent buyout by VSKK. No connection existed between them and the commissioner either, and no link between them and the West City Archives. None, except for...

Kirsten's hand fell out from under her chin and slapped onto the desk.

Konstantin was the CEO. She fired an awkward glance at Dorian as something did a backflip in her stomach. After a few breaths, she grinned. Of course, if someone knew EnMesh was about to be purchased by VSKK, they might try to sabotage things by killing one of their scientists. That made sense. If there was anything in VSKK's network, Konstantin would be able to find it.

That left EnMesh and Kukla disconnected from everything else.

Kukla, why does the name sound so damn familiar?

Her mind raced as she thought about the phrase 'Kukla Investment Corporation.' She heard the voice of an Eastern-European man talking about corporate property. In silence, she stared at the ceiling lights for several minutes before it hit her: #1998 City Road 130, the building where she'd found the silver circle... and later fought Charazu. *Purchased by Kukla Investment Corporation.* She sat back in the chair, arms limp at her sides. *Is it a coincidence? They buy all sorts of things.*

She pulled her legs up, resting her chin on her knees. *No, too much of a coincidence. Kukla buys a building where Charazu is summoned. Then, they buy out a company that has an employee murdered by someone summoning demons. Hang on. I'm reaching. RedEx has thousands of employees. Even a random killer could have chosen one of their employees by chance.*

A smiling, balding face with large ears flashed in her mind. Yevgeniy Suvorin, majordomo of Kukla Investment Corp. Friends with Konstantin. Kirsten bit her fingers. The link. Coincidence became too much to ignore. Everything swirled around those two men. It had to be Yevgeniy, or at least someone working under him. They wanted to take over VSKK and destroy Konstantin. That's why he researched ancient Sumerian. Someone must have been after him since before he left the ACC. He needed to learn how to defend himself against it.

There had to be a proof trail somewhere in the system. Some transaction, some communication, something that would lead her to evidence the Council would accept. Konstantin has been dealing with it for years. Commissioner Vernon only had a few days left.

Sudden loud ringing from her NetMini ringing all but knocked her out of the chair screaming. Kirsten fumbled to answer it, so wound up with worry she couldn't stop shaking. When Konstantin's holographic face appeared, she squeaked.

"Is everything all right, *Lyubimaya?* You look quite... what is the word, frazzled?" He glanced around before raising an eyebrow. "You're still at the office?"

"Yes. This case is really kicking my ass. I only have a few days left to save the next victim."

"Oh?" He raised an eyebrow. "You know who next victim will be?"

"Not who the killer is going to take next, but..." She bit her lip, lowering her voice. "I shouldn't say anything..."

"Not over the line then. I would like you to accompany me to a boring event I must attend tonight. It would be intolerable without you."

Kirsten whined. "I want to, but I have so much I have to get done. That woman is going to die if I don't find some kind of proof. The reports alone will take hours."

"I'm sure your captain will understand. He wouldn't want his best astral sensitive to burn herself out. Surely, he does not expect you to work all night without at least having dinner?"

The idea of forgetting entirely about the investigation and enjoying a night with Konstantin tugged at her. So tempting, yet so selfish. Vernon would die in mere days if she didn't come up with something. It gnawed at her to abandon her duty, but she couldn't stop thinking about how wonderful it would feel to be with him. She twisted the bracelet around and around her wrist while staring at the screens. "I…" *Can't, shouldn't, mustn't…*

"I'll send a car for you."

Kirsten couldn't help but shiver at the thrill he wanted to spend time with her. The case could wait. "Okay."

THE LIMOUSINE CAME TO A HALT AT THE END OF A PIER, AGLOW IN THE CAST off light from a large corporate yacht. She hadn't said a word the whole ride, since Konstantin had only sent his driver to pick her up. Kirsten stepped out after the automatic door swung open and adjusted her dress. Two silver disks on each shoulder held a drape of black cloth across her chest, an extra mantle over a high-necked black gown that hung to her ankles. Of all the expensive dresses he'd had bought her, this one, by far, covered the most skin. Konstantin waited at the dockside end of the boarding ramp, holding his arm out to her as she approached.

A sudden upwelling of joy propelled her up to a brisk stride. Nothing mattered but his being happy to see her. She hurried over and grasped onto his arm, feeling like a princess clinging to her prince.

"You look radiant, my darling." He kissed the back of her hand. "Quite fetching with your hair wild. It suits you."

Her cheeks warmed. She lost a few seconds staring at his firm jawline, perfect nose, and smoldering eyes. "You are quite handsome yourself tonight."

He started up the ramp, but paused two steps later, glancing down with a grin. "You're wearing flats?"

Princess Kirsten shrank back to just Kirsten. She blew air out of the side of her mouth. "Every time I wear heels, I wind up running around barefoot and getting shot at. I'm hoping to skip that part tonight."

He nodded. "Fair enough."

When they reached the top of the ramp, she froze, gripping Konstantin's arm hard enough that he glanced at her with concern. Yevgeniy stood at the rear of the boat's open deck, flanked by three young women and two men of similar age. She looked away before he noticed her staring, tucking into Konstantin's side.

"What's wrong? I'm rather worried about anything that could frighten you."

Tell him. Wait, no… Yevgeniy might hear me. If he's the one, something might lurking nearby. She peered around Konstantin, opening her mind to the paranormal. The briefest trace of abyssal energy right beside her on the right made her whip her head in that direction, but the darkness receded. Kirsten let go of his arm and stood her ground, glaring around at the rich people in search of the demonic entity she felt certain she'd missed seeing by less than a second.

"Are you quite sure you're all right? A moment ago, you appeared ready to hide under your covers. Now you look ready to arrest someone." Konstantin chuckled.

She swept her gaze around the boat again, but nothing paranormal appeared. Her mood sank back to worried contempt. *Ugh. What am I doing here? I don't belong with these people—and Vernon's going to die if I don't find something.* "Oh, I'm not good on boats. I never learned how to swim."

"Swimming? Isn't that mandatory training?"

"Maybe for tactical. I went right from a school desk to a patrol craft." She narrowed her eyes at a woman wearing a serpent of shimmering silver fabric and more credits in jewelry than she made in a year. Any one of these people could feed a homeless child and not even notice the drain on their finances… but they didn't. *Selfish, arrogant, puffed-up—*

"Come." Konstantin grasped her arm.

Her imminent explosion of disgust burst into a bubble of apathy. Mute, she offered no protest as he tugged her by the arm to a table in the shade of an overhanging upper deck. Soft music filled the space, barely loud enough to be noticeable over the constant sound of the ocean. She picked a seat with her back facing the wall, giving her a view of the entire main deck save for one row of tables behind her. He sat beside her and waved at a steward who approached to pour them both champagne.

"We seem to continue to have these strange, difficult situations. I didn't realize you had a fear of water travel."

The entire room lurched slightly as the boat got underway. She didn't react much other than to stare curiously at the slight tilt in the champagne.

He smiled. "If not being on a boat, perhaps there is some company here you are not fond of?"

She found no answers waiting in her lap. *Yeah, you're still a rotten liar, K.* "I'm a mess about the case. I've found some evidence that has me worried about you. The bodies we keep finding all have the same kind of writing on them as the circle I asked you about."

"Hmm." Konstantin gazed out over the water. "Really? They found writing on them? How... curious. You think there is a connection to Charazu? I thought you banished it?"

"Yes, that particular demon is back where it belongs. But, I'm sure there's more involved—at least one living person responsible for summoning things. Every time they kill someone, they're sacrificing them to something bigger than Charazu. I don't want to say anything here. Too many ears."

"Charazu is a true demon, older than all of humanity. Older than the Earth. It never lived a mortal life. However, I wouldn't consider it powerful." He offered a pleasant nod. "I shall trouble you no more about it tonight. At least, not while we are here." He winked.

She eyed the partygoers, fighting the urge to scowl. "So, what are they celebrating?"

"My company has evidently purchased some shipping outfit. These decisions are made by people a few levels down."

Kirsten stared at him in disbelief. "Aren't you the CEO? Didn't you have to approve it?"

"Such innocence in your eyes." He chuckled. "Your naivety is beautiful, Kirsten. I have a majordomo who handles most of the day-to-day decisions. My role is more one of appearing at droll functions like this and smiling for the NewsNet. Without you here, I could not tolerate it."

An hour of random conversation about vacations at a mountain chalet and other fanciful things he planned once she could take time off passed in a blur. She held his hand for most of it, forgetting about the case, Commissioner Vernon, and all the work she still had to do. Did it really matter? She could quit; Konstantin had so much money she would never have to work again. Her mind filled with a daydream that involved her, Konstantin, a fireplace, bear-fur rug, a little house on an island somewhere—and it didn't involve clothes.

He excused himself to make some brief remarks at a podium about the acquisition of RedEx, assuring everyone that no significant personnel changes were planned for anyone in upper management. As far as the company was concerned, the only thing to change would be a name somewhere in a records system no one but lawyers ever look at. To the outside world, the company would remain 'RedEx.'

Kirsten spent the time of his speech watching Yevgeniy. The man's surface thoughts went by in Russian. The only emotions and images she could make sense of focused on the breasts to his left and right. She scowled at him. *Pig*. Her angry glare lingered until Konstantin walked in front of her, blocking her view. She smiled up at him.

"Well, now that the unpleasantness is over with, we have the rest of the night." Rather than sit, he extended a hand.

The boat had returned to port, timing its arrival within a few seconds of him concluding his remarks. She took his hand, involuntarily clinging to his side as if he would protect her from Yevgeniy. Surprisingly, the man she knew responsible for allowing demons into the world didn't remove his stare from his two female companions once the entire time, save for a brief handshake when Konstantin had taken the podium.

He walked her to the limo, holding her hand as she got in. After easing her door closed, he joined her via the other side and resumed holding her hand. "See now, Kirsten. No one is shooting at you, and you still have your shoes." He stroked his thumb over the back of her hand. "Are you sure you would rather be alone tonight? Perhaps we can seek the sanctuary of my estate and discuss the particulars of your investigation. I might be able to make sense of the inscriptions you found on the dead, if you have images."

Talking about dead people wasn't the preeminent thought on her mind at the mention of going to his mansion. Her mind took her back to that night on the curb when he kissed at her neck.

"I'd love to." She stretched her right arm out to cradle his cheek, the dragon ouroboros bracelet glittering in the moonlight.

She kissed him as best she could, but felt like a clueless teenager. He eased her into a more passionate, more adult kiss without once chuckling at her obvious inexperience. When they pulled apart, she shrank in on herself, overcome with shame. The man who'd given her beef stew had kissed her like that, too. Kirsten fidgeted at the bracelet, expecting he'd demand it back and kick her out of the car right there.

I didn't know what I was doing at twelve. I just laid there like a corpse. She kept petting the gold dragon around her wrist. *Konstantin's a real man. I'll do much better for him.* Shame peeled back, and she lifted her head, attempting a smile that asked if she did okay.

He smiled the grin of a man about to get something he had waited long for. His proximity filled her with warmth. The thin black dress became stifling. Her mind raced. Would he try to get her in bed tonight? Could she say yes? Her breathing sped up in time with her heart. She fidgeted, finding it strange how worked up she became at the mere thought of it. If she didn't find something to distract herself, mere desire would push her to the edge and back again before they ever made it to the manor house. She squirmed in her seat as need battled embarrassment. Her body wanted what her mind dreaded.

Not growing old alone had been one of Kirsten's primary goals for the better part of the last three years. Whenever she came close to finding someone, the P word (psionic, that is) brought things to a flaming halt. Now, she'd found a man who didn't care about her gift. The prospect of being *with* a man grew closer. Wonder at how different it would be than her first time made her tremble. This wouldn't be an act of desperation; this would be pure bliss.

A veritable force punched her in the gut. She clenched both hands over it, barely suppressing a groan of discomfort. Her arousal crashed to dread. The heat in her face flashed ice cold. Her thoughts shifted to Evan, an out-of-nowhere sense of horrible trepidation that something bad had happened to him. Konstantin's hand on her back snapped her out of the daze but made the queasiness worse.

"Are you feeling well, Kirsten? Please don't tell me the fish was bad."

"You're going to be mad at me. I have the worst feeling about Evan. It's too strong to be nerves. I... he's clairvoyant. He could be calling me for help. Something's wrong."

Konstantin's eyes narrowed to slits. He spent a moment staring out the window to his left.

A loud gurgle from her stomach made the driver glance back. Konstantin brushed the hair off her face, his expression softening. "You are a devoted mother. I would very much like you to have some of your own one day." He nodded. "Very well."

She grabbed his arm. "I'm really sorry, Konstantin. I don't know why this keeps happening. Maybe he's having separation anxiety. Maybe I could call him and we could still"—she doubled over from pain—"no, please, I have to make sure he's okay."

"I understand, *Lyubimaya.*" He patted the hand resting on her thigh. "I shall make arrangements for a private night, only the two of us. Tell me when you are ready."

Kirsten blinked. "Of course. I want to be with you so much." She fell against him again.

He held her until the limo stopped outside Nila's building. After they landed, he escorted her into the lobby.

"Perhaps I can wait here?" He winked. "Go, check on him. If all is well and you are feeling better, we could yet continue our special night."

Kirsten stared into his eyes, the strength leaking from her legs. "Okay, that—"

"Mom!" yelled Evan.

The boy squeezed himself past the elevator doors before they opened all the way, and ran to within ten paces of her, bare feet smacking loud over the lobby tiles. Powder-blue pajamas hung loose around him as he came to a halt and stared at Konstantin, a mixture of dread and challenge in his eyes.

"Mom, I need you." He shivered, balling his hands into fists.

The sight of the boy twisted the knot in her gut. His calm, almost threatening, tone scared her and washed any thought of a romantic evening out of her mind. She over and scooped him up, holding him tight.

"You shouldn't be out here with no shoes. The floor is ice cold. You're shivering."

He held onto her shoulders, never once taking his eyes off Konstantin. Kirsten kissed Evan on the side of the head, stroking his hair and offering an apologetic look to the man she adored.

"Do not worry." Konstantin smiled. "He is at that age. He does not like having competition for such a remarkable woman. Soon, he will understand it isn't competition. Perhaps our next night should include the boy?"

Evan's body tensed.

"It's something to think about," muttered Kirsten, unable to look at him.

"Excellent." Konstantin bowed. "Do let me know what he is fond of so

I can treat him on his birthday. Shall I drop the two of you off at your apartment?"

Evan let his head rest on Kirsten's shoulder and whispered, "Can we take a Pubcar?"

Kirsten winced. Her helpless expression asked a question her lips couldn't.

"All right. It will take the boy time." Konstantin stepped closer and tugged Kirsten into a brief kiss by one finger on her chin. "I shall see you soon."

"Thank you," whispered Kirsten.

Evan made a soft *blech* noise after Konstantin walked outside. Kirsten stood in place for a moment, waiting for a sudden bout of headache and nausea to pass. She clung to Evan until she felt at ease again, then carried him into the elevator.

"Let's grab your things from Nila's place and we'll go home. Did something happen? Did you have a bad dream?"

"No."

"You don't like him." Kirsten exhaled.

Evan shrugged. "He's old. You're too pretty for him. I don't trust him."

She laughed, making a goofy face as she tweaked his nose. "He's not that old."

He resisted her attempt to set him on his feet inside the elevator. "Sorry for bein' squeezy."

Dread wrapped around her heart. It probably wouldn't be long before she had to make a choice between the two of them. She gazed at their reflection in the silvery doors, and patted him on the back.

There is no choice.

KIRSTEN SPRAWLED ON THE FLOOR AT EVAN'S SIDE AFTER TUCKING HIM INTO his sleeping bag, stealing a few minutes of time with him before he passed out. She smiled to herself about Doctor Loring's nod of approval and thought about how best to give him a real bed. That would likely involve moving. This cheap apartment barely had enough room for her living alone.

The sound of him breathing in his dreams made her feel tired. With heavy limbs, she forced herself up, staggered to her cabinet, and peeled the expensive dress off. She squinted at herself in the small mirror, taking note of the dark smears under her eyes. After checking to make sure Evan remained asleep, she slipped out of her undies and into her pajamas. The bracelet snagged on the sleeve, causing her to hold her arm up and stare at the carved serpentine dragon eating its own tail.

Konstantin told her the ouroboros symbolized life, the endless cycle of death and rebirth. She tugged at it, twisted it, and found herself unable to remove it. She pinched the head, looking for a mechanism to unclasp the fangs from the tail. After fighting with it for ten minutes, and realizing she came close to falling asleep on her feet, she gave up.

Screw it, I haven't taken it off since he gave it to me... Sleeping in it one more night won't kill me.

She looked at her home terminal, thinking about the reports she needed to type up. "To hell with reports. They can wait. I'll be no help to anyone as a zombie."

Kirsten tiptoed to bed and all but melted into the Comforgel pad. For once, the damn thing lived up to its name. Sleepy Evan peeked over the side a moment later. She gave him an approving wink, and he climbed up to cuddle against her. He hadn't said much about that night, only that he'd had another bad dream about twin gold metallic dragons devouring her.

Curled up upon the warm semiliquid mass of Comforgel, with a contented Evan tucked under her right arm, Kirsten almost felt blessed.

INVASION

Kirsten's eyes opened with a mild stab of pain as thick eye-crumbles peeled apart. For some reason, she had trouble drawing a breath. She wheezed, gasping for air. Her mind took a few seconds to process the reason for her sudden consciousness—sixty-some pounds of terrified boy shaking her via a two-fisted grip of her pink pajama top.

She vaguely remembered him being unaffected by Theodore's presence. Obvious fear on his face meant one of two things: either he had a nightmare, or something more dangerous than a perverted ghost was nearby. Worry and protectiveness kicked the fog away from her brain., and with it came an explanation for why she could not breathe. Evan sat on her chest.

"Mom," he whispered, "there's a monster in the bathroom."

She clasped his hands, extricating his fingers from her shirt. She heaved a sigh of relief, but didn't relax all the way. Nightmare or actual monster remained up for debate. "Okay, I'll check."

He scooted around behind her as she sat up. She slipped out of bed and grumbled at the clock showing 3:06 a.m. Her body protested the tease of only five hours sleep as she plodded over to the bathroom door and pulled it open.

Amid a swirl of black vapor, a humanoid figure glared at her with bright white eyes. Its skin had the sheen of polished black leather, muscles angular and thin. Insectoid mandibles opened, peeling skin away from a more human-like set of silver teeth concealed by the flaps. Rather than feet, its legs ended in sharpened bone spurs. In the hollow of where intestines should be, several infant-faced serpents writhed, each as big around as a man's forearm. White skin striated with dark veins stretched, dripping dark violet ichor as the demonic cherubs snarled.

Kirsten had about enough time to blink before it raised two three-fingered hands in a shoving gesture. Telekinetic force slammed into her, hurling her off her feet and out into the main room. She smacked into the wall above the bed and fell face-first onto the Comforgel pad as Evan scrambled out of the way, screaming.

The impact knocked her senseless. Her mind shouted at her to move, but the muscles didn't listen. Evan's continuous howl moved from right to left in a circle, followed by hissing and the scraping of chitin.

"Mom!"

His shriek pushed aside her full-body pain. She gathered her feet under her and jumped to her feet. The creature held Evan upside down by his right ankle. He held his hands out, fingers splayed, focusing his astral power at the mass of serpentine hell-babies. They emitted disharmonic gurgling coos tinged with irritation as they writhed about in an unsuccessful effort to bite him. The

"Put him down!" shouted Kirsten while staggering toward it.

Flashing a toothy grin, it drew back its free hand, about to plunge long, black talons into Evan's exposed belly.

"No!" Kirsten roared. She wrapped her astral power around the abyssal's essence shoved with all of her desperation.

The demon blurred into a streak of black, rocketing into the wall as if hit by a nonexistent PubTran bus moving well past a hundred miles an hour. It mashed into the wall as if solid, black gunk spattering everywhere and dribbling out of its mouth. Evan fell on all fours, and scrambled upright. The creature peeled away from the wall and flopped to the ground in a tangle of broken limbs. Bones crunched and snapped as it twisted its head around to face her, eyes narrowing.

Evan started to run toward her, but skidded to a stop with a look of terror on his face and diverted to the bathroom. Hurt by the fearful look he gave her, Kirsten took a step to follow him but spun at a shadow moving behind her. The bed sheet loomed over her, wraith-like. Before she could process the sight, it pounced and engulfed her. She screamed with anger as it dragged her onto the bed, coiling around her in a boa's embrace.

Cloth covered her head and tightened around her neck. The sheet constricted around her from neck to ankles, grinding her knees together, pinning her arms, forcing the air from her chest. Kirsten squirmed, fighting to slide a hand up to her throat. She grasped the coil of linen around her neck and pulled, trying to ease the suffocating pressure.

Heavy thuds moved past her, bone spurs stabbing carpet-covered concrete. The light slap of Evan's feet on the bathroom floor punctuated his continued screams. She thrashed, losing a second or two to panic before her training took over. *The sheet isn't physical.* Kirsten shouted Evan's name in her mind and released a blast of psionic energy, shoving at anything paranormal. The sheet billowed out to a sphere around her, trembled, and popped like a bubble fluttering to the bed. She flung it off not a second before a tremendous *boom* reverberated from of the bathroom, followed by an uneasy child's squeal.

"Evan!" Kirsten shouted, leaping off the bed as she called the lash.

The sheet whipped at her, tightening around her ankle the instant her foot hit the floor. She caught a fleeting glimpse of the creature smashing its fists against the shower tube, the glimmer of an astral blockade flickering in the plastic. Her rush of pride that Evan had managed to do that gave way to anger at the beast threatening him. She flung the twelve-foot-long lash at the beast, but the sheet yanked her leg out from under her and hauled her backward. The tip of the energy stream missed the abyssal by an arm's length. Thunderous pounding continued in the bathroom, the noise as loud as cannons.

Kirsten clawed at the rug, trying to pull herself toward her son. She rolled onto her back and whipped at the bedclothes. The shimmering energy cord passed through the sheets with no discernible impact, but the sense of a tiny oblivion echoed in the back of her mind. The sheet ceased moving and went limp. She kicked it off her leg and sprang upright. When she whirled toward the bathroom, she came nose-to-chest with the large demon. Six pallid white serpents dangled from its abdomen like disemboweled intestines with demon-baby faces. They screamed in tiny high-pitched wails all at once and surged toward her, mouths open.

"Gah!"

She tried to jump back but tripped over the Comforgel bed and landed flat on her back. The abyssal descended on her. Hot, bone-hard hands clamped around her wrists, claws piercing her skin, pinning her down.

The serpents twisted and wound about each other, stretching longer. Malformed faces of six demonic horrors somewhere between infants and little old men hovered close to her face. Tiny lips twisted into sinister grins, revealing blackened gums studded with rotting teeth. They wavered about as each nudged the others away in an effort to get a closer look at her.

All six screamed and lunged forth to devour her.

Kirsten cringed away, feeling nothing but a faint awareness of slime running over her neck. Weight no longer held her down; claws no longer pierced her arms. Her head rolled straight, gaze fixed upon the ceiling. Calm overtook her, as if everything now made perfect sense. She knew exactly what needed to be done.

"NO, NO, NO!" SCREAMED EVAN. "STUPID MACHINE."

Soaking wet in his pajamas, he pressed his face into the tube wall trying to see into the room outside the bathroom. Everything had gone quiet, but he didn't trust the sound as much as he did the feeling in his gut. A shadow changed; Kirsten sat up, pivoted, and planted her feet on the carpet.

"Did you kill it?" he yelled, to no response.

She grasped the E-90, lifting it from the nightstand and caressing like a beloved kitten while clutching it to her chest. After a moment, she pivoted toward the bathroom with a military heel turn. Evan backed into the other side of the tube, squinting at the assault of soap-laden water drenching him. Something didn't feel right.

"Stupid shower came on." He grumbled, banging his elbow on the console twice.

Kirsten stepped into the light, a bruise around her right ankle visible under the pink leg of her pajamas. Her sleeves had soaked with blood from midway between wrist and elbow, crimson lines trailed over the E-90 and dripped on the tile floor.

Pat... pat... pat...

He stared at her face, at the horrible, evil, murderous grin. She raised her weapon; jet-black eyes sighted over the laser pointed right at him. Mom wasn't Mom right now.

Pat... pat... pat...

"Mommy!" he screamed, slapping his hands on the tube. "The demon got you!"

She became super-squeezy every time he called her Mommy. He hoped it would be enough to snap her out of it. The weapon trembled. He remembered her saying she could never hurt him. Evan stood his ground, growing angry at the creature for attacking his *real* mother.

"Mommy!" He roared, as much as a nine-year-old could roar. A wave of psionic energy flew out of him, trying to knock the bad thing out of her.

KIRSTEN BLINKED. WARM LIQUID, TEARS PERHAPS, RAN DOWN HER CHEEKS. One second she lay on the bed with those horrible little faces hovering over her. The next, she stood in the bathroom—with a gun pointed at Evan. Her breath sputtered in an erratic gasp. She forced her arm down. Black vapor gathered around her body and fell to the floor, drawing backward into the outer room.

Evan started to smile, but his eyes shot open wide. "Behind you!"

She whirled. The abyssal dragged itself up behind her, crawling over the rug. The sudden ejection from a possessed host seemed to have crippled it. Kirsten shuddered in rage at the idea of what it almost made her do. She tossed the E-90 to the bathmat and summoned the Astral Lash.

One of the baby-serpents poked out from beneath the creature and spat a stream of black gunk. She charged past it, emitting a furious scream while raking the glimmering whip in a downstroke straight into the slinking abyssal's face. The infant-headed serpent flopped about as if electrocuted. A deep bass howl accompanied by a cacophony of tiny infant-like screams tore the air.

Overcome with grief and anger, she grabbed the lash in both hands, striking out again and again in a blind rage, barely aware of anything more than a dark mass in front of her. The fourth time she whipped the energy stream into it, the abyssal exploded into a cloud of inky fog.

A sense of obliteration blasted outward along with the headache which so often followed a hard mind blast. She fell to her knees and went over forward. Bloody hands clutched at the carpet; the sight of red ignited fires in her arms where claws had pierced. A rush of warm, humid air hit her from behind. Evan emerged from the tube through shimmering flecks of light from the dissipating blockade.

"You're bleeding," he said.

Kirsten crawled around to face him and sat back on her heels. He looked miserable, soaked and dripping in his wet pajamas. Such guilt came over her, she cried.

"You said you couldn't hurt me. I knew you wouldn't." He leaned forward and kissed her on the cheek.

She pulled him into her lap, cradling him, water and all, and mumbled apologies into his hair.

"Mom?"

"Yeah?" She sniffled, and raised her head to look him in the eye. "Yes?"

"You're still bleeding. Take a stimpak before you get sick."

Kirsten made a noise somewhere between laughing and bawling. Evan tugged at her until she stood, and dragged her to the bed. Numb, she sat on the edge of the Comforgel pad in dazed silence watching him fetch a handful of stimpaks from her belt. While she jabbed herself in the arm with one, he stripped off his soaked PJs, and dried off with a towel before wrapping it around himself and walking over.

"Coffee?" he asked.

"It's not even four in the morning."

Arms folded to his chest under the terrycloth wrap, he stepped up until their foreheads almost touched, his expression serious. One droplet of water fell off his nose. "Are *you* going back to sleep?"

Kirsten leaned out and ruffled his hair. "Mocha."

MENTAL NOTES

The din of voices tugged at the edges of Kirsten's consciousness. She moaned: a noise that began deep in her brain as a request for a few more minutes of sleep, but entered the world as a monosyllabic grunt. Her right forearm balanced over her face. As her sphere of awareness widened, she noticed the absence of Evan. He should've been curled up next to her. With another groan, tried to lift her arm, but it flopped on her stomach and slid off. Cold floor across the back of her knuckles reminded her she'd crashed on a sofa in the squad room.

She pawed at the cushions, searching for the missing boy, sitting up after she found no trace of him. White socks at the end of her black leggings confused her. She didn't remember taking her boots off, or even putting her uniform on. The desks all sat empty except for Morelli's. As usual, he made it a point not to look directly at her.

"Dorian?" she rasped, forcing herself to swallow.

Morelli fumbled something small and plastic, which clattered to the floor.

"Evan went to school about an hour ago. Someone from the dorm came to escort him over." Dorian coalesced beside her. "I'm to tell you Eze wants to see you when you wake up."

Kirsten held her face in both hands, elbows on her knees, trying to rub wakefulness into her eyelids. "How long was I out? Wait, Eze can see you?"

"No, he just spoke assuming I was here. It's about ten now. The two of you arrived a little after five in the morning. Bad night?"

She stared at her boots, unable to fathom how to work the fasteners along the outer edge. Confusion lasted only until she slid her legs into them, at which point, the task became automatic. With another groan, she stretched away the discomfort of a five-hour sofa nap.

"An abyssal came after us in the apartment last night. Bastard thing got me half-awake, slipped into my head. My defenses weren't ready."

Dorian put his hands on his hips. "Evan gave me the rundown."

"Someone tried to get me to..." She pivoted toward Eze's door. "Now I'm pissed."

"Oh, shit." Dorian held his hands up. "Look out."

"Dammit, I'm serious." Kirsten managed to stop glaring by the time she entered the captain's office. "Sorry for passing out like that, sir. I had an event at home last night."

"Yes, so I hear." Eze looked up from his terminal, chair creaking as he leaned back. "The boy filled me in."

"Did he sleep at all?"

Eze laughed. "He said he'd nap in math class. To be honest, I'm not sure if he was kidding."

Sounds like something my kid would say. Kirsten smiled. "Sir, I'm at a loss. I have scraps of things that don't make sense and some theories—but no evidence I can take to the council."

"Alright." Captain Eze steepled his fingers to his chin. "Let's hear it."

She sat facing the desk, casting a brief glance over the row of four-inch ceremonial African masks at the edge. "Okay, I went to the morgue..." *Shit, I forgot to type the reports.* "I had a suspicious feeling about some recent killings. I went to the RTC to follow up on it, and found evidence of what appears to be some kind of ritual murders. While I was there, one of the clerks called to warn someone I was getting too close. Then he tried to kill me. I chased him, but he shot himself and destroyed his NetMini in the process."

Eze reached toward his terminal, swiping past a few screens. "I read what Div 2 filed. However, the investigation has stalled pending your reports. Do you think Hassan acted of his own volition?"

"I never got the chance to find out. I didn't see a spirit lingering after he died, nor did I feel Harbingers around. If he had a ghost, he ran off before I entered the room."

"If?" Eze leaned back with a raised eyebrow. "I did not think spirits were optional."

"I…" She gazed into space. "Dammit, I have so many reports to catch up. The incident at the Pentecostal place, B. G. Wallis. Those idiots with the knives had no ghosts. I think they were bodies worn by demons. I still don't know if they were killed ahead of time, displaced, or stolen from a morgue."

"So these 'abyssals' were inside them?"

"I think so, yes. Perhaps not abyssals, but definitely dark spirits. Weak, too. The people ran at armed officers with nothing but knives. I'm thinking it was some kind of trap, like the entities *wanted* to be killed. Maybe they somehow fed off the aggression of murder."

Captain Eze shifted his gaze to his terminal again, staring at it for a few seconds before saying, "I spent two hours with Chandrasekhar yesterday afternoon."

"Who?"

"Division 1 Bureau Chief. I had to give a statement about what happened at the church. He asked how you were doing."

Kirsten frowned at the little masks. "I couldn't save Womack. The man was so strong, he threw me around like a rag doll."

"They don't blame you. You tried everything you could think of to keep them outside. It was my error insisting they accompany you." He tapped his finger on the desk and met her stare. "I wanted to apologize for over-coddling you."

"No offense taken, sir." She couldn't quite smile so soon after remembering the death of a police officer. "It's nice to be cared for. In your place, I probably would've made the same decision. I'm sure you didn't fully believe my story about demons at the time. But, back to the case, I think the nexus is a man named Yevgeniy Suvorin. He's the majordomo of Kukla Investment Corporation. I can't see any other common thread among the dead."

Kirsten explained her findings on the bodies. Arris, the security guard from the Archives. Connected to VSKK via Konstantin having an office there. Donn, the engineer, worked for EnMesh, which Kukla recently purchased—direct connection to Yevgeniy. The woman, Munoz, worked for RedEx, which VSKK just acquired—connection: Konstantin. The two men appeared to be friends, which linked both spheres together.

"What of Mr. Rosa?" asked Eze. "Did he not manage security at the Municipal Complex?"

"Yes." She nodded. "Commissioner Vernon is under the influence of a paranormal entity, much the same way one tried to make me hurt Evan." Kirsten scrunched her fingers into the seat cushion. "I bet they took Mr. Rosa first to get inside, and got rid of him when he was no longer useful. The trade deal being pushed around now would benefit the entire ACC."

"Need I remind you your friend Konstantin's company *is* based in the ACC. Sure, they are in a moderate quasi-republic, but they remain loyal to the ACC when push comes to shove."

Kirsten's head shook with an emphatic negative. "That's the whole point. Yevgeniy is trying to ruin him! He's the majordomo for his company, and he wants the whole thing."

Captain Eze tilted his head. "Didn't you just say Yevgeniy is the majordomo for Kukla?"

She bit her lip, absentmindedly fingering the dragon bracelet. "Sorry. I misspoke. He's Kukla. And he's trying to take Konstantin's company away from him."

"What has you so convinced Konstantin is a target and not an actor?" The holo-terminal bathed Captain Eze in light from a new page tinting his face from deep chocolate to light brown. "He does possess familiarity with the archaic language you keep finding, does he not?"

She gawked at him. "How could you even suggest that? He loves me!" Kirsten covered her mouth with both hands and swallowed. "Sorry, sir." Her gaze fell into her lap. "I mean, if he had anything to do with it, why would he try to cuddle up to me? I'm the one chasing the abyssals around. Hell, he gave me Charazu's name—I couldn't have destroyed it without that. I think Yevgeniy has been after him for years. He had to learn Sumerian to protect himself. Over there, the government kills people for being psionic. Who knows what the hell they'd do to a person for claiming to be at war with demons. It's probably no big deal to him anymore."

"Keep your friends close, and your enemies closer."

"Sun Tzu?" she asked.

Eze smiled. "Not exactly. It's from *The Godfather*, I think. Did you ever consider he may just want you where he can watch you?"

Kirsten shuddered. "No, that can't be true. He's so sweet. I feel safe around him."

"Have you considered the possibility he is influencing you?"

"I'm a Grade 3 suggestive. If he was doing something to me, I'd feel it. I'd know." She twisted the bracelet around her arm feverishly.

"Perhaps a telempath?"

"I..." She stared down. "I don't think so. Telempathic manipulation feels false once they stop concentrating on it. If it's powerful, it feels genuine in the moment, but the victim always gets a sense they were manipulated later. I don't feel that from him. I saw one of the murders happen in the memories of a witness."

"Oh." He perked up. "What did they see?"

Kirsten relayed the scene of Alaina Munoz's murder: the four men, the mask, the chanting, and rambled over a ten-minute grumble about Lace and Brooke's plight. When she reined in her runaway emotion over that poor girl, she gave him a forlorn pout. "There are two other men involved in that murder. I can see them in my head, but I have no way to connect them back to anyone."

Eze spun in his chair. He took a small black case from the shelf behind him, then whirled back, peeling plastic film bearing a Teradyne logo away from the thin box, which he opened. She sat, quiet and patient, as he unpacked a blank holodisk and inserted it into a writer on his desk. The spindle of four two-inch silver disks sank into the device seconds before a motorized hatch closed and it spun up to speed.

He leaned forward, left hand on top of the holodisk writer. "Focus on the memory, Kirsten."

She sat up, hands on the edge of the desk, and locked eyes with him. Relaxing, she let his telepathic feelers enter her thoughts. Kirsten called Brooke's memory of the attack on Ms. Munoz to mind, trying to pay attention to the faces of the two men holding her arms. A sense of light-headedness came on, a 'heavier' sensation than what happened normally when someone read from her thoughts. The pupils and irises of Eze's eyes had faded away, leaving them all-white. The small electronic device beneath his hand whirred and beeped.

A little over a minute later, the writer wound down and stopped. He put a hand to his tired face and rubbed his forehead. When he lowered his arm, his eyes had gone back to their normal deep brown. He ejected the holo-disk, popped it into its case, and handed it to her. "Here, you should be able to get a searchable face print from this."

Kirsten accepted the holodisk as if it were a holy relic, cupping it with reverence in both hands. "I had no idea you could do that."

"It is a simple thing, Wren. No different than someone with a wire." He poked himself behind the ear. "It is a link between my mind and a device. The writer did all the real work." He winked.

She stood, still cradling the disk, and ferried it out to her desk and popped it in her terminal's reader. Eze had transferred the images from her memory onto the disk, creating a video recording that appeared taken with an old, blurry lens. Kirsten spent a few minutes scanning frame by frame to a point she could isolate a still image of the suspects' faces. The distant city had strange artifacts, products of blurry memory or random subconscious flights of fancy. In almost all glass surfaces, a phantasmal version of Konstantin appeared, gazing at her. The faces conveyed no emotion, but every one of dozens stared right at her. *He's watching me.* Warmth swirled around her insides. She smiled to herself while absentmindedly stroking the bracelet. *I guess I'm thinking about him when I don't realize it.*

Aside from mild graininess due to the nonstandard interface between Eze's brain and the writer, the video surprised her with its clarity. She drew a box around the face of both men. The one holding Alaina's right arm had his back to Brooke for most of the event; however, she managed to grab a profile image when he shifted to walk away.

She set the system going in search of a facial match and started on the reports and incident forms for everything that had happened thus far. For quite a few minutes, she glanced at Eze with envious squints. Before he made Captain, he could fill out reports in mere seconds. Then again, most non-psionic cops who opted for an M3 port in their skulls could do the same. Having a wire connecting them to cyberspace made a lot of things easy and fast. Kirsten shuddered at the thought.

No metal inside me. I'd rather type all day.

Two hours later, she left the search going and took a break to meet Evan in the dorm area for lunch. After a pleasant forty minutes, she returned to find a red square flashing on two separate display panels. On the left screen, a close-up of one man from the telepathic transfer was frozen at the precise instant he appeared to make eye contact with the viewer. The other pane contained a dozen possible matches.

It took only a minute of running down the short list for something to jump out at her. A coincidence too glaring to ignore—a man by the name of Randall Morris was a ninety percent match on the face and a security guard for EnMesh Corporation. Kirsten leaned back in her chair, squinting at he still-flashing images where system still attempted to match the other man.

"Think that's the guy?" asked Dorian.

She glanced up at him, then back to the employee record for Mr.

Morris. "Nothing in his file says anything about him having lost an arm or gotten a cybernetic prosthetic. Am I losing my mind or is the relationship to EnMesh strange to you?"

He glanced at the estimated progress bar on the other process. "We probably have enough time to pay this guy a visit and come back before that finds anything. What about the other close matches?"

"Morris is the second most likely match at ninety percent. This guy," she said, flipping two images to the left, "has been on Mars for the past six months working for a geological survey company."

Dorian chuckled. "He doesn't look like a scientist."

"Private security force." Kirsten locked her terminal and stood. "Most of the hits are either mercenaries, criminals, or military. Four of them have been in prison for more than a year."

"Well, then… let's go talk to Mr. Morris."

She took a step for the door, but did a one-eighty toward the locker room. "Yeah. Be right out, gonna grab armor."

"Ahh, she's learning."

Kirsten sighed. "I'm much happier chasing the dead. *Ghosts* I'm equipped to deal with."

HELPING HAND

Three minutes into the flight, the location of Randall Morris's NetMini appeared on the navigation console. Kirsten pulled back on the stick to climb out of the traffic lane, and hit the bar lights. Blotches of abnormal color shimmered on nearby buildings, aftereffects of the windscreen filtering out glare. She lined up on the glowing yellow line stretching off over the city courtesy of her electronic windshield.

Her course resulted in a slalom path between buildings, cutting diagonally across the city's grid layout. A quarter mile into the flight, a young man with light brown hair appeared as a holographic floating head in the middle of the console.

"Unit 1815-014, request verification for noncompliant traversal of Sector Grid. I'm not seeing any incident alarms active in accordance with your vector at this time." He blinked at something to his left. "Uhh, 014... Division 0?"

He looks seventeen. "You look new, Lumford. Is this your first week?"

"Holy shit! You *are* psychic."

Dorian and Kirsten spoke at the same time, though Junior Tech Lumford only heard her. "Your name is on your uniform." She steered into a left swerve around a black glass tower. "Not bad. You're right about Zero. Do you know what the 1 stands for?"

"Uhh..." Lumford's eyes shifted around as if hunting for something around his terminal. After two seconds, he locked onto something. "Investigation, uhh investigative operations."

"Ooh, you really are new. Still have the cheat sheet on your cube wall." She smiled. "Yep. What else does that tell you?"

"You're going to *retire* someone?" He turned pale.

Kirsten glared, making him jump back in his seat. "No, Lumford. That's Division 9. Zero doesn't assassinate anyone."

"We're here to usher in a new era of service." Dorian spoke in the cadence of a used-hovercar salesman, fists on his hips while wearing a plastic smile.

"Ugh, I hated those commercials," whispered Kirsten.

"Uhh, I-Ops..." He stared into space for several seconds before looking up. "You're a detective, not enlisted—an officer." Lumford remained pale, and fumbled with a salute.

She returned it. "I'm trying to intercept a potential suspect, Lumford. I'm not pulling a Division 1 and using the lights to race home for a mid-day fuck break." The same hand she used to salute cut the comm.

"Wow... that's kind of unlike you. Bad mood?" Dorian raised an eyebrow.

"Maybe I'll send him a text later and apologize for giving him a hard time. It just pisses me off that these jackasses from Div 1 skirt traffic protocol *constantly*, but when I do it for a real issue, I get the just-out-of-the-academy radio guy who wants to boss a couple of beat cops around."

"So what's got you in the bad mood?"

"I just have this feeling Morris isn't going to get me anywhere."

Dorian's eyebrows crept upward a tick. "Really? There's nothing more than that?"

"I'm worried about Evan, alright? A demon got into my apartment last night and tried to kill us both. I had six little creepy-ass snow-white babies from hell trying to bite my face off at three in the damn morning. So yeah, maybe I'm a little on edge when I get shit for driving diagonally across the city." She grumbled a few non-words while twisting her hands around the control sticks. "It's like whoever is doing this is two steps ahead of me every bit of the way. I feel..." Kirsten's gaze fell to her lap.

"You're not helpless, Kirsten. You never were." He pointed. "Umm, building."

The crash avoidance got emitted two warning beeps before she swerved, still faster than the automatic override. She rolled out of the maneuver, pulling up past the hundredth-story mark and gliding in a graceful arc over the last two miles. Off to the left, the Y-shaped road bisecting this sector into three small districts gleamed in the waning midafternoon sun. On final approach to Morris's apartment, she shut off the bar lights and circled.

"Wow, I thought I lived in a crappy area. The map must be wrong. This looks like a grey zone."

"Nah, Sector 40 is just a bad part of town. There's no disavowed sector anywhere near here."

Landing on the roof proved easier than expected. While not designed for residents to own hovercars, the building did have two landing pads for emergency vehicles. Kirsten glanced at the slab of light bobbing over her left arm and confirmed her target—or at least his NetMini—was still here, quite a distance below on the fifth floor. After pawing the 'shutdown and lock' button, she hopped out and hurried to the roof access elevator.

She stared at the floor ticker counting down.

"Something wrong with your arm?" asked Dorian.

"No."

"You keep fidgeting with the arm guard."

"Oh, just Konstantin's bracelet." She smiled at the sound of his name.

"You should have left it in your locker. It's as thick as a finger. It could break your wrist if you take a hit in the arm."

"Someone might steal it." She put the uncomfortable tightness under the rigid armor out of her mind. "Besides, it will bring me luck."

"Are you feeling alright, K? I'm not used to seeing you go from anxious and moody to grinning so fast."

"You grumble at me for being short with the radio guy, and now you're grumbling at me for being too chipper?" She blinked. "What do you want me to do?"

"Now I know something's wrong with you, K. You're not this belligerent."

She drew in a breath, finger up, but stopped when the doors opened. "Maybe I am just shitting bricks that I'm not gonna be able to save Vernon. Stupid council."

Kirsten stomped past six apartment doors before hanging a right and passing three more. Turning on her heel, she raised her boot to smash the door in. *Wait.* Foot down. She tried to rub her face, but couldn't with the sealed helmet. *I don't even know for sure this guy is involved yet. Slow down.*

"I think you might need a vacation, K—after we figure this one out."

"Yeah, maybe." She pushed the door buzzer.

A double-blink of her eye aimed at the right spot switched on tactical mode. Sensors in the armor rendered the apartment on the other side of the wall in a wireframe of glowing lines traced over the real world. Toward the back right corner, a hazy figure loped out of a hallway and leaned into the living room.

"Fuck off, I'm not buying shit."

"Mr. Morris, I'm with the police. I have a few questions to ask you."

The amber ghost of a man sprinted across the room to what appeared to be a closet door. When he leaned back, he fumbled with a large rifle.

"He's going for a gun!" Kirsten backed away from the door.

"On it." Dorian leapt through the wall.

"Console, command override." Kirsten looked at the apartment door and blinked. A rectangle of yellow light flickered over it, as if the door reacted in the manner of a clicked-on desktop icon. "Shit, this is a lot faster than my armband."

The door snapped open, allowing the sound of Randall Morris's muttered cursing into the hall. He rattled a power-drained rifle, smacking it with a metal right hand. Kirsten ducked in, E-90 aimed.

"On the floor, Morris."

He hurled the firearm at her, making her flinch enough to foil her aim as he ducked around a corner into a hallway. Kirsten chased, nearly sliding into a fall on a loose throw rug. Rapid motion and numerous walls caused the ghost of his estimated position on her HUD to falter. She rounded the corner and skidded to a stop, staring at a small, black canister bouncing toward her.

"Shi—!"

She crossed her arms over her face and poured mental energy into the psi armor. A second later, the deafening explosion of a stun grenade threw her to the ground in a sliding skid. The visor blocked out most of the flash, though the concussion left her disoriented until a large, meaty hand clamped around her neck and lifted her into the air. Her mind snapped out of the daze, but her body didn't want to move yet. She moaned, trying to raise the E-90, but flopped around like Brooke hopped up on muscle relaxants.

Randall grinned at his helpless target, taking his time to flutter the fingers of his cybernetic left arm before balling it into a fist. He drew his arm back to pound her in the face, but Dorian flew by attempting to grab him, passing through without contact. The big guy twitched and glared around in confusion.

Kirsten concentrated on Randall's thoughts and lit off a Mind Blast. Her rapid assault of psionic energy knocked him loopy. His hand opened and she fell straight down like a sack of meat packed in armor.

A little cartoon face surrounded by animated sweat droplets appeared on the right side of her HUD. "Stim-suit not detected, automatic adrenaline cannot be deployed."

"Fuck you, too," muttered Kirsten.

Randall staggered down to one knee, holding his head. "Ngh, what the hell?"

Dorian continued trying to apply a technically perfect police ass whipping, but the minimal solidity he generated didn't have much effect on the seven-foot Morris. The instant a little control returned to her body, Kirsten dragged herself away, fear and anger conspiring to force her stunned muscles back into compliance. Hundreds of tiny metal dots littered the floor and walls, spent electrodes from the stun grenade. She pulled herself up with the help of a small table, and whirled into a kick. Her boot caught Randall on the side of the head, knocking him flat. Added to the effects of a Mind Blast, the hit made him to vomit.

She pounced on his back, gathering his still-human right arm in a chicken wing hold.

"He's gonna snap the binders with that thing. You need a medusa." Dorian scowled at his inability to do more than offer advice.

"Don't have one." She held the E-90 to the back of Randall's head. "Don't move shithead. Ops, request backup, my location. Suspect augmented."

A woman's face shimmered in on the left side of the HUD long enough to speak three words. "Copy that, agent."

She leaned forward, bracing her left arm across the back of his neck. Her weight balanced half on her knees and half where she sat on the small of his back. Morris grumbled and coughed up a bubble of puke. Kirsten grinned to herself. *Even if this idiot won't talk, all I have to do is ask and he'll think about it.*

"Who are you working fo—"

Seething hot pain exploded in her left thigh.

Question became scream.

Kirsten gaped in shock at the vibro-blade embedded in the armor on her leg. The two-inch wide weapon had sprung to the rear from the elbow of the cyberlimb, and gone deep enough in to find bone. As if the pain of a stab wound didn't hurt enough, the hypersonic oscillations heated the metal beyond agony.

Randall twisted his body, simultaneously yanking his left elbow blade out of her leg while bashing his right elbow into her face. Kirsten flew backward and bounced off the wall. The scent of burned blood and cooked meat rose into the air. He whirled around and pounced on top of her, covering her helmet with his metal left hand, squeezing. Aiming with hope, she twisted her E-90 upward and fired. It missed, but came close enough to make him release her helmet and grab the gun.

The instant she could see, Kirsten pounded him in the brain with another Mind Blast. Morris emitted a grunting screaming squeal and staggered away, grabbing his face.

"I don't have a Medusa, but…" Kirsten two-handed the E-90, and aimed at the start of the metal by his armpit. She fired a long beam, raking it over the limb and slicing it off. A small burst of orange sparks leapt into the air as the metal limb ceased moving and fell to the floor with a *thud*. "Randall Morris, it's a violation of UCF law, Section CI-42 D, for a felon to possess a cybernetic prosthesis with a rating beyond rehabilitative. You've committed attempted murder on a police officer, which is a felony. So… I can't let you keep that thing."

Howling, his cauterized stump wagging, an enraged Randall Morris palmed the top of Kirsten's helmet and rammed her head into his knee. She bounced away and fell, dazed. Her armor absorbed most of the energy of the impact, but the hit left her staring at a spinning hallway.

Dorian shouted as he forced himself into the world of the living, a trace of glowing skull shimmered from beneath his skin. "Get away from her!"

Seven-foot, 340-pound Randall Morris shrieked with the voice of a six-year-old girl. After soiling himself, he sprinted down the rest of the hallway and dove headfirst out the window. Several seconds later, the deep, echoing *whump* of a body striking a dumpster rang out. Kirsten tried to stand, but collapsed with both hands on her left thigh, screaming. Dorian dropped to one knee and grabbed her shoulders.

"Go, chase him. Find him. There's no one else here."

"I can't leave you."

"I'm not helpless. Go. Don't let the fucker get away."

Dorian closed his eyes, shaking his head. He leapt to his feet and sank into the floor. Kirsten dragged herself against the wall, unable to hold back wails of pain as her leg moved. Outside, sirens closed in on the area.

Captain Eze's face appeared on the left side of her visor. "Wren, your armor's transmitting crazy bio readings. What happened?"

"Got stabbed in the thigh. Bleeding a little." Kirsten glanced at the scarily large stain on the rug under her. "Shit, I'm in trouble. He must've hit the femoral. I shot a cyberarm off this bastard..." She slumped to the ground. "Make sure it gets to Div 2."

Dorian's face came out of nowhere, filling her vision. She looked up, unable to speak. He leaned closer, his hands settled on the sides of her head and slipped down to her shoulders. Lightheadedness came on worse. A blanketing of coldness washed over her.

The tromp of approaching boots barely reached her consciousness.

WARM.

Weightless.

Goop.

Yay. Naked time. A brief check with her hand confirmed it. *Well, at least I'm alive.*

"Agent Wren," said a woman's voice from everywhere. "We're about to drain the tank. You may experience some lingering discomfort in your thigh. The pain is only in your head. Your leg is no longer injured."

She reached up and gathered her hair tight to her neck, leaving her eyes closed, and let gravity take her down to a seated position at the base of the medical tank. Before the doctor said a word, she assumed the position: head down, ass in the air. Choking the breathable gel out of her lungs felt less like drowning and more like a bad flu this time. The clear glass barrier rotated a quarter turn then sank into the floor. Cold air washed over her. She sat back on her heels and wiped her mouth off on the back of her arm. After a moment of savoring the breeze on her face, she opened her eyes.

Her left thigh sported a two-inch strip of pink, a scrap of brand new skin that didn't match the paleness around it. She held her arms away from her body, cringing at the sensation of the gel all over her. Trying to be casual at wearing only slime, she tried to walk unassisted like a normal person—which proved incompatible with slippery goo and bare feet. Halfway to the shower tube, she wiped out and landed on her ass. A medtech and a doctor ran over and helped her up while wrapping her in a towel. The tech swabbed a smaller towel around her face.

She coughed, spitting up more into a teal tray one of them handed her.

"You may be woozy for a few hours, agent. You lost quite a bit of blood. In some ways, it was good he had a vibro blade. It partially cauterized the vessel and slowed the bleeding. Also, whatever psionic talent you used to cool your body off helped. I think it made the difference."

"That would be a ghost saving my life." She offered a weak smile, and accepted their help for balance on the way to the autoshower.

The medical staff exchanged a glance.

"After you clean up, you should eat something." The doctor pulled her robe open and gestured at her ribs and hips. "Preferably something with protein."

"Thanks." Kirsten blinked as she reached out to activate the wash cycle, surprised to find the gold bracelet still on her wrist. Not even one carved scale appeared out of place. She glanced at the medical tank for a moment, then back at the jewelry.

Strange. I guess nanobots don't have a taste for gold.

Kirsten looked up from the tray of food, flashing a silly grin at Evan.

He stared at her, still red-eyed. The smile he cracked was only for her benefit.

"Sorry I scared you."

Evan pushed mashed potatoes around his tray.

"Hey, you helped. They know you're clairvoyant, sweetie. When you got scared, they came looking for me."

He pushed his tray away, next to hers, and crawled under the table to her side. She squeezed his shoulder and ran her hand through his hair. He nibbled on a nugget of battered vat-grown chicken. Watching him tease his food around for another few minutes without eating was too much for her. She broke into sobs and pulled him into a hug.

He eventually squirmed around and stared intently at her for a long moment. His expression of worry became one of calm, and he smiled. Kirsten composed herself and let him cling, continuing to stroke his hair while he ate as though nothing was wrong. His sudden acceptance made her feel uneasy. *Well, I guess it's a good sign when a clairvoyant stops worrying about you getting hurt.* She smirked. *Guess that means I'll live at least another few months.*

28

MISPLACED

K irsten fell back in her chair with both hands over her face, a little after eight at night.

The last of the reports done, she finally had a moment to breathe. At a chime from her terminal, she spread her fingers apart to stare between them at the window that popped up. Her Citycam search came up blank for hits on the second face; however, a cross-division feeler received a hit from Div 9: an eighty-two percent match on a man named Nafiz Ajouri, suspected of being involved with international smuggling.

She scooted up to her desk read over various details. The man trafficked in art objects, historic relics, corporate intelligence, even humans in a handful of cases. Fortunately, they listed him as 'low' for risk of violence. Kirsten narrowed her eyes at the file image, trying to reconcile it against her memory of reading Brooke's mind. It seemed as likely to be him as not. *Profile searches suck. This is next to useless.* Kirsten tapped her fingers on the desk, frowned, and cross-checked Nafiz Ajouri against any ACC affiliation with Kukla or VSKK. Kirsten stared at the spinning 'please wait' icon, her head spinning around involuntarily.

Somewhere, deep in cyberspace, hundreds of thousands of transactions collided in a spectacular storm of electrons. Vid calls, financial exchanges, medical records, all possible points where the entity of Nafiz Ajouri may have had contact with either company. She imagined a CPU core two hundred miles away in a GlobeNet cluster ticking one degree warmer.

"Why are you comparing him to those two companies?"

Kirsten shot upright in her chair, screaming at Captain Eze's voice coming out of nowhere from behind. "Holy crap..." She grabbed her chest. "Sir... Sorry." Blush. "Umm, because I don't have ninety-one days to check him against *every* Russian corporate entity."

He allowed a trace of apology to leak out in a smile. "I think you should trust your instincts."

Beep.

Kirsten squinted. "What the hell is Koloss Venture Capital? How did the search give me that?"

"Probably a few layers in," said Eze, rounding her desk on the way to his office. "Let me know if you need any assistance."

"Can you ask the council to let me sneak up on Commissioner Vernon?"

Eze's voice echoed from inside his office, a baritone half-shout. "I said assistance, not act of God."

"I didn't think you believed in the sky wizard?" said Kirsten.

Eze poked his head back into the room. "I don't. But it's more likely he exists than the council will let you near Vernon without concrete evidence."

She sighed.

He ducked out of sight into his office.

Kirsten poked the line on the holo-panel. Koloss VC had issued a payment to Nafiz for C400,000 five months ago. The comments held little of use, something about an expedition to North Africa. *Probably smuggling some priceless national treasure into Russia.*

The VidPhone on her desk went off, scaring the second shriek out of her in five minutes. Eze stood to give her a quizzical look via his window.

Wren, are you alright? You seem wound rather tight lately.

She looked up with a sad stare. *I have three days left to stop Division 9 from murdering an innocent woman. Can't you call that off?*

He sent a defeated gaze at the floor, shaking his head.

"Kirsten?" Samuel Chang's smiling face shimmered into view over her desk, a life-sized hologram.

"Hi, Sam."

"How are you doing?" He leaned on his hand, wearing an enormous—and slightly dazed—grin.

She tried not to take out her mood on him. "I'm having a shitty week. Quite shitty actually. Post-bad-Mexican-food-with-a-heavy-flu shitty. I almost bled to death a few hours ago, got attacked in my own apartment by a demon a day ago... Oh yeah, in three more days, the government is gonna murder someone unless I prove them wrong. So, yeah, I'm peachy keen."

"If there's anything I can do for you, Kirsten, please ask. I..." He looked to his right, and spun back with a smile. "I have a hit on the cyberarm you recovered. It's an Intera Iron Claw series. Very similar in handprint to a NinTek Warrior. Factoring in that bizarre withering effect, this arm is a ninety-four percent probable match. It's only a little weaker than military grade and a competent tweaker can boost it up to mil-spec. Civilians need a permit for these bad boys, like energy weapons. I traced the lot number for this puppy to a shipment headed for a body shop called Plastisteel Dreamz. With a z."

"Of course they mangle it." Kirsten rolled her eyes. "I'm sure that z increases revenue by twenty percent over an s."

Dorian cracked up laughing, appearing in the chair at his desk behind her.

"Even when you are angry, you are pretty." Sam paled, clearly embarrassed at having blurted.

Kirsten smiled back at him, finding him endearing. The sudden pain in her stomach barely registered compared to her leg. "Thanks. I need to locate this shithead." She grabbed her thigh. "This time, I'm inclined to interrogate his ghost. Can you send me a pin for that store?"

"Sure thing." He managed a feeble smile. "Let me know if there's anything else I can help with."

"Thank you, Sam. I definitely will." She got up, locking her terminal after the call dropped. "Crap, my tac armor is still in the shop." Kirsten pulled her NetMini out. Two seconds later, Evan's face appeared above it. "Hey, kiddo. I'm gonna go to a store and check something out. You feel anything bad?"

He made a series of faces, calling to mind his autoshower impression of the wizard Monwyn. "Nope."

"Okay. See you soon."

She went to hang up, but he blurted, "Wait! The cat is hurt. Be nice to the kitty."

Kirsten stared at him. He grinned, waved, and kissed his NetMini. A holographic lip print hung in midair for a few seconds before he hung up.

Dorian raised his hands in a gesture of surrender. "Don't look at me, I have no idea. Maybe they're putting some interesting vitamins in the school lunches these days." He let her walk past him toward the door. "Wow, that Sam guy... He's really smitten with you."

She shook her head. "So are most techies. What the hell is a 'high elf' anyway?"

"Where did you hear that?"

"First time I ever went into the RTC, one of the network boys asked me if I was a high elf."

Dorian chuckled. "I'm pretty sure he thought you were pretty, if not a little thin and on the short side."

She smirked. "I shouldn't lead him on. I'm going to marry Konstantin."

He followed her into the hallway to the parking deck, walking through a wall and three people to stay alongside her. "You're so sure of that? I've been keeping quiet up 'til now, but I gotta say there's something not right about him. I swear he saw me when we first went to the Archives."

Kirsten stopped, whirling on him. "All these months you've been telling me not to worry, telling me I'll find someone out there who will love me and not care I'm psionic. Now, I find someone, and you're telling me you don't like him?" A collision between anger and wanting to cry turned her face red. "I had a thing for you, Dorian, I really did. I"—she flashed a coy smile—"still kind of do. But, as you keep reminding me, you're dead."

A few people stopped what they were doing to look at her.

He grasped her shoulder. "I'm not jealous, Kirsten. I'm worried."

"You've been spending too much time with Eze." With sudden acute awareness of all the eyes on her, she lowered her voice to a mousy squeak and speed-walked into the parking deck. "He's the perfect man, and for some stupid reason I can't even begin to understand, he chose me. Why can't you let me be *happy* for once in my damn miserable life?"

When she stopped at the side of the car, he stood in silence, sadness on his face.

"I..." For an instant, she resented Konstantin for making her snap at Dorian. A blast of queasiness almost took her off her feet. "Ugh. I'm sorry, Dorian. I'm stressed out, I shouldn't have snapped at you like that." *What's gotten into me?* "You just saved my life..." She willed herself solid to spirits and held on to him, whispering, "I'm scared, Dorian. I don't know what's happening to me."

He patted her back. "I asked you to promise me you wouldn't do anything stupid to get a man." Dorian put his hands on her shoulders, pausing until she looked into his eyes. "All I ask is for you be careful. Maybe I'm overreacting, but after eighteen years as a cop, I tend to trust my instincts when I'm suspicious of someone. Something isn't right with that man."

Evan doesn't like him either. Neither does Captain Eze.

She stared at the wall, trying to swallow the nausea. She absentmindedly fiddled with the bracelet.

They're just being overprotective of me is all. Konstantin loves me.

PLASTISTEEL DREAMZ OCCUPIED THE FIRST FOUR FLOORS OF A CENTURY tower at the approximate center of Sector 1105. The polished white walls gleamed in multicolored light from ten-foot-tall holographic people modeling various pieces of cyberware. All of the holographic giants had cybernetic enhancements: arms, legs, full-body conversions, tails. Some danced, some engaged in choreographed martial arts displays with implanted blades, and others showed off work-enhancing parts designed to boost white-collar productivity.

The two floors above the shop held a parking deck, while the remaining ninety-four stories appeared to be run-of-the-mill offices. She flew into the parking area, landed, and drove on the ground wheels to a marked space a few rows in from the edge. Still guilty about snapping at Dorian, she ignored a number of cheerful ad-bots on her way to the elevator, which she took to the ground level.

When the elevator doors opened, she cringed from the simultaneous assault of too-loud music and brilliant light. Aside from the dull blue floor, everything in the place was hospital-white. Shelves of model cybernetics stood interspersed around strange sculptures that reconfigured themselves every several seconds in an endless arrangement of stacked geometric shapes.

A smiling woman approached her, wearing a skimpy dress consisting of narrow cloth strips: one around the neck, one around the breasts, and a strap running down the center of her torso to the top of a tiny skirt. She started to ignore the woman until she picked up surface thoughts.

"Wow, you're alive?" Kirsten blushed. "Sorry, the outfit and that smile, I thought you were a sub-sent. Only a doll could stay upright on heels so extreme."

The woman's smile broadened; her eyes grew intense.

Kirsten stopped, pinching the bridge of her nose. "You're right. That was bitchy of me to say. I'm sorry. I've been having a rough week, and I guess I am a bitch right now."

The woman's smile flattened into a line.

"Yes," said Kirsten extending a hand. "I'm with Division 0. I did just hear your thoughts. I'm sorry. Again, it's been a horrible week for me, and I'm just not in the mood for the usual corporate nose-to-ass dog circle."

Dorian put a hand on her back. "Rein it in, K. Cripes, what's wrong with you?"

"Uhh." The saleswoman fussed at her hair, glancing to her right at a regal woman behind the counter. The last two inches of her snow white hair cycled among various shades of glowing blue. "Can I help you, officer?"

"Agent. I'm basically a detective. Look, I'm not here to buy anything. I'm trying to track down a component I believe was sold here. I don't want to take time away from you that you could be using to earn a commission, so if you could point me at a manager or someone..."

The smile returned, genuine. "Mirabella will be able to help you."

"White hair?"

"Yes, that's her."

"You know," said Dorian. "Half of our job is to make people at ease with psionics, not freak them out."

Kirsten put on a normal, pleasant face while walking to the counter. "She'll be fine; I just caught her off guard. I would have let it go, but she called me a bitch." She glanced up at him. "Don't say it—I know I was being one."

"Hi, are you Mirabella?" Kirsten stopped by the counter with her right hand on her belt, perhaps a little too close to the E-90.

The white-haired woman stared in shocked silence. "Uhh, I'm sorry. It was just a little Flowerbasket."

"Relax, I'm not here about anything you did. You haven't committed any major crimes have you?"

"No..."

"Good." Kirsten held her left arm up, accessing the data from Sam via her armband terminal. "I'm trying to find out who purchased an Intera Iron Claw cybernetic arm with a specific serial number. More specifically, I'd like to know how he got it without any record of it being added to his medical file. Even better would be if you could tell me if he has scheduled an appointment for a replacement."

Mirabella leaned over the counter to read the floating holo-panel, and a wire connecting her head to the desk terminal slipped off her shoulder. The serial number appeared as if typing itself on the store's screen. In a few seconds, a long list of red text appeared with several bits flashing.

"I'm sorry, Agent. The arm you're looking for was part of a shipment of parts we reported stolen."

Kirsten squinted. "It was not reported stolen. There's nothing in our system about a theft."

Mirabella swiveled the ethereal screen around so Kirsten could see it. "I don't know. It says here the entire shipment was flagged stolen-in-transit. It never arrived at the store. Our computer should automatically transmit the loss report to the police after the insurance claim is generated."

"When did it go missing?" Kirsten looked around the room for any unusual reaction to her presence. All seemed normal.

"According to this, three weeks ago."

"That report should have hit our system by now. Dammit." She poked at her arm until Sam Chang appeared. He looked thrilled to see her again so soon. "Sam, can you do me another favor?"

"Yes, of course!"

Dorian gestured at him. "See…"

29

GREY AREA

Schematics of a PGM Model 14 long-haul cargo transport bathed the patrol craft in a calming shade of cyan. The image of a sixty-foot long truck hovering next to the NavMap console rotated to face her and then to profile—an animation it had been doing for the past fifteen minutes. Text nearby gave details about the maximum load capacity, turning radius, armor thickness, and top speed of the vehicle. Only one piece of information on the screen mattered to Kirsten: the transponder code.

"Damn nice of Sam to hack into Intera's system and find that code for you."

An upwelling of indignant rage came out of nowhere when she glanced at Dorian, but before she bit his head off, she realized the oddity of it. Rather than vent at him, she settled for a giant worry moth bouncing around in her gut. "Yeah."

"You're sweating. I've never seen you so uneasy without armor before."

"It's not the armor." She banked the patrol craft into a rightward descending turn. "It's the stress. I don't know what the hell is wrong with me or how much more I can take this case. You'd think after what Mother did to me, a little stress wouldn't change my personality so much. I feel so guilty for how I've been acting to you."

"Can I say something at risk of starting an argument?"

She poked the button to deploy the ground wheels. "Sure."

"I think you don't feel like you are part of Konstantin's world. Sam is closer to your societal comfort zone. He doesn't make you feel like you're betraying yourself by joining the upper crust you have so much contempt for."

"Dorian…" Kirsten glared at him as expected, but as long as she'd known him, he had always been genuine and protective of her. He'd saved her life yesterday. She couldn't scream at him for saying something bad about Konstantin. A ball of needles replaced the moth in her gut. Instead of yelling, she burst into tears and clutched her stomach.

Dorian reached over and gripped her shoulder. The tears subsided in less than a minute, leaving her gasping.

"Ow. I might be getting a stomach bug or something. I'm getting so sick all the time. Feels like I have a little monster clawing me up inside."

"It hurt enough to make you cry?" He shook his head. "That's not good. The doctors didn't find anything when you were in the tank."

She became angry, but not at Dorian. "I keep having this sense something dark is following me. There's gotta be a spirit somewhere messing with me."

He glanced at the back seat. "Yeah, I feel it too sometimes."

"Figures," she grumbled, staring at the NavMap. "They ditched the truck in a grey zone."

"Well it's not like whoever stole the transport is going to park it where we'd trip over it. They didn't want it to be found."

"Good point. I'm gonna stash the car out of sight."

A Nippy-Nom convenience store occupied the entire ground level of a four-story building on the corner. One face abutted the grey zone and had the bullet holes to prove it. She landed on the roof and jogged down the fire escape to the street level. Bathing in the garish pink and orange light of the sign made her hungry for an instant burrito, her old staple. It remained an appetizing thought for several more seconds until worry about the case took over.

Her armband display relayed the tracking information from the patrol craft's computer. A yellow thread traced out into the dark blue wireframe model of the city, leading her toward the transponder.

"Keep alert. This is still a grey zone," said Dorian.

She didn't look up from the map. "Evan said I'd be fine."

Dorian tugged at her shoulder until she glanced at him. "Kirsten, even if he *is* a precog, it is far from infallible. They see a most-likely future that assumes you proceed with due diligence. If you go carelessly stumbling around and inviting trouble..."

Kirsten bit her knuckle, glaring down the street. "I'm terrified he might be a precog. So far, when it seems like he's seen the future, it's always been something happening to me. Not even himself."

"Maybe more than chance made him astrally wander the alley that night." Dorian grinned.

"Doubtful. He had no emotional attachment to me then. How could he have known I'd be there?"

"That wouldn't have been you. Precog's strongest visions involve threats or benefits to their own lives. Being there to have you find him saved his life. He wouldn't have lasted much longer there."

Kirsten folded her arms over herself and choked up. She couldn't get the memory of how skinny he'd been that night out of her mind. "I don't wanna talk about that. If I start throwing the word 'precog' around, C-Branch is going to interview him and test him, and..."

"I wouldn't worry about it. He might have a little bit of precognitive ability, but remember. Something on the order of one percent of psionic individuals do. Of the one percent, only three percent of precogs receive untagged visions."

"Yeah." She exhaled.

"All of Evan's supposed bouts of pre-sight have been tagged to you. The two of you have a strong emotional bond." Dorian interlaced his fingers in front of his chest, tugging as if he couldn't pull his hands apart. "He hasn't seen acts of random violence or anything regarding total strangers. If all he can see is *your* future—and his own—they won't be interested in him. Plus, he seems to be getting visions in real-time. He freaks out *when* you're in danger. That's not too much *pre* in the precog."

Beep.

Kirsten had walked off-route, distracted by the conversation. She doubled back and jogged around a corner to street blockaded with a wall of destroyed ground cars. Thirty yards past the barrier, the lower floor of an old parking garage flickered orange in the glow of several fires and thrummed with heavy techno music. Enough gaps existed in the impromptu wall for people to slip through without much trouble, suggesting it had been put up to block vehicles.

Dark buildings with broken windows and the occasional crater from a small missile lined the street to her left and right. Two blocks away, the road ended at a T in front of an enormous statue of a stylized metal hawk flying through a ring of circuit-inscribed metal. Firelight glimmered over the wet street surface, brighter in patches of silvery plastisteel where the traction coating had peeled away.

With a hand on her weapon, she crept among the flickering shadows toward the source of the light and music. A ramp wide enough for three cars abreast led from the street level down to a basement garage. Repetitious bass thrummed within the plasticrete walls, magnified by the resonance chamber of a mostly-empty space. Kirsten gazed warily at the ceiling, wondering if the vibrations might threaten the integrity of the building.

At the bottom of the ramp, she tucked up to the wall on the left and peered around at an assembled crowd. Ten men, ranging in age from later teens through early thirties, lounged around on old sofas and recliners. Their hair represented every shade of color imaginable. Most of the people held containers of synthbeer and dressed in the uncoordinated manner of street toughs who couldn't agree on a common theme. That, at least, eased her nerves. *Not a gang, just fringers.* They bobbed their heads in time with the beat; one guy with black and red streaked hair shouted over it asking about someone they had sent off for food. Dark grey metal horns, about an inch long, jutted out from his temples.

Several small metal cargo boxes littered about the area contained fires, one of which serving as a grill as well as a heat source.

At the back corner of the 'furnished' area, a group of four women sat around a table—rather, a repurposed industrial wire spool—cleaning rifles and pistols. The oldest, maybe twenty, held a partially disassembled rifle up to the light with a metal arm that mostly matched the contours of a normal arm. It struck Kirsten as creepy, like the skin had been removed to reveal metal underneath. Engravings of winding ivy covered the entire limb from shoulder to fingertip.

The missing cargo transport took up the remainder of the ground floor beyond them, parked along the rear of their encampment. Cloth fluttered from the open trailer, resembling a shy spirit peeking around the metal wall. Kirsten took a deep breath and walked toward the group. Acrid fumes rolled by in clouds from whatever they burned for heat. Plastic sheeting hung over gaps to the street level high at her left scratched in the wind, a somewhat futile effort to make the area more habitable.

One by one, the fringers took notice of her. Kirsten stopped to let the awareness of her presence spread over the group, an impulse racing along a nerve to their collective brain. One of the women at the table grabbed two halves of rifle and rushed to put them together. The metal-armed one held her hand down and gave her a shake of the head.

Kirsten waited until a fat man in a long coat cut the music. "I'm not here to give anyone a hard time. I'm just trying to track down what was on that cargo transport."

She weathered appraising stares, while the fringers appeared to search for a wordless consensus on how to deal with a solitary police officer. The man with the red/black striped hair slid off the hood of a wrecked car, tugged a crimson leather jacket tight to his shoulders over a dark turtleneck, and sauntered over.

"You got some set on you, *chica*, coming here alone." He reached a slow hand up and flicked a finger at the strip of black plastisteel on her chest with her name and rank etched on it. His roundish face and short hair made him seem boyish. "Wren… That's a little bird, isn't it? What's the zero for?"

The thought Dorian could appear and likely scare the room empty in seconds brought a smile to her lips.

"Careful, Ink, them is psionic cops," said a voice from the crowd. "Gonna melt your brain."

"How 'bout it, *chica*? You gonna melt my brain." He touched his fingers to his jacket and flicked his arms to the sides.

"Ink? You must have a lot of tats." Kirsten regarded him with an unimpressed expression.

"Short for Incubus." He winked, a trace of red light glowed from his eyes.

Kirsten swiped the lash through him from crotch to head. He reacted with a mere shiver. All the bravado fled from his face at the glowing whip. A few of the fringers dove behind stacked boxes or destroyed cars.

"Fuckwazat?" he squeaked, body motionless, eyes locked on the white light trailing from her hand.

"I'm also trying to send a couple of demons back where they belong. Incubus is a kind of demon. I didn't want to take a chance. Did that hurt?"

He swallowed, still frozen. "No. Little cold actually."

The lash receded once she stopped concentrating. "Good, that means you're just a poser with cybereyes and not a real demon. We can be friends." She patted him on the shoulder, and stepped around him. "Look, people. Barring Lace, I really do not care what drugs you have stashed around here or what small-time bullshit skimmers you're running."

Dorian stifled a chuckle.

Incubus faced her with a slow turn, cybernetic vampire fangs retracting as he smiled. "Uhh, yeah. So, about that. She said it was fine. Was supposed to be out of the system and empty. We wanted the truck not what was in it."

"Who is *she?*"

"Skittles," said the woman with the cybernetic arm, pointing it at the truck.

Kirsten nodded, edging in the direction of the truck. "Everyone just calm down, okay? If I was here to make trouble for you, I wouldn't have come alone."

The fringers traded stares as she slipped into the shadow of the cargo-mover's cab. Inch-high letters spelled out Peterbilt-Grumman-Mack along a strip below the windscreen. She edged past the corner and passed a primary drive wheel half again her height. Handholds in the stationary central hub offered a way up to the cabin door nine feet in the air. Someone had used them as storage bins for small bits of electronica. The heavyset kid turned the music back on, but at a less oppressive volume.

"Dorian, keep an eye on them, please."

He nodded, allowing Kirsten to turn her full attention to the massive transport. Behind the huge drive wheels, the truck had two axles of load-bearing tires as tall as her chest. Fifty feet of trailer stretched toward a square of light on the concrete wall, within which sat the shadow of an enormous cat. She expected to peek into the trailer and find a housecat perched next to a lamp.

Kirsten hurried to the end and leaned around the corner of the truck, ducking the wavering cloth that acted as a door. Bunk beds lined both walls, reminiscent of the sleeping quarters of a military starship. A small crew ladder on the left side took her up to the cargo deck, six feet off the ground. As soon as her face cleared the level of the floor, she froze. Next to the second pair of bunks on the left, a slender woman sat cross-legged as if meditating, perched on a pile of dingy pillows, wearing nothing but the hair draped over her chest and prominent ribs.

Two large, fuzzy cat ears sprouted from a fluffy slate grey mane long enough to drape on the floor. Her feline ears twitched in time with the beat of the music outside. The woman was fashion-model thin with a graceful face like a toy doll. Her delicate features looked as though she would crack at the slightest touch. Fangs peeked out of her parted lips, and her eyes—right one gold, the other green—were half open, the left much wider than the gold. Vertical feline pupils closed to thin streaks of black amid the color, and drool fell in drops from the end of a tongue resembling a larger version of a cat's.

Kirsten looked to the side, embarrassed as though she'd walked in on someone in the bathroom. On the floor behind the cat girl, a grey-furred tail swished, crinkling amid plastic wrappers. A standard M3 interface wire continued from the end of the extra appendage, circling the lower bunk before plugging into a battered cyberspace deck. Large and boxy, it resembled military surplus hardware. The words *Titan Alchemist* ran across the front in steel letters made to look bolted on.

"Be nice to the kitty." Evan's voice whispered in her memory. *Son of a bitch.* Kirsten shivered with worry. *He is a precog.*

"Excuse me?" whispered Kirsten. When the girl didn't react beyond twitching ears, she repeated it, louder.

The slender woman shook her head as if shrugging off the effect of a sedative. Her eyelids equalized level, slit pupils widened. After a few seconds of woozy staring, metal claws sprang out of her fingertips. Ten six-inch blades glimmered in the light of a portable electric lamp. The woman raised her arms and, much to Kirsten's surprise, hissed.

"*Calm* down." Light danced over Kirsten's eyes.

The Neko-Chan's tail tripled in visible width as all the hairs stood on end. Her ears went back, then swiveled one after the other to face forward.

Kirsten climbed the rest of the way into the trailer. "Sorry for walking in. I'm not here for you. Someone said you might be able to help me with something." Kirsten glanced at the wall. "Uhh, go ahead and get dressed."

"Why?"

Oh, brother. One of those. "Umm, because you're naked in public?"

"This is my home. It's not public. And it's not against the law to not wear clothes."

Fine, whatever, I have better things to do than argue with an exhibitionist. "I'm Kirsten. I guess you're Skittles?" Kirsten jumped at the *snap* of claws retracting into the woman's fingers.

Skittles shifted around and sat sideways, draping herself over the pillows. "Yeah."

"I'm trying to figure out what happened to the cargo this truck was carrying when it went missing. It's obviously not here. Ink implied you were the one who stole the truck?"

Skittles gasped, sliding backward under the bed until the wire coming out of her tail almost pulled the deck to the ground. "Please don't arrest me. They'll kill me."

Kirsten squatted to look at the woman cowering under the bed.

Dorian stooped, snapping his fingers and making a *pspspsps* noise, as if trying to call a cat.

Red-faced, Kirsten thumped him on the thigh, turning so Skittles couldn't see the desperate need to laugh on her face.

"She's not really a cat. An actual cat would be going nuts at me," said Dorian, standing straight again.

Once she had 'serious face' back, Kirsten skimmed the Neko's surface thoughts. The woman's mind-voice narrated in calculated French, forcing her to rely on images and feelings. "Oh, no, Miette. I'm not here to take you back to Europe, and you can lay off the scared shitless act. I know you're faking it for sympathy."

"How do you know who I am if you're not here to take me back?" Acted terror thinned out to contained aggression. "You working for him? Ambassador Montpierre owned me for three years. When he came to UCF, I run away. I will die before I go back."

I can see you thinking about it. Sorry for invading your privacy, but I'm in a rush. I won't take you back. I'd arrest the bastard for human trafficking if I had the jurisdiction.

Skittles's jaw gaped, eyes all the way open. "You're psionic?"

Kirsten braced for it. "Yeah, but I'm not gonna hurt you."

"Oh. It is okay, he has gone back to Europe." She crawled out from under the bunk and sat up, fear and aggression gone—replaced with sudden cheeriness. "You're one of those special cops, right?"

"Yeah…" Kirsten raised an eyebrow. *Is this girl nuts?*

"Good, that means you don't give an excrement about cyberspace." Skittles examined her fingernails with a devilish grin. "I'm a naughty kitty sometimes."

"Well, as long as you haven't hurt anyone, I can overlook it. I really need to find out what happened to the cyberware this truck was carrying."

Skittles folded her arms, pouting. "That copulating illegitimate person."

"What?" Kirsten blinked.

Dorian laughed himself to tears.

Skittles grumbled in French, sighing as she turned her head to the right. A thin sliver of silicon slid out from behind her jaw with three square sockets on the upper surface and the underside. Only one of the six receptacles had a chip in it. As soon as it finished extending, it slid back into her skull. Kirsten covered her mouth to hide the gasp of shock at the lack of a human ear.

"English is a chip. I don't really learn it well yet. It does not give me the good naughty words. I stole this cargo for a cyberdoc in trade for work. My friends got truck, he got 'ware, I got parts. Only, the feces-head did it wrong." Skittles grabbed her tail and shook it at Kirsten.

Dorian cackled.

"You're hurt?" *Just like Evan said.*

"It has the fire of nerves when I plug in and plug out. I like this more than wire in head, but he did not put it in right."

Dorian examined the tail. "Synthetic. Very expensive. Almost indistinguishable from real living tissue. Looks like her ears are the same way."

Skittles ears thwapped backward in two quick motions, angling in the direction of Dorian. She squinted at the far end of the trailer, as if searching for the source of a sound.

"Guess that's why her tail fluffed up when she got scared," muttered Kirsten.

"Who are you talking to?" Skittles' ears went back. "I hear someone whispering."

"A ghost. Are you psionic?"

"The ears could just be that sensitive," said Dorian. He yelled, "Hello?"

Skittles whirled toward him, tilted her head left, held it there for a few seconds, and tilted it right.

"So, you gave the parts to a cyberdoc here?" asked Kirsten.

"Yeah, but he did bad job. I will show you where he is if you psionic him. Make him fix my tail. He won't do it for free, even though he copulated upwards."

Dorian laughed.

Feline ears thwapped.

Kirsten debated the ethics of her request for a few seconds. "So he paid you for work by installing your tail, screwed it up, and then wants to charge you more to fix it? Okay. If the story is true, I will talk to him."

Skittles wrapped herself around the largest pillow, poised to chomp on it with feline fangs. She scooted around to expose her back to Kirsten and raised her tail. "Pull wire out so I can leave trailer." She bit down.

The fur-covered appendage felt eerily natural, complete with body heat like the tail of a great cat. Kirsten cringed inwardly at the warmth in her hand, unsure if she should be repulsed or intrigued. Skittles whimpered pitifully when Kirsten grasped the M3 plug inserted in a concealed socket at the tail's tip. The cat girl trembled, her fear genuine.

"Just pinch the little release button there and pull the wire out," said Dorian. "Standard neural interface port. Kind of clever actually, tapped right into the spinal cord via the tail extension. Not having the socket in the skull is fairly ingenious. Some of the more deadly net attacks make them spark. Keeping it away from the head is a novel idea."

"You know how I feel about cyberware," whispered Kirsten.

She squeezed the little buttons, then pulled the wire and tail apart.

The woman screamed into the cushion, shuddering and sweating for several seconds before the wave of pain subsided. Her right ear flapped with sporadic twitches mirrored by facial tics and a bouncing leg on that side. Once the storm calmed, she sat up with a puff of pillow-foam stuck to her fangs. While giving Kirsten a pathetic stare, she huffed and launched it onto the bed.

Kirsten clasped Skittles by the head and thumbed her eyelids open wider. The right eye dilated more than the left. "That looked like it hurt. I don't like the way it only affected one side of your body. I should take you to a hospital."

"It only hurts when I plug in or plug out. Electricity leaks to nerves. It copulating inhales."

"That's going to cause brain damage, if it hasn't already," said Dorian.

Kirsten checked the woman's pulse. "Are you certain this cyberdoc of yours can fix this?"

Skittles stood and stretched. Kirsten whirled away, embarrassed. "He has to. I do not have money for legal doctor. I do not have job for health plan, and am too old for free help. Ready?"

"Uhh, aren't you going to get dressed?"

"Why?"

Kirsten, flailed. "Because you have to. People don't just walk around outside with no clothes. That's just inviting creeps to…"

Skittles' fingers sprouted metal claws again. She grinned. "Can try. Can die."

"Actually, exhibitionism is rather common among people with an addiction to feline body modification." Dorian shrugged. "Technically it's illegal, but who has the time to bother with streakers when there's a dozen murders a day. Only rookie Div 1 cops bother busting Nekos for public indecency."

The slender woman pulled the hanging plastic to the side, about to exit the trailer. She shivered in an oncoming blast of outside air. "Okay, okay. It's cold, I will do the clothes." She rooted around under her bunk, sniff-testing several garments before settling on a loose-fitting tank top with a metallic cat face on it, a knee-length lacy black Goth skirt (with tail hole) and combat boots.

Dorian grinned. "If you ever decided to buy cyberware, this is kind of what I pictured you looking like."

Kirsten glared at him.

"You have sneakers that meow, cat stickers all over your locker, that giant pink sleeping shirt with the white cat head on it, a kitten on your NetMini—"

Making herself solid to spirits, Kirsten grabbed him by the arm and pulled him to the far wall. "Liking cats and wanting to *be* one are two entirely different hobbies," she mumbled.

Skittles giggled.

"She's got copulating great hearing," said Dorian, pointing over Kirsten's shoulder.

"I am not the offended," said Skittles, after springing to her feet. "At first, Montpierre forced me. His men took me from the street, and I woke up in a cage with ears and tail. He is a very strange man." She ran her fingers through her fluffy pewter-grey hair, grooming her ears in the process. "I have decided to like it."

"You could always get the stuff removed…" Kirsten flashed the bastard offspring of a cringe and a smile. *You poor girl.*

"*Non.* Too late. My old ears are gone, my eyes are changed—DNA surgery. Too costly to undo. And, normal Miette would not survive on street." With that, she pounced, flying over Kirsten's head and out the back of the trailer, landing on all fours in a wary crouch. A few seconds later, she sprang up and beamed.

"Guess she's ready to go," said Dorian.

Kirsten followed the fast-walking, occasionally skipping, Skittles down streets packed with ruined cars and broken storefronts. The reek of the piss-soaked stairway at the far corner of the parking garage painted the back of her throat with a scratchiness she couldn't cough away. Four blocks away from the parking garage, Kirsten put her hand on her sidearm at a noticeable worsening in the surroundings.

Skittles paused, squatting to examine a dandelion sprouting from a wind-collected pile of dirt. She leaned in and sniffed at it. The more Kirsten watched a grown woman act like some combination of oversized pre-teen and feral animal, the more pity she felt for her. She half-expected her to eat the plant.

"Even in this place, we find a way to live." She glanced up at Kirsten. "Like this weed."

"Miette?"

"Hmm?" Skittles stood and continued in her previous direction, walking backwards with a fang-baring smile.

"Why didn't you go to the police?"

The woman spun forward, adopting a stiff-legged, arm-swinging fascist march. "They don't give one copulation what the executives do to little people. Montpierre could have shot me in the head right in front of them, and they would have only female dogged and complained for having to make the cleanup."

Dorian laughed himself to tears.

"I mean here. There are programs for women who— "

"I wouldn't give him the satisfaction." Skittles bounded to the top of an overturned cargo-hauler, glancing down past her dangling tail at Kirsten. "I already paid him back."

Not feeling up to the task of a fourteen-foot vertical leap, Kirsten walked to the cab end and squeezed through a gap between it and the wall. Skittles dropped down as she emerged and led the way into the ground floor of an abandoned building, and out the other side to an alley packed with wrecked cars. Smoke wafted by, scented with burning plastic, charred meat, and a hint of wood.

Skittles squatted low to the ground, her body below the waist vanished amid her billowy skirt.

"I don't mean to sound insensitive, but you seem rather blasé about what he did to you."

Skittles gave her a measuring look, frowned, and gazed off at the road while stroking her hand repeatedly down the length of her tail. "I maybe said more than was. I got caught with my claws in the data jar. Montpierre chose me from a line of people to be sent to a work camp. He paid my sentence, so I was his pet for a couple of years."

"That's slavery!" blurted Kirsten.

"Bleh. So was camp, but it would have been much bad. He did me a favor, really. As much illegitimate person he was, he never did the hitting. I almost feel the sadness for making it look like he supported the resistance." Skittles climbed over a dead car.

Kirsten, with more effort and less grace, followed. "What happened?"

"I spent months making a false GlobeNet person and using it to help the resistance. I left clues to make seem tiny errors each time I went in. When the BSE closed in, I had left enough trail so they think like Montpierre was behind the avatar."

"BSE?" asked Kirsten.

"*Bureau de la Sécurité Èlectronique.*" Skittles flipped about, walking backward a few paces. "Police on the Cyberspace."

"*In* Cyberspace," said Dorian.

Skittles's left ear thwapped against her head twice. "Whatever... in, on. Stupid chip."

Dorian jumped at the shock of being heard.

Kirsten laughed a live person making a ghost startle. "Augmented hearing has been known to pick up ghosts. A long time ago, they used to record them with sound equipment."

Skittles stopped short, raising a hand. She crouched and stared at the mouth of an alley two blocks away. A whispery rush came from behind. Kirsten and Dorian turned to the rear at the noise the cat girl didn't appear to notice. A shadowy transparent figure with two glowing red spots for eyes raced past them, its long, spindly arms trailing to the sides. The entity zoomed by, Kirsten whirling to follow it with her gaze. It glided to a halt by the alley that had captivated Skittles.

A man cackled. Quiet murmured voices gained in volume. The shadowy figure waved its vaporous hands in a beckoning gesture. Men wandered out of the alley to the street, all in black coats emblazoned with a calligraphic red D—a pack of Diablos. Numerous weapons, including pistols, submachine guns, and swords of various sizes glinted in what little moonlight made it past the glowing indigo smog.

Kirsten's breath stalled in her throat. Her muscles locked in fear. Two women would be an irresistible treat for that gang. Rumor had it they abducted women and held them for weeks or months. That they frequently *didn't* kill their victims may or may not have been a good thing.

The wisp waved its hands again in a gathering gesture at the gangers before extending a long pointing finger at Kirsten. "Kill... Kill..." The phantom whisper scraped over the back of her mind. Skittles' ears thwapped.

"Damn, it's not gonna take much to drive them over the edge," said Dorian.

The Diablos swayed on their feet, shaking their heads dizzily. A few stumbled into nearby wrecked cars and held on to keep from falling over. In seconds, the disorientation faded to murderous rage. Guns came out, faces twisted with diabolical glee.

Kirsten grabbed Skittles by the shoulders and pulled her down to the street, taking cover behind a crushed passenger van. "Stay down." She popped up, aiming over the smashed front end at the gang. "Don't you dare. Put those things away and keep walking."

"K, they're Diablos. Even without that shadow, they would be a problem. They shoot at cops for fun. Division numbers to them are point scores."

"But they're compel—" She dove as four men raised submachine guns and lit up the van with automatic fire.

Fragments of metal, upholstery padding, and glass rained down over her.

Skittles sat, back against the van, picking at her nails and brushing the occasional scrap of car off her skirt. Except for her ears folded backward, she looked calm. "Want me to help?"

"No, stay down. You're a civilian."

The wispy shadow zoomed out of the van wall, tackling Dorian backward. Keening wails echoed into the distance as they sailed through one destroyed vehicle after another. Glass frosted over wherever they passed. Kirsten huddled against the side of the van. When the shooting ceased, she popped up mostly to get a visual on the scene, still, she fired twice to make them duck. Neither shot hit anything, but she got a general idea of where threats were. In typical Diablo fashion, none had bothered to take cover behind the cars.

They opened fire again, laughing.

Kirsten yelped at a fleck of hot shrapnel catching her across the cheek as she ducked. Fragments rained around them.

Skittles swatted some glass off her hair and examined her fingernails. "Want me to help now?"

"What are you, nineteen? Stay down, don't get hurt."

"Thank you, but I'm twenty-six."

"Why hello, sir!" cheered a male voice, its electronic nature obvious. "You appear to be running low on ammunition. Minos Corporation is running a special on Class 4 M55 PDW ammunition. The 11.5 mm penetrators are precision milled from the finest high-density synthetic metals and would be a perfect complement to your compact personal defense weapon. We even have a discount on M40 PDW for your friends with the 10mm firearms. Act now, and you can get 100 rounds for the price of 70. Only seventy-six credits."

Kirsten gripped the crumpled hood of the van and pulled herself up, ignoring the sting in her cheek and gawking at the ballsy advert bot hovering among the Diablos. Fortunately, it had their attention for the moment. Somewhere behind her, Dorian growled and cursed. He sounded frustrated, but neither scared nor worried.

"Hey, bot!" she screamed. "You can't sell them ammo."

The large floating sphere pivoted to face her. "Of course we can! Especially because they are almost out. They have credits; we have bullets. It's a match made in heaven."

"They're shooting at me."

If the orb had arms, it would have shrugged. "I am sorry, miss. What our customers do with their ammunition is not our concern. It is a (mostly) free country."

"I'm a goddamned police officer! Your company will get shut the hell down if I report you."

The Diablos seemed amused enough to watch this unfold, and not resume shooting at her at that moment.

One tapped the metal ball with his gun. "Only if the bitch lives."

"Do you have identification?" The bot wobbled, simulating nervousness.

Kirsten held up her armband as the orb zipped over. It chirped once it read her Police ID codes. "I am terribly sorry, Agent Wren." It pivoted as if to look at the gangers for a second before swiveling back to her. "Can I interest you in any E-mags for that E-90?"

"Get the hell out of here!" she snarled.

It recoiled and glided back among the gangers. "I am sorry, gentlemen.

By law, since you are engaging in a violence event with an employee of the police services, I am unable to—"

"We'll pay double."

The orb hesitated. "I..."

"Hey, ball... we ain't shooting at anyone right now, we're just standing here with our cocks in our hands," roared one.

"A valid point. I shall process your order straight away. How many boxes would you like?"

Kirsten fired, skimming a burn over the side of the orb. It careened into the night, trailing sparks and emitting a digitized scream of "eeeeeeeeee."

Dorian's head came out of the wall. "Nice shot." A black hand wrapped over his face and pulled him back in.

"I was trying to blow it up." She dove for cover again as the hail of bullets resumed. "I hate orbs."

"Break's over!" yelled one.

"Want me to help?" asked Skittles.

Kirsten ducked low, looking to take a shot under the van at a boot; however, it had collapsed to the point where no gap remained between metal and the road surface. A meaty *smack* came from the right seconds before the wispy shadow slid out from the same patch of tarnished plastisteel wall where Dorian appeared seconds before.

The shadow spun over in midair, hissing at Kirsten. It whirled to flee, but Dorian zoomed into another tackle, holding it down while it flailed at the air trying to get away. He punched it repeatedly; it clawed in a wolverine's frenzy at his side and back.

At a break in the constant automatic fire, Kirsten sprang up, catching the Diablos reloading. She fired, winging one in the arm. With his coat on fire, he dove for cover. She aimed at where she figured he landed and put a shot through the wreck. Rage on the other gangers' faces confirmed a kill.

"Now you did it, bitch," growled one. "Now we ain't just gonna kill you."

"Like they were going to be cordial before," she muttered to no one in particular.

"Mind taking a swipe at this damn thing?" grunted Dorian.

Kirsten ducked a second before the gunfire resumed. The cold from the van seeped past the thin cloth on her back, a reminder of her lack of armor.

She concentrated on the lash. Skittles gasped at the ten-foot-long tendril of scintillating white energy stretching out from her right hand. The woman crumpled her hands to her mouth, cat-eyes flicked left and right, locked on to the tip of the wavering light, tail thrashing with anticipatory waves.

Dorian flung the shadow at Kirsten, distancing himself. She swung the psionic whip at the screaming entity, which crossed its insubstantial arms across its face in a feeble defense. Her lash sliced the creature in half, almost in the middle. Both halves broke apart into shreds of vaporous black ether that fell to the ground in jellying tar-like blobs that exuded smoke. Kirsten blinked.

That thing was either weak as hell or I'm scared out of my mind and don't realize it.

Skittles emitted a frustrated noise that sounded like *myarp* and sprang at Kirsten. She swiped her hands at the air four times, at a speed turning them to a flesh-toned blur. Yet, for all her effort, the lash had no solidity for a living woman's hands to grasp. She ended up kneeling on Kirsten's lap with two fistfuls of uniform, nose to nose with a manic smile.

"Oh, you have got to be kidding me. Does she chase yarn too?" Dorian snickered.

Cat ears flattened. "Your no-see person thinks he is funny. I cannot do the resisting. It is from the DNA surgery. Fast small things are"—she shivered—"*sooo* irresistibly fun." She climbed off Kirsten, whining in a demure tone. "Especially shiny ones."

Bullets continued to snap and ping around them, tearing long streamers of mangled metal out from the side of the van.

Dorian stepped over beside Kirsten. She looked up at him, brushing bits of glass and paint flakes off her sleeves. He raised his arms and fixed a determined stare at the Diablos. Soon after, tiny threads of wispy white energy trailed into him. Some of the scratch marks on his arm and face faded away.

The Diablos started bitching about their guns.

"Thanks." Kirsten smiled, and leapt up with her weapon trained. "Okay, shitheads. You caught me when I'm crunched for time. A spirit just made you want to kill me, so I won't hold it against you. You have four seconds to disperse."

"You bein' a cop makes us wanna kill you. Spirit ain't got shit to do with it." The largest of them pulled the trigger of his dead pistol, and growled.

"I am so glad we shifted over to electronic firing circuits," said Dorian.

"Dorian, that happened before you were born."

"Want me to help yet?" asked Skittles.

Kirsten grumbled. "Stay down. I don't want you getting hurt."

The Diablos tossed their firearms to the side. Kirsten's forming smile dropped to a look of abject horror as eight men drew swords, axes, and other nasty pointy things. Like something out of a Monwyn video, they roared battle cries and charged at her. At least two of the swords coming at her emitted the high-pitched whine of vibro inducers. Dorian sapped the power from them as well, turning them into normal composite blades. Kirsten's heart resumed beating.

"Run." Kirsten waved at Skittles. "They're charging."

The Diablos swarmed around and over the smashed van, oblivious to the Neko girl sitting in perfect calm behind them. Backpedaling, Kirsten fired six times, killing two and wounding one before the other five backed her against a dead car. The lead man roared, hauling a two-handed sword up over his head. Kirsten dove out of the way; the blade stopped six inches deep in the vehicle. The horrendous screech of it sliding loose drew a pained scream from Skittles as she covered her ears.

Another leapt at her with a smaller sword, knocking the E-90 out of her hand before chasing her against the side of a building. She got a grip around his forearm, diverting the blade into the wall inches left of her head. With a grunt, she drove her knee into his groin. His eyes half-closed, his mouth agape, he sucked air in his nose. Dorian dove on him from behind; the spectral assault did little other than make his coat flutter.

"He's on Zerk," yelled Dorian. "Pain causes euphoria and increased adrenaline. Don't hurt him, just kill him."

"*Again!*," he rasp-screamed. "That was beautiful. Do it again." Eyebrows flared up as he leaned his weight into her. He dropped the sword and overpowered her until he had her by the throat. His other hand pawed at her chest.

"Want me to help now?" asked Skittles.

The other four Diablos at last noticed her.

"Uhh, sure," gurgled Kirsten, feeling proud of herself for not succumbing to panic. A contest of strength was not one she could win. "*Stop.*" Her eyes glimmered with light.

The ganger froze in place, keeping her pinned to the wall, but no longer strangling or fondling her. Kirsten started to issue another command, but stopped at the sight of Skittles walking toward the gangers without fear.

"You boys have ten seconds." She counted from one to ten. With each spoken number, a single eight-inch claw, curved to a wicked point, sprouted from a fingertip.

The Diablos didn't look impressed.

At ten, Skittles blurred into a smear of grey hair, black cloth, and pale skin. She weaved among the Diablos, going from where she'd been to a few steps past them in three seconds. Thin trails of blood spatter stained her cute, once-white tank top. Her motion ceased before any of them reacted to it. Three of the four Diablos fell to the side, covered in numerous scratches. The first clutched a throat sliced into several flaps, blood gushing past his fingers. The next sported four burbling puncture wounds between ribs where a straight four-claw stab found his heart. Number three scrambled to keep his intestines inside a shredded abdomen. The Diablo in the middle of the alley had so many claw wounds on his chest he seemed skinless, but only laughed at her.

"Shit, that one's got a subderm weave." Skittles hissed at him, tail flared and circling.

"That is utterly psychotic," said Dorian.

Kirsten locked eyes with the man holding her and snarled, "*Let go.*"

He ripped his hands away from her as though she were a boiling-hot pan.

She leapt in a somersault at her E-90 and rolled up on one knee, aiming at him. "Dorian, I can't just kill this guy."

Skittles blurred again, shredding a hole in the other ganger's coat. Blood sprayed, but her attack didn't do much beyond expose the sheen of dark metallic threads between his skin and muscles.

"Here, kitty, kitty," he growled, and lunged into a swing with a two-handed sword.

Skittles flowed out of the way like a liquid, making his strike appear ponderously sluggish.

The force of his swing and the mass of the weapon pulled him staggering two steps when it hit nothing but air. "Bitch! I'm gonna make boots out of you."

"Bind the pistol. I'll do it," said Dorian.

"He's not a threat now."

Dorian gestured at the dodging cat girl. "What do you think he's going to do to the next innocent person he runs across? Diablos are probably one of the most dangerous non-aug gangs in the city. They don't usually kill their victims because they want to savor the psychological damage they cause. They are *evil* if anything ever deserved that word."

"I am still not going to shoot a defenseless man."

"What about him?" Dorian pointed at the walking wound chasing Skittles. "He's trying to kill a 'helpless civilian.'"

Kirsten sighed. "Helpless…" She squeaked in an attempt to raise her voice, coughed, then yelled. "You! Asshat! Drop the sword."

He ignored her, and hurled all his strength into another swing. Skittles slid under it, scratching at his chest with both hands so fast they blurred. Blood flew everywhere, but her thin metal claws didn't seem capable of penetrating his subdermal armor.

"I said, stop!" shouted Kirsten.

The man faced her and roared. Evidently realizing he had little chance of cutting the cat, he raised the sword and shifted his weight as if to charge at Kirsten.

She shot him once in the chest, sending bloody steam out both entry and exit wounds. The sudden release of tension within the fibers of his armor implant caused strips of meat to snap free, flopping as he crashed to the ground. Skittles seemed unaffected by the gore, as if she had seen far worse in her life. As casual as anything, she walked over with her hands held up like a surgeon after scrub.

"Oh, please tell me you're not going to lick yourself clean." Kirsten stared.

Dorian cracked up.

"Uhh, no. That's nasty." She went over to one of the first Diablos killed by a laser blast and used his shirt as a rag to wipe herself as clear of blood as possible without a shower.

Kirsten searched the last man and removed several more weapons before spinning him around and staring into his eyes. "*Go to Sector 1.*"

The man trudged off like a zombie.

"What was the point of that?" asked Dorian. "That's hundreds of miles away."

"He's going to walk out of a grey zone and Division 1 will find him somewhere between here and the southwest corner of the city."

"The doctor is another block that way." Skittles pointed with her tail, trotting over while working her improvised rag around her fingers. "Ready?"

Kirsten smirked at the ghostly Diablos trying to figure out why they couldn't pick up their weapons. "One minute, I need to call some associates."

An eerie quiet came over the area as she closed her eyes and beckoned.

SKITTLES SLID DOWN A METAL RAILING WHILE KIRSTEN TOOK THE STAIRS. The cat girl sprang off at the bottom, a story and a half below street level in a dingy corridor of white tiles part way between abandoned subway station and decrepit hospital. Ten feet from the last step, a curtain of heavy black plastic sheeting blocked the way. Skittles fussed at it until she found the seam. Bright light leaked out from the room beyond as she pulled half the tarp aside and held it for Kirsten. She ducked in, squinting until her eyes adjusted to the glare.

She gazed around at a room that had been decorated in a style of bloody-street-doc chic with a side of former boiler room. Two procedure tables occupied the center of the area, flanked by tall shelves of cybernetic parts—some of which still had blood on them. The more distant table contained the corpse of a filthy dark-skinned man with his chest cut open. A doctor in a bright green chem suit with an electronic visor hovered over the corpse, ripping threads of neuralware wiring from an exposed spinal cord.

"Hey, Doc," chirped Skittles.

The man jumped, taking a step back and grabbing at an armband terminal. Two tracked security bots, miniature tanks with assault-rifle mechanisms mounted to their chassis, rolled into the room from an inner hallway and aimed at the cat.

"That's close enough," said the doctor, pointing at her.

"I am curious, doctor..." Kirsten stalked closer. "It is 'doctor,' isn't it? Why would you assume she wants to use you as a scratching post?"

The man screeched; spittle coated the inside of his faceplate. "The police? You brought a goddamn cop here? Are you insane? Now I'm going to have to burn the whole place."

"I'm Division 0, Doc. I'm only looking for information."

"Fucking psionic?" He shook his finger at Skittles. "You *are* fucking nuts. A god damned psionic?"

Dorian walked toward the man, causing the overhead lights to falter and dim. The doctor looked, shivering. Despite knowing her partner affected the lights, the sporadic flickering added to the already creepy ambiance of the room made the hairs on Kirsten's neck stand up.

The trembling doctor took a step back, looking around at the sparking, sputtering LED tubes. Blood dripped from the strands of neural wiring still clenched in his fist. He jabbed a finger at his arm-mounted control unit. Both bots swiveled to aim at Kirsten, but Dorian glared at them, drawing all their power away before they could do much more than emit the squelching angry buzz indicating they could not fire on a cop.

With a terrified scream, the doctor abandoned the wiring and sprinted down the corridor the bots came from, swatting several layers of transparent plastic out of his way. Bloody wires swung back and forth from the table, dribbling blood on the floor.

Skittles put her hands on her hips. "Wow. You know how to make an entrance."

"That was all Dorian."

The cyberdoc returned with an energy rifle, which he aimed at Kirsten.

"*Drop it,*" said Kirsten, a white glow in her eyes. "Now *get over here.*"

The weeping man shuddered in place for barely a second before his hands snapped open and the rifle clattered to the floor like a plastic toy. He staggered toward her, fighting it every step of the way, and came to a spasmodic halt a few feet in front of her, casting mournful looks back at his abandoned weapon.

"Good." Kirsten put a hand on his shoulder. "Now, despite your opinion psionics should be rounded up and launched into space, I'm not going to get mad at you. In fact, I'm not even going to arrest you for trading in black market cyberware. That is, of course, *if* you can assure me all of your hardware is scavenged from the already dead. You don't kill people for parts do you?"

"No..."

His surface thoughts matched his words. "Good. In exchange for letting you slide on tax evasion, I want two things."

Skittles crossed her arms, hip thrust to one side. She sported a sly smile and swished her tail back and forth.

"W-what?" stammered the doctor.

"First, I want to know what happened to an Intera Iron Claw cyberarm with serial number"—she glanced at her forearm terminal—"IC-018-AFC0:1723:00E2. Give me everything you know about the man who used it, and I won't also charge you as an accessory in the attempted murder of a police officer."

The doctor gulped. His coffee-hued face all but vanished behind a thick layer of fog on the inside of his chem suit mask. His breaths wheezed, straining a respirator not meant for the speed at which he tried to take on air.

"Secondly, I need you to fix the botched installation you did on her tail before it causes permanent brain or nerve damage."

He babbled, waving an arm at Skittles. "You did, didn't you? You called the damn cops because of a stupid short. We had a deal. You have to pay for additional work."

Skittles popped a single claw from her right index finger, wagging it back and forth. "Oh, no, no, no. Not *additional* work. Fixing the broken feces. Those two bots were all that stopped me from boning you like a fish last time." She gestured as if inserting the claw and slicing him open. "I could show you what it feels like whenever I use this damn tail. Just stick this right up into the base of your spine and pull…"

"The only question, Doc, is if you fix her willingly or under compulsion." Kirsten folded her arms, hoping he believed the attitude she faked.

"That… you can't do that! It's unethical. It's illegal."

Dorian howled with laughter.

"As if what you do isn't?" Kirsten glared, trying to ignore her partner for the moment. "Look, just fix what you screwed up. I'm not asking you to give her free parts. Take a little pride in your work, maybe she sends you more customers instead of plots to slice you open from ass to skull. And you did try to sic those bots on me. You're damn lucky their failsafe wasn't removed or you'd be looking at a summary execution."

"You're encouraging the trade of illegal cyberware? How do you think Miss Kitty obtained military-grade speedware?" asked Dorian. "I don't think she's got a permit for that."

"I'm more worried about demons right now," grumbled Kirsten. "And speedware isn't *that* illegal. It's not like she's using Nano claws."

"Demons?" The doctor gawked. "You are nuts."

"If you'd rather go down for attempted murder of a police officer and trafficking illegal 'ware, keep on talking."

"Fine, fine." He held both hands up in a gesture of surrender for a few seconds. Once he gathered his composure, he fiddled with a holographic panel projected from the metal band around his right forearm. "What was the serial number?"

She read it off again.

The doctor looked over his screen for a moment before tapping it. "Randall Morris. Used to work for EnMesh security. Told me he was let go for taking side-jobs of 'questionable legality.' Frequent client of mine. He gets shot up pretty bad all the time, needed it strictly off the books to hide it from his employer. Last I heard from him, he had a rather large paycheck waved over his head from some Russian. He never mentioned a name."

"Damn," grumbled Kirsten.

"I can go digging... See if I can find anything on the 'net once my tail is fixed." Skittles stripped and stepped up on the raised base of the cleaner medical tank.

Kirsten shivered at all the dirt and junk piled around it, wondering how voracious the nanobots within the gel could be. Could they destroy *all* the contamination here? "Go on, Doc. Please fix her. I trust you will work better under your own steam than as a mind puppet."

He gulped, and hurried over to the control box for the tank. The clear plastic tube sank down from the ceiling and sealed her in. Skittles bounced on her toes like an eager kid about to go on an amusement park ride.

"Mind puppet? Really?" asked Dorian, a hint of a chuckle in his voice.

She offered a weak shrug and whispered, "It worked, didn't it?"

Skittles held her breath until the peach-colored gel reached the top of the tank. A tremendous plume of charcoal-grey hair rose upward like an ink cloud in the upper third of the tube. Bubbles streamed out of her as she exhaled hard and sucked in the oxygenated slime as though it were no big deal. Within seconds, her body went limp as she slipped into the painless grasp of anesthesia.

"She's rather used to the stuff," said Dorian. "Wonder if she has military training to be that accustomed to the transition to gel. I bet she's former Resistance. I wouldn't be surprised if she got herself sent to the ambassador's estate on purpose to spy on him. Hell, maybe she was there in case they wanted him dead."

Skittles' back split open as if cut by an invisible knife. Inch by inch, her tail peeled away until it floated free from the body. Synthetic nerve connections wrapped around the M3 wire trailed like threads of molten cheese to the base of her modified spinal cord. One by one, they broke away and reattached.

Kirsten cringed and looked away.

"You've seen worse than that walking around after death," said Dorian.

"Ugh. I know. But she's still alive. Somehow, that makes it worse." She positioned herself so she could watch the doctor without having to see the tube.

"This will probably take a little while." Dorian patted her on the shoulder.

"Yeah. I know." She kept a link open to the doctor's surface thoughts, making sure he didn't do anything sketchy.

30

DRAGONS

Impact knocked Kirsten out of a deep sleep. Spots of light danced around above her, meaningless to a brain struggling to adjust to a rapid transition from dream to wakefulness. A few seconds later, she realized what had hit her: Evan. He clung to her, trembling.

Kirsten embraced him and rubbed her hand up and down his back. He whimpered. As warm as he felt, her touch had to be icy.

"Evan?" Kirsten patted him, and used her other hand to wipe her eyes. "What's wrong? Is there something in the apartment?"

He shook his head. "No, 'member we blockaded it."

She sat up, shifting him to sit sideways across her lap. "Bad dream?"

"Yeah."

"Do you want to tell me about it?" She kissed the top of his head and rocked him back and forth.

"Dragons were trying to eat you."

Oh... She heaved a mental sigh of relief. *Not a precog flash, just an ordinary nightmare.* "Oh, sweetie. There's no real dragons. Are you sure you haven't been spending too much time with Monwyn?"

Evan glared at her for a second or two before his expression of panic returned. "It's not Monwyn's fault." He cuddled against her side again. "These dragons were gold. Metal ones. Long and thin like the ones on the Chinese food bots, not fat like fantasy dragons."

Kirsten peeked into his thoughts, catching a fleeting glimpse of two golden dragon-heads shooting toward her like coiled serpents. She couldn't really gauge their size since they filled the entirety of the mental image, a burgundy-brown blur behind them... perhaps an out-of-focus door. Evan's dream showed the final two seconds before large metal-toothed maws engulfed the point of view. Her voice shrieked in the darkness that followed.

She took a breath to clear her mind. "Evan. You don't have to compete with Konstantin. There's no choice. You are the most important person in my life."

He stared at her arm, frowning at the bracelet. "I don't like him. He feels weird." Evan shied away from the ouroboros.

Upon noting the dragon bracelet looked quite a bit like the ones in his nightmare—only tiny—she tucked her arm out of sight under the blanket so he couldn't see it. She squeezed him. "Evan. Look at me."

He looked up, staring at her with wide, innocent green eyes.

"There is nothing in this world, or the one after it, that could ever lessen how much I want you to be my son. I won't let anything or anyone hurt you ever again."

His eyes reddened, but he didn't cry. At least, if he did, the tears waited a few seconds until after he leapt into a hug and she couldn't see his face. "Are they gonna let me stay with you?"

"I got a positive evaluation from Dr. Loring last week. I won't know for sure for a little while yet, but... Captain Eze said he'd raise hell if they don't."

Evan laughed.

WHAP.

The noise made her eyes pop open.

Whap.

The noise took on a plastic tonal quality.

Wiff.

Kirsten sat up in bed and stared over her feet at the bathroom door. Evan stood near the fogged-up autoshower, whipping a towel at the tube as if practicing with a lash. She covered her mouth to hold in the laughter from the sound effects he added. He tried a few more times before giving up, dropping the towel, and climbing the sink to reach the clean-underwear dispenser. He stepped into them and came trotting out before he had them on all the way, heading toward her.

"Mom, can you show me how to do the lash?" He climbed onto the bed.

"Did you skip the rinse cycle? Your hair smells like soap."

"No. The new stuff you got is strong. It hurts my eyes. I wanna learn how to do the lash so when the next demon comes after you I can protect you."

Kirsten giggled into a sigh. "It takes more than astral to do that. You're not a mind blaster, thank goodness."

"Why?"

She ran her hands through his hair, trying to avoid the disaster it would be if she left it to finish drying uncombed. "Even other psionics are afraid of people who can Mind Blast. When someone is powerful with that talent, they can permanently erase brains. It scares them more than death. I don't want you to get stared at the way I do." She hugged him. "I'm not very good at it, and Morelli still can't even bear to look at me."

He pouted. "I hate not being able to fight. What good is seeing ghosts if I can't stop them from hurting you?"

She bit her lip, thinking about how the East City astral sensate had to constantly use a bound sword to deal with ghosts.

Evan blinked as if an idea hit him out of the blue. "What's a bound weapon?"

Kirsten shoved him face-first into the pillow. "Don't do that." She attacked his bare back with tickles until he wailed for mercy. "It's rude to eavesdrop on someone else's thoughts."

Out of breath, he curled fetal and giggled. When he regained the ability to speak, he pushed himself upright. "Just for 'mergencies."

"It's dangerous, Evan. A bound item becomes solid to both spirits and living people, but it's only as useful as what you bind. If you want to hurt a ghost, it has to be a weapon. A sword, a bat, a knife, something like that."

"Can't bind a gun?" He made a finger pistol and accompanying sound effects.

"Sure, if you plan to hit them with it. You'd have to bind each individual bullet for it to work. They are small, so it wouldn't do much to them anyway. The hydrostatic shock effect doesn't work the same way as it does on a person."

He made the blankest face she had ever seen. "Hy... dro... static?"

Hello, K. He's nine. "Bullets don't hurt ghosts as much as they do people. Plus…" She put a hand on his shoulder and squeezed. "I told you I could never hurt you. In order to bind something, you have to use your own blood. It allows your spiritual energy to remain on the item for a few hours."

"I still wanna learn."

She stared at him, thrilled his ribs no longer stood out so much. He remained on the 'too' side of thin, but much closer to healthy compared to the boy she found in that dingy apartment. "All right, but you are only going to watch me do it. I am not going to cut you, and I am not going to allow you to cut yourself unless it's an absolute emergency. Do you understand?"

He nodded. "'Kay."

With the help of a steak knife, a few spoons, and a stimpak, Kirsten demonstrated binding. Much the way she picked up the nuances of astral projection from him, he skimmed her thoughts as she focused the power to see how it *felt* to do it.

"'Kay. I think I could do it." He smiled. "If I had to."

She collected the empty coffee mugs. "I'm going to hop in the tube now. Promise me you won't try to do this while I'm in the shower."

"'Kay."

"Evan…" She squinted.

"I promise." He held his hand up. "Really. I don't wanna cut myself unless it's a 'mergency."

Kirsten pounded her desk terminal. A still-talking man's holographic head imploded into a speck of light and winked out of existence. Several of her squad mates jumped at the sudden noise. Morelli lapsed into choking on his tea.

"That went well," said Dorian.

Nicole glided by while packages of food floated out of a box she carried and glided to various desks.

"Thanks for meeting the 'bot outside." Kirsten took her breakfast burrito.

"Mmm!" Morelli saluted Nicole with his sandwich.

Nicole flopped in her chair. "You look pissed."

"EnMesh couldn't give me a damn thing I didn't already know. They terminated Morris five months ago for 'conduct incompatible with employment.'"

He exhaled. "Wow, just when I thought the euphemisms were out of control, you find a new one."

Kirsten drowned her chuckle with a mouthful of jalapeño-laced egg. "Mmm. I love these things, but they are annoying."

"How's that?"

"I can't enjoy coffee for a while afterward, mouth is sore."

"Iced coffee?"

"Dorian, you're a genius." She swiped her hand at the immaterial panels floating over her desk. A moment later, Samuel Chang's head appeared. "Sam, I hate to bother you... can I ask you for a fav—"

"Sure." He grinned. "You look good today. Less stressed out."

"Hah." She rolled her eyes. "I'm only hiding it well."

"The color in her face is from hot peppers," sang Nicole.

"Hush, you. You're whiter than I am."

Nicole gave her a raspberry. "Not my fault I go from ghost to sunburn instantly."

Dorian glanced at her. "Didn't gingers go extinct a few generations ago?"

"Umm. I think that's only a rumor. But..." Kirsten leaned back in her chair, whispering. "Her dad really wanted a blue-eyed redhead. Cost them a hundred grand in embryonic gene tweaking."

"So, what do you need?" asked Sam.

"Can you get into the system at EnMesh Biomed? I need anything you can find on an employee by the name of Randall Morris. I'll send over his file now."

Sam bowed. "Your wish is my command."

"Thanks." Kirsten jumped at finding Nicole close enough to breathe on. "Gah!"

Nicole grinned. "Here's your iced coffee." She struck a pose. "Not bad for a hundred grand, eh? At least I'm a little exotic. Not everyone gets to be carried to Earth by angels."

Kirsten went red-faced, exasperated at Nicole's continued mental eavesdropping. "I didn't have an angelic parent, Nikki. I only met *one*, and they called themselves Seraph."

"What's the difference?"

"Umm. I dunno."

"Potato, po-tah-toe," said Dorian.

Sam looked up all of a sudden. "Oh, Kirsten, I found something on your other suspect. Last night, a Citycam picked up a hit on the unidentified man in that video. I managed to find him in the system under the alias of Ajit Emir. He's a perfect match for your Nafiz Ajouri. Mr. Emir, or whatever he goes by, has quite a record. Nothing individually alarming, but it's full of small-time burglary charges and tax pops. He sells weapons and drugs and doesn't claim it as income. Div 1 has him listed as an opportunistic warrant."

"So they'll grab him if they spot him, but they're not searching." Dorian shook his head.

Kirsten blinked. "Sells guns and drugs and all they get him for is not paying tax on it?"

"He sticks to under-the-radar military stims, Flowerbasket, Sandman, and a couple of the harder things like Nightcandy, but he won't touch Lace or Phindara. All the weapons he sells are civ-legal. All he's really *doing* is evading tax. Anyway, I got a hit on a NetMini. CR 408 and Lake Street, sector 418."

"Thanks, Sam." She stood. "I haven't forgotten. I will make good on my promise for dinner. I've been so damn busy with this case…"

"I understand. I heard about the commissioner."

"You did?"

Sam winked. "I have level 4 clearance."

KIRSTEN FLEW IN SILENCE FOR ALMOST AN HOUR BEFORE SETTING THE patrol craft down in the parking lot of a nameless six-story commercial structure. Subdued red light leaked out from curtain-covered windows on the ground floor. She jogged to the door, mechanically reaching for the handle—but stopped inches short of grabbing an enormous bronze phallus.

"Oh, ick." She reached for the center, hesitated, went to grab the top, paused again, considered the bottom, and sighed. "Seriously?"

Dorian cackled.

"What are you, twelve?" She scowled, shooting him the side eye from hell. "I wasn't expecting that."

He gestured at the door. "Does anyone ever expect a giant bronze dick in their hand?"

It's only metal. She grabbed the middle and flung the door open. "You…

are… impossible."

Two men, one behind a front desk and one standing in front of it, stopped kissing to look in her direction, both giving her the head-to-toe appraisal. The one behind the desk raised a light brown eyebrow.

"Good morning, officer. You're a few days early, but I have all the employee records ready for you. I assure you, all the vaccinations and immune-boosters are up to date."

"The only thing louder than his shirt is the pattern on that tie." Dorian held his arm over his eyes as if staring into the sun.

"I'm not here about your service." She offered a pleasant smile. "I need to have a word with a client of yours. He's wanted for questioning in a murder case."

Both gasped. The man in front of the desk paled a little.

"Need me to do anything?" asked the clerk.

She shook her head to the negative. "If things get nasty, hit the deck and stay down 'til the dust settles."

The NetMini trace on her armband display led her down a dark hallway of polished wood and blood-red carpet. Every several meters, a table held a vase or small phallic sculpture. Despite the unassuming exterior, the discrete adult club appeared to cater to men with an excess of money. She stopped outside Room 8 and readied her E-90. Azure dots swept back and forth along the barrel, lighting her face in pulses.

Dorian poked his head into the wall. "Looks like one guy. Right of the door. He seems to be waiting for you. Hmm. Someone tipped him off."

"Got it." She kicked the door in and dove to the left, aiming at where she expected him to be.

His ambush foiled, the dark skinned man stood motionless, and held his hands up. A black leather mask covered his entire head, open zippers over his eyes. Tight, shiny black pants left little of his scrawny glory to the imagination. He clutched a stunrod in his right hand, the tip glowing dark blue.

Two seconds of silence passed before he let loose a war cry worthy of a mujahedeen and leapt at her. Kirsten ducked to the right, cracking him across the back of the head with the handle of the E-90 as he went past. He stumbled, gouging a dent in the drywall with the stunrod before he fell to his knees, free hand clamped over where she'd hit him.

She backed up a step and levelled off her laser at him. "Drop the stunner and get on the floor."

The man stood, wild eyes glaring at her from behind tiny slits. He took a step closer.

This guy wants me to kill him.

He lunged, stabbing the stunrod at her gut like a sword. Kirsten spun into him, slamming the hardened armguard into his wrist to deflect the attack while seizing the offending limb in both hands. With a graceful twist, she ducked under his arm and redirected the weapon into her attacker's throat. Bright blue light gleamed from the eye-slits. Spittle foamed out of the bottom of the mask. As tingles reached her hands, she let go, leaving him convulsing on his feet for several seconds before his twitching body collapsed. The stunrod had disrupted communication between his brain and muscles for several seconds.

She wrenched the stunrod out of his grip and held it aloft. Images of the murder of Alaina Munoz flashed in her mind, the struggling young woman held down by this man while his accomplice plunged a dagger into her heart.

"You son of a bitch!" Kirsten shrieked, cracking him twice across the chest with the metal baton.

Brief contact with the stun element caused pain over the entire body, but fell short of the all-out paralysis of a proper application. The man curled up on the floor. She kicked him twice in the gut. "Who are you working with? Why are you killing those people?"

The man wheezed, coughing. "W-wait."

"Whoa! Kirsten, calm down." Dorian leapt between them. "You're acting like me… a few months before my first summary."

She exhaled, tossing the stunner over the bed before pacing in a tight circle. "Thanks." None too gently, she rolled the man on his stomach, sat on him, and pulled the mask off. The face staring back at her wasn't Nafiz. Too young, only her age. "Damn." A different sort of nausea settled into her gut. "Who the hell are you?"

"Tariq. I"—he coughed—"work here."

Kirsten stood. "What the hell did you attack me for? I could have shot you."

"Nafiz said you were an assassin. He said the Syndicate was sending a blonde woman to kill him."

"I'm not an assassin. I'm an actual cop." She squinted. "You did see the uniform, right?"

Tariq wiped foamy spittle off his chin. "I… He said the assassin would dress up like a cop so they could just walk in and kill him and no one would care."

"Where did he go? Do you know where he lives?"

"No," said Tariq, arms limp across his lap. "He saw me a few times, once every couple of weeks. He took a vid call from some this nasty old Russian guy a few minutes ago." He rolled his eyes. "I swear. *Some* people just don't know how to take care of their skin. The guy had a gorgeous Tanaka Mori. Oh, to die for."

Kirsten blinked. "What the hell is a Tanaka Mori?"

"Sounds like someone's name," muttered Dorian.

"Designer suit. At least sixty grand to start." Tariq fanned himself. "You don't want to know the things I'd do to get one of those."

"I can imagine." Dorian cringed.

"So… about Nafiz?" asked Kirsten.

"After he hung up the vid, he asked me to buy him some time. Left his NetMini here so you would find it. The old guy seemed pretty upset."

"Nafiz told you to attack a police officer. He could have gotten you killed." She stomped to the nightstand and grabbed the NetMini.

Dorian stuck his finger through it. Seconds later, the security screen faded out to the desktop image of a calm tropical beach scene. Kirsten went to the vid call app and checked the history.

"That call came in about four minutes ago." She grumbled. As expected, trying to trace it came back with 'unknown device.'

Dorian narrowed his eyes. "It would have been right when we left the PAC. The only way he could have known is if he is watching you."

"Or has my phone tapped." She kicked the bed. "I'm confiscating this." She waved the civilian-grade stunrod at Tariq, and stormed out.

Tariq grunted and wobbled to his feet.

Kirsten stopped, spun around, and looked at him. "Sorry for getting a little rough with you, but… you did attack me. Do you need a medic?"

He poked at his bruising ribs. "I think so."

Dorian chided her with a look as she called it in.

31

WANT

The Division 2 Regional Tech Center hallways seemed even colder than normal, the air conditioning working as much overtime as the techies. Kirsten trudged down the four black stairs to the network operations room. The pink-haired tech woman fired off her usual sharpened glare, while Neal refused to acknowledge her presence. Ever since Dorian shut his terminal down, he'd gone off the deep end, believing his workstation cursed. He'd evidently moved on to Shinto, decorating his desk area with various hanging ofuda and paper charms. On her previous visit, The last thing he'd said to her involved something about how nothing could exist that was inexplicable to math or science. She grinned, remembering the face he made when she asked him, via telepathy, to explain *that* with math.

"Hey, Sam." She fell into the chair, staring at his desk.

"Geez, Agent Wren, you look like a zombie… just cuter."

The pink-haired woman emitted a quiet, but unmistakable, gagging noise.

"I just had Div 9 wrist-deep in my ass, and elbow-deep in my terminal." She didn't react to the gasps. "Metaphorically speaking."

"What happened?" asked Sam.

"A suspect had warning I was coming for him at about the same moment I left my squad room. They're checking for hacks, bugs, or listening devices. I couldn't do what I need to do there, so I'm here. Mind if I use your equipment?" She twisted to point. "Not a word, Dorian."

He whistled, pacing around.

Sam blinked at Dorian, or rather the empty bit of air she'd spoken to. "Sure. Ghost?"

"Yeah."

She pawed at the screens, going for her file node where her notes resided. "I've been trying to find some kind of a pattern to these companies, but the only connection I keep coming back to is this guy, Yevgeniy. I've been staring at pages and pages of financial records."

"You guys don't have a Gnome?"

She buried her face in her hands. "Is that something from the Monwyn franchise?"

"No, it's an analysis AI, specifically developed for forensic accounting." He slid closer to reach the holo-panel, his proximity triggering a spike of awkwardness. "One moment."

Kirsten smiled at him as an overwhelming sense of guilt fell on her; the discomfort of having him near enough to feel body heat seemed traitorous but also welcome. She didn't mind Sam so near. Something about him *was* charming in an awkward sort of way, but she didn't want Konstantin to get the wrong idea. Dorian had a point, Sam was 'from her world,' genuine and sincere. She never got the sense he wanted anything from her but attention. With Konstantin, she often felt like either a street waif who didn't belong or a possession. A sudden storm exploded in her gut, and she clamped both hands over her stomach.

An elderly gnome appeared, all two feet of him standing on Sam's desk —complete with pointed hat and green tunic. Top-of-the-line holo projectors made him appear solid enough to be real.

"Give him the particulars," said Sam.

The gnome rotated to face her, and bowed.

"Can you please look for relationships between RedEx, EnMesh, Kukla Investment Corporation, VSKK, Yevgeniy Suvorin, and any security employees thereof?"

The tiny old man nodded. He clasped his hands behind his back and gazed upward as if staring into the heavens in search of truth. His eyes glowed in flickering shades of amethyst and green, creating matching coloration on the sides of his long nose. Kirsten jostled to the side as the pink-haired techie bumped into her chair from behind. Her shirt open far enough to display the lack of a bra, she dropped a datapad on Sam's desk, then leaned forward, over Kirsten.

"Well, that's subtle," muttered Dorian.

"Sam, Lieutenant Saunders asked me to remind you about your end-of-year self-review. It's late. He wants you to do it before you leave today."

He glanced at her, offering no reaction whatsoever to the pair of almost-exposed tits in his face. "Uhh, sure. I'll do it right after we're done."

"I'll let him know." Ignoring Kirsten entirely, the woman wandered off.

Kirsten glared at the woman's back. "She must like you."

Samuel Chang blushed. "No, it's not like that. She's a friend. Guess she's jealous of you. It is rare to be beautiful on the outside as well as on the inside." The earnest look in his eyes almost made her suggest they go out for dinner that night.

Fire swam up the back of her throat. Kirsten clamped a hand over her mouth in an effort to avoid throwing up all over his desk. A little metal dragon ripped around in her stomach, biting and clawing at her from the inside out. When the initial urge to vomit retreated to a grinding, she doubled over and gasped. *What the hell is wrong with me?*

"I'm sorry." He offered her tissues. "I did not mean to offend you."

Dorian put an amazing, cool hand on her forehead. "Kirsten?"

"I'm fine. Had to be bad fruit." She re-swallowed her breakfast. "I'm glad I got the oatmeal today instead of the usual spicy eggs. Sam, that's very sweet of you." She winced. "I'm sorry. I'm just sick with stress over this case. It's not you."

"Do you need water?"

She forced a smile past the pain. "That would be wonderful."

Sam ran off to the break room.

"Kirsten, you're sweating and feverish. Every time you look at him, you grab your gut. Now, either you're allergic to what he's starching his shirt with, or you are taking the phrase lovesick too literally."

"Dammit, Dorian, I belong to Konstantin," she hissed, managing to avoid screaming it at the entire tech crew. "Why do you keep trying to pull me away from him? You just—" She gawked. "Sorry. Shit, twice now I've snapped at you."

"That's not you talking, K." He held her head in both hands, peeling her eyes open one at a time to examine them. She shivered at the icy fingers encircling her skull. "You are growing more and more defensive whenever someone suggests that fancy billionaire might not be an ideal match."

She glanced at the unmoving gnome with its light-eyes, then at the floor between her boots. "Maybe I want it too bad. Having that kind of security for Evan, it's more than I could have ever dreamed."

"You don't make bad money with the department. Remember that whole 'merit pay' thing?" He winked. "It's not like you to care so much about the size of a bank account. And since when do *you* belong to anyone?"

"I don't..." She blinked. *I said that, didn't I?* Her cheeks flashed warm. "Umm. I dunno. This case is driving me crazy. And, I've never had to worry about a kid before. If I have my way, he'll never want for anything."

"You know it's a recipe for a spoiled brat. Sooner or later, his gratefulness for getting him out of the situation you found him in will wear off. As soon as he feels comfortable, he'll be just like any other whiny, needy, foul-mouthed teenager. The day will come when you will count down the days until he's old enough to move out."

"He's not just being super-nice to thank me for saving him. That's who he is."

"Kirsten?"

"Yeah?" She looked up.

"I suggested you might think Sam is cute and you were ready to rip my head off. I just said, more or less, Evan is only acting sweet so you don't get tired of him and kick him out. That, you brushed off. Does it seem a little odd to you?"

"You didn't mean it."

"Meaning it is beside the point. I said it to poke you. I'm worried, Kirsten. You're not acting right."

Sam edged out of the breakroom, desperate to extricate himself from a heated discussion with a short, wide-bodied Hispanic man harassing him about his end-of-year appraisal.

"It's gotta be all the stress: the adoption, the case, the demons. For shit's sake Dorian, I almost tried *praying* the other day. I think I'm losing it."

He chuckled, still looking worried.

Sam hurried over, handed her a water bottle, and flopped in his seat right as the gnome came out of its trance. Kirsten sucked down half the water bottle in a single gulp. The diminutive AI waited for her to recover.

"The corporate entities you mentioned are connected. Kukla

Investment Corporation has recently acquired EnMesh Corporation. VSKK has recently acquired RedEx. Money has flowed in a back channel between Kukla and RedEx as well, siphoned through accounts linked to another entity: Koloss Venture Capital. Koloss has contributed funds to both EnMesh and RedEx, as well as significant contributions directly to both VSKK and Kukla. Further research indicates Koloss VC owns a majority share in Kukla Investment Corporation. By means of four shell corporations that exist only in Cyberspace, it is also listed as the owner of VSKK, a result of some very obscure accounting."

"So... basically you're saying Koloss owns everything related to this case?"

"It would seem that is correct," said the gnome, nodding for emphasis. "Also, I have found evidence Koloss, via Kukla Investments, has acquired numerous properties in Northern Africa, specifically Egypt. The trail led to thirteen small businesses engaged in historic preservation initiatives, Egyptology, and archaeological expeditions. There have also been significant donations arranged via a network of smaller business entities to the West City Archives as well as the *Büro für Geschichte* in Berlin, and the *Ministerstvo Istoricheskikh Sokrovishch* in Moscow."

"Huh?" Kirsten blinked.

"Museums," huffed the Gnome, with crossed arms. "Didn't you receive an education?"

"Enough to put me on duty when I was sixteen. More or less only what I needed to know to do my job."

"Criminal." The gnome's stubby arms flailed. "Is there anything else I can do for you?"

"Where is this Koloss VC?"

"It is a phantom. It occupies no physical real estate. However, the corporate registry is in Eastern Siberia, ACC."

Kirsten lifted the bottle to drink more. "Any idea who's running it?"

"By virtue of a chain of ownership among six other companies, including VSKK..." The gnome rocked heel to toe. "A man by the name of Konstantin Dobrynin."

Kirsten threw up.

SAID THE SPIDER

K irsten paced back and forth in the ground-floor lobby of her
apartment building. Being at home on a Wednesday, earlier
than sundown, lent a bitter edge to the flutter of worry
bouncing around her stomach. The strong orange light in the sky
exacerbated the *wrongness* of her feelings, as if something had lifted her
out of the real world and planted her in a false world that looked and felt
in every way the same except for a series of tiny flaws that escaped
conscious notice but agitated her subconscious mind into believing
something was wrong.

Then again, something *was* wrong.

However, no matter how much she studied the data dump from the
gnome, it still circled back to the unbelievable. She stared down the
length of her shimmering, sapphire-blue gown, self-conscious over the
milky whiteness of her legs. Thin straps held silver high heels to her feet.
They made her think of Armando/Brian/Douchebag, the last time she'd
worn them. *Why am I wearing these damn things? This isn't a date, it's an
investigation.* Her stomach churned. *He'll know something's wrong. Ugh, I'm
going to blow chunder all over him.* Thinking of vomiting made her think of
a worried Sam dabbing at her face after she decorated his desk. That
brought on another twinge of pain, a dagger in her stomach.

She walked to the glass, staring at the street while clinging to the E-90
in her purse under her left arm. The dull, silvery rectangle spanned

sixteen inches end to end. She should be able to get the weapon out in a hurry—and the bag matched her shoes.

A black limo came in for a landing outside, tossing debris and dust in all directions from the ion drives surging to arrest the effect of gravity. She put on the best smile she could muster. Her gait wobbled, partly from her continued hatred of high heels, the rest from feeling like she had been hung from the ceiling and used as a punching bag.

She made it to the car without tripping, close to fainting when Konstantin appeared out of thin air, opening the door for her. *Hologram... Just a f—hologram.*

"Such a pleasant surprise, *Lyubimaya.*" The false image pantomimed shutting the motorized door for her after she gathered the gown around her legs and got in. He vanished and reappeared on the seat beside her. "I am finishing up a business meeting. We should arrive at the restaurant close to the same time."

"I can't wait to see you," she said, past a Cheshire smile.

He bowed and faded away. She spent the remainder of a fifteen minute ride in silence, concentrating on unwinding the knots in her gut. Barfing all over Sam's desk was embarrassing enough, but if she did that here with Konstantin, she would never want to go outside again.

As good as his word, Konstantin emerged from the gold-rimmed doors of The Five Corners. Another place where normal people had to wait three months for a table—normal in the sense of being merely wealthy, as opposed to Konstantin's ridiculous fortune.

As soon as she saw him, the nausea faded. She ran to his side. The closer she got, the better she felt. By the time they settled into a table in the shadow of an enormous ice swan, she shivered with giddiness. Holographic wings around the sculpture moved up and down in time with distant violin music emanating from everywhere. Terraces lined the sides of the dining hall, each of the restaurant's five floors themed to a different geographical motif. Yellow and cream, the vault ceiling made her feel as though she sat inside an immense lemon meringue pie.

The floor around them consisted of a winterscape with staff dressed in white and blue, bedecked with sparkling crystal sequins. Bright azure holograms zipped here and there, snow faeries or fireflies. Above them was Ancient Rome, with waiters dressed in period garb. The third floor contained an amazing collection of African artwork and colorful dashiki-clad waiters. She leaned half out of her chair to peer over the edge of the fourth floor, catching glimpses of Chinese décor.

Konstantin chuckled at the girl-in-wonderland face. "This place is quite astounding, isn't it?"

"Yeah. What's on the top floor?"

"Pompeii, I think. Mostly Italian cuisine. It might be Mediterranean though. They change the themes every few months."

A beep from her purse distracted her. The past twenty minutes, long enough for their appetizer to come out, had gone by in a blur of small talk. Her NetMini flashed an incoming text from Nila: ‹Evan in panic mode, be careful.› She tucked the device past the pistol, sliding her hand onto the grip for confidence.

"Can I ask you something?"

"Of course, *Lyubimaya.*" He raised his hand, wobbling his empty glass at a nearby waitress with long white hair, bedecked in diamond snowflakes and swan makeup.

"Do you know anything about a company named Koloss... It owns Kukla Investment Corporation. That's where Yevgeniy works, isn't it?"

"Koloss... I can't say I've heard the name." He smiled at the ice-princess, thanking her for the refilled drink. "Is it something I should know?"

Her grip clenched. Soft, rubberized handgrips squished between her fingers. She flicked a finger at the trigger. "It turns out you own it. I think..." Dizziness swam over her brain, splitting her silverware into three copies, a mesmerizing dance that held her gaze for a few seconds before the utensils merged again. "I think... Yevgeniy is trying to hurt you. He's calling demons, isn't he? You know it. That's why you studied ancient Sumerian stuff." She withdrew her hand from the E-90 in her purse and clasped the edge of the table. "You've been sending money to treasure hunters in Egypt. You've been searching for old books, maybe something that can protect you."

Konstantin glanced at her with an unreadable face for a moment before the slightest trace of a smile curled his lip. He took a sip of his drink, straight genuine vodka, and set the glass down. "I am impressed, Kirsten. I didn't think your people would give serious credence to the existence of such creatures. Yevgeniy thinks he is a threat." He waved her off. "In truth, he is but a nuisance. I have learned enough mysticism in my years to keep his efforts at worst annoying and at best amusing. His desperation will reach the point where he calls on something he cannot control. Then"—Konstantin seized a stuffed mushroom from the plate and held it up, staring over it—"then, they will devour him."

Chomp.

Despite it being only a mushroom that died, a chill ran down Kirsten's bare back. Within a few seconds, his mirth infected her and she grinned. After the arrival of the main course—fish for her, pelmeni for him—their conversation wandered far away from anything to do with demons, about-to-be-executed commissioners, or finance. By the time he walked her to the limo, she found herself wrapped around his arm. She had managed to limit herself to one glass of white wine, albeit a large one. *Am I drunk? Why do I feel like I'm going to fall over if I let go?*

"Mmm," she cooed. "I'm so happy right now, I feel like nothing matters but being with you."

"*Lyubimaya*, you can free yourself from such unhealthy stress. As my wife, you would never need to work again. You could spend your days with your boy, and your nights with me. You could sleep the sleep of angels, free of worry."

Kirsten closed her eyes.

"Alas, I fear you are quite dedicated. I would invite you to my home, but I expect your work calls you."

She bit her lower lip, pulling herself up by the grip she had on his arm. "I want to go with you."

"You know not how long I have waited to hear those words leave your lips." He brushed his cheek across hers and placed a gossamer kiss on her mouth.

He held her hand as they climbed the steps of his manor house. White walls shifted with shadows cast by imitation firelight from numerous holographic lanterns. Kirsten shivered, gathering her coat close to her back as a shield against the wind. The estate, east of the northern edge of West City, had open grounds free from the burden of city plates. Trees, streams, and several constructed ponds dotted the landscape.

"This is so beautiful. The only times I've seen real ground, it's been desert or covered by city."

"Nature has created many things of wondrous beauty, Kirsten. Far from the least of which I find on my arm at this moment."

A rush of warmth ran to her face and she found her legs unsteady. Konstantin drank in her adoring stare for a moment before ushering her through the door. Inside, the warm air of a cavernous foyer banished the cold northern wind. A man in a dark suit approached without speaking, taking both their coats.

Led by the hand, Kirsten followed him up a long, curved staircase to a second-floor hall. The extravagance lifted her out of the real world. She slid into the fantasy of a princess in her castle, her doe-eyed gaze unable to believe the paintings, statues, polished rosewood floors, and carpets that passed her on both sides. He stopped at an archway. A fireplace waited at the far end of a room full of medieval weapons and several sets of armor arranged on pedestals.

"Would you care for some hot cider by the fire, perhaps cognac?"

Kirsten leaned into him, palms flat on his chest. Hand over his heart, she listened for several beats while staring into the distant hearth. She caressed him, once again startled by the firm, statuesque muscles beneath his shirt. His arms wrapped her in a sense of safety. She enjoyed the quiet embrace for a while, then leaned up and kissed him.

"I want you to be my first," she whispered, shrinking down off her toes to cling to him again.

He swept her into his arms and carried her. She folded her hands to her heart, barely noticing the paintings, candles, and little statues drifting by. Another stairway took them up to the third floor. She floated in a haze of contentment. He shifted sideways to navigate a set of double oak doors engraved with squares reminiscent of a castle portcullis and into a room larger than her entire apartment. Konstantin set her on the edge of a great canopy bed with a carved cherry wood headboard in the image of a pair of entwined Chinese dragons.

She pushed her hands into the burgundy silk, astounded. "A cloth mattress?"

The smile he gave her said 'of course.' An expression she once thought contemptible and arrogant. She slipped out of her shoes, stood and shrugged one shoulder out of her gown. Shimmering azure cloth fell away in a second, gathering around her bare feet. Not a synapse wasted its time on embarrassment at a man seeing her in only black silk panties and a gold bracelet. She *wanted* him more than anything she had ever wanted in her life.

Konstantin stepped to her, hand behind her head as he tilted her into a long kiss. She swayed, arms lax, surrendering her body to wherever he moved it. The smooth silk of his shirt brushed her nipples and stomach. She inhaled his scent. Their kiss paused long enough for him to gaze into her eyes. He tilted her over, leaning with her until she slid onto the bed. He sat up, coarse worker's hands touching her pale, silken skin, sliding around her breasts and pausing above her hips. He twirled a finger around the band of her panties, lifting an eyebrow in question.

Kirsten couldn't believe this man wanted her. A man like him, so handsome, so powerful, so rich, had the pick of any woman in the world —and he wanted *her*. She reached her arms over her head, managing a quick nod before closing her eyes. A weak gasp escaped her lips as the elastic tugged past the crown of her hips and cool air brushed her intimates. Silk slipped down her thighs. Kirsten pulled her right leg free, and shuddered as he used both hands to guide the material all the way down to her other foot, so slow she almost screamed. He cupped her heel and raised her leg to his lips, bit the panties in his teeth and tugged them off over her toes. Kirsten slid farther into the plush bedclothes, squirming, eager for him to take her. She closed her eyes and moaned.

A minute passed without contact. Only the cool fabric touched her nakedness.

Impatient, she peeked. Konstantin unbuttoning his shirt in a methodical manner that ended with a neat folded garment set on a nearby ottoman. The sight of his bare, muscular chest pulled a gasp of desire from her throat. Such a body belonged to professional athletes, not billionaire playboys. Regardless of how much surgery this being sculpted from tanned flesh-colored marble may have endured, his physique stole the breath from her lungs.

Konstantin strode to the foot of the bed and crawled forward until he hovered over her, kissing his way from thigh to the base of her neck. He lowered his lips, attending to her right breast. She grasped handfuls of bedding, clenching and releasing from the sensation. The scratch of unshaven man on her flesh, the warmth of him all over her, the scent of his breath—she drowned in Konstantin. He leaned upward, again kissing her lips while he caressed her other breast. Rolling to the side, he slid his hand down her back, over her ass, and back up the inside of her thigh.

The beeping NetMini fifteen feet away didn't exist.

She squealed at his touch. Arching her back, she squirmed and begged him not to stop. When sensation faded enough for her to notice his hands no longer made contact, her eyes fluttered open. He stood beside the bed, draping his black dress pants over the back of a chair. Violet boxers hugged the kind of contours Nicole so often gawked at online. Kirsten bit her knuckle at the sight of how ready he seemed to be.

A demure shiver ran through her at the size of the bulge. "Oh, my... Konstantin."

He shed the last of his garments, and slid onto the bed at her side. His length brushed across her thigh as he leaned down to kiss her on the neck.

"I can't believe this." She closed her eyes. "Why me? You are so perfect..."

Konstantin guided her hand to him, grunting when she gripped a little too firmly. "This *is* your first time. Are you sure you want to continue?"

She caressed his alarming size, gasping. Compared to her, it came a little too close to an awful memory. Then, she had cringed and waited for it to be over as fast as possible. But here, she wanted to enjoy every second.

He let her examine it, mouth curled back and eyebrow raised as if showing off a priceless artifact unmatched by anything in another's collection.

"If you promise you won't hurt me," she whispered, biting him on the ear. "My body or my heart." Her eyes opened with a sliver of guilt. *He's going to know he's not the first. He's going to throw me out. I'm such a whore.* Kirsten burst into tears. "I'm not good enough for you."

A kiss took the tear from her cheek and put it on her lips. "*Shh.* I know." He ran a hand over her head. "You were an orphan doing whatever you needed to do in order to survive." The next kiss brushed her neck. "To me, you are still unsullied."

Surging with adoration, she sat up and cuddled to his chest, letting him hold her for a moment before she reclined and offered herself to him. "I want you to make love to me for the first time."

Konstantin shimmered with an angelic aura; his face, beaming with passion, seemed even younger. In this light, he looked no older than twenty-five. He prowled over her, a stalking panther. Kirsten shivered as *it* dragged over her thigh and across her belly. She tensed, waiting for the feeling of him inside her.

The room flooded with an eruption of classical Russian music.

Konstantin froze, not moving a muscle for twenty-six seconds until it stopped. Anger swam over his face. It took him a moment to relax, helped along by her hands on his chest. A second after as he eased her onto her back again, the music returned.

"Someone wants me to cut their balls off," he growled. "I am sorry, *Lyubimaya*, I must take this call. It is a special line." He slid from the bed, lifting her hand and kissing it before setting it between her legs. "Keep yourself warm. I will be only a moment."

Kirsten barely noticed him grab a silk robe and storm out. She rolled on her side, snuggled in the thick comforter. Her gaze settled on a hazy silvery blob atop the desk, though she couldn't quite tell what the strange object was.

Beep. "Incoming Vidcall from... *Evan.*" The digital voice gave way to a little boy's gleeful chirp of his own name.

Evan. Kirsten grinned, licking the taste of Konstantin from her finger. *I know someone named Evan.* She laughed.

Beep. "Incoming Vidcall from... *Evan.*"

She scrunched up her face at the bag. *I'm busy, kiddo.* Kirsten shot upright. *Kiddo. Boy. Evan! Holy shit! What the fuck is wrong with me!* Kirsten leapt from the bed, tearing at her purse to grab the device. She pulled it out right as the ringer ended.

Redial.

"I'm sorry, I'm inside school now and not 'llowed to have calls. If this is a 'mergency, call my mommy." A link popped up on the screen to contact her.

Kirsten's head swam in a nauseating spiral that left her on her knees. She sat back, covering herself with her arms. Her clothes had vanished: heels, panties, dress, as well as Konstantin's. Stifling a squeal of embarrassment, she pounced on the bed and gathered the comforter around herself. The enormous, thick blanket would be far too heavy to carry. She gazed around the room feeling trapped by her shame. When her gaze fell on a pair of ornate wardrobe doors, an inexplicable urge pulled her to her feet. She dashed across the room and swiped one of his silk jackets from the cabinet. The garment fit her like a short robe, its sheer fabric cool on her skin. She bundled it closed and tied a quick knot in the belt before dropping her NetMini in the pocket.

E-90 in hand, she peered out into the hallway. Nausea pummeled her in the gut so hard the walls swayed back and forth. The paintings seemed to animate and mock her. Little voices from figures within them called her disloyal to Konstantin. They ordered her back to the bedroom. The grinding of tiny teeth in her stomach intensified.

She clung to the doorjamb to keep from falling down again, and searched for somewhere to go. To the right, past a long red carpet, stood a fancy set of red-stained, wooden double doors with solid gold doorknobs in the shape of Chinese dragons. Something about them drew her, beckoning. Left hand pressed into her belly, right clutching the E-90, she staggered toward the doors, determined not to let the churning sickness inside her win. A few feet from the doors, her balance returned. Intricate workmanship on the handles rendered every scale in precise detail. Ruby eyes gleamed such that she couldn't tell if they reflected light or created it.

Each dragon had a movable pointed tongue that curved out of the gaping maw. Depressing one opened the latch. She opened it to reveal a small chamber containing only a spiral staircase and drab walls. *I know I'm at least on the third floor. I gotta get out of this house. I'm suffocating in here. Did he slip me something?* Metal stairs at her bare feet chilled a gasp out of her. Kirsten hurried down the spiral stairs, going around and around. The instant she worried she might've gone deeper than the first floor, she arrived at a plain door. She wobbled upright, abandoning her friend the railing, and pushed the door open into a small room with a table, couch, and holo-bar projecting a hundred-inch screen of a live Gee-ball game.

Basement? Man cave? She ignored a small leather-covered door behind the couch, heading for a larger one opposite the way she entered, hoping plain meant a better chance of it leading to the outside. It opened into darkness. *Damn.* Behind her, a toilet flushed. She darted into the black and edged the door shut behind her, heart racing.

Colder air wrapped around her. The floor felt like bare concrete with a dusting of grit. The scent of wood, straw, and strange spices hung in the air. She fumbled, searching the wall near the door for the expected panel. A tiny electronic chirp followed her finger meeting a smooth surface. The lights came on.

Piles of wooden boxes, many with Arabic writing on them, stood in stacks in front of her. Thirty feet to the right past a large conference table, several steel cabinets stood against the wall. The sound of breathing attracted her forward and left, around a pile of coffin-sized crates. Several had customs imprints from the Middle East. When she reached the edge of the boxes and peered around, her heart almost stopped.

Between the two large metal cabinets, a squat table held a carved box she initially mistook for an Oriental shrine. On the wall above it hung a solid black mask with gold filigree around the eyes and two thin lines falling like tears to the jawline. Sickness hit her in the gut with the force of a cyborg's punch. Her mind dove into the scene from Brooke's memory —the man with the knife. The same knife she somehow knew sat inside the fancy carved box at the center of the table. Brooke's vision zoomed in, as if a camera rushed at the man in the mask. She peered close, staring at the holes.

Konstantin's red-brown eyes glared at her, lit wild with bloodlust.

"No!" She covered her mouth to mute the wail. "No," she cried, in a breathy rasp.

Kirsten stumbled around the corner and a thousand credits-worth of half-digested fish exploded through her fingers. She landed on all fours, retching for a moment before the heaving stopped. *Ugh.* She shuddered, sick to her stomach at the thought the man who'd murdered Alaina Munoz had *touched* her. A trail of bile still clinging to her lip, Kirsten lifted her head and peered down a short hallway that ended at a barred door lifted from a medieval prison. Inside a small prison cell, a naked woman lay on the ground bound hand and foot with metal restraints.

Exactly like Alaina Munoz had been.

She appeared to be sleeping or drugged. Her shoulder-length black hair greyed from a coating of the ubiquitous dust, which also highlighted her musculature wherever her brown skin had touched the floor.

Shuddering with the continued desire to vomit, Kirsten half-crawled, half-walked to the cell door. Aside from the woman, it contained a large pan of cat litter. She aimed the E-90 at the shiny bars, hesitating at the fear the laser would reflect away without harming it. Despite being modern plastisteel, the polished cell door used a mechanical key and had no electronics programmed to accept police override codes.

Kirsten reached between two bars and grasped the woman's foot. Slapping her several times, she whisper-yelled. "Hey, are you alive? Hey? I'm gonna get you out of here." She huddled against the wall outside the bars and pulled her NetMini from the robe pocket. A red icon at the bottom caught her eye that she hadn't noticed before. Email. Based on the timestamp, it arrived while she had been at the restaurant. She didn't recall hearing the chime. Three flicks of her thumb opened a message from Samuel Chang.

‹Kirsten, I went looking for Nafiz online. I managed to trace the call that warned him. It looks like it came from a manor house way out in the north. It's owned by Enigma Capital, of which eighty-two percent controlling interest is owned by Davosk Shipping. Davosk shipping is… you guessed it… owned by Kukla. I've attached the email.›

Her heart pounded in her head as she scrolled down.

‹She is coming here, go, now. Do it.›

At the bottom of the ominous email, she found three still images. In the first, she led Evan to the patrol craft on the parking deck of Nila's apartment building. In the second, she opened the patrol craft's door for him. In the last photo, Evan sat in the driver's seat, saluting her while she laughed.

The nagging sense of a paranormal presence that had dogged her for days reverberated in the back of her mind, pulsing in time with the nausea which kept her legs from supporting her. Driven by fear for Evan, her mind lashed out, grasping at thin air. A sense of tangibility led her to the gold serpent bracelet around her right wrist.

I couldn't take it off that night. She grabbed it, twisting and squeezing. Her skin reddened as she tried to pull it over her hand. One of the horns nipped her finger as she tried to find whatever mechanism released the metal teeth from the tail. *What the hell is this thing? Is he... what is he doing to me?* She thought back to the restaurant. Her hand had been on the E-90, about to challenge him, but on came blind adoration. *He's* making *me love him.* Hot tears ran down her cheeks as she twisted her arm at the cursed jewelry. *Get off.* She shook her hand. *Get off me! He can watch everything I do. Oh, shit!*

She held her fingers over it and focused. The bracelet levitated around her wrist, spinning and wobbling. Paranormal energy imbued within it reacted to her ability to manipulate astral forces. She grunted, trying to will it open. A sense of panic came from it. The ouroboros whirred around her tiny wrist as if under the force of an invisible magnet. When the direct psionic assault failed to do anything more than spin the bracelet, she fell into a primitive physical tug of war with it. She pulled at it as though she'd been physically chained to Konstantin. Somehow, this bracelet affected her. Fishy bile blasted past her teeth on a cough at the thought of what almost happened upstairs. Far more than what she did ten years ago, *that* would have felt like rape, had he gone all the way.

Anger swam to the surface. Her brain switched gears and she held her right arm out at length. She called the glimmering lash from her left hand and swiped it at the bracelet, striking something faintly solid within. A wave of energy rocked her with the sense of a soul meeting obliteration. The crippling pain in her stomach stopped in an instant, leaving only the sort of dull ache normal after a bout of vomiting. With a shaking hand, she pinched the now-hot horns of the bracelet, and the tail of the ouroboros slipped loose from its mouth. She hurled the unclean thing down the hall as hard as she could throw it.

Her thoughts jumped to Evan. *Oh, no. Nafiz. Calm down, K. Evan's with Nila. She's a pyro. She'll end anyone that tries to hurt my son.*

Kirsten stood, glaring at the 'no signal' error on the NetMini. She backed to the end of the corridor away from the cell, finding a connection as soon as she stood in the wide open basement.

"Hello, *Lyubimaya*."

The voice accompanied an assassin's embrace from behind. Rather than a knife at the throat, the tiny nip of an autoinjector found her neck. He released her and she slumped to the ground, rolling onto her back. A mild burn spread over her body, stealing her ability to move or even speak. Melting walls drooped around her, swirling into a spiral surrounding the face of a man in his seventies. Darkened teeth appeared within a dour smile. His robe hung open, proving his face wasn't the only thing idealized by enchantment.

"I am sorry it came to this, my love. I was so enjoying your company. I am impressed, Kirsten. I thought you had pinned everything on that smiling drunken playboy, Suvorin. Fortunately"—his voice echoed as her ability to see faded away—"your little friend is the last piece I need."

"Charazu?" she wheezed.

Konstantin's blurred face smiled. "Ahh, yes. An early effort that proved too difficult to control adequately. I should thank you for helping me clean up my error. The ancients are so much more difficult to control than a returned mortal."

Kirsten tried to fling herself at him, but couldn't even make one of her eyelids open. All her attempts to scream happened in her mind. Vision faded to darkness, and sound swirled as if she went underwater. A scuff of a foot came from beside her head. Konstantin's rough, calloused hand patted her on the cheek.

"I promise, he won't feel a thing."

PREMONITION

Evan crossed his arms over his face and screamed as the enormous fanged, pink rabbit engulfed him. He pulled the senshelmet off his head and pouted at the giggling girl on the other side of the sectional. The cartoon rabbit on her nightgown mocked him more than her pointing finger. He sulked. The hand-to-hand fighting game was too simple. Evan had spent an hour searching for effective combos of moves, but his efforts at strategy continued to succumb to Shani's random flailing.

"You're not even playing. You're just doing random stuff as fast as you can."

She pulled her senshelmet off and set it on the couch next to her. "That's playing. If I wasn't playing, I wouldn't do anything."

"That's not how you play! You're s'posed ta use moves an' combos and tactics. Countermoves and attacks."

She stuck her tongue out at him. "I'm winning, aren't I?"

Evan frowned. "Wanna play *Colony Commando 9*? We can be on the same team there."

Shani scrunched her face. "Are there bunnies?"

"No."

"Cats?" She tilted her head left.

"No."

"Puppies?" She tilted her head right.

"No, it doesn't have cute stuff. It's about soldiers and aliens."

A series of contortions worked their way around her lips while she ground the gears of her little seven-year-old mind. "Do the soldiers shoot bunnies?"

"No!" Evan threw his hands up in the air.

"Okay. As long as they don't kill bunnies."

He glared. "'Kay, lemme put in my EGM username. We can play co-op on this one."

"You're just tired of losing to me."

Evan's eyebrows formed a flat line across his brow. "Yeah, I'm just tired of losing a fuzzy bunny fighting game to a button masher."

She gave him a raspberry. "There's no buttons."

"It's just a term. It means you're doing random attacks without any attempt to do any specific moves."

Shani tilted her head. "Huh? I think you're just tired of losing."

Evan started to sigh in frustration but wound up laughing. The game had been made for little kids, so maybe it didn't even have combos.

He punched in his PID, logged into Electronic Game Megaverse, and connected Shani's Neurocaster IV to his account. Nila's apartment filled with the sound of a dropship overflight, knocking small objects off shelves in the rumble of starship-sized ion thrusters. He sat there patiently waiting for the animation to finish, but before the option to start a game popped up, a chill washed over him, rapidly worsening to sharp nausea and full-body numbness. Evan broke out in a cold sweat and crossed his hands over his belly, shivering.

"Turn that down! What the hell are you doing?" yelled Nila from the back.

"Volume twenty percent," chirped Shani.

A green line appeared on the holographic display, which shrank to the left.

Shani stood on the couch, leaning over the back to yell, "Okay, Mom!" When she flopped back down, she stared at Evan. "What's wrong?"

Evan looked at her, searching for words he couldn't find. His hands shook, sweat ran down the back of his neck.

Fear.

As soon as it had come on, it faded. He looked around, fixating on the cartoonish huge-chinned soldier grimacing at him from the screen. Giant machine guns sprouted from both hands and a ridiculous amount of mini-turrets dotted his powered armor. Letters resembling cut steel spelled out *Colony Commando: The Last Hope* on the right half of the screen. Nine large bullet holes underlined it—the ninth in the series.

She made a face at the image in the goggles. "The first one and the ninth one are the same game with little bit better graphics. His armor is silly. If he fired all those guns at once, he'd fall over, and where does he keep all the bullets? This is the ninth one? Why do they keep making these games?"

New maps, new weapons, new aliens. Evan answered in his head. The impulse to speak became lost trying to wander from brain to tongue. "S-something's wrong."

"This was *your* idea, Evvie." Shani grabbed her senshelmet and popped it on. "You're not afraid of some slimy aliens are you?"

The doorbell chimed, something musical. Nila had said it came from a big guy named Ben, in England. Evan whipped around to stare at the door. The tones vibrated his bones. Shani tossed the senshelmet to the couch cushion, leaping to her feet while cheering "I got it! I got it!"

"Shani, no! Don't open the door!" Evan screamed and started to climb over the couch to get away, but froze the instant Shani's hand touched the knob. He screamed, "Nila! Help!"

PRINCESS ALSBETH

Cold grit ground into Kirsten's skin with every breath. Her head felt as though someone inflated it to many times its size. Numbness manifested in patches over a body she couldn't move. The taste of dust made her sputter, and she gathered every ounce of conscious willpower into the task of getting her lips away from the floor. Her weight shifted onto her side. Air washed over her bare front. Freezing metal spots found the small of her back—rigid bands locked about her wrists. Her eyes snapped open.

She stared at the wall of a small prison cell.

Short-chain binders pinned her ankles together and kept her hands behind her back. Some manner of rubbery cord linked the two restraints, allowing her little range of motion. Devoid of reason, Kirsten thrashed in an effort to break free. Her struggle ground more painful particles of grit into her unprotected skin. She knew she wasn't strong enough to crack plastisteel, but some primal instinct urged her to try. Lying still would be like accepting her captivity.

She had to try. Konstantin had emailed pictures of Evan to someone.

"You fucking bastard!" she screamed. "Don't you dare touch him!"

Her voice echoed back from the basement until only the rasp of her own breathing broke the stillness. She struggled until she flopped over, exhausted. The elastic strap drew her hands and feet close behind her back once more. The memory of Konstantin's touch between her legs brought hot anger to her face. Her attempt to cover herself came to a halt with a metallic *click*. Kirsten wobbled into a kneeling position, wringing her arms in an ineffectual attempt to slip loose.

"Lay off the yelling or they'll gag you," a voice whispered. The woman who had been in the cell before had come to. She sat up, leaning against the far wall. Like Kirsten, she wore only metal binders.

Kirsten's face burned red. She twisted around to examine the cuffs locked on her legs. They appeared devoid of electronics, fully mechanical, and almost a half-inch thick. The logo of an online kink store had been engraved along the hasp. Whoever put them on her tightened them too much, enough to break bones if she twisted wrong. *At least the only person who can see me is another woman.* Kirsten let her head sag forward. She'd felt helpless when Mother dragged her into the kitchen by her hair. She thought about waking up in her own cuffs when Templeton found her. That had been scary, but it had not topped Mother. Hiding under a SUV in a parking garage to elude a man with vibro claws—that made her feel more vulnerable than Mother ever had. Having nothing between her and a hail of bullets but a fast-disintegrating concrete support pylon had surpassed the SUV.

Kirsten stared at herself. Naked, hogtied, and trapped in the basement dungeon of a manor house where no one knew she had gone. *I've gotta stop trying to one up myself.* She squirmed, brushing hard grainy bits from her back as best she could. *Crushed soy hull.* A glance left at a litterbox sent her into another fit of struggling. *The bodies had soy hull and cat litter in their skin.* She dry heaved twice before working up a sweat from trying futilely to pull her hands out of the cuffs.

"You're wasting your strength," said the other woman. "The guy they had here before you was huge, and he couldn't break them."

That must've been Arris.

"I gotta get out of here. That piece of shit is going after my son." Kirsten stared at the ceiling, thinking about what the Seraphim told her, something about being out there to protect her. She curled into a ball, shivering from shame as well as the cold. Where were they now? She started down the path of 'where are they when I need their help,' but put the brakes on. *They're not here. They gave me a boost off the parking deck. I must not need their help now.* "There's a way out."

"Good fucking luck finding it." The woman puffed at a stray bit of hair over her eyes.

Kirsten wobbled onto the balls of her feet and hopped twice toward the door before the elastic pulled her off balance. She fell forward, whimpering from the strike of her knees on hard plasticrete.

The other woman shook her head. "What 'chu gonna do? Bite the bars out? You can't even stand up to see the lock."

"I'm not helpless."

"Yeah, you sure as hell don't look it. Skinny ass bitch trussed up like a Thanksgiving turkey."

"They didn't blindfold me. I'll kill the first son of a bitch I see." Kirsten snarled, falling over backward in a failed attempt to get back on her feet.

"You go, girl. Kick some ass. We halfway out now." She laughed at Kirsten's ungainly roll. "So what are you doing here? They grab you just like the others?"

"I'm with Division 0." Kirsten grunted, taking another futile stab at breaking the restraints, or at least snapping the elastic. She got one hand around the rubber cord; which had to be at least an inch thick.

"That sounds kinda military."

"Police, actually." After rolling back on her belly, she rested her head sideways on the cold floor, panting.

"You're a skinny little thing for a cop. Thought all cop chicks were like dudes with boobs."

"Maybe in Div 5 or 6. I'm more of a detective." *You're keeping secrets, K? Neither one of us has much to hide at this point.* She blushed again.

"Oh, so you gonna detect our asses out of here? I've been stuck in this cage for two weeks. Guys are real assholes, too. They haven't taken these cuffs off once. Least they haven't dragged my ass out yet. Guess they're strugglin' to find a buyer. My brown ass ain't so exotic, but a pale thing like you oughta be outta here real fast."

Kirsten rocked until she wound up seated again. She glared at the wall beside the woman's head, jealous for a moment her cellmate wasn't hogtied. "They're not going to sell us. We're going to be used as human sacrifices to summon demons."

"Yeah, right." The other woman stared down. Ten seconds later, she snapped her head up and gazed wide-eyed at the barred door. "Shit!" She fell over sideways in a furious effort to break her cuffs. "You're right, these weird motherfuckers are gonna kill us." She stopped fighting when she ran out of breath. "Why the hell did they take our clothes if all they wanna do is kill us? You got a point though, the one dude was a little harsh to look at. Guess they didn't sell him as a sex toy."

Kirsten didn't want to admit to being about to get it on with a seventy-year-old man. The mere combination of her last glimpse of Konstantin's face coupled with remembering his rough hand touching her brought back the dry heaves. She leaned forward, face on knees, breathing. When the wave of nausea subsided, she spent another minute searching for a voice. "It's probably to reduce forensic evidence, or maybe some weird ritual requirement I don't understand. All the victims found so far were nude. I dunno, maybe the bastard likes the view or maybe you get bigger demons for sacrificing naked virgins. Name's Kirsten, by the way."

"Miranda. Heh, guess that's why I'm still here." Much of the cockiness had vanished from her voice. "I haven't been a virgin in a long time. Shit, are you really a cop? That means you got backup comin' right? You're gonna get us outta here? I don't wana fuckin' die."

"I... I didn't tell them I was coming here. It was sort of on a, umm... date." She shivered, unable to tell what would win a contest: cold or shame.

"Date?" Miranda wriggled herself seated again. "You were dating an old geezer?"

Kirsten went pale. "Don't remind me. He had some kind of spirit embedded in this bracelet he gave me. I think it made me see him as if he was perfect." *As if being chained up in here isn't embarrassing enough. They were all right. Everyone was trying to warn me. Evan called him old... To a nine year old anyone over eighteen is old... but did he see him as he really looks? That guy at the male club said 'old Russian.' Dammit! I'm so stupid. He was too good to be true.* Tears fell from her eyes and slid down her shins.

"So, cop chick, how are you figurin' our asses are getting out of here? I don't know about you, but I feel pretty damn screwed. Your ass is thin, but you ain't making it through the bars."

Nothing to lose now. "I'm psionic. Division 0 is a special branch of the police commissioned to deal with psionic criminals. I happen to be the one who gets stuck with all the other stuff, like ghosts."

"You're psi... psionic?" Miranda squirmed against the wall until she stood on tiptoe in the corner, chains rattling. "Please don't kill me. Papa warned me about psionics. Said you come from the Devil."

"I'm so tired of that bullshit!" Kirsten shrieked. "Fucking made up Satan has nothing to do with it."

Kirsten's growling struggle to free herself made Miranda whimper as if trapped in jail with a hungry lion held back by a leash that could break at any second. Finding the effort futile, Kirsten glared, lost somewhere between crying at old wounds and becoming so furious her heart felt like it would explode. She closed her eyes, seething. Chaos swam around in her mind until the all-consuming need to find Evan took over.

Kirsten narrowed her gaze at her whimpering cellmate. "Not every psionic can kill people with their mind. Some only play with emotions, see ghosts, or hear what you're thinking. No, I'm not reading your mind right now. I try not to invade people's privacy. My mother was like you, thought psionics were the Devil's work. Bitch almost killed me when I was ten."

"I'm sorry." Miranda closed her eyes, crying, whispering to God for help. After a moment of nothing happening, she sniffled and glanced down at the floor. "Can you kill people?"

Kirsten took a deep breath, bristling with anger at the fear in the sound of Miranda's clattering handcuffs, and let it out in a long, drawn-out groan. "I technically have an ability that *can* kill, but I'm nowhere near strong enough at it to do that. I got *lucky* enough to be one of the few who can. However, I don't *like* using it. It hurts me, too… and it just feels, I dunno, *wrong*."

"Oh, God. Oh, God. Please don't hurt me. Now I know why I'm stuck in here. God wanted me to stop being afraid of psionics."

Kirsten shifted. Between the unforgiving hogtie and tiny little painful things all over the freezing floor, she couldn't find any position even tolerable to sit in. "Ugh. Look, I don't have time to fucking debate theology with you. We're both stuck in this place, and I know for a fact we can get out of here."

"How could you know that?"

I bet I could tell this one an angel told me and she'd believe it. "I'm psychic."

Miranda giggled nervously, still trying to squeeze herself into the wall.

Kirsten shivered with rage. Evan was in danger and she couldn't do a damn thing about it. Like Princess Alsbeth in the Monwyn vid, she sat locked in a long-forgotten dungeon. At least Alsbeth had a beautiful white robe. Unfortunately, no great and powerful wizard was on the way to save Kirsten. *No, Princess Wren gets stuck saving herself. You fell for the Prince Charming routine and he turned out to be a geriatric maleficar.* For a moment, she pondered trying to use Beacon to call Theodore or Dorian, but decided against it. Konstantin might have things in this house capable of destroying Dorian, and she did *not* want Theodore to find her like *this*. She studied the lone LED bulb, the walls, the floor, and the bars. *So damn cold.*

"Hey, these cuffs came from a sex shop right? Maybe they have a safety release?"

"You into that weird shit?" Miranda blinked.

Kirsten had gone well past blushing. "No, I hear stories from the Div 1 guys who find people in compromising situations. This one guy was hanging from his ceiling for twenty-seven hours before he realized the cuffs had a thumb switch." She scooted over and studied the restraints on Miranda's legs. They'd locked her in the same type of short-chain binders, gleaming mirrored chrome. "Shit, just keys. Dammit."

"Can you, like, maybe scoot back to your side?"

"What, you don't want me to get any psionic on you?" Kirsten squinted. "We're trapped in a cell together with nothing but chains on, kidnapped by people who plan to murder us, and all you can think about is not wanting to touch a psionic? Really? Are you that damn shallow?"

"Sorry, I didn't mean to offend you."

"Too damn late. So, how'd you wind up here? All of the other victims had no family or anyone to notice them missing. You got people looking for you?"

"I can't tell you. Please don't read my mind, it's not admissible."

"Did you kill anyone? You gonna kill anyone?"

Miranda shook her head. "No, uhh, I did fantasize about shooting the bastard who put me in this cage."

"I'm currently fantasizing about shooting the bastard who put us in this cage."

Miranda managed another nervous giggle.

"Look, I couldn't care less right now what you did. I need to get out of here and get to my son before that motherfucking, lying, cheating, son of a bitch, bastard..." Kirsten strained against the cuffs with each curse word, until she broke down and sobbed. The remembered touch of a calloused hand sliding up inside her thigh flashed from handsome highwayman to horror-vid walking corpse. She gagged.

"I snuck in to rob the place. This guy has a lot of expensive shit. Some of it supposed to be priceless. I dunno what happened to me. I'm creepin' around this museum-like room, right?" She made hand gestures behind her back while speaking. "Then there was this, like, cold on the back of my neck. Like some kinda hand was made outta ice grabbed me, and everything went dark. I woke up like this." Miranda fidgeted, her fear ebbed enough to let her heels touch the floor again. "Hey, how good are you with your tongue?"

Kirsten's bawling shut off as if by a switch. "What did you just say? How can you think about *that* at a time like this? I don't even like women. Hey, wait a sec. You're all into the God thing, but you were gonna rob the place? What happened to thou shalt not steal?"

"It took a back seat to 'thou shalt not starve.' Anyway, that's not what I mean. If you promise, and I mean swear-promise not to arrest me, I might be able to help us get out."

"If you could escape, why are you still here?"

"'Cause, you dumb bitch, I can't reach." She bounced like an anxious kid begging for a treat. "You swear-promise?"

"What are you, twelve? This isn't a goddamned sleep over." She exhaled hard enough to blow cat litter across the floor. "Fine."

Miranda swung her head to the side, tossing her hair off her neck to expose a small half-inch black square behind her right ear. It bore an icon of a stylized snake-headed woman's face.

"A medusa." Kirsten blinked. "You have a Loki Blade don't you?"

Miranda looked down. "They're not illegal. Just, well... frowned on."

"Yeah, I know. Div 1 loves to do awful things to people who have them. Come on, get down and scoot over—if you can stand to let a psionic touch you."

"Soz." Miranda slid down the wall until she sat on the floor, shifted onto her stomach, then slithered closer, trembling.

Kirsten fought her way back to a kneeling posture and tried to get her hands on the Medusa plugged into the woman's head, but between the elastic strap and her feet getting in the way, she gave up. In a fit of desperation, she tried once more to break her restraints.

"Those things hold one-ton cargo boxes down, you ain't snapping it. Use your teeth," said Miranda.

Kirsten slipped, falling face-first into the ground. With thoughts of Evan driving her, she ignored the pain. Dazed, she repositioned herself and eventually scooted close enough to nuzzle up to Miranda's neck.

If Theo sees this, I will obliterate him. I'm not dealing with that taunting for the rest of my life.

"Okay, don't move," whispered Kirsten. "This thing is gonna shock the shit out of both of us if I touch your skin with my nose while I'm pushing the buttons. Security feature to prevent self-removal."

Kirsten waited. "That means stop shivering."

"I'm freezing, terrified, and there's a nugget of cat litter digging into my ass."

"Miranda?"

The woman looked at her. "Yeah?"

"*Stop shivering.*" Kirsten's eyes gleamed with paranormal light.

Miranda went still.

"Was that psionic stuff?"

"Yep."

Kirsten tilted her head in her best effort to keep her nose away from Miranda's neck. The tip of her tongue found the Medusa box and she bit down on it, squeezing the release buttons on the upper and lower edges. For several seconds, she stopped breathing and tugged. A half-inch metal prong, asterisk-shaped like an M3 jack, gleamed on the reverse side. As soon as the tip cleared the socket behind the woman's ear, a spark leapt from her to the prong, hitting Kirsten in the nose with the force of a light punch. The flavor of tin filled her mouth and her eyes watered out of control. She rolled off Miranda and spat the device into the litter box. After a few breaths, she curled into a ball and tried using her knee to cradle her face.

"Shit. Ouch."

Miranda lapsed into mild convulsions, face-down and flopping. When the fit subsided, she lay still and breathed hard.

Kirsten blinked past the pain, unable to cradle her face in her hands or stop her eyes from watering. She flopped onto her back and stared between her knees at Miranda. "Well, what are you waiting for? I swear I won't arrest you." The sight of metal on her ankles lit the fires of rage, but no matter how hard she pulled, the refused to snap. *I'm gonna kill him.*

"It hurts so much."

Another attempt to break the cuffs with brute force failed. "Dammit, bitch, come on. Does it hurt more than a dagger in the heart? They're going after my son! I swear I won't arrest you for breaking in here, having a Loki, or whatever. Dammit, woman, I'll help you rob the place myself if it saves Evan's life!"

Miranda battled her way into a sitting position, legs straight forward, and closed her eyes as if meditating. Seconds later, she whimpered and gasped. A line of blood ran into her right hand as small Nano blades pressed a half-inch out of the skin on both sides of her wrist. A few seconds later, the cuff around her right wrist popped open, cut in two neat halves. She whined as she moved her arms around front, stretching.

"Come on, come on." Kirsten rolled on her side and rattled her cuffs.

"I'm so sore. I've been chained for weeks. They never took them off."

"Hurt later, free now."

Using the tiny Loki Blade like a saw, Miranda hacked at the restraint on her ankles, whimpering. It didn't take much force to push the Nano edge through the metal, but she mewled and cried with every ounce of pressure. After cutting the cuffs from one ankle at a time, she held the blade over the cuff on her other wrist. A series of pitiful whimpers and gasps came out of her as she scraped her arm back and forth. Once she freed herself of all metal, Miranda kicked the binders to the corner and curled up in a shivering ball. Trickles of blood ran down her legs, dripping from her wrist and fingertips.

"Ow. It's s'posed to push against each side of the cuff. Not cut things like a knife. Shit, that hurt. It's like I stabbed myself through the arm and wobbled the knife back and forth."

Kirsten rolled onto her belly and tugged at the elastic cord. "Please..."

It took Miranda a moment to gather the nerve to move. Eventually, she crawled closer and knelt next to Kirsten. Droplets of warm blood patted on her back when Miranda stooped over her. The elastic cord gave way with ease. Kirsten stretched out flat with a sigh of relief.

"Okay. Now it's your turn to stay still. This thing'll go through your arm before I realize it."

"Yeah, I know how Nano works."

Kirsten held as still as possible while Miranda used the tiny synthetic diamond blade sticking out of her arm to cut the cuffs. She rolled over and sat up, rubbing her wrists while Miranda attacked the binders on her legs. Streaks and smears of blood covered both of them by the time she was free. Miranda held her right arm out and made a fist. The transparent blades sticking out of both sides sank back inside, the faintest trace of a whirring motor audible. She slunk away and curled up in the corner, cradling her bleeding arm. Some seconds later, the blood stopped seeping.

"You okay?" Kirsten crawled over, examining the cuts.

"Yeah. It's got nanobots to repair the skin. It didn't do it all the way on account of me using it to cut so much. I tore the skin more than it would have just going on and off. Nano don't usually make much of a hole, ya know?"

She grasped Miranda's right hand in both of hers. "Thank you. I'm sorry you had to hurt yourself, but we are going to get out of here."

Miranda stared in mute silence.

Kirsten stood and looked down at herself. No clothes, but also, no chains. "Perfect. One step closer to out." She went to the door. After a moment of stretching away the pain of spending hours stuck in a tight ball, the sense of being locked in a cage overwhelmed her. She tried to tear the bars down with her bare hands, thrashing and rattling the heavy barrier until she ran out of energy. Exhausted, she slumped against the cold metal, panting. "Well, now that I got that out of the way... we only need to get this door open. Can you cut out a bar or two?"

Miranda whined. "No, they're like an inch thick. The blade's too short, and it will hurt like fuck."

Kirsten paced. The need to get to Evan and the frustration at being trapped became painful. "You're a thief, huh? Can you pick this lock?"

"Can you psionic me up something to pick it with? Oh, there's some robes in the cabinet by where the mask was. They put one on the dude they had in here when they took him out."

Where the mask was. The spot of wall lay bare. She forced the image of a mask-wearing Konstantin hovering over Evan's helpless body out of her mind. Kirsten wasn't sure if she wanted to waste the ten seconds it would take to put even a robe on. She had to get to him. She would streak the city if it would save Evan. *Streak the city...* She sat still and closed her eyes. *I'll project and go to him. Wait, no. I'll just see them, I won't be able to save him as a projection; all I'll do is waste time. Calm down, K. Stay professional. Remember Shani. Get emotional and someone's gonna die. If they grab him, he will project and come home. He can lead me right to the bastards.*

Her sudden spin toward Miranda made the other woman jump. "You said something about a gag before?"

"Uhh... yeah. I thought you weren't into—"

"I'm not!" yelled Kirsten. "What did you mean?"

"The creep they have watching us wants us to stay quiet. First day I was here, he said he'd gag or drug me if I didn't stop screaming."

"So if we make too much noise someone will come in here?"

"Yeah." Miranda wore a face like a child about to be scolded. "But you don't want 'em to."

"Perfect." Kirsten grabbed the cell door, and shouted at the top of her lungs.

SORCERESS

Hands clasped on the bars, Kirsten rattled the barrier. Ten minutes of shouting had thus far produced no effect other than echoes, and Miranda giggling at insults that ranged from juvenile to crass as desperation increased. Frustrated, she let go and paced for several seconds before flinging herself at the door for another try at tearing it down. Their prison wasn't getting any warmer, but at least fruitless exertion took the sting out of the chill.

Miranda put a trembling arm around her from behind, attempting a hug. "Hey, calm down."

Kirsten tensed at the touch. *Oh, please don't let Theodore find me now.*

"Sorry. I'm freezing."

They huddled together against the wall, shivering.

"So, who are you to him?"

"What?" Kirsten glanced at her for an instant before attempting to stand for another round with the bars.

Miranda clung. "The old man, Konstantin. I heard him tell the guards you were not to be killed under any circumstances. He said something about keeping 'it' where he wanted it, and if you died, he'd have to go out and find the next one."

How could he know that? Kirsten blinked. *He doesn't even know I'm a suggestive, or he would have blindfolded me.* "It's a long, complicated story. Some entities from the next world want me to help them."

"Oh." Miranda shot her a look that called her nuts.

"You don't have to believe me." *Shit, I can't just sit here and wait.*

Frustration at being separated from Evan manifested as tears. She had to do something. Trusting Dorian not to do something stupid, Kirsten concentrated on him. The sense of power emanating from her mind unwound like a thread from deep within her skull. She beaconed, calling to the astral realm for him. After she felt certain the message had gone out, she relaxed her power, but grew worried. *Please let him be careful.*

"Umm, what the hell was that? Your hair moved like there was a breeze and your damn eyes glowed behind your eyelids." Miranda disengaged from their share of body heat.

"I have a ghost friend. I just tried calling him."

"What's he gonna do? Scare the bars open?"

"No, but he can take a message to my captain. Even if he can't see him, he can type it on his terminal." Kirsten tolerated idleness for less than twenty seconds before leaping to her feet. "Oh, goddammit! I can't take this. Wait, I got an idea."

"What?"

"Something an old spirit once annoyed the shit out of me with. When I was little, I tried to ignore them so I didn't get punished. Ghosts always came asking for help, but it made my mother angry if I used my abilities. This one ghost refused to be ignored." She grabbed a fragment of the handcuffs and raked it back and forth across the bars while shout-singing "Henry VIII."

"Stop it, that's annoying." Miranda covered her ears.

After two verses, a distant slam echoed from the basement. Kirsten sang louder. Stomping approached. Seconds later, Randall Morris rounded the corner of the boxes and stared down the short hallway to the cell. His missing arm had been replaced with a common civilian prosthetic. Flesh-toned plastic approximated the shape and contours of an arm, separated into visible panels by gaps that left the black interior visible. He froze.

"Hey, what the hell are you two doin' loose?" He pulled a pistol off his belt and aimed at them. "Put those damn cuffs back on."

Kirsten dangled the broken thing. "Sorry, we broke your toys. Now bc a good little boy and *Unlock the door.*"

The force of her suggestion hit him like a punch to the head. His gun fell to the ground as his arms went limp. He tottered around the stacked crates out of sight. Miranda ran up behind Kirsten, clinging to her from behind. Kirsten sucked air in past her teeth, tensing at the intimate contact.

"Was that some kinda psionic shit?"

Kirsten's knuckles went white on the bars. "Yeah."

Miranda clamped tighter, resting her chin on Kirsten's shoulder. "I swear if that psionic stuff gets us out of here, I'll totally change how I feel about them. Maybe my parents were wrong about hating you guys."

"Gee, thanks."

"Where's he going?"

Kirsten shifted left to try and get a better look at the shadow creeping across the ceiling. "To get the key, I imagine."

"Oh."

Miranda's grip forced much of the air out of Kirsten's lungs when Randall appeared at the corner, zombie-walking to the cell with his right arm held forward. He stopped, six feet away when he stepped on his pistol. He looked down at it and broke out in a cold sweat. Veins in his forehead swelled. His face turned purple. He bellowed and threw the key behind him. Kirsten stared at the gleaming metal, tracking its bounce into a patch of shadow by a wooden crate painted with Cyrillic letters.

"Bitch!" Randall fell on his knees, seizing the pistol in both hands.

Kirsten planted her feet in a wide stance, still holding the bars. Her overwhelming need to protect Evan coalesced into the energy of a Mind Blast. Disgust at Konstantin and humiliation at her current incarceration added to it. She may have tried to say something coherent, but the noise that came out of her didn't even come close to speech.

Randall Morris twitched, his eyes rolled back into his head, and he fell over backward like a plank. A rancid smell wafted by a few seconds later. Kirsten rested her forehead against the cold metal bars, trying to ease the throbbing migraine forming in the wake of so much power. Her legs went slack. Miranda's arms around her middle held her up for a moment before letting her slump to kneeling.

"You're bleeding!" cried Miranda, wiping her hands at Kirsten's face.

"I don't think I ever threw so much effort into one of those before. I feel like I got hit in the face by a PubTran bus."

"Pretty sure he got the worse end of the deal." Miranda went up on tiptoe to peek for a second, then sat on the floor next to her. "I think you killed him." She shivered. "I smell shit. Umm, remember when I made fun of you when you said you weren't helpless. You know, when you were rolling around. I take it back."

"Thanks," said Kirsten, not bothering to conceal the sarcasm.

"So, yeah. Asshole is dead and we're still a pair of locked-up bitches. That worked."

"You know, for a psionic-hating religious idiot, you sure don't have much faith."

Miranda pouted.

Kirsten rubbed her eyes, shook off the headache, and crawled back to the bars. When her vision adjusted to the light, she stared at the key and focused on the want of it to come toward her. *I can pull grenade pins, so I can drag a damn key across a concrete floor.* She slid a hand out between the bars, reaching for it.

"What"—Miranda's words stalled as the key twitched and pivoted to point at the cell. She leapt on Kirsten's back, chin over her shoulder, ear to ear with her. "Are you doing that?"

"Thanks for drilling my skull into the bars. Yes, I'm doing that. Don't shake me, I suck at Telekinesis, but I should be able to move a key."

"What's uhh, Telekinesis?"

Kirsten glanced at her. "You are terrified of psionics to the point you hate them, but you don't even bother to learn what they are?" She scowled. "Typical."

"I'm sorry. I didn't hate them as much as they scared the shit out of me.""

Kirsten focused on the key again, willing it toward her.

Miranda squeezed Kirsten in bursts of fleeting joy each time the key scooted closer in a series of sporadic jerks and skids. When Kirsten thought about how only a tiny strip of metal kept her away from Evan, it sailed into the air and went over their heads. Miranda let go and scrambled after it, not caring it landed in the tray of kitty litter. She ran back to the door, reached through the bars, and after a moment of fiddling, unlocked it.

Kirsten shoved the door open and vaulted Randall's body. Miranda stopped to grab the pistol and tugged at the dead man's coat, too weak to move the cybered-up corpse to get it off him.

"Hey, wait. Help me get his coat."

"I gotta get to my son." Kirsten kept running.

"Wait! We can't run outside naked. There's robes." Miranda scurried to one of the metal cabinets.

"I've already lost too much time." Kirsten ran for the exit.

"Hey, there's a picture of you over here."

Kirsten stopped with a hand on the doorknob. Curiosity, or perhaps a need to understand what happened to her, muted her haste. She jogged over to Miranda. On the altar, beneath where the mask had been, a sheet of plasfilm bearing a photo of her lay beneath an ancient wooden bowl that contained several strands of blonde hair as well as ashes of something burnt. To the right, an old book sat open to a drawing of an ouroboros, surrounded by writing she couldn't decipher. The fancy box was empty; Konstantin had his knife as well.

Son of a bitch. She swiped the hairs out of the bowl. Her hair.

Miranda pulled the cabinet open, revealing several black silk robes on hangers.

Wham!.

Miranda screamed. Kirsten jumped. They both whirled around to stare at a man in a black suit and blood-red shirt one step in the door to the little 'man cave.' He'd slammed it against the wall on his way in. After a brief pause, he raised a stunrod and ran at them.

Kirsten's eyes glowed pure white. A stream of erratic images and thoughts crashed into the charging giant's brain, shutting down. He went from full run to sliding on his chin in the span of an eye blink. One hand slid to the side of his head, lacking even the coordination necessary to put his hand on his face. Kirsten ran to the stunrod, stooping to pick it up before thrusting it into his neck in one fluid motion.

The large man convulsed and went still.

Miranda's face emerged from black silk as she let a one-piece robe fall around her. She grabbed another one. "Kirsten, here."

Before she could turn away, the large man's body swelled. His suit split open down the back, seconds before a gory explosion of blood splattered into the ceiling and all over Kirsten. Miranda screamed, dropped the extra robe, and jumped into the cabinet. Dark vapors coalesced upward from the cavernous hollow in the corpse, forming into a chitinous humanoid figure that resembled a skeleton with a crown of short horns.

Glowing red smoke welled out of its eye sockets. Dry crunching ran down its spine as limbs solidified and it set its shoulders. Kirsten squinted up at the eight-foot demon and folded her arms.

"I don't suppose you'd give me a minute to put something on before we start this?"

The polyphonic voice reverberated over the basement. "I shall rend the flesh from your bones and drink the essence of your suffering."

"Didn't think so." A flick of her arm sent the lash outward.

Kirsten swung in a wide right-to-left arc. The tip scored a light grey burn across the black, leathery ribcage. Growling, the abyssal stumbled away, unable to hide the surprise at the amount of pain her attack caused. The demon snarled, yellow-green fumes leaking through its teeth.

"Not the easy meal you were expecting?" Kirsten circled to the right, keeping the energy whip moving. *No wonder it's scared. I must look like a Seraphim to it right now.* She didn't exactly have much on. *All I'm missing are the wing-like ribbon things.*

It reached to the side closed a fist around empty air, and made a throwing gesture. A crate flew at her. She crossed her arms in a block, the wooden box breaking apart as it smashed into her and knocked her onto the table. Her chilled skin squeaked as she skidded across the table and fell off the far side. Stunned from pain, she curled up on the bare plasticrete floor and plucked a few large splinters out of her forearm.

Miranda poked out of the cabinet, pointing the pistol at the giant skeleton.

The demon laughed and loosed a low, throaty growl.

She screamed slammed the wardrobe cabinet door. Kirsten grabbed the top of the table and pulled herself standing, leaning on it for a few seconds until her legs decided to work again. The creature spun on her, palm extended. Another crate leapt into the air. This one flew too high and smashed against the ceiling above her head. Kirsten ducked the shower of soybean shells and wood fragments. She ran forward, shoving at the abyssal's paranormal essence.

A contest of strength, tilted in her favor by her need to protect Evan, flung the dark spirit into the wall with enough force to crack cinder blocks. The abyssal bounced to the floor and rolled onto its chest with the scrape of shell on stone. Kirsten padded up beside it, the coiling lash stretching to a length of almost fifteen feet. The shimmering blue-white light added to her illusion of feeling like a Seraphim.

One black-clawed hand sprang forth and grabbed her leg. With a contemptuous sneer, she pulled the lash around and whipped it down at the demon. The tendril struck it with a loud *whap*, and coiled around its chest, wrapping and lifting it off the ground. She swung her arm around, flinging the enormous skeleton first into the ceiling, then the ground. *The entire damn house is going to hear this.* She took a step back, grabbed the lash with both hands, and spun in a motion that hurled the demon across the large room. It hit the wall headfirst and smashed a new hole in the cinder blocks.

Groaning, the demon floundered, arms scratching at the ground to pull itself upright. Kirsten charged after it, the slap of bare feet running on concrete drowning beneath her angry roar. A surge of psionic power intensified her weapon to a blinding glow. The abyssal teetered up to its feet barely a second before she jumped into a two-handed overhead strike. It tried to lurch to the left, but she twisted to compensate, whipping a diagonal shot into its body that vaporized the demon into a hanging cloud of blank smoke.

Kirsten stood there covered in blood and dust, gasping for breath as the inky smear drew into itself with a great rush of inhaling wind.

Miranda peered past the cabinet doors, her face lit by a narrow strip of light. "A-are you an angel?"

Kirsten let the lash dissipate and walked over. "No. I'm only borrowing the uniform." She picked up the robe and pulled it over her head, letting the cloth fall around her body. "Though, I think I saw one once." She ran to the door. "Come on, I'm leaving."

Miranda recovered the pistol and followed. "Sorry I didn't help you with that... thing. You want the gun? You're the cop."

"Don't be sorry. The gun wouldn't have done a damn thing but piss it off. You better keep it so you're not helpless; I have a weapon."

She stomped, as much as she could stomp barefoot, into the man cave. Two men in black business suits went for handguns at the sight of her. Kirsten held her arms out and knocked the one on the right to the ground with a Mind Blast. Miranda shot the other one. Kirsten caught herself subconsciously gesturing like the sorceress from the Monwyn world with each blast and blushed. *Must be the robe.* The noise of Miranda firing at another man dispelled her fleeting amusement. He dove left, triggering twice as he fell. Miranda hit the ground screaming. Kirsten thrust her arm at him, rising onto her toes as she channeled another Mind Blast. For an instant, *his* eyes glowed white as his brain absorbed the psionic energy she pumped into it. The attack left him limp and drooling. That time, she almost chanted *Invocatus Penumbratus.*

"You hit?" yelled Kirsten without looking back.

"No, but I just about pissed myself," said Miranda. "I think a bullet nipped my hair. I just steal stuff. I don't like to shoot people."

Kirsten ran up the spiral stairway, and stopped short with a gasp at the top, staring at gold dragon doorknobs. *Evan saw gold dragons devouring me...* She shivered, her eyes started to water, but worry became angry. The basement could've been the dragon's 'belly.' She shoved the elaborate doors open and strode into the corridor. Security guard after security guard emerged from side rooms, falling one after the next to a series of mind blasts. A few bullets whizzed overhead.

I'm barefoot, in a black robe, waving my arms around and 'slaying' the bad guys with magic.

The scene felt like some twisted cosplay LARP based on Xiana, the Black Sorceress—only her *magic* wouldn't make them get back up as skeletons. Some of Xiana's lines from the vid echoed in her head, but she choked on them. Thinking of the Monwyn franchise made her miss Evan more. The more she thought about that fantasy world, the more she *needed* to have him next to her on the couch, watching one.

Miranda followed close, aiming her gun at each man, but not firing as they went down. "Are they dead?"

"No, but when they wake up, they'll probably spend a few hours wishing they were." *Just like I will in the morning.* The women fought their way across the mansion to Konstantin's bedroom. Kirsten slumped into the wall beside the door with a hand on the side of her head. *Oh, yeah. It hurts.*

"You okay?"

Kirsten cringed at the voice throbbing in her head. "Yeah. Just need a sec. Mind Blast is not a warm fuzzy power. Feedback migraine."

"Oh. Sorry." Miranda rubbed her shoulder.

The spiky headache ebbed after a few seconds. Finding the doors locked, Kirsten leaned back and kicked. They rattled. "Ugh, this is so much easier with heavy boots." She threw her shoulder into the doors, but bounced away. Another kick stunned her foot and left her hopping. "Give me a hand?"

Miranda nodded.

They backed up against the wall on the opposite side, and rushed it together. The door gave out under their combined weight. Kirsten stumbled to a halt three steps into the bedroom. Miranda wound up falling over. The stink of burned hair hung in the room. Her purse, and the E-90, sat at the center of his desk as if dropped in a hurry. She reclaimed her weapon, refusing to look at the bed, and kissed the NetMini when she found it in her purse, turned off.

"What stinks?"

Kirsten tapped the NetMini, willing it to boot up faster. "Some idiot tried to fire my service weapon."

Miranda's face gave away she knew all about police trigger interlocks. "Ouch."

"It's no worse than a stunrod to a grown man."

Chimes came from the NetMini.

"Suri, send a call for backup right away. Try to call Nila or Evan too."

"Why did you turn me off, Kirsten? You know I don't like it when you turn me off."

She pointed the E-90 at her NetMini. "I wasn't the one who turned you off."

"Calling now."

"Girl," said Miranda. "Time for a new phone. That one's got attitude."

"Don't get me started."

"So, umm. Thanks for busting me outta there. I'm gonna get lost before the place is swarming with blue and whites."

"You've got probably eighteen shots left in that thing. We don't know how many men are on his security team. Are you wanted right now?"

"I don't think so." Miranda gnawed on her knuckle. "I don't want to risk it… What's the point of getting away from one cage only to wind up in another?"

"The police won't sacrifice you to demons. Oh, and you get clothes."

"Good point." Miranda plopped down on the end of the bed.

WORST FEARS

Chattering teeth seemed loud as thunder. Kirsten paced in a circle. Men shouted downstairs, barking orders to search the grounds and ensure no one got out. From the sound of it, Kirsten decided her odds improved if she remained in the bedroom as a defensive position. *They think we went outside already.* She shivered each time her foot hit the rug, each time the sheer silk robe brushed over her body. Whenever she glanced toward Miranda seated on the foot of the bed, she cringed. Kirsten tried biting her nails, but the sight of the redness around her wrists made her angrier.

Rage and shame got into a fencing match over what Konstantin did to her. The worst part of it was he made her want him to. Mercifully, much of what happened came back muted by the effect of his mental influence. Blurry bits and pieces of her interactions with him over the previous few weeks fast disintegrated into a haze of amnesia. With each passing minute, he seemed less and less real. *I should be happy he charmed me. Maybe when it wears off I won't even remember how rough his hands are.* She gurgled.

Sirens emerged from the distance, drawing Kirsten to the outer window. Most of the horizon glittered violet with the mixture of red and blue lights. Kirsten spun away from the view and grabbed the NetMini. She swiped at the screen, placing a vid call to Operations. The holographic face of a dispatcher appeared.

"This is an official—"

"Agent Kirsten Wren, Division 0. ID W396-I0039. I just called in for a backup request at this location. Patch me through to the senior. I have visual on what looks like twenty units approaching."

"One moment. Verifying your ID." The color of the hologram head changed, as her file photo lit up in front of him. "Sorry, Agent. What the heck are you wearing?"

Her face flushed red. "It's a long damn story."

"Fair enough." The hologram changed to a black woman with crimson hair, a small scar from left eye to chin. "Agent? Good to see you alive. What happened to you?"

"Sergeant Reed?" Kirsten squinted at the barely-visible nameplate.

"Yes. What's your situation? Your Suri said you were abducted?"

"Yeah, this asshole has a private dungeon, but I got out of the cell. I'm on the third floor now with one other victim. We are both armed, so please don't shoot any females in black robes. All the security people here are in business suits."

"Ma'am, please remain at your current location until we secure the area."

"Hurry up! He's going after my son."

"Understood."

She stuffed the NetMini back in her purse and threw the bag on over her shoulder. Pacing again, she squeezed the rubberized handle of her weapon like a stress ball. Thudding footsteps in the hallway grew louder. She raised the E-90, aiming it with both hands at the door. When they opened, a man in a dark suit carrying a rifle froze in his tracks, staring at her.

Kirsten squinted. Her eyes flickered. "*Drop it.*"

The rifle clattered to the ground.

She pointed. "Go *surrender* to the police."

He slumped and trudged out with the stagger of a zombie.

"Damn, that's fucking handy." Miranda stood and got clingy again. "Shit, I could make so much money with a trick like that."

Kirsten didn't so much mind the woman clinging to her now that they had robes between them. "Psionics who do that run into us." She winked, then sighed. "It's also why no one trusts suggestives. We tend to get shot in the head from long range when the government declares us dangerous."

"Like animals." Miranda sent a guilty look at her toes. "I'm sorry."

"Human nature makes people fear what they can't explain or think they can't defend against."

Police loudspeakers shouted outside, demanding surrender.

"My parents thought psionics were evil," muttered Miranda.

"You may have been raised to fear us, but at least you have the choice to learn." A few gunshots popped in the distance; Kirsten glanced at the window. "Wow, idiots. Look, I won't BS you. Some psionics are every bit as dangerous as people fear. That's what my unit is for. It just pisses me off when the bible-beaters get all high and mighty. One kook kills people in the name of God, and the religious wingnuts say not to judge them all by the actions of a single person. When a psionic does something wrong, those same people demand rounding us all up and executing us to the last for being too dangerous."

"It's just the one guy. Reverend Harris or whatever. People know he's crazy. I grew up terrified of psionics, but I never met one before you. I mean, we met under some pretty crazy, fucked up circumstances, but you're nothing at all like I expected. You're pretty cool."

"Thanks." At the sound of the downstairs doors being kicked in, Kirsten squirmed out of the hug and ran to the hallway. "Come on."

She went right, toward the sound of fighting. Around a corner, two men with rifles fired down over a railing into the open center of the house. Kirsten sighted and shot before they could turn on her. The first laser seared a fatal path through the chest of the near man and burned a hole in the other one's thigh. He crawled away, raising his hands. Kirsten padded toward him, but after taking three steps on frigid hardwood, stopped at what his surface thoughts gave away.

Desperate to get to Evan, she hammered him with a Mind Blast perhaps a bit harder than intended. Her eyes flared white; the man grabbed his head, howled, and passed out.

"What the fuck?" Miranda gawked. "He was surrendering."

"No, he wasn't. He wanted me to get close enough for vibro claws." Kirsten dashed forward, taking cover against the wall and aiming over the railing at the ground floor. Several of Konstantin's security men traded bullets with the police, shredding the front windows. "He's not dead. Stay back, get down."

"How did you know? Did you read his mind? What about privacy?"

Kirsten shot a man downstairs who ripped full automatic out the window at the Division 1 group, catching him in the lower back. He hit the ground screaming, bloody steam pouring out from where his kidney used to be. "I tend to bend rules a little when people try to kill me." She fired again, wounding another. "And threaten my son."

A man leapt over his cover, trying to put a column between himself and Kirsten. She shot straight into it. The laser penetrated the column, the man, the wall behind it, and probably two more rooms. Random luck caught the guy in the right arm. He fell out into view, dropping his rifle and howling in pain.

"You have two seconds to surrender." An amplified man's voice shook the windows from outside.

Two men downstairs fired up through the floor. Kirsten, shrieking, dove away from a geyser of plaster and wood fragments. She rolled into the corridor, dragging Miranda behind.

"Damn. I hate real wood. Epoxil traps bullets."

Shimmering green light flooded the area, followed by howls. All firing from downstairs stopped at once. Men shouted their surrender. Kirsten crawled to the railing. A haze of smoke filled the main foyer, spewing up from a long burn mark on the floor. Outside, a Division 1 patrol craft hovered, Starburst laser extended from its pod and glowing. Apparently, they fired a warning shot before trying to hit someone with it. The remaining nine or so security men threw their rifles aside and raised their hands.

Miranda squeezed Kirsten from behind. "They... shot that at people?"

"Cops get a little testy when people throw bullets at us. We don't really like it much." Kirsten shoved off the floor and stood, running for the stairs. "Technically, they fired it at the floor. The first one's a warning."

Kirsten dashed down the stairs to the ground floor and ran outside. Since none of the advancing blue-armored offers even gave her a second glance, she figured they'd all tagged her on their heads-up displays and had been watching her already.

Sergeant Reed stood from a crouch behind the hood of her patrol raft, rifle still trained at the building. The police swarmed inside, taking the remaining private security men into custody. Kirsten skidded to a halt on the wet grass outside by Reed. She'd run outside with almost nothing on, forgetting how far north she'd gone. Her toes had already gone numb. She resisted the instinct to scream at the sudden shock, but couldn't stop her teeth from chattering.

"Reed, thanks for the save. This is Miranda; Konstantin kidnapped her as well. I saw nothing to indicate she was abused while in captivity, but I am confident he meant to murder her at some later date."

"Serial?" asked Reed.

"No, maleficar. He sacrifices his victims to summon demons."

"Agent, we have a MedVan on the way. You've obviously been through a traumatic experience."

"I'm not crazy. Dammit, the man is after my son. I need your car."

"I can't let you run off half-naked and obviously in a state of mental distress."

"*Car, now.*" Kirsten's eyes glowed.

Reed blinked and moved away from the driver's door. Kirsten pushed Miranda into her. "Let the medics check her out. She could be traumatized. Oh, and if you see anything in her record, as long as it's not big, please let her skate. She saved my ass."

Kirsten jumped in, pulled the door closed, and chucked the E-90 into the passenger seat. With Sergeant Reed staring dumbfounded, Kirsten hauled the patrol craft into the sky and swerved south. The rugged rubber floor mat felt bizarre under bare feet. A long time in service left the carved diamond-pattern on the control sticks worn smooth. The Starburst laser and its assorted components added weight, which made the handling more sluggish than a Division 0 car.

After keying in a nav pin for Nila's apartment, she climbed past the altitude of the highest building and rammed the left stick all the way forward. Numbers fluttered by on the windscreen, rapid cycling slowed as her speedometer edged into the upper three hundreds. Hot air from the heating system brought feeling back to her toes. Alone at last, with nothing to do but wait for her travel to end, she cried from worry and kneaded the joysticks. Her NetMini AI had failed to reach either Nila or Evan; attempts to call both of them rang to vidmail every time.

Captain Eze's head shimmered in above the center of the dashboard. "Wren, what the hell happened to you? They're telling me you took a Div 1 unit?"

"Commandeering, sir. You were right about Konstantin. You were all right." She gathered herself, shaking from the effort it took her not to break down. "He was manipulating me." She showed off her bare right wrist. "That bracelet he gave me… I don't know what it was. Half of me wants to call it magic, but that's fucking crazy. There was an entity in it, making me do things."

"Are you hurt? Why didn't you stay on the scene?"

"He's going after Evan, Captain. He said my 'little friend' was the last thing he needed for his plan. He's gonna kill my little boy and…" The car took over driving while she covered her face with both hands. The autodrive slowed her down to 250 mph—for safety reasons.

"Wren, focus. Stay with me. Where are you?"

Kirsten sucked in a breath and wiped her eyes. She grabbed the sticks and went back to almost four hundred miles per hour. The acceleration pinned her in the rigid rubber cushions. Seats made for armored bodies weren't too kind to an ass protected only by a layer of thin silk. "Nila's. Evan would be there; she takes him home if I'm working late."

"We haven't received any alarm calls. I'll meet you there."

"Sam Chang in Div 2 has all the file details. Konstantin's the one who's been summoning this shit all along. I'm so fucking stupid. The whole time I'm investigating this case I was holding hands with the son of a bitch responsible for everything." Every ounce of her loathing for the elite, wealthy bastards that she'd been forced to suppress came back at once in a tidal wave of fury. Kirsten punched the dashboard, then cradled her throbbing fist to her gut. "I should have listened to someone."

"It was the charm." He stared at her. "Evan needs you to be calm right now. I'll see you there."

Alarms went off from the navigation system. She yanked back on the left hand stick. Automatic passive restraints wrapped her torso as airbrake flaps opened all around the exterior of the hovercar. Her speed plummeted. Once it dipped below two hundred, negative thrust kicked in and brought her to a near standstill. The car had gone from 390 miles per hour to nothing in a little over five seconds. Kirsten wheezed, gasping for breath. She swung the car around and steered for the pool platform. Downdraft from her rushed, reckless landing interrupted an evening party and blew six people into the water and sent a dozen more falling over each other to get away.

She grabbed the E-90, flung the door open, and sprinted for the entrance. The sight of a crazed woman in a black robe leaping out of a police vehicle spurned one man into attempting to block what he likely assumed to be a thief. He tried to grab her, earning a knee in the balls and a pistol whip to the side of the head for his effort. The man hit the ground, clamping one hand on her ankle as she attempted to run. She caught her fall on her hands and spun over, aiming the E-90 at him.

"*Back off.*" The flash in her eyes brought a gasp from a couple in formal dress climbing out of the water.

The man let go, crawled away, and cradled his crotch. Kirsten scrambled upright, almost tripping on the robe, and darted to the elevator. No amount of screamed threats made it move any faster to the thirty-ninth floor. She squeezed past the doors before they finished opening, shoving them aside. A hallway and a half later, she came to a halt. The sight of the door to 3918 hanging open hit her like an icicle in the heart.

Kirsten trudged up to Nila's apartment, shoving the limp flap of Epoxil out of her way with the tip of the E-90. The apartment appeared trashed, as if a gang war broke out inside. Scorch marks on the wall brought Nila's pyrokinesis to mind. Evan was gone. For that matter, she didn't see any sign of Nila or Shani either.

The boy's shoes remained tucked against the wall by the door where Nila asked visitors to leave them. She fell to her knees, dropping the E-90 in her lap. It slid over the smooth silk, clattering to the ground as she picked up the small, blue sneakers and cradled them to her chest.

"No..." she sobbed. "Please, no..."

CAT AND MOUSE

Evan huddled in a dark corner, peering past a tangle of pipes at a sliver of light. Chemical vapors brought reflex tears to his eyes, and he tried not to pay attention to the slimy stickiness he walked on. Shani pressed herself against him, trying to whimper despite the hand he kept over her mouth. Both children looked as though they had gone for a roll in a tray of coal dust.

Shani squirmed to look at him. *I'm sorry.*

Stop whining, they'll hear us. He narrowed his eyes at her.

She nodded. The girl stopped making noise, but shook harder.

Evan let go, leaving a grimy, hand-shaped smudge around her mouth. She gathered her hair off her face and tucked it behind her ears. The scuff of boots on the hard floor drew near, and with it, the scent of burned meat.

The girl scooted behind him. *I'll get the gun. You shoot him, you're a better shot.*

He gave her a pathetic stare. *This isn't a video game. I don't want to kill people for real.*

Shani glared. *They're trying to kill us! You won't get in trouble.*

Both kids froze as a charred man rounded the corner of an enormous air-handling unit. The September chill had it running almost constantly. The mechanical thrumming drowned the noise of their breathing. His handgun glinted in the dim basement light as he searched back and forth among the pipes and ducts. A burned swath of shirt exposed a swath of skin. Most of his hair was gone. Only one fuchsia spike that remained of a once-grand mohawk. Smoke still peeled from his leather vest and pants; a portion of his right boot had melted to his leg. Anger and frustration conspired to keep his face in a perpetual state of twitching.

Evan narrowed his eyes. The second coolest thing he'd ever seen in his life had been Nila pointing at people and lighting them on fire. The *coolest* thing he'd ever seen in his life had been Kirsten walking into his crappy little room in the bad place. He wouldn't let these turds take him away from his mother.

The man swung his handgun to the left again, straining to see in the dark. He faced right at them, but didn't react. He advanced while peering every few steps under a pipe or duct to either side. Shani's fingers dug into Evan's side. He held on to her every bit as tight, staring agape at the approaching thug. The sight of Nila tossing fire everywhere had almost gotten him caught when he stood there gawking. She had told them to run: probably meant outside and keep going, not run to the basement.

He can't see us, don't make a sound and he'll go right by.

Shani squeezed him in response to his telepathic voice. *Okay.*

Evan stopped breathing as the gang punk came within four feet of them, still peering into the dark. Shani clung tighter. The man leaned forward, swaying his head from side to side.

"There you is. I see pink."

Shani trembled.

He's lying. Evan's firm grip told her not to move. *He's trying to scare us.*

Lips twisted to an anticipatory grin, twitched, then flattened into a sneering frown. "Little bastard," he grumbled. "Yo, Roy, you got anything by the stairs?"

"Ain't seen shit," shouted a deep voice from far away.

"I know yer down here, ya little shits."

"Yo, Parrot, hurry the fuck up before that freaky fire bitch gets here."

The man less than three feet from Evan gestured to his side at the darkness with his gun arm. "Aww, man, don't worry about her. The crew's gonna treat her real nice."

Shani dug her fingers into Evan's side, almost hard enough to make him yell. He turned his head toward her, eyes still on the ganger for all but the two seconds it took to send a telepathic message.

Your mom's badass. These morons won't hurt her.

Evan jumped as the thug took a step, boots peeling away from the sticky floor. When he had gotten too far to the right to see them, the boy stood and hauled Shani after him. He held a finger to his lips in the universal gesture for 'don't make a sound,' and crept out from under the pipe nest. He gripped her by the hand, leading her along the outer wall in the shadow of the HVAC unit. Sticky chemical slime oozed between his toes with each step, making him shudder. He looked down, cringing at the dark gunk. Shani, her face twisted with an expression of disgust, bit her lip.

Sorry for opening the door. Are you mad at me?

No, they would have kicked it down. He looked right, left, and up. *We could climb up on top. They'll never find us before your mom realizes where we are.*

I don't like it down here. It's scary and eww. She peeled one foot from the floor. *We're gonna get sick.*

Evan leaned around the edge of the machine, trying to get a look at the stairs almost sixty meters away. He settled back on his heels in the dark and looked at his friend. *There's a man with a rifle at the stairs.*

If we sneak up on him, I can get the gun and pull down his pants. Shani grinned.

He smirked. *Why do you think they're trying to kill us already?*

Police don't stop being police because the bad guys get mad at them. She stomped her foot with a faint *splat.* Her expression said she immediately regretted the feeling of it.

We're not cops. We're kids. If we get shot, my mom is gonna kill me.

A dull metallic *clank* made them jump. The thug had doubled back, perhaps hearing Shani's foot hitting the slime. Evan clenched his hand around hers and sprinted past a patch of light where a passageway led between rows of steel behemoths. Banging and squishing from behind made him think the ganger gave chase, and he ran harder.

At the far corner of the second machine, the substance on the floor went from sticky gunk to slick. Evan's feet shot out from under him. He slid into a roll, tumbling into an array of spare pipes leaned up against the wall. Shani crashed into him, having also wiped out, and screamed at the sudden clamor of falling metal. Evan leapt on top of her, and took a falling pipe to the back of the head.

The thug rounded into view and pointed his gun at them, grinning.

Pinned under a stunned boy and several dozen pipes, Shani screamed, "Mommy!" as loud as she could.

"Got you now, you little fu—" His voice cut off to a squeal as one of the pipes leapt up and smashed him between the legs hard enough to bend. The hit lifted him up on tiptoe.

The pipe clanked to the ground while the ganger, gaping mouth drooling, landed on his knees, both hands over his crotch. Shani looked at Evan, patting him on the cheek.

"Ev... Ev... wake up."

"I'm awake, just... ow." He moaned.

She reached an arm toward the murderous thug, yanking the gun from his weakened grip with ease. It spun through the air into her hand. Like she'd touched a piece of dog poo, she hurriedly stuffed it into Evan's gut. He gathered it in a double-handed grip and pointed it at the man's head.

"Leave us alone."

The ganger picked up the pipe that had felled him, and stumbled forward, clapping his hand on the metal while glaring at Shani. "I'm... I'm gonna"—he gasped and panted—"take this fuckin' pipe and I'm gonna jam it—"

Blam.

Evan shot him in the thigh.

"You got em, Parrot?" shouted the distant, deep voice.

Parrot crumpled to the ground, roaring and growling in a voice teetering on falsetto. "Oh, you little fucker... oh, I'm gonna... oh, yeah. So much pain. Magnitudes of pain. Infinite universes of suffering."

Just for spite, Shani levitated the pipe, whirled it around and beaned him. Parrot went to sleep.

Evan aimed high, and shot out a light.

"What are you doing?" whined Shani, sounding panicky.

"Hiding us."

"I'm scared of the dark," she whimpered.

He concentrated, trying to remember what Kirsten showed him. Within a few seconds, the world around him shimmered into a wavy sepia-toned nightmare version of reality.

Shani gasped. "Your eyes are glowing."

"Shh!" Evan put his hand over her mouth again, lowering his voice to a whisper. "Don't yell. Yes, they are. I can see in the dark. They're right by the stairs."

She grabbed his arm with both hands and pulled it down. "Won't they see your eyes?"

Evan cringed at the oily puddle coating the floor beneath him, leaking at a slow drizzle from a large machine housing nearby. His feet and hands couldn't get any traction, making it hard to even stay upright on all fours —forget standing.

He locked eyes with Shani. *Don't try to stand up. It's slippery. We'll hurt ourselves and make too much noise.*

Okay, replied Shani, also using Telepathy.

Inch by inch, he dragged down the passageway, trying not to think about the scary giant machines surrounding him. Once clear of the oil slick, he grasped a rusty railing and pulled himself upright. A coating of oil on his feet kept him slipping as though he tried to walk on ice. Shani stood behind him, waving her arms as her legs slid apart. She grumbled and floated off the ground. Evan scraped his feet on the dry plasticrete for a few seconds before risking a step. He found his balance and crept to the end of the row, Shani gripping his shoulder while drifting behind him like a balloon. He peered around and shot out another light to darken the center of the basement.

Shani jumped at the sudden bang. Her telekinetic levitation died with her concentration and she fell straight to her butt, oily feet shooting out from under her.

"Parrot, what the fuck is going on?" The man with the deep voice moved away from the stairs, but only took two steps before another man came down behind him.

"The little bastard still down here?"

"Yo, Zee. Yeah," said Deep Voice.

"Where's Parrot?"

"He's searchin.' He been shootin' tho. Maybe he got 'em, maybe he just tryin' to scare 'em. Yo, I don't like this, man. It ain't right to do kids. What the hell did the little bastard do that you wanna pop him?"

Shani scrambled upright and peered around the side of the old heating machine beside Evan, her head right under his chin.

"Little fucker got me arrested. Do you have any idea what that did to my rep, gettin' taken down by a goddamn little kid? I can't show my face anywhere without getting laughed at."

"Yo, I'm just sayin'. You wind up in the tank again as a kid killer, you done. You only makin' your rep worse."

"You going chickenshit soft on me now, CyberB? Too many double orbitals?" Zee patted the man on the potbelly with three loud claps. "I'm gonna saw that little son of a bitch's head off and mail it to his cop mommy with a camera drilled into his forehead so I get to see her face."

"Man… that's some messed up shit," said CyberB.

Evan ducked out of sight and ran deeper into the basement, pulling Shani along.

"I hear you runnin', brat," yelled Zee. The tromp of boots echoed over the basement, drawing near. "Wanna make a deal? How bout I let your little girlfriend live if you come over here right now."

Evan slowed to a jog, glancing back.

"You're a liar!" shouted Shani, pouncing on Evan's back.

The boy ran through a maze of passages, stepping over and around debris he had no trouble seeing. Zee chased. Crashes, clangs, and swear words whenever he tripped over things in the dark gave little clue how far away he was.

After a bunch of random turns, Evan spotted a thick jumble of pipes connecting a large cylindrical tank to the wall in a corner. It looked like a safe refuge only a small child could fit in. He rushed over, dropped to his knees, and guided Shani in before scooting after her. They crawled in against the wall, huddled together under the tangle of metal tubing. Evan nudged Shani into the deepest corner, put himself in front of her, and kept the handgun pointed at the aisle leading up to their hiding place. Shani clung to him from behind.

Fear mixed with the imagined reaction of his new mother finding him dead made him cry, but he kept himself silent. He only had to wait for her to find him—if she was still even alive. Before the drug dealer and his men showed up at Nila's apartment, he'd been sick to the point of vomiting about Kirsten. Such an awful feeling of worry had taken him, he could barely contain it. He knew *something* bad was about to happen to her, but not exactly what. An image of gold dragons accompanied the smell of that stupid old man she liked, some nasty cologne. Evan's dislike for the man became dread. Somehow, he *knew* the man wanted to hurt his mom. As soon as he saw her again, he'd beg her to get away from him.

Evan's tears fell like a flood. *She's still alive. She's gotta be. Please still be alive.*

Boots crunched in the dark. Shani pressed her face into the back of his shirt to muffle her breathing. Evan wanted his mother. A tingle of energy swept over the tip of his brain. The new sensation confused him for a second, but he ignored doubt and pushed at the thought.

Mommy! Help!

The distant clatter of a rifle striking the ground startled him into opening his eyes. Zee, only ten feet or so away from their hiding place, jumped back with a gasp.

"What the fuck is that?" He squinted, aiming. "Oh, you little sneaky fucker. Glowing friggin' eyes. You're one of them psionics, aren't you?"

Zee raised his weapon at the kids in a shaking grip. Abject fear in his stare said he didn't want to give them any chance to do something to his brain. Evan tensed his finger on the trigger, but before he pushed aside his hesitation at killing, Shani snarled. Zee lurched forward as if something strong yanked on his right arm. He fired, the bullet hitting the floor in front of him, pinging off two pipes and disappearing into the far end of the basement with a *clank*.

"Ain't fallin' for that shit twice. I know your damn tricks now." Zee showed off a metal forearm brace to which he had bolted the gun, then plucked at suspenders made from chains. "Time to die."

Growling, Shani thrust her hands forward. The muscles in Zee's arm swelled as she pushed his aim off to the side. He shot the ductwork. His face reddened in anger. Spittle, mixed with a liberal amount of curses, flew from his teeth. Zee grabbed his forearm with his left hand and strained to pull his aim back toward the kids. Shani released her telekinetic grip. Zee overcorrected spinning wildly to the left and putting a bullet into a fan motor on the other wall.

For a half-second, Evan pondered giving Zee the opportunity to surrender. The murderous rage in the man's eyes directed at Shani scrubbed the thought from his mind. If he didn't do it, this man would kill Shani. He clicked the trigger as fast as his finger could move it. Though the gun weighed like a plastic toy, it kicked him back with each shot. Only three bullets struck Zee, all in the chest, staggering him.

Evan stopped firing once his shots went high. Zee gurgled, a trickle of blood leaking from the corner of his mouth. Shani let out a grunt of exertion and shoved at his weapon arm. A disoriented Zee whirled in a full three-sixty, almost aiming at the children again before she forced his arm straight up.

Shani shuddered from the exertion, and whimpered in fear.

Evan shot him again.

Clack. The bullet ricocheted off his chest into distant pipes, clattering and clanging.

He aimed up, trying for a head shot, but missed.

Shani panted, shaking. Zee growled, gradually bringing his arm down, overpowering her. Seconds before his weapon pointed at her face, Evan slid in front her.

"Don't look, Shan…"

A streak of green light burst out of Zee's chest, igniting the armor around the hole. Another brief streak of emerald laser pierced his head, leaving two tiny holes on either side of his skull wafting smoke. Zee crumpled in place. Nila rushed over and shot Zee once more through the chest from two feet away, but the body didn't react.

"Police. Drop your weapon," deadpanned Nila.

SANCTUARY

"Wren?" Captain Eze's voice barely reached Kirsten's awareness over her sobbing.

She pushed herself off the floor, sniffling, and stared up at him with such a pathetic expression he ran over and took a knee.

"Are you alright? What happened?"

"It was Konstantin." She wiped her face, unable to stop crying. "He's got Evan."

Eze gathered her in his arms and carried her to the sofa. "We'll find the son of a bitch. Hey. Look at me."

She sat up straight, fists on knees, inhaling deep breaths.

"Don't mourn someone who isn't gone. You haven't seen Evan's ghost, right?"

Kirsten nodded. "No... You're right." She wiped her face. "I shouldn't give up yet."

Captain Jonathan Eze patted her on the back. He stood and crossed the room to the door, placing his hand on the panel beside it. In seconds, his eyes became all-white and gave off a faint glow. The clamor of additional police units shuffling down the hallway pulled Kirsten to her feet. She looked down at herself. Despite escaping from an abduction, she felt foolish as if she'd forgotten her uniform. She paced a figure eight, gazing around at the random burn marks on the walls.

Two Division 1 officers entered. They started to survey the scene but both fixated on her with tilted heads.

Eze snapped out of his trance. He strode over to her and placed a hand on her shoulder.

"Kirsten, it's not what you think." He smiled. "The building's security system shows a bunch of street toughs. Nila held them off, the kids ran."

"A gang? Why the hell would gang punks come after Nila at home?"

Eze glanced at the Div 1 cops and pointed. "There's a body in that hall. Secure the area and don't let anyone out of the building."

"Sir." The closer one nodded and moved into the apartment while muttering into his comm about setting up a lockdown on the building.

"I don't know..." Eze looked at the wall.

"What is it? Why are you hesitating?"

"I have the feeling they were after the kids more than her, and that doesn't make a lot of sense."

A sudden wave of inexplicable panic washed over her, sapping the energy from her legs and sending her onto the couch. When the paralytic spike of worry passed, she looked up at Eze, tears streaming from the corners of her eyes.

"Evan needs me. He's terrified. He..." She stared into space. "He's in the basement."

"In the basement? How do you know that?"

"He's calling me." She leapt off the sofa, hiked the robe up to her thighs, and sprinted out of the apartment.

Kirsten dashed down the corridor to the elevators. The robe might've billowed a little but she didn't care at all who saw what as she zoomed past a dozen officers from Divisions 1 and 0. A middle-aged man moved to step into an arriving elevator, but she body-checked him, knocking him aside, then mashed the B on the console with the grip of her E-90.

"Ugh. Hey what the hell!" shouted the man, picking himself up off the floor.

"I'm really sorry, police emergency."

The doors hissed closed. Kirsten jumped up and down, trying to kick the elevator into a faster descent. She gripped her weapon in both hands, aiming at the frigid floor between her feet. She couldn't tell if her shaking came from cold, fear, worry, shame, or anger. So much had happened to her over the past few hours, her mind floated in limbo.

When the doors opened, she jumped out and ran down a short corridor toward a body. A young man in a tattered vest, dark pants, and mismatched boots lay dead on his face against the wall. The smell of charred flesh in the air said 'death by laser.' *Nila came this way. Oh, please let her have found him.* She ran past the corpse, heading for two pairs of doors at the end of the corridor. The one on the left was open already, so she went that way. The urge to yell for Nila or Evan came on strong, but she checked her emotions—she might need the element of surprise.

A short stairway led into the dark; a heavyset man lay on the ground near the bottom on his chest. Despite having his arms trapped behind him in police binders, he seemed calm. At the sight of Kirsten, he did a double take. She ignored the confusion on his face and stepped over him. A few paces later, she grimaced at the stickiness of the floor while throwing desperate glances at four possible ways to go. Left, right, or two forward passages between rows of enormous machines.

At a sudden eruption of gunfire, she ducked—but nothing pinged nearby.

The muzzle flare was strongest to her right, but sounded distant. She went for the straight-ahead aisle on that side. A moment later, green light flashed in two pulses one after the next. Kirsten sprinted hard down the narrow passageway and almost wiped out as she rounded the corner. She stopped short at the sight of Nila squatting on the far side of a dead man, with two relieved children clinging to her.

"Evan…" Kirsten wanted to shout, but only whimpered.

"Mommy!" he cheered, and ran to her.

Kirsten fell to her knees, wrapping her arms around the shivering boy, so overwhelmed with relief that the boy wound up supporting all her weight for a few seconds. His terror and tears evaporated in an instant. He bounced, squeezed, and cuddled.

Nila picked Shani up and carried her over, glancing at the sound of more police flooding the basement. "The heavy guy at the steps surrendered."

"He didn't wanna shoot us," said Shani.

Evan leaned back enough to make eye contact. "Yeah. That guy tried to change Zee's mind." He furrowed his brow. "Why are you dressed up like Xiana?"

Her cheeks burned with blush. "Uhh, someone stole my clothes. This was all I could find."

Nila raised an eyebrow. *What the fuck happened?*

Oh, not much. Kirsten found the floor rather interesting. *I almost had sex with a seventy-year-old man, realized I've been quasi-possessed for a few weeks, wound up naked in a dungeon... you know, the usual bad shit that happens whenever I wear high heels.*

Nila grimaced. *I'm sorry I asked.*

I feel like such an idiot, Nila. Kirsten squeezed Evan. At last, her brain processed Evan knowing the dead man's name. "Zee?" She blinked and twisted around to look at the corpse. "You know this son of a bitch?"

Soft clicking came from the right.

Kirsten twisted her head that way and found Zee's spirit attempting to fire a spectral gun at Evan.

"The drug guy from Sector D, you remember?" said Evan. "The one Shani pantsed. In the cartoon underwear?"

The ghost snarled.

"Oh," said Kirsten, eyes narrowing. "Him. Didn't he go to jail?"

"Drug charges and assault on a chem-user? He probably did two weeks and got out. If they even kept him that long. Overcrowding." Nila grumbled.

Kirsten stood, keeping a hand on Evan's shoulder. Shani shivered at a sudden chill in the air while Nila raised an eyebrow.

"Is he still here?" asked Evan.

Kirsten beckoned for *them.* "Not for much longer."

"Mom," said Evan.

She looked him in the eye. "Yes?'

"I don't like Konstantin. He scares me. I think he's gonna hurt you. Will you please stop seeing him?"

Kirsten choked up. "You're absolutely right, Ev. But... I want to see him again."

He blinked in shock. "What? No!"

Nila tilted her head. "Seriously?"

Kirsten held up her E-90. "Oh, I'm quite serious."

CLOUDS OF MIST WASHED OVER THE HOOD OF THE BLACK PATROL CRAFT AS Kirsten guided it in for a landing in front of the Five Hundredth Street Sanctuary. A handful of people in line for free food waved at her as she got out and adjusted her utility belt. Never before had a hot shower felt so good—even a rushed one after a medical evaluation. Not content to wait for her to open the back door, Evan climbed into the front seat and joined her outside the car.

Nila, now in her tactical armor, let Shani out of the rear passenger door on that side. Despite the current situation, Kirsten couldn't hold back the giggle at the kitten mewls coming from the girl's sneakers as she ran to her mother. The dire look Nila gave Kirsten only made her laugh louder.

"Thanks for that, by the way. She saw your Nomz and *had* to have them. I hear little electronic cats in my sleep now."

Shani, with a big grin, shifted her weight from leg to leg to keep her shoes mewing.

"I dunno. It is kind of cute that the kid-sized ones sound like kittens."

Nila narrowed her eyes, but grinned. *I'm going to find the most obnoxious toy I can find and give it to Evan for his birthday.*

Kirsten laughed, took Evan's hand, and led the group into the building. "I hope this will only be for a few hours. Maybe a day or so. Father Villera has agreed to let you stay."

"I never thought you'd drag people to church," said Nila, with an eye roll. "You don't seriously buy this crap do you?"

"Not like that, no. But…" Kirsten smiled at a man who moved to create a gap in the line for them to get in. "There is at least enough to it that abyssals won't walk in here."

"I guess… if you think so." Nila held tight to Shani's hand. The girl clung to her mother, uncharacteristically shy around so many vagrants.

"The bad ghosts don't like it here," said Evan. "I pushed one in with the car and she 'sploded."

Father Villera came around from behind the food-serving table and walked with them to a room in the back with two cots and a desk. Shani dove on the left-side bed. Nila folded her arms, remaining in the doorway where Evan clung to Kirsten.

"I don't know how I got to you before his men showed up." She ran her hand over his hair. "Maybe those gang idiots scared them off. Stay here with Nila until its safe."

Evan looked up at her, eyes wide. "The bad ghosts can't get in here, but what if he just sends people?"

Kirsten patted Nila on the arm. "That's why Nila's here…" She thought for a moment and raised her forearm guard. Within a few seconds, Captain Eze's hologram appeared. "Captain, can you request a Div 6 security detail? I've found a place where they are safe from demons, but Konstantin might still send ordinary thugs. Most of the security men at his estate were normal."

Eze glanced left at another screen, and both eyebrows crept upward. "You're at the church on 500th street?"

"Yes, sir. Abyssals can't get in here. They're safe if he sends one of his pets, but he's also got a lot of money and resources. He could send ordinary mercenaries, maybe even a borg."

"Alright, consider it done. The raid found no trace of Konstantin at the manor. Div 9 is getting ready to go after him at a property belonging to Koloss Venture Capital. They're picking up activity inside on the sensors and the senior-in-command has requested you on-site to handle anything... weird."

Kirsten hugged a gasp out of Evan. "Understood, sir. Do I have time to wait for Div 6 to get here? I don't..."

"It's okay, Mom. I don't feel scared. Don't let him get away." He squirmed up and kissed her on the cheek.

She held back the urge to cry. "Tell them I'm on the way."

Nila put a hand on Kirsten's shoulder as the light from Eze's hologram flickered out. "Go get that bastard."

Evan folded his arms and nodded. "I'll keep them safe."

CHARTER TO MIAMI

E van's last comment kept Kirsten on the verge of tears for the entire ride to the nav pin. She wrung her hands on the control sticks, alternating between shivering worry and seething anger. The image of the boy's confident smile and bright hazel eyes wouldn't leave her mind. She wanted nothing more than to go home, plant him in her lap and watch Monwyn vids until he grew up.

Kirsten glanced at the empty passenger seat, but a beep drew her attention to the center console.

"Agent Wren?" an anonymous black helmet appeared floating in hologram.

"Yes, who are—"

"My designation for this operation is Whisper 3. I'm in position over the target location. Please follow this waypoint."

A neon yellow stripe appeared in midair, courtesy of the electronic windshield. It traced a path into the distance, ending on the roof of a corporate tower two-point-six miles away.

Ugh Div 9 always plays by its own rules. "Understood."

She clung to her anger at Konstantin and flew hard, perhaps a bit fast for the area. Upon reaching the building, she throttled back, lifting the nose and setting the patrol craft down beside a row of four other black hovercars that looked like hers only they didn't have police lights across the roof. *Why do we call all big buildings century towers? Like half of them are taller than a hundred stories.*

Kirsten hopped out, leaving the door to close itself, and jogged over to a black-haired woman in a light, sand-brown coat. Her heavy side-buckled boots looked quite similar to Kirsten's. The woman turned at her approach, and made Kirsten feel tiny, having about eight inches on her in height. Dark blue eyes set in the face of a black-haired porcelain doll triggered a spark of familiarity. *Nina! Don't offer a handshake first. It'll make me look like an eager rookie. She's a lieutenant.*

Kirsten saluted.

"Thanks for coming, agent." Nina returned the salute. "Are you okay? Heard you had a rough night."

"I'm fine, Lieutenant. Thanks. Yeah, bit of a bad night. Sorry if I'm on edge here. I feel a bit out of my league. Oh, did that info I sent you a week ago help? That body looked like the work of the sick freak you've been looking for."

"Lieutenant Duchenne, we're in position," shouted a man by the roof access.

No emotion showed from Nina's face. "The scene was cold. Too much time passed. Bertrand is a slippery bastard. I think he's hiding in The Beneath."

"Oh. Sorry. Hey, you know ghosts have strange talents. If I run into another one of his victims, I'll ask them if they can help me track him down. I might be able to lead you right to him."

Nina nodded. "Thanks. That would be helpful."

Kirsten blinked. *Someone in Division 9 believes in ghosts?*

"I still owe him." Nina glanced at the door. "Okay, people, in we go. We have a Zero along for the ride in case we run into something we can't explain." She lowered her voice. "Just stick close to me. We'll do the heavy lifting."

"Seriously? You expecting a psionic?"

Nina walked over to the stairwell access. An unfamiliar *bwee-oop* came from Kirsten's earbud around the same time the security code on the door panel flashed from red to green. "If we run into anything fucked up, Agent Wren gets to give orders until the scene is unfucked. Everyone understand?"

A series of affirmatives filtered over the comm. channel. Kirsten bit her lip at hearing a Div 9 channel. More likely they'd set up a special loop for her, and could still talk about their super secret stuff without her hearing it.

With that, Nina entered the stairwell and descended four floors. At the bottom, another access panel opened on its own. Kirsten eyed a cam bubble in the ceiling, wondering if someone back at Div 9 Net Ops followed them virtually.

"We're in position," said Nina.

Kirsten suppressed the urge to shiver at hearing her voice without seeing her lips move. Telepathy wouldn't have bothered her, but knowing this voice came from metal installed in the woman's brain unnerved her.

"Copy that, Lieutenant," said a man. "We're going in three… two…"

At the one count, Nina shoved the door open stepped inside, surprising three men in suits. She waved her arm from left to right, her giant pistol releasing a short burp of automatic fire. Somehow, each man had a bullet hole center mass.

"No warning?" Kirsten blinked, offering an apologetic look at three confused ghosts.

Nina moved up to a corner, firing two shots into an armored man thirty meters further ahead, both drilling neat holes in the composite vest. He gurgled, slumped against the wall, and sank to the floor with an astonished expression.

Nina glanced at Kirsten. "They abducted a law officer with intent to kill. They are, according to your statements, responsible for manipulating government and corporate officials via paranormal means. Also, Konstantin Dobrynin is a foreign national." Another man rushed the corner, blades sprouting out of his forearms. Nina swung her arm into a clothesline move, crushing his body from shoulder to rib. The corpse convulsed on the ground, most of the bones in his chest shattered. "So, no. No warning."

"How can you assume their entire security team is culpable?" Kirsten grimaced at the sight of the most recent ghost. The upper half of his body flopped forward as if on a hinge. Upon noticing she could see him, he gave her a bewildered look. "You just tried to attack a Division 9 doll with claws, jackass. What did you expect would happen?"

Nina squinted. "That thermal anomaly behind you… is that his ghost?"

"Yes, ma'am. No, ma'am, you don't have a line of them following you. Most don't linger around much past an hour or so."

A section of wall exploded inches from Nina's face. She bent away as more gunfire came down the hall. After a pointed stare at solid drywall, she mumbled.

"Wait here. I'm gonna scrub the hallway."

Kirsten crouched against the frosted glass wall of an executive office while Nina edged to the corner. After the bullets stopped hitting the floor, Nina leapt into a blur of tan coat and black bodysuit. In the span of three seconds, she came to a halt at the far end of the hallway. Six men with rifles fell to the ground. The closest (and first to die) hadn't yet hit the floor by the time her fist launched the sixth corpse into a vendomat.

Nina waved at her to come over, but the screech of vibro-claws sent shivers down Kirsten's spine. A man rushed out of a doorway by Nina, arms held to the side with a trio of fourteen-inch blades sticking out between his knuckles. Kirsten backed up a step, raising her E-90.

The man sprang at Nina. She moved as though she didn't exist in the same flow of time, blinking out of existence a second before reappearing two steps behind the man. He swiped his blades at empty air.

He lunged with a wild, frustrated roar, stabbing at Nina's face with white-hot blades. To Kirsten, the fight from that point forward played out as a series of still images flashed in sequence. Nina leaning left. Her hand on his wrist, his broken arm twisted at an impossible angle. Nina's left forearm slamming down onto his back. The body, now missing its right arm, embedded hip-deep in the wall.

Nina's movement smoothed out, returning to real time. She dropped the ripped-off limb with a squishy *plop* and made a 'come here' gesture with her unbloodied hand. Kirsten blinked. *Lucian had no damn idea.* She couldn't help but stare at Nina as if getting too close to her would be fatal. *They thought I was Division 9? Nina would have destroyed those idiots in two seconds.* She imagined the attack at Henry Motte's house happening with Nina in her place, and laughed.

Nina lifted an eyebrow. "Are you okay, Agent Wren?"

"Yeah… just a funny thought." Kirsten grimaced, losing her smile as she stepped over a severed leg. "Ma'am."

After a glance around at the carnage, Nina continued down the hallway at a brisk stride. "Zeroes find strange things funny. Did one of the ghosts say something?"

"No, they're either confused, still trying to hit you, or giving you the finger." Kirsten jogged to keep up. "Intera tried to kill me awhile back."

Nina fired into the wall twice. The massive handgun pounded the air in Kirsten's lungs. A man's wheeze and the thud of a body hitting the ground followed. "That's still not very humorous."

"I was just... they thought I was Division 9 because my uniform is black. One of their assassins taunted me for fighting like a little kid. I was laughing at what would have happened if those idiots attacked you."

A tracked security robot the size of a one-seat car rolled around the corner behind them amid the smoke and plaster dust at the same time three men with rifles appeared in a glass-walled conference room further down the hallway. They raised their weapons, intending to fire despite several layers of floor-to-ceiling glass between them.

Nina spun, gathering Kirsten into her chest before leaping backward through a solid wall. The sudden motion jerked her breath away. Stunned from the near-instant transition from standing to lying on top of Nina, Kirsten made a noise like a honking goose as they landed, clutching at the arm across her body. Bullets chewed up the rug where they'd been standing seconds before.

Her brain didn't have a chance to consider said arm could crush her before Nina pushed her aside.

"Think you can take out that rover?" asked Nina.

Kirsten gawked. After that maneuver, she barely knew her own name.

"Hey." Nina patted her on the cheek. "You still there?"

"Uhh." Mechanically, Kirsten drew the E-90. "Yeah. Sorry, disoriented from the... How did we get in here?"

"Start firing at the bot in two seconds. I'll deal with the three on the right."

After crawling behind a desk, Kirsten draped herself over the top and fired at a dark spot visible beyond frosted glass walls. Shimmering streaks of azure light connected the tip of her weapon to the huge robot. Geysers of sparks and molten glass sprayed as the sentry bot staggered, its heavy frame shaking the floor. Static and digital warbles emanated from it, though she couldn't tell if it tried to scream in pain or if she'd blown out its voice processor.

Nina leapt back out the hole she'd first made in the drywall and ran off to the right. Kirsten kept firing, hoping to keep the robot occupied so it didn't shoot Nina in the back. A piece of assault rifle bounced past the hole in the wall, a hand still attached to it. A wet, splintering *crunch* cut off a man's scream. Something clicked off the desk Kirsten hid behind; a bloody tooth rolled to a halt on the carpet.

Holy shit.

She ducked a hail of plaster dust and flying glass shards as the rotating security rover machine-gunned the frosted glass wall to shards. Angry whirring noises came from its tank treads as it rotated to face Kirsten. Small patches of fire and sparks flared out of laser holes all over its hull, though it didn't appear seriously damaged. Without a wall blocking her view, she had a clear shot at the thing. As fast as the E-90's core could cycle, she put six beams into it. Four in the central body and two into a boxy part in the back she hoped contained the ammunition for its guns.

The robot sputtered, twisting side to side in erratic jerking motions. The rear end exploded in a ball of green flames. Nina, bloody up to both elbows, came out of nowhere and landed on top of it with a heavy *whump*. A pair of Nano blades emerged from between the knuckles of her right hand, which she drove into the forward end of the main body. One twist rendered the bot silent and dark.

"Control box on these Sentinel-4s is right here." Nina pulled her claws out with an ear-bleeding squeal of synthetic diamond on plastisteel. The ten-inch blades slid without a sound back into her forearm as she leapt to the ground. "Decent job of keeping it occupied though. I think you hit the targeting system."

Kirsten pushed herself to her feet with two handfuls of desk. "Are those things legal?"

"The weapon systems are civilian grade, but it was hacked to disregard police transponder signals."

"Wow... Bots that size aren't prohibited?"

"Not purely from size," said Nina in a tone that shared Kirsten's distaste for the idea.

A man's roar preceded an enormous aug rushing into the hall. Both arms, his entire chest, and most of his neck consisted of jet-black plastisteel armor. He charged at Nina, raising a six-foot-long Nano sword in a two-handed grip. She almost rolled her eyes and shot him square in the forehead. The sword fell out of his grip, spearing into the floor behind him and standing straight up as the man slid the last few feet to Nina on his face.

"Where did your ex-boyfriend find so many idiots?"

Kirsten stared at the gleaming sword, the dead man, the sword again, and Nina.

Voices on the comm. from the rest of the team called in reporting eighteen unarmed civilians taken into custody, eleven armed individuals terminated—no sign of Konstantin downstairs. Screaming came from farther down the corridor. Kirsten leaned out of the room to peek. A handful of orb bots and another large tracked unit chased two security men down an intersecting corridor.

Nina laughed. "We won't have to worry about the automated security anymore. Looks like DeWinter's got it under control. You see anything weird?"

"Demons?" Kirsten looked around. "No, just a handful of new ghosts... and one suspiciously absent old one." She gawked at Nina while listening to voice chatter about zone clearing. "The Archives. I have to go to the archives!"

HISTORICAL INFLUENCE

Greyish smog peppered with staccato bursts of blue light rolled past the patrol craft's windscreen. A yellow wireframe model of the surrounding city shimmered, allowing Kirsten to fly despite a near-total lack of visibility. Alas, the flight computer had difficulty rendering small objects (like advert bots) fast enough to avoid the occasional minor collision. Fortunately, the bots too small to register in time presented little threat to the armor plating.

Clank.

She yelled, "Your damn fault for ignoring the emergency transponder and not clearing the lane."

"Dorian? Come on, where are you? Wake up." Kirsten pounded her hand at the center console. "Did you try to come after me when I was stuck in his basement? Where the hell are you?"

A dotted line led in an arc from the hood, plunging into the city of pixilated a few miles ahead. From this altitude, the West City Archives complex resembled several stacks of hatboxes linked by archways and elevated, enclosed bridges. She nudged forward on the right stick, diving closer to the ground. Below the thirtieth story, she emerged from the underside of the smog layer. The weak gloom of an overcast day glowed along the silvery glass canyon around her, hundreds of near-identical century towers.

Two minutes later, she circled around and brought the patrol craft to rest in the central courtyard. She leapt out of the car, worry and fury in her eyes daring anyone to give her crap for landing there. Two steps later, she faced the car and closed her eyes. Beaconing for Dorian, she spent a minute projecting the want for him to come to her into the astral realm, with no luck.

William Arris was a security guard here. Konstantin used him in some ritual. There has got to be a connection. She stormed in the nearest door, past a handful of security guards who all backed off with raised hands. Holographic signs led her through an atrium, two hallways, and up a flight of stairs to the office of the curator.

Kirsten barged in, disregarding the security desk in the antechamber. A slender middle-aged man with touches of grey hair half-stood up, tilted his head and appeared about to say something, but ducked down when she unfurled the astral lash. The scintillating cord sent harsh shadows skittering over the wall. At the inner door, she waved her forearm guard at the panel. The guard pursed his lips, shook his head, and sat back down as if she didn't exist.

"I'm sorry, the Curator has asked that—" A thirty-something man of Indian descent stood from behind the executive assistant's desk in the next room, his protest cut off by a lash to the chest.

Her strike found no resistance, destroying only the man's ability to speak. She paid him no further attention and stepped up to a run. With a growl, she shoulder-blocked a set of carved wooden double doors open and sprinted at a big fancy desk in the middle of a huge office. A slender, dark-skinned man with a greying afro behind the desk barely had a chance to open his mouth before she sliced the ethereal tendril into him.

The man sailed to the right from the force of the hit as if weightless, landing in a heap. A baritone wail of pain startled her for only an instant as he fought to crawl forward. She tapped into the shame and anger from what Konstantin did to her, and brought the spectral whip down on top of him a second time.

Two security guards plus the executive assistant ran in, and stood aghast at a blast of jet ichor spewing from the curator's mouth, nose, and ears. Some of the liquid coalesced into a legless humanoid shape that flopped its arms at the floor, making a series of splats. Kirsten swung the lash again, blasting the apparition into a cloud of fine mist that settled over the new arrivals, staining them indigo.

One more swipe of the energy tendril through the curator found no trace of resistance. Satisfied, she released her power and the cord dissipated. Kirsten glanced at the desk, specifically the nameplate, then crouched over the shuddering man. "Mr. Annan, are you okay?"

He convulsed once, vomiting more inky water. After a few heavy breaths, he wiped a line of drool from his lower lip and sat back on his heels. "Please explain what in God's name just happened to me."

She tried not to look at the dark stain spreading over the crotch of his pants. "You may want to change before I go into great detail. A paranormal entity had possessed you. I have reason to believe it may have been used to influence your decisions." Kirsten helped him up. "Sorry to barge in on you. The last one of these I tried to destroy ran off when I simply walked in to talk. Wanted to make sure I got the bastard if you had one."

"A paranormal..." He stared at the ceiling.

Kirsten looked up at the oddly tall man, trying not to let the height disparity intimidate her. "Paranormal entity. Ghost. Maybe even a demon. Doesn't matter what you call it, it's gone now. Mr. Annan, can you please look back over the past few weeks. Any decision you made in that time is suspect."

He wiped his face with a burgundy silk handkerchief. The tool proved inadequate for the amount of sweat and post-possession slime. "Please, call me Kwadwó, Miss..."

"Agent Kirsten Wren. National Police Force, Division 0."

Kwadwó Annan excused himself to a small, attached bathroom. She paced in an anxious circle. The security officers wandered over, more casual upon realizing she had come to help the curator. Her brain flew on autopilot, navigating the small talk the men made while she waited for Kwadwó. Some minutes later, he emerged from the bathroom in different pants and a sleeveless undershirt. After draping his suit jacket over the back of his chair, he took a seat at the desk and opened his terminal. Kirsten went to his side, gazing at the dozen grey holographic panels that unfolded in midair. A few small portrait holo bars on a table behind the desk projected still images of a younger Kwadwó: sitting among pyramids, a camp in a jungle, a red stone cave somewhere on Mars, a barely-recognizable man encased in a heavy coat at a place covered in snow. The man had been to so many places she figured him for a globetrotting archaeologist.

"I'm not exactly sure what's going on here, Agent." Kwadwó scratched at a salt and pepper goatee. "Most of the past two weeks feels like a disembodied dream." He looked over at her. "As though I watched myself from the outside."

Kirsten put a hand on his shoulder. "I'm sorry I didn't show up sooner. It's important. I need to know what Konstantin Dobrynin did here."

"Konstantin..." Kwadwó grabbed at an icon in the light panel and tossed it to a larger screen. When the face of a hard-eyed man in his later seventies appeared, Kirsten looked away and blushed. "Let me see... the only thing. That son of a bitch." He slapped his desk. "I remember telling him we didn't have the resources to give him an entire wing for his exhibit, yet here is my signed approval for it."

She refused to look at the wrinkled face on the terminal. Shame came over her, making her want scrub memory of his touch from her body, but she instead out a hand over her mouth. Two hours in an autoshower would do the job, but she couldn't think about that now. Kirsten closed her eyes and thanked the Seraphim that someone had called him before he had gone all the way. His hand touching her down there was bad enough. Even if the Seraphim had nothing to do with it, she felt grateful anyway.

Kirsten forced that memory aside and put on game face. "What did he install in that wing?"

"There's no inventory in the catalog. It *should* be empty. But I have a suspicion it won't be." Kwadwó stood, throwing his blazer on. "Let us go."

It took about six minutes to walk from the curator's office to the private wing. A holographic panel, six feet tall and two wide, advertised a one-of-a-kind display of ancient artifacts with a focus on forgotten cults and mysticism. The giant holo-panel tinted the walls different colors as it cycled from blue to desert brown to red with different versions of the same advertisement.

Kwadwó swiped his ID at the door, but it buzzed. "Damn. My pass should open everything here."

Kirsten's police ID triggered the same buzz. Despite all the crap going on, an illegal hack on the door to bar the police caught her off guard. She squinted, drawing the E-90. "Take a step back, Mr. Annan."

"But—"

On the lowest setting, a pip from the weapon burned the locking bar and lit the marble floor behind it aglow. Kirsten booted the ornate doors open. They hit the wall with a *slam* that echoed within an open chamber beyond. Dozens of crates littered the room. Pulverized soy shell and dust smeared in whorls on the ground. The shapes of exhibits lurked in the darkness, mostly incomplete, but a few had display cases or non-sentient doll 'actors' portraying ancient mystics.

Surrounded by velvet ropes in the center of it all, a black pillow with a fist-sized dent sat within a two-foot clear cube. Whatever it had been meant to hold had either been removed, or never placed there. She stepped over the barrier and put her hands on the bullet-resistant plastic box. A strong wave of paranormal energy filled her mind with a dozen screaming voices. Terrified women, frightened men, and one angry roar. The angry one sounded familiar. She'd heard that exact sound before.

From Dorian.

Your little friend is the last piece I need. Konstantin's voice, withered and old, rasped at the back of her consciousness.

Kwadwó's hand on her shoulder made her realize she had slumped to her knees. "Are you alright, Agent Wren?"

She let him help her up, wanting to back away from the touch of a man in his later fifties. Dark brown eyes beheld her with a look of a concerned father, easing her mind. "What... what was in there?"

"Terminal," said Kwadwó, reaching up to enter his password on a transparent white slab of hologram that appeared next to him. A few finger swipes later, he pointed. "That. Looks like some manner of gemstone."

While the curator opened a second panel and scrolled over reams of text, Kirsten stood and peered at the first screen. Security camera images of the case from two days ago showed a violet jewel set in the hollow spot on the pillow. A teardrop cut the size of a man's fist pulsed with amethyst light in a way that conjured the sense of a heartbeat.

"The Heart of Eannatum," said Kwadwó. "It was recovered from a dig site in Iraq years ago, but stolen before it made it out of the country. There are all manner of rumors about what happened: cultists objecting to it being unearthed, mercenaries, even the local government was purported to be involved."

Kirsten poked a finger at the screen. "I think cultists came closest, though I doubt they were motivated by protecting cultural heritage." She took a step toward the door, but stopped short when Brooke's memory came back to her: the glowing crystal in Konstantin's hand that appeared to consume Alaina Munoz's ghost.

It's some kind of soul trap. She bit her knuckles, fighting the urge to cry. *It can't devour them. It's gotta be a trap.* Her eyes widened. "He didn't need to kill people... he needed *spirits!* I destroyed his harvester when it tried to take Allan, so he had to start making new ghosts, weak enough for him to catch himself. Shit!" She spun, and took the curator's hand. "Thank you, Kwadwó. Sorry for the mess. I need to go."

He's not after Evan at all. I'm coming, Dorian.

41

DECOMMISSIONED

Electronic thrumming flooded the cabin. The noise verged away from the realm of pure sound into something tangible—a vibration teasing at Kirsten's presence. Silence from the passenger seat seemed more vacuous knowing Dorian was gone. *Stay professional.* The words manifested in his voice at the back of her mind. She picked her thumbnails at the control sticks. Captain Eze hadn't received any updates about where Konstantin ran off to, and Division 9 had all the starports and shuttle terminals under tight surveillance.

On an upwelling of sudden confidence, she jabbed her finger at the console. A few seconds later, Division 0 Chief Jane Carter appeared. Confusion settled into an expression that conveyed amusement.

"Agent Wren. I trust you know it is quite irregular to call me directly."

"Yes, ma'am. I'm sorry, ma'am. This can't wait." She glanced at her forearm. "Uplink, official log." The armband beeped and twittered. "Thirteen hundred hours, fourteen minutes to fourteen hundred hours, nine minutes. Transmit."

The right side of Carter's face changed color as the video of Kirsten's time at the archives played.

"I destroyed an entity influencing the curator. I know the same damn thing is in Vernon, ma'am. I've got no idea where Konstantin is and only hours before Div 9 puts a bullet in that woman's head. I'm going there now, ma'am. If it has any warning, it'll hide again."

Carter's fingernails clicked, tapping on her desk out of sight. "I have the feeling a direct order to stay away will only generate some paperwork later while we have a hearing about why you disobeyed it."

"I'm sorry, ma'am. I don't know how to get a demon on camera to admit it's influencing a government official. All of Konstantin's notes look like stick men doing aerobics. I... I can't let him play with our government and I can't let our government kill an innocent woman. So, yes, ma'am. I'm going there anyway. I had hoped to get your approval first... or at least give you a heads up."

Carter leaned back in her seat, trying not to smile. "Please send me the same visual records when you are done there. I'll need it to deal with General McDonnell. I assume you're not going to be gentle with the security detachment. I'll send a tactical team to back you up as well."

THE ELEVATOR DOORS PARTED TO REVEAL THE EXPECTED HORSESHOE OF soldiers in assault armor. Sergeant Gerard moved in her path as soon as she emerged. Kirsten surveyed the men; her gaze lingered on the one that seemed most eager to shoot her.

"Hold it right there, girlie. We didn't get any auth—"

"Sergeant Gerard, I'm shocked you're still able to work with Corporal Fuentes after what he *did to your little sister*." Kirsten's eyes glimmered.

Gerard froze, jaw twitching. His face warped with rage as his mind conjured up some horrible event. Four seconds later, Sergeant Gerard pulled a vibro-knife from his belt and pounced on Fuentes. The two troopers on either side of Fuentes tried to hold him back, while the three on the other arm of the horseshoe raised their weapons.

"*Freeze!*" She yelled, taking a step at them.

All three had clean eye contact, though her suggestion power lacked the strength to fully affect more than one person at a time. Spreading it over three brains diluted it into a momentary confusion instead of a minutes-long compulsion not to move. Kirsten avoided the brawling soldiers to her left and sprinted for the door at the far end of the lobby, calling the lash.

A chubby woman with dark hair and a plum dress dove for cover behind the reception desk, screaming at the energy tendril fluttering behind Kirsten. She dove shoulder first through the door into Commissioner Claire Vernon's office. After three strides, she leapt into the air and brought the lash up in a long overhead, making contact with Vernon the same instant her boots alighted upon desk.

Thunder erupted behind her.

Kirsten's arm snagged as the glimmering thread found solidity within the woman. Fire lanced her left thigh. A burst of Epoxil fragments flew. Another stab of heat caught her in the right shoulder. Kirsten pulled at the lash as she spun around in the air, falling. A flash of green armor at the door gleamed in strong overhead lights. The man on the far left shouted at the other two, shoving their rifles to the side. His voice blurred as time seemed to slow down.

"You'll hit Vernon…"

Kirsten landed atop the desk, the impact filled her mouth with a burst of blood. She kept going, sliding off the desk to the floor. Snarling, she yanked at the lash, dragging Vernon to the ground with her. Black fluid burst out of the commissioner from both ends, spraying from her nostrils as well. Another distant pop preceded a dull *clank* somewhere above her.

The women landed almost nose to nose, neither with the energy to move. Dark liquid bubbled from Vernon's mouth, blood from Kirsten's. Their eyes met—brown to blue.

Demon… forcing you to approve trade deal. Division 9… will to kill you to stop it.

Claire Vernon tried to gasp, managing only a bubbling throat noise instead.

They won't kill you now.

Vernon slid a hand over the carpet, and grasped Kirsten's. She glanced at her hand, alarmed at not feeling the woman touch her. Her entire body had gone numb. She coughed up more blood.

Please tell Evan I'm sorry…

Commissioner Vernon slid out of her vision as something pushed her over onto her back. The ceiling rolled into view beyond the tip of a rifle in her face. The helmeted man above it blurred too much to recognize.

Too late, asshole. I got the demon. Vernon's safe and Carter's got the video. You've just murdered a police officer. Enjoy life without parole in an asteroid mine.

She tried to blink, but the blurriness became darkness.

42

PARAMOUNT

Consciousness returned with a great breath. Kirsten's lungs filled with warm, syrupy, breathable gel. The unexpected sensation triggered a fit of the closest a person could get to coughing while submerged. A white blur neared, flooding the tube with reflected light.

"Agent Wren, please calm down."

Kirsten attempted to grab her neck with both hands, but only her left arm moved. She rubbed her throat. *I'm okay, wasn't expecting gel. I'm just coughing.*

The telepathic transmission caused a headache of near-migraine proportion. When she went fetal, the woman's voice again reverberated in the fluid.

"Please, Agent Wren. I need you to relax."

Kirsten uncurled from the fetal pose. Her right arm floated, separated from the rest of her body at the bicep. Only a few strands of tissue connected it to the stump. The sight was the last straw her beleaguered mind could handle, and she fainted.

When she regained consciousness, she grabbed at her arm. It had become whole again, tender, but otherwise normal. She could move, and sensation had returned.

Palms on the glass, she cringed. *What happened?* Ow. Sore... but I'll deal.

An Asian woman in a white doctor's coat almost fell out of her chair at the sudden voice in her head. She looked around the room for a moment before realizing it came from Kirsten. The doctor who told her to keep still must've left already, making her wonder how long she had been unconscious. The new doctor walked over to the tank and pushed a button on a control panel beside it.

"You were shot multiple times. Your right humerus bone was completely shattered. We had to detach it the rest of the way to allow the nanobots to clean bone fragments out of the muscle and reconnect the nerves and blood vessels. I would not advise you put a lot of stress on it for a few hours, but you should retain normal function."

Kirsten sagged with relief. *This is still my arm. No cyberware.*

"You're almost done in there, Agent Wren. Should be another ten minutes or so. Would you like me to put on some music?"

Kirsten shook her head. *How long was I in here? I have to find my partner!*

The doctor glanced at the terminal before looking back at her. "You should be thrilled we saved the arm. If you didn't get here so fast... You've been in there about two hours. Nanobots are currently regenerating your blood supply and performing some final repairs at the cellular level to grow you some new bone marrow. You may notice mild discomfort in your arm and left femur."

Kirsten fidgeted, biting her lip while she hung weightless in fluid. Within a minute, 'mild discomfort' translated to the sensation of a series of needles jammed into the bones of her arm and leg, twisted back and forth, and lit on fire. The twinges came and went too fast to make her want to scream, not that she could with liquid-filled lungs. In a few minutes, the torture subsided to a dull overall sense of warmth.

She pressed herself against the tube as the doctor picked up a robe, a puppy eager to be let out of her crate. The doctor fiddled with the controls, and a patch of cyan light flashed on her face. Her voice saturated the gel yet again.

"Agent, there's someone here asking to see you. Do you mind if they come in?"

Kirsten sighed. *Fuck it. Maybe he'll be cute.* She gave the doc a thumbs up, thought for a second, and sent a message: *As long as it's not a reporter.*

Laughing, the doc nodded at a terminal out of sight. Nina walked in as pumps kicked on, drawing the gel into vents in the tank base. As usual, Kirsten remained limp and let gravity take her down until she sat on the floor. Once the last of the peach-colored gel slurped into the vents, the clear tube wall sank out of the way. *I'm winding up inside the tank way too often lately.* The doctor draped the wonderful warm robe over her as she assumed the pose and choked out the gel.

"Well," she rasped, coughing again. "I guess I know how I got here so fast."

"Director Carter was on the line with my boss while you landed, trying to call us off sending Vernon to Miami. I had a feeling things wouldn't go smoothly with Gerard. For what it's worth, the idiots who shot you got some tank time, too."

Kirsten's laugh devolved into more coughing. The doctor handed her honeyed tea, earning an adoring smile. "That's a bad sign. They know me here well enough to have the tea waiting. Guess I should be happy they're bad shots. Only hit me in the arm and thigh."

"Thank Vernon. If she wasn't in the line of fire, they wouldn't have tried to leg you. Why didn't you wait for approval?"

Hot tea ran down her throat. Soon, relaxation radiated from the node of heat forming in her stomach, spreading over her body. After a second big sip, Kirsten hocked up a wad of phlegm and B-gel and spat it into a waiting teal tray. "Whatever was inside Vernon had a way to hide from me once. I wanted to catch it off guard. I couldn't take the chance one of her security people would tell her I was coming." After another long, closed-eye sip of tea, she looked up. "How is Vernon?"

Nina dropped a bag on the Comforgel pad next to her. "Your gear. Vernon's as good as can be expected after projectile vomiting a few gallons of black gunk. She wanted to thank you for saving her life."

"There's at least two more. Someone at RedEx and Graeme McCullough at EnMesh Biomed are compromised. Probably whoever made the decision to accept the buyouts."

"We're in the process of freezing those transactions now. I do have some good news for you. We found Konstantin."

Kirsten snapped her head up. She set the tea down and jumped to her feet, flinging the robe off on the way to the autoshower. "Where is the bastard?"

"Paramount City. We're leaving in fifteen minutes."

She punched the fast-wash option. "Thanks for not making me beg to be there."

Nina laughed. "I half-expected I'd have to drag you onto the shuttle."

Sitting in the passenger seat was strange. Being in the passenger seat and not having Nicole driving was even more so. Kirsten glanced over at Nina. Two dots swirled around her NetMini's physical screen, refusing to align.

"Damn, how fast are we going? It's having a problem connecting."

"Only 418."

"Wow, it doesn't feel like it. Where's all the fancy super-secret government stuff? This looks like a civvie car."

Nina smiled and tapped the wire coming out of the back of her neck. "Need one of these to even know it's got special systems. Though, not many civilians drive these beasts."

Kirsten shivered.

Evan's face blurred in above the NetMini, red-eyed and sniffling. "Mom!"

Nila Assad squeezed into frame. "Dammit, Kirsten, what the hell did you do? The boy's been going completely batshit for hours."

Guilt hit her heavy. "Took a couple of bullets, saved someone, killed some demons. You know, my usual Tuesday night."

"Mom..." Evan sniffled, unable to say more.

"Is it over? Did you get the bastard?" Nila tried to comfort him.

"The good news is, he is not going after Evan, or you, or Shani. You don't need to keep hiding at Father Villera's place."

Nila breathed a gasp of relief. Shani's hand invaded the image from below, waving. She tried to jump up higher to get her face in view, but couldn't reach.

"The bad news is he's got Dorian, and he's on the damn Moon. I'm going there now."

Evan glared at her for an instant, but his face softened. His pang of need managed to come through loud and clear via a VidPhone link.

"I'm sorry, Ev. There's no time. I have to stop him before he hurts Dorian." *Dorian could already be gone. Could already be loose energy.* "I..." She swallowed the lump. "Have to..."

He wiped his face. "It's okay, Mom. I'm scared, but I trust you." His attempt at confidence still leaked tears.

Kirsten glanced sideways at the creak of the control sticks in Nina's hands. The woman hadn't looked in her direction since the boy appeared. "I'll get back as fast as I can. Be good to Nila."

"I will."

The call ended. Kirsten sat quiet for a moment before she spoke at her lap. "I adopted him. Well, technically, I'm trying to adopt him. You could—"

"We're almost at the starport. You ever fly on a DS4?"

"Sorry. No. Just a DS2."

"The fours give a better ride. They're about quadruple the size and can jump. Largest deep-space vessel that can breach atmosphere."

"Seems like overkill for a Moon hop." Kirsten stuffed her NetMini back in a pocket.

"Fastest way up there."

Sudden deceleration made Kirsten drift forward in her seat. She grabbed the 'oh-shit' handle and held on for dear life as Nina whipped through a series of turns no human had the reaction time to cope with. Kirsten didn't open her eyes until the whine of ground wheels deploying vibrated the car's frame.

Nina landed on the pad, twenty yards away from a vessel the size of a three-story building. About fifty yards nose to tail, it had a shape akin to a fighter jet that went on a sumo diet. The front end extended out over a belly-door with a ramp leading into a space capable of holding two DS2s or about a dozen armored vehicles.

Kirsten followed Nina up the ramp to a narrow metal ladder on the side of the otherwise empty vehicle bay. A short climb up a narrow vertical shaft led to a hallway on the top floor. Staterooms and bunks were to the right, a small ready room to the left, beyond which a cramped tunnel led to the cockpit.

Nina moved to the lounge, past a few personal weapon lockers, and flopped in a seat between two assault infantry troops. Kirsten shivered at the sight of about twenty soldiers, though these men and women seemed many degrees more welcoming than Gerard's team. Kirsten forced a pleasant smile as she crossed the room to the nearest empty seat. A moment later, the ship began vibrating from the engines powering up.

A small area between lockers across the room held a micro-kitchen with a food assembler.

Kirsten pointed at it. "Does that thing make coffee?"

43

THE RITUAL

K irsten sat beside Nina in the rear row of a six-wheeled open-top transport. The long barrel of a double Starburst laser hovered over the passenger compartment, mounted to a turret at the back end. A dozen soldiers filled the rest of the seats. Kirsten looked up past the laser at the Earth amid the darkness of space, a striated blue-white marble far larger than anything Kirsten had ever seen in the sky before, and prettier than anything else in sight.

Paramount City struck Kirsten as underwhelming.

Bleakness spread out around her. The city housing the UCF Senate held the mood of a grey zone, without all the broken buildings. Unadorned plastisteel structures stood in clusters under a massive transparent about twenty miles across. Some resembled ordinary high-rises, but most looked halfway between crashed spaceship and engineering failure. A distant gleaming sliver of jade jutted up from the bland greyness at the center of the city dome, tall enough to almost touch it. The Senate Chambers, and approximately six square miles of 'upper class' living around it, stood in harsh contrast to the outer rim. Evidently, the farther away from the center one lived, the poorer they were.

She gazed around at the squalor, heartsick for the rag-clad people congregating near the starport. The beggars ranged in age from six to sixty, and approached tourists asking for food or money.

"Why are there little kids begging at the starport?"

"Their parents refused to sign on for habitat reassignment," said one of the soldiers.

"You want to force them to move to colonies? Why doesn't the government at least take care of the kids like on Earth?"

"No one sees them up here," said Nina, her tone flat. "They look and act in worse shape than they are. The whole thing is a propaganda campaign put on by the MLF."

Kirsten blinked. "Seriously? Why would the Martian Liberation Front be active on the Moon?"

The soldiers shifted, keen on what Nina would say next.

"Their goal is to divest Mars from Earth government. The UCF is part of Earth government. It's basically the seat of it since the Senate is here. They work to foment discontent within the UCF to weaken our resolve on Mars."

With a belabored moan from its e-motors, the rover slowed and pulled into a parking space in front of an unremarkable building, five stories of tiny, narrow windows that could have been either an apartment or an office.

"I need a few minutes to coordinate with the local infrastructure," said Nina, before vaulting out of the rover. "Wait here. This won't take long."

Kirsten climbed down over a tire that came up to her chin. No sooner had she let go of the boarding ladder, a fourteen-inch silver orb bot floated up to her. The iris within a glass dome whirred open, letting more green light out. The words 'NewsNet: Lunar Edition' circled along the metal around the clear lens.

She held a hand up to shield her eyes from the light, and the orb backed up. The silhouette of a short-haired woman darted around the end of the military rover as the NewsNet's Lunar correspondent ran up on her, as if trying to figure out where the bot had gone off to. A tiny audio boom popped out from the top of the orb and angled to point its microphone at her.

"Amy Gordon, NewsNet," said the woman. "Can you tell me anything about why a member of the shadowy psionic police corps is on the Moon?"

"Shadowy?" Kirsten blinked, still squinting at the overly bright glare coming from the orb. "Where do you get that from? I'm assisting in the apprehension of a fugitive, just like any other cop."

A few of the soldiers jumped down, moving to grab the reporter. Her hazel eyes narrowed, daring them to try it.

"Before the government censors the media, what do you have to say about reports that psionics are taking over the government?"

Kirsten raised a hand at the soldiers, who—much to her surprise—paused. "Look, first of all, psionics are not some kind of evil Devil-sent cult. We are people like anyone else, with a few extra bells and whistles. Secondly, my organization is not 'shadowy.' There are too many closed-minded idiots out there looking for any excuse to lump everyone with mental abilities in the same bucket and label us all dangerous."

Amy's face shone with anticipation. Her lack of shrinking away from a psionic's advance created a twinge of unease in Kirsten and took the defensive tone out of her voice. The vid-bot drifted in a slow panning circle.

"Are there bad psionics? Of course, they are human. There are bad humans, right? My department is here to deal with them. Ordinary criminals have guns, so society has other people with guns to stand between the nuts and the citizens. We're no different. Being psionic does not make a person bad, no more than having a weapon turns a person into a crazed murderer."

The orb drifted closer, close to jabbing Kirsten in the head with the microphone. Amy swatted at the orb. "Paul, back off."

Kirsten blinked. "You... named your camera bot, 'Paul?'"

Amy shrugged. "It's kind of got a personality... seemed like a good name for a little guy that keeps generating more work for me. I had no idea you were here until he zoomed off."

The bot waved its mic boom at Amy, wobbling side to side in midair in an effort to radiate happiness.

"So are you, right now, doing something to my brain to make me like and trust psionics?"

Kirsten pinched the bridge of her nose. "No, I'm psionic, not religious. I don't freak out when people disagree with me."

"Is it true psionics have influenced the Senate?"

"Not to my knowledge, no."

The reporter raised an eyebrow. "Division 0 does not have a large presence on the Moon, how can you be so certain?"

Kirsten frowned. "Due to Senatorial security protocols, Lunar citizens, and all visitors, are required to undergo psionic testing. Anyone with even mild scores is denied access to the government building."

Amy tilted her head. "You don't seem too happy about it."

"Name a single minority group in human history that was ever happy about being the victim of stereotypes."

"That's not quite a fair comparison, Agent Wren. Historic minorities could not, by virtue of what they were, infiltrate the minds of others or force them to do things."

"Miss Gordon," said Nina, swooping around the back end of the rover, her coat fluttering behind her. "I'm afraid I must end this interview now."

"The government can't keep the citizens in the dark forever... whoever you are."

Nina folded her arms. "Four."

Amy leaned toward her. "What's going on? Why was a psionic brought to the Moon?"

"Three."

Paul the orb shuddered, gliding backward.

The soldiers moved around Kirsten and converged on the reporter. None pulled a weapon. They all seemed calm, almost apologetic.

"Fine, fine." Amy walked backward, shook her head, and trotted off grumbling. A few yards away, she faced the bot. "I'm here at an undisclosed location in Paramount City, where government agents have just ordered me away from where they have brought a psionic to the seat of the United Coalition Front Senate. Are they up to something? Will someone's brain get scrambled? We'll just have to wait and see. I'll be here when the grey matter flies. Coming up later: Meet Lieutenant Alton Lamar. Fifty-seven years ago, the jump drive on his exploration vessel malfunctioned. I'll be with you tonight for the emotional moment when the still-twenty-five year old flight officer is reunited with his eighty-one year old wife and an adult daughter who looks old enough to be his mother. But now, back to Kimberly on Earth with a great, inexpensive way to add some zing to an OmniSoy omelet."

KIRSTEN CLIMBED BACK TO HER SEAT, NOT QUITE SURE HOW TO PROCESS what she witnessed. Once all the soldiers climbed back in, the rover lurched into motion, jostling her about. She stared at the reporter, who teased a future story about the latest way to die in your own kitchen. The green bobbing helmet poking up over black headrest in front of her became mesmerizing. Within a minute, the overall melancholy within the rover came to a burdensome, claustrophobic head.

"I wouldn't have hurt her," said Nina.

The sudden interruption of silence made Kirsten jump. "W-what?"

Nina continued to stare forward. "I saw the look on your face. The reporter. I wouldn't have hurt her. I wasn't chasing her away to protect some big secret, Agent Wren. We don't have time to waste."

"Oh." Kirsten stared at her pale hands on black uniform-covered knees. Something about the lighting made her feel even whiter. "She was hoping you would. Wanted to get it on vid."

"We usually cut the feed before killing reporters."

Kirsten shivered at the coldness from the woman to her left.

Nina smiled. "Teasing. We only kill reporters when they point guns at us."

Shimmering jade rose higher and higher into the sky on the left. The senatorial tower appeared to be the only item of color in an otherwise greyscale world.

Oh, yay. "Right. So, umm. Where are we going?"

"We have tracked Konstantin Dobrynin through the underground of Paramount. He's infiltrated an abandoned level of a disused defense department installation. Despite there being thirty meters of solid Moon rock between him and the Senate chamber, command is concerned about him being below it."

"Below it?" Kirsten blinked. "What genius decided to put a military base right *under* the Senate building?"

"When the UCF first established itself on the Moon, the situation was even worse than it is on Mars. We had ACC everywhere, open war for control of the lunar surface. Paramount City was the first settlement, and that base, the first installation. They built it underground because atmo-fields only existed in theory back then and the situation demanded an operational presence faster than it would take to construct a dome. We dug in, and they kept throwing all they could at us. Fortunately, a number of clandestine operations back on Earth caused enough damage to their launch facilities that it slowed them down. We seized the advantage on the Moon and they ultimately gave up. That's probably why they're fighting so hard on Mars."

"In the dorm school, they said the ACC honored the old flag that went up hundreds of years ago." Kirsten grabbed her stomach to fight a twinge of unease.

Nina glanced over, no readable emotion on her face. "What else did they teach you?"

"Umm..." She looked way, watching stark buildings and narrow streets slide by.

"Not everything's information control. Conceding the truth of the moon was done as part of some back room deal. The ACC didn't want to admit they lost because it would make them look bad to their people. Our side agreed to keep it quiet as a condition of their cessation of hostilities."

"That's... wow. You know some of the conspiracy people out there think the UCF and ACC work together all the time to create an illusion of conflict."

"It's not as bad as it looks," said Nina, while checking her immense handgun. "These are dangerous times, and there are far, far worse places to live than the UCF."

The lesser of two evils is still evil. Kirsten took out her NetMini and stared into the black glass. *What's the alternative though? Living like tribals out in the Badlands? Or moving to a lawless colony?* "Yeah." She traced a finger over the smooth, black surface, causing the holographic panel to appear. The last application she'd accessed, her email client, popped up with images of Evan. Confident Konstantin posed no threat to him, she allowed herself to smile at his excitement playing with the patrol craft.

"Guess you like your car."

She glanced at Nina, raising an eyebrow. "These are of Evan."

"Oh," said Nina, leaning closer. "I thought the car was the focus of the image, the boy is off to the side."

Kirsten flipped over the pictures, first to last and back again. *Dammit! She's right. They were scoping Dorian, not Evan. Konstantin knows about the car.* Relief at Evan's safety clashed with worry about Dorian, leaving her hands shaking.

Nina spoke on the comm channel, giving orders and arranging teams and people around the destination. At the same time, she spoke in the real world. "Fear or anger?"

The oddity of hearing her carry on two conversations at once caused a face that made Nina laugh.

"Uhh, yes." Kirsten looked down and curled her hands into fists. "Both."

"We're almost there." Nina took a wire out of her coat pocket, then plugged one end into the back of her neck and the other into Kirsten's NetMini. "Here, you should see this."

The Vidmail client vanished in a smear of pixels as a full-panel feed took over. The room in the image had the look of an empty garage with enough space for numerous armored vehicles among reinforced pillars. Silver markings, a familiar circle, surrounded a dark metal disc at the center, likely an old lift platform. Within the ring, a pentagram filled with ancient writing, unreadable from the ceiling-mounted camera, shimmered in the light of five candles. Around the center, five dingy jumpsuit-clad people hung from handcuffs on the columns. Two women and three men writhed in synchronized motions, all reacting to the same, invisible energy. None appeared cognizant of their surroundings, as if sharing a mutual pleasant dream.

Konstantin paced at the edge of the circle, adding a symbol here or a pinch of silver powder there. Bile rose in the back of her throat at the sight of the elderly man. Dozens of weird stares people gave her when she'd been out with him made sense now. They'd must've thought the worst of her, a girl young enough to be his granddaughter chasing money. She squirmed, attempting to force away the memory of that rough hand sliding up inside her legs.

"I agree. Looks like a clusterfuck in there."

Heat fell over Kirsten's face like a curtain. "Uhh, yeah."

"You alright? Your heart rate spiked."

Kirsten looked away, blushing harder. "Fine."

"Well, I ain't psych, but I know when something's not right. Are you going to have any hesitation in there?"

Shame morphed to anger. Kirsten glared forward. "No. I don't think so. In fact, I can't wait."

"Good. He's got some armed sentries on the outside. They are unaware of our operatives already in position. As soon as we're ready, we'll neutralize them. How do you want to play the inside?"

Kirsten thought back to the Pentecostal church. "I'd prefer to go in alone, at least at first. I'm not really too fond of the idea of having to deal with a Division 9 doll who's been possessed by a demon." She forced a weak smile. "No offense."

Nina nodded. "I can't say I believe you, but I'll trust you for now."

"What do you mean by neutralize?"

The Lieutenant glanced up and left, as if examining a screen only she could see. "There are eighteen sentries posted around an upper level maintenance corridor and five outside. We have shooters in position for a simultaneous kill."

"Nina—sorry—Lieutenant, I don't know if that would be a good idea.

Whatever Kon—the bastard is doing, it feeds on ghosts. Killing them all might make my job harder."

"It's okay, Kirsten. Nina is fine. I owe you at least that for trying to help out with Vincent. Do you have anything concrete to base your opinion on?"

She's smiling. Now I'm scared. A blur of motion went past Konstantin on the floating panel. "Oh, hi, Nafiz. Two men inside, I should be able to handle them." Kirsten rubbed her right wrist. *Now that I'm off his damn leash.* "Umm, no. I'm only theorizing. Recently-deceased ghosts will probably be too weak to matter. I guess I just don't like killing."

"Neither do I." Nina stared up at the stars. "I hope I never start to."

Kirsten opened her mouth to speak, but lurched up in her seat when the vehicle pitched down at a forty-five degree angle on a long, curving ramp. Gleaming green went by in a flash on her right—the Senate Tower. It remained visible for a mere second before a tunnel swallowed them. Whirring motors faded to silence as the driver let off speed, allowing gravity to take them forward. Four of the Marines stood in their seats, compact rifles at the ready. Seconds stretched to minutes in Kirsten's mind. Anxiety over Dorian, fanned by the fires of feeling like a fifth wheel, set her leg bouncing.

"We are go on my mark," said Nina over the comm. "Three, two, one… mark."

Nina said 'mark' at the same instant the rover reached the end of the curve and a door guarded by several men appeared in front of them. A faint electronic noise, a rippling thrumming, emanated from the soldiers in the front of the rover. Flaming holes like laser wounds appeared in the chests and heads of the men, without visible beams. Twitching, smoking bodies collapsed to the ground in front of a pair of great, armored doors. Only one of the sentries managed to yelp before he died.

Over a dozen voices said 'target clear' in rapid succession on the comm. Kirsten sent an apologetic frown at six ghosts standing around in total confusion. Their plain suits, much like the security team at Konstantin's mansion, caught fire.

"I hate these IR lasers," said a gravelly voice over comm.

A woman replied. "Why's that?"

"Winston likes the blood spatter from slugs," said a different man.

"Yeah, but we need quiet," said a female voice with an Asian accent.

"I got a knife for that." The man emitted a sinister, throaty chuckle.

She squirmed. *He likes killing* way *too much.*

"You sure you still want to go in alone?"

Kirsten jumped at Nina's voice. "Uhh, yeah. You're watching right? Just come in if I need help."

"Opening these doors will make a lot of noise and give away any surprise we have. However, I've already found a way for you to go in quiet." Nina handed her a sleek military knife in a black nylon sheath. "You're not claustrophobic, are you?"

"As long as it's not a closet, I should be okay." She took the huge blade in both hands, grasping the rubberized grip. "A combat knife?" A whistle slid past her teeth when she pulled it an inch out of the sheath and noted the blade had the appearance of bluish glass. "Nano?"

"Call it a key." Nina walked to the wall and peeled a section of metal paneling open with her bare fingers.

Kirsten gulped at the sight of plastisteel bending like foil.

Nano claws sprang from Nina's right hand. "Like this."

She punched the blades into a large pipe concealed within the hollow. The inch-thick plastisteel cut like soft foam. A deft motion excised a plug big enough for a body to slip through. Kirsten crept over, leaning into the hole and looking left and right. The conduit appeared empty save for a thin strip of grime down the center. The reek of ancient air brought a dry tickle to her throat.

"Crawl until I tell you to stop. You'll be right under them. Best get moving. I have a feeling those hostages aren't intended to be used for negotiations."

Kirsten clipped the knife to her belt and braced her hands on the sides of the hole. A quick jump and knee tuck brought her boots over the rim and she set her feet in the pipe. After a brief glance at Nina, she shook her head and slid flat into the tube. "No, they're sacrifices."

Nina held out a set of goggles. "Need night-vision?"

Kirsten concentrated and activated Darksight. Her eyes glimmered with whitish energy. The soldiers all leaned back simultaneously.

Nina just laughed. "Guess that's a no."

THE ENDLESS TUBE SHIMMERED IN WAVERING SEPIA. DESPITE KIRSTEN'S surroundings being quite stationary, the visual effect of the real world and its astral echo not quite lining up made her feel as though she crawled along a swaying hose. She hardened her stare, pulling herself along arm over arm.

"Damn glad I don't get motion sickness." The narrow pipe made her doubt even psi armor would've fit. For once, she appreciated the thinness of her I-Ops blacks.

"I'm coming, Dorian. Hang on."

Perhaps sixty meters after entering, the pipe inclined, then leveled off a few meters later, giving her a view of an end. Only the sound of her faint grunts and scuffing body accompanied her over the last thirty meters. What she thought to be an end turned out to be an elbow making ninety-degree turn upward. She rolled on her back and dragged herself into a seated position, rocking side to side until she pulled her boots under her. After standing, she turned to face her original direction of travel and reached up to grab the bottom edge of the next section.

A dam of crystallized muck crunched at her touch, resulting in cold, greasy slime dribbling onto her face. Her squeak, what bit of a scream escaped before she clamped her mouth closed, reverberated in two directions. She stood there cringing as the substance slid over her hair and down her back. The scent of metal filled the air.

At least it doesn't stink like the sludge from the Beneath. She shuddered at the memory of that particular horror, and pulled herself up. Once her hips cleared the edge, she leaned flat on her chest in the higher section. A boot to the wall propelled her forward, and she continued to crawl.

"Twenty more meters," said Nina in her earbud.

"Okay," she whispered, voice quivering.

"What's wrong?"

"Nothing. Guess I don't like being trapped in tight spaces."

Nina grinned. "Who does?"

Movement had become more difficult. Whatever substance dribbled all over her lubricated the pipe here to the point her hands slid more than pulled her along. After a laborious several minutes, the nauseating sound of Konstantin's voice murmured in from above.

"Stop. No, back up six feet... There."

Kirsten shimmied around to lie on her back, and bit her lip. "There's nothing here, just pipe." She couldn't sit up, turn around, or run away from danger.

"Use the key I gave you."

"Duh." Kirsten wiped the sweat from her face with her right sleeve.

She drew the Nano knife and shivered at a sense of dread emanating from it. Sure, she had used a Nano-edged uti blade before, but the cutting edge was tiny—barely two inches long—and encased in a protective shroud. That thing existed to cut seat belts, chain, rope, whatever.

The sliver of transparent doom she currently held consisted of eleven inches of synthetic diamond, a close-quarters military weapon of last resort. *I wonder if it's really true the edge is only a single atom wide. Sounds like marketing bullshit.* Kirsten stuck the tip in the pipe over her head and braced her left hand under the handle. She grunted and pushed, expecting to feel foolish. Though it took a bit of strength, she shoved the blade to the hilt, piercing the half-inch thick metal.

Holy shit.

With extreme care, she worked the knife forward. Stabbing proved far easier than cutting—at least, to a non-doll. However, cut she did. She rocked the handle back and forth, inch by tedious inch. A surrealist's impression of an oval fell onto her when she connected the line, pinning her under twenty pounds of plastisteel. Fortunately, her body prevented it from making too much noise crashing down. She propped the cutout up with one hand while her other trembling arm put the combat knife back in the scabbard. As soon as a reassuring *click* said she was no longer in danger of sneezing and lopping off her own arm, she resumed breathing.

Kirsten worked the slab past her head, easing it down and pushing it out of her way. Squares of light gleamed above, some manner of grating. Kirsten blinked, releasing Darksight. She sat up out of the hole, slid her boots underneath her, and squatted. Her hair teased at the underside of a metal grating. She peered up at the underside of a four-wheeled moon rover left over from when the installation was operational. Its shadow kept her out of sight in a drainage trench meant to catch spills or runoff fluids from vehicle maintenance. Judging by the discolored wall in front of her, she would have been neck-deep in lubricant years ago.

No wonder Nina was so precise about where to stop.

After lifting a the grate, she eased it to the side and slipped into the room with a belly crawl that took her out from under the rover and behind a mass of boxes covered in grey tarpaulin.

Konstantin paced at the edge of the pentagram, orbiting a metal podium that held two datapads and some old papers. Gleaming light caught her eye amid the strange writing. At the center of the glyph, the fist-sized violet gem lay surrounded by a swirl of phantasmal energy, emanating a pulsing light reminiscent of a heartbeat.

The gem didn't show up on vid. That's really weird.

She couldn't help but stare into the energy surrounding it, noting whispery voices begging to be set free. Amid the wailing and crying, one stood out as different—cursing.

Dorian.

Kirsten almost leapt over the boxes, but ducked when Nafiz approached bearing the black mask. She tugged her E-90 out of the holster and aimed. If she fired at Konstantin, the laser would penetrate him and strike a dazed, black-haired woman dangling from a column. The hostages all wore yellow-orange jumpsuits marked with the logo of Lunazoom, a trans-city tram system.

Shit. Konstantin, you bastard, I'm gonna make you pay for what you did to me. Her hand shaking from anger, she put that awful, wrinkled face right in the center of her gunsights.

Mom, you should break Konstantin's heart.

She scowled at Evan's words drifting across her memory. *Breaking his heart is the least of his worries now, kiddo. Come on, you piece of shit, one step to the left.*

Konstantin accepted the mask from Nafiz and held it aloft in both hands, chanting in some unknown language. The sight of his aged skin burned blush into Kirsten's face. She scooted to the side in search of an angle to fire from that wouldn't kill a civilian. She lined up a clear shot, but the E-90 didn't chirp when the tip of her finger touched the trigger. She tilted her hand and looked. The blue light no longer slid up and down the barrel, and the ammo display had gone dark.

I didn't forget to charge the E-mag. God dammit. She squeezed the release and caught the dead Meissner cell, trading it for one from her belt. *Still dead. Oh, shit, whatever he's doing is sucking power like Dorian can... just from everything. Fuck. It's gotta be that gem. What did Kwadwó call it... the Heart of Eannatum?*

Feelings of blind idiocy slapped her into an open-mouthed gawk. *Break Konstantin's heart. He didn't mean love... Oh, no. He really is a precog. I can't tell anyone.* Elation and worry sparred. *Wait, no, this involves me. It could still just be strong emotional clairvoyance.* She clung to the edge of the pile, leaning around the side and staring at the glimmering jewel. Lightheadedness came on as her feeble telekinesis gathered itself around the sense of the stone's weight. When Konstantin looked away to bow at Nafiz, Kirsten let a surge of psionic energy go. The gem swiveled in place, wobbled up on end, and fell toward her. She strained, and the fist-sized rock came bouncing, rolling, and skittering across the floor into her hand, trailing a shroud of wispy energy.

No sooner had she touched it than her head flooded with voices: two men wailing, two women screaming, and one man, Dorian, cursing. Terror, pain, and anger almost overwhelmed her. The last moments of life from several viewpoints flashed by in a cascade of horror. Cold metal tightened around her wrists and ankles. A masked, cloaked figure plunged a frigid knife into her heart over and over. Kirsten gritted her teeth and collapsed on all fours, but forced herself past it.

Spectral winds whipped up around her as the Heart of Eannatum seemed to sense her intent to destroy it. She set the gem on the floor, bracing it with her left hand and brought her weapon down to smash it. The E-90's handle bounced off it with a rubbery *thud*. The sound of the strike echoed, drawing Konstantin's notice. Nafiz snarled; fortunately, the electronic firing circuit in his pistol was as dead as her weapon.

"Shit," she rasped, dropping the laser and going for the Nano knife.

She grasped the blade with both hands and raised it over her head. The unnatural wind whipped hard enough to kick away her hair clip. Blonde flapped into her eyes. The gem glowed brighter, the whorl of phantasmal energy blew bone-chilling cold right through her flesh. A vortex of darkness tugged at her life essence, as if the Heart of Eannatum tried to drag her soul out of her still-living body.

"*Nyet!*" shouted Konstantin.

Kirsten screamed from the pain, ignoring him as she drove the tip of the transparent blade into the wobbling violet rock. The weapon glanced off, sending the gem skittering away, and dug four inches into the plastisteel ground. Bouncing farther and faster than it should have from the force of the strike, the gem appeared to be running away from her.

Dammit, how do I break this—?

"You are too late," howled Nafiz.

A fist hammered into Kirsten's nose when she looked up. The hit knocked her flat to the side; warm blood dribbled over her lip. He yanked a short vibro knife from his belt and tossed it to his left hand. She rolled on her back, crab-walking after the gem.

Grr! Kirsten gathered a Mind Blast and pounded it into Nafiz. Her eyes flashed bright white; his skull snapped backward. Coppery blood dripped onto her tongue as numbness throbbed through her cheek. Nafiz twitched into a seizure, pawing at his face in a repetitive, spastic motion. He wilted to his knees, staring into space, drooling on himself.

"Do not kill her, Nafiz!" shouted Konstantin, before throwing a pair of metal restraints to him.

The man twitched and convulsed, oblivious to Konstantin. The binders smacked him in the side of the head and knocked him cold.

Konstantin roared, "Clumsy fool!"

Again, Kirsten drove the Nano knife into the Heart of Eannatum, but it deflected with a brilliant flash of energy that blasted her onto her back. Konstantin laughed, not bothering to chase her with urgency. He strolled from the center of the ritual circle as though he had all the time in the world. She rolled onto all fours and crawled to where the knife remained stuck in the floor.

"*Lyubimaya*, would you be so kind?" Konstantin picked up the binders and dangled them at her as though suggesting bedroom kink.

"Go to hell!" she screamed. Tears of anger streamed over her face as she tried slashing the stone.

Another blast sent her sliding on her back, headfirst into a pile of metal crates.

Konstantin clucked his tongue at her. "You cannot destroy the Heart, my love. It has endured for thousands of years. It will not let you harm it."

My love. Bile seeped into the back of her throat. She had all she could do to keep from vomiting at the thought of that man touching her. The mere memory of his fingers inside her made her dry heave. She crawled with one hand pressed to her stomach to where the Nano knife lay abandoned.

"You are most determined, but I am afraid this has gone on too long," he said, swinging the cuffs around his finger and whistling. "Do not worry, *Lyubimaya*. You will not be harmed."

When she grasped the rubber handle, droplets of blood fell from her nose onto the knife. The sight stalled her, staring at the little crimson dots floating above the floor on a transparent blade.

She touched her face, tender from where Nafiz had hit her, then glanced at the blood on her fingers, as if mesmerized by the sight of it. A light came on in her head. Having her hand so close to such a weapon terrified her, but Konstantin strolling ever nearer frightened her more. She smeared her blood across the Nano knife and concentrated. Her blood flared to brilliant white energy and wisped off.

"What are you doing!" shouted Konstantin, his casual walk stepping up to a run. "No!"

Kirsten leapt at the helpless gem, shrieking with joy and rage. Two-handing the weapon, she stabbed it down at the heart. This time, the point pierced the violet crystal as if it were made of marshmallow, sliding to the hilt and pinning it to the ground. Konstantin pounced on her, grabbing her shoulders in a futile effort to stop her.

Intense light flared from cracks racing through the gem.

A sharp crack preceded a roaring explosion that flung stinging shards of gemstone everywhere. Konstantin flew off to one side while the energy shoved her in a different direction. She abandoned the knife and crossed both arms to shield her face from the peppering of tiny needles.

When she came to rest, the room hung in eerie silence except for the disoriented moaning of the hostages. Kirsten stared up at the ceiling three stories over her head, grinning to herself at sweet revenge. She'd ruined his plan—now, she had only to find enough strength to stand up before he came over to kill her.

Dorian slid to a halt at her side. The naked ghosts of the four prior victims flew by.

He sat up and gasped at her, surprise and relief in his eyes. For the tiniest instant, he looked about ready to yell at her for being blind, slow, or cutting it too close.

Kirsten blushed. "Sorry I'm late. I was a little tied up on Earth."

He opened his mouth to respond, but pointed past her. She turned her head. Konstantin stared at her and the freed spirits, eyes bulging behind the mask, clenched fists shaking. With a primal howl, he yanked the ceremonial dagger from his belt and ran toward the nearest hostage.

"Shit." Kirsten forced herself upright.

Nafiz moaned, dragging himself to his feet and flinging his arms to the side. Three narrow, ten-inch blades slid out from his knuckles and locked, a trickle of blood running down each one.

Kirsten drew her E-90, aimed at Konstantin, and squeezed a useless trigger. The woman he charged at remained delirious and unaware of death coming for her. Kirsten would never be able to catch him before he killed her. She couldn't suggest without looking into his eyes. She had no way to save that woman's life.

Kirsten clicked the trigger over and over, screaming, "No!"

44

SACRIFICE

D orian thrust his hand into the E-90, focusing. The blue lights flickered to life in their endless march along the sides. The weapon spat a thin streak of laser. Kirsten's frantic trigger clicking made the shot go high.

Konstantin ducked the brilliant azure beam, and made the mistake of looking back where it came from. She fired again, nailing Konstantin in the cheek. Sparks and smoke sizzled from the jet-black mask. He staggered to a confused halt. She shot him again in the face, knocking the deranged maleficar two steps back. Smoke poured thick from the eye sockets. Seconds later, the stink of burned flesh reached her.

Despite failing to create a hole, the interaction of laser and paranormal artifact had apparently stunned him. A thumbprint-sized patch glowed red-hot, searing his cheek. Kirsten fired again into the mask, but the glittering silvery sparkles embedded in the black material seemed to diffuse the beam, heating the mask without allowing it to penetrate.

Konstantin spun on the hostage, knife raised. Kirsten aimed lower and fired another shot.

Her laser blast caught him in the lower chest, piercing his torso and hitting the far wall. Flames licked at the edges of a finger-wide tunnel through his body. Konstantin froze, the blade slipped from his grasp, and he sagged limp. A second later, blood squirted out of him, spraying several feet in front and back. With a wheezing moan, he collapsed over. The mask bounced loose when his face hit the ground, but didn't go far, clinging to his cheek by a strand of molten skin.

Nafiz came out of nowhere and tackled her. He raised his implanted blades, but Kirsten rammed her knee into his side, sending him sliding away before his claws tasted blood.

She sat up, scrambling to her feet as the near-skeletal man flipped over and sprang through the air, blades first. She lit off a blast from the E-90 in time to scorch his leg. He fell on his front, his claws sparking the ground inches away from her. She scooted backward as he crawled, kicking at his arms to deflect blades. Her thick boots spared her a few slices when he landed an edge on her shin. He tried to leap on top of her, but she stomped him in the face, knocking him on his ass. Moaning, he rolled to the side, claws retracting so he could cradle his nose. Blood gushed out between his fingers.

Nafiz muttered in Arabic.

She glanced to her left. "What's he say—"

"You don't wanna know," said Dorian. "Something rather nasty to call a woman."

Kirsten pointed the E-90 at him one-handed, using the other to steady herself as she wobbled to her feet. "It's over, Nafiz. Don't make me shoot you."

The five hostages came out of their hypnotic state. One by one, the realization they were fixed by handcuffs to metal columns in the middle of a garage hit them, and they shouted and struggled. The woman that Konstantin had meant to kill gaped at the dead man on the ground, screaming.

Nafiz peeled his red-stained hands away from his face and held them in a gesture of surrender. She met his wild stare. Wet-looking black hair shimmered in the light. Though he flashed a 'trust me' smile, deceit flashed in his thoughts. The Arabic words in his head she couldn't make sense of, but the imagined feeling of a mechanism in his teeth came with the taste of something noxious. She cringed away a second before he leaned up, spraying clear liquid out of holes in his canine teeth. The attack missed her face, instead saturating the cloth of her upper chest. Biting fumes robbed her of the ability to see anything but blobs of color.

Shink. Claws popped out.

Her mind had one proverbial foot in the door of his from eavesdropping on his surface thoughts. She didn't need sight to aim a

Mind Blast. Kirsten staggered away from the sound of his growling, gathering a psionic assault that slapped all reason from Nafiz's consciousness when she let it loose. Random images, sounds, feelings, and tastes smashed into the man's brain.

He moaned.

Kirsten swooned, cradling her head in both arms. Using that power again so soon after overdoing it at the manor brought on a near-migraine. Pain like a lava spike rammed into her skull mixed with burning in her eyes, leaving her praying for death to escape it all. She slumped to her knees and covered her face with both hands. Somewhere to her left, a body hit the ground amid the clatter of claws on metal floor.

"Hey, get us out of these cuffs!" William Arris, or at least his ghost, shouted.

Kirsten pawed at her eyes, blinking away tears while trying to clear her skin of the toxic agent. *I don't even want to know what this would have done if it hit me in the face, the fumes are bad enough.*

"Can she see us?" Alaina Munoz asked, hopping closer.

Kirsten's sight returned a moment later, everything hazed as if behind a blurry curtain. Dorian had helped the ghosts stand. They remained as they had been at the moment of their death, naked and locked in metal binders. *Ugh, I think I'd rather face obliteration than eternity in handcuffs.* She pondered an old East City spirit she once met and shivered.

The woman had spent centuries trapped in a crude wooden device that kept her hands trapped together in front of her face, locked around her neck. The persistent binding manifested from her psyche, burned in due to a cruel execution for being a witch. Perhaps in the case of recent haunts, she might be able to help them change. Kirsten shook her head, blinking, wiping the last bits of chemical burn away.

"If any of you hear voices of your family calling you, go to them. If not, hop outside and I'll help as much as I can once this scene is cleared. Yes, I can see you. Yes, I can hear you. No, I don't have time right this second. I can't remove the binders because they aren't real. You are uhh… 'dressed' like that because it is how you were at the moment of death. Stop thinking of yourself in that way and they will disappear, and please, think on some clothes. I'll be outside in a few minutes." She pointed at the door and retrieved the Nano knife from the floor.

Nafiz moaned and sat up, snarling an Arabic word at her.

"Oh, fuck you too." Kirsten frowned over the E-90 at him. "What did he call me?"

Dorian, still cringing, shook his head. "I told you, you really don't want to know."

Konstantin emitted a sudden furious roar that echoed, as if over loudspeakers, shaking the entire room. Lights faltered and distant electronic components throughout the ceiling exploded in a series of bangs. Venom fled Nafiz's eyes. His claws retracted. Hands raised, he backed away from the pentagram. Dark red smoke billowed out of Konstantin's remains, gathering in a whorl that re-formed into his apparition. He attempted to stand, but couldn't rise beyond a stoop, tethered to the mask by the same thread of skin holding it to the corpse. He pointed at Kirsten, and shrieked barrage of Russian invectives.

Nafiz gestured at Konstantin's ghost, babbling. When the specter glared at him, he sprinted away, shrieking like a schoolboy.

Kirsten faced him. "You're in my world now, Konnie." She squinted and called the lash. It unfurled to the floor and coiled around her boots. "Now it's my turn to touch *you* in a bad place."

Konstantin grew angrier, but only for a few seconds. He looked down, then howled in pain. His legs skidded together, pants bunched around his shins as if a giant invisible fist seized him. After a look mixed of pleading and hatred, the ghost of Konstantin Dobrynin vanished down into the floor. She ceased concentrating on the lash, and the thread of energy dissipated from the tip, as if retracting into her arm.

"That's not going to end well," said Dorian.

"No..." Kirsten glanced around. "No, I don't think it will."

Dorian moved to her side. "The ritual demanded a sacrifice... I think we just fed it Konstantin."

Every light overhead exploded at once, raining a dazzling shower of sparks and flecks of red hot glass. She ran shrieking for cover with her arms over her head. The air at the center of the ritual circle shimmered, expanding in a nimbus of faint energy. Shattered fragments of the Heart of Eannatum rattled on the floor before skittering into the whorl and vanishing in a series of indigo flares. Dorian ignored the raining embers, shouting at the other ghosts to hop out of here as fast as they could until the wave of paranormal energy smacked him to the ground.

Konstantin's corpse shifted, sliding around in a wide circle two feet off the ground. It skimmed the pentagram, head in line with the outer edge. After making a full circle, it rose and floated above the middle, upright. Flames from the candles surged upward into three-foot hissing jets. The hostages all screamed. Dark smoke billowed from the center of the glyph, forming into the silhouette of a massive humanoid cloud.

Kirsten grasped the edge of the metal box she hid behind, easing herself up until she could see over it. The apparition flung its arms out to the sides, thrusting its chest forward. Konstantin's floating corpse glided backward into the smoke, engulfed in seeking tendrils of shadow until it vanished. At that instant, the mass of vapor solidified into jet-black flesh, glistening and scaled.

To Kirsten's horror, its face took on a nauseating familiarity as the demon absorbed Konstantin's essence. He had completed the ritual, though not the way he had hoped. Rather than having control over a powerful spirit of the Abyss, it had consumed him and stepped into the world with free rein.

"Oh, that thing's going to be a ball of happiness," said Dorian. "Any ideas, or are we screwed?"

Faint wisps of grey energy trailed from the chest of each hostage to the huge demon. It leaned backward, inhaling the streams with a moan of savoring delight.

Kirsten shivered. "I think it's gonna siphon their spirits. Did you have to use that particular expression?"

"Which expression?"

"Screwed." She shivered.

"Wha—?" Dorian scowled at the demon. "What did he do?"

"It was just his hand…" Heat flooded her cheeks. "What he did to my head is worse." She held up the knife, letting the light play off the edge for a second before she offered it to him. "Here. Get the people out. I'm the one that should be sorry"—she glanced at him—"for not really hearing what you tried to tell me."

He clasped the bound knife, squeezing her hand into the soft grip. "You couldn't. He had you enthralled. I knew it wasn't you talking."

"Thanks."

Kirsten vaulted the cargo boxes while Dorian ran through them, holding the knife over his head so it passed over the top. The demon drew back a handful of claws, ready to slay one of the male hostages who had fainted at the sight of it. She jumped from the box to the floor, calling the lash as she sprinted toward the demon. Sensing the energy pouring out of her hand, the creature spun to face her, facing her with one room-shaking step.

Dorian snuck around to the left, evidently amused at having to use physical cover to stay hidden.

She stared up at the fiend, close to twice her height. "You know what this is, don't you, bastard? You can feel it." *Holy shit this thing is huge. I wonder if he's strong enough to attract direct intervention.* A shiver ran down her body. *Maybe if I fail.* She thought of Evan. *I can't.*

It leaned back, emitting a deep laugh.

Kirsten swiped the lash, scoring a pale burn mark across the jet-black skin of its chest. The demon's laughter cut short to a wail of pain. It staggered back a step, nearly falling to one knee. Her arm throbbed from power back-feeding down the tendril. Kirsten clamped her hand to her right bicep in an effort to dull the ache.

"Hurt, didn't it?" She scooted to the side. "You shouldn't have made yourself look like him."

The demon surged to its feet lunging at her with an upward rake of its claws. She hurled herself into a somersaulting dodge. Talons peeled several plates out of the floor as easily as fingernails on foil. It spun to follow her, raking again. Kirsten ducked behind a cargo box, barely suppressing a shriek of alarm as the plastisteel container burst apart in shreds.

A screaming woman in dingy worker coveralls went silent at the sight of a floating knife as Dorian ran toward her. When it came within a few feet of her, she begged for her life.

Dorian forced his voice into the mortal world. "Calm down."

A quick swipe of the synthetic diamond blade cut the chain. The woman dropped to the ground on all fours. He gestured with the knife in the direction of the exit, stabbing twice in a pointing motion.

Kirsten ran ahead of the demon, trying to keep out of reach. She spun, taking a few backward-running steps long enough to swing the lash before whirling to face forward again. The abyssal avoided the attack by stopping short, then pounced with a closed fist as big as her entire torso. It missed by inches, slamming into the floor and launching her into the air. She flailed and came down on all fours. Close to the rover that concealed her initial entry, she scooted under it. Before she could take even one relieved breath, the demon grabbed the front end, sinking its claws into the armor plating, and flung the six-wheeler aside like a plastic toy. It landed in a crumpled heap of twisted metal some ten yards away.

Huddled on the floor, she found herself eye-level with the creature's knee. It roared, stretching both hands over its head. When it raked its claws down, she leapt forward, diving between its legs as it shredded the floor. She dashed straight ahead, shocked into a panic-driven sprint. The demon stood in no great hurry, its massive hands ripping up the floor. It chuckled in a low, rolling rumble, and flicked its claw to toss a stuck piece of pipe aside.

The next nearest hostage soiled himself when the floating knife approached him. Dorian cut him loose and he ran whimpering after the first woman.

"Come on, come on," shouted the other woman, two columns over. She rattled her binders, staring at the floating knife with desperation. "I don't know what the fuck you are, but hurry the hell up."

Dorian shot her a look and moved to the next-nearest person, one column away from her.

The floor behind Kirsten shook from the enormous demon's run. She dove to the left not a second before it leapt at her. Kirsten hit the ground on her side as the demon slid past her on one knee, failing to stop after missing. She reined in her fear, shoving herself upright and raking the lash across the back of the demon's legs. It howled and fell to its knees. She leapt up, poised to whip it in the head, but a bony onyx sphere caught her in the side of the head and sent her skidding and tumbling over the smooth metal. She rolled to a halt some distance away, too dizzy to comprehend which way gravity pulled.

"Oh… he's got a tail." She cradled her head.

Pain shot in threads over the left side of her skull; warm blood tickled at her ear despite the numbness. Rapid images flashed in her mind: Mother smashing her headfirst into the kitchen floor, a fistful of hair pounding her head against the fridge, the tub, the wall. *Thanks, Mom.* She shook off the disorientation and pushed herself up to her knees. The grey streak her whip had left on the creature's chest had disappeared, leaving it unhurt. Her second wind faltered.

In the distance, the third hostage tumbled away from the column and ran for the doors. *I have to keep this thing's attention away from them.* She dragged herself up to her feet and charged, an attempt at a battle cry sounding more like a war-squeak.

The demon swung its right arm in a wide arc. For once, being short helped. She darted under it and dragged the energy tendril over its abdomen. If she leapt through its legs again, it would turn and see the civilians getting away. She hesitated.

Growling, the giant demon raked its left arm at her, twelve inch black claws gleaming. With no time to move, she focused on its supernatural presence, attempting to catch its attack with her psionic ability. Overwhelming paranormal energy slammed into her. While she managed to push against it enough to keep its claws away from her skin, the impact of its presence on her mental power swatted her to the side. She sailed into the air, landing in an uncoordinated roll that left her spread-eagled on her chest some distance away.

Ow.

Her mind throbbed, her body ached, and her nose wouldn't stop bleeding. *I'm wasting my time. It's a true demon like Charazu. I'm only causing pain, not really hurting it.* Her eyelids tried to close as futility loomed. It would be so easy to lie there on the nice, cold metal. Standing up again would only bring more agony.

Evan must be losing his mind right now. She sucked in a breath, and pushed herself upright.

The second female hostage held her hands apart, waiting for the knife. Dorian slashed the chain between her wrists. She collapsed to all fours but sprang back up. With one hand on her face, she wobbled toward the exit. The last hostage, a hulk of a man, had fainted. All three hundred and change pounds of him hung like a deer ready for cleaning.

The knife cut the plastisteel chain with a faint *click* and little discernible resistance. Once the man hit the ground, Dorian looked from the abyssal to the blade and grinned.

Kirsten eyed the fourth hostage, tracking the woman until she ran out of sight down the access ramp. The energy thread connecting her to the demon faded away. Wondering if it had been leeching from them all along, she threw herself into another attack with renewed hope. She tapped the memory of Konstantin's hand touching her between the legs, feeding off her anger at him manipulating her for so long.

The Astral Lash glimmered with emotion, growing brighter as she rounded it overhead and snapped the tip into the demon's chest. A great booming crash shook the hangar. The strike launched the creature off its feet. It slid, rubbery skin squealing over the metal floor, until it smashed into a column, leaving it bent from the impact. Kirsten took two steps, stopping when a sudden shriek came from behind her as if a bucket of ice water had been poured over a man. Disregarding the odd noise, she advanced on the prone demon.

"Wren, what's going on in there? Cams are out." Nina's voice crackled in her earbud. "We took out one suspect attempting to flee via a service tunnel. What kind of idiot runs at a full squad with only claws?"

Bye, Nafiz. "Someone in the midst of a panic attack. He saw something he couldn't handle. Hostages are clear, they're inside the door. Open it, let them out, but stay back."

"Sounds like a full-on war in there, are you sure?"

Kirsten whirled the lash into the air. "Yes, I'm sure. Your people really don't want to see this."

"See what? There's nothing on the video feed but you and that... laser whip or whatever you're using."

"Be glad it's not showing up on video."

She snarled, slicing the whip across its face. The hit sent the abyssal sliding off to the side with a deafening roar of agony. However, its tail caught her in the boots and pulled her feet out from under her. She landed flat on her back, stunned.

A few seconds later, the demon sprang into the air above her, fist cocked back. Kirsten screamed, flinging herself to the side as it drove its arm elbow-deep in the plastisteel. Crimpling metal catapulted her into the air. She landed in a tumbling roll a few feet away.

It stormed after her and punched again, but she scrambled out of the way. The instant she got to her feet, it lunged with a sideways claw swipe. She ducked the arm, then jumped the low-swinging tail. She whipped the lash to the ready, but a sudden backhand strike caught her off guard.

The hit launched her flying onto a cart used to load missiles the size of caskets onto combat aircraft. Kirsten landed draped across two C-shaped rings. One hit her in the back, the *crack* of a breaking rib jolting her body. The other caught her legs behind the knee, leaving her dangling with her ass suspended above the body of the automated ordinance mover.

Her ungainly pose left her helpless long enough for the demon to close the distance in a quick stride. Once again, the pale burns the lash caused had vanished. The distorted face of Konstantin laughed at her. Stuck in an awkward position as though the missile cart offered her up as a sacrifice to its master, she could do little more than glare as it reached for her.

It stopped, claws only inches from her cheek, gazing wide-eyed into space.

Dorian hung on its back, all his weight on the bound Nano knife. The weapon sliced abyssal bone and muscle with little effort; however, the wound closed as fast as it opened. He ripped open a ten-inch deep cut from the creature's shoulder to the middle of its back.

"Damn, it's restoring itself," he said.

"It's…" Kirsten rasped, and coughed. "Like Charazu. You think Konstantin will help translate the circle this time?" She tried to smile, blood leaked between her teeth.

"I wouldn't count on it." Dorian backed away as the demon turned on him. "I'm not sure if this knife hurt him enough to worry about, or if I just look tasty…"

Kirsten groaned. The pain grinding in her back from the cracked rib flared as she strained to get the uncomfortable C-ring out of her armpits. The attempt to move hurt so much she let herself sag there, cradled in two unmoving metal half-loops. A cough covered her mouth and neck with blood. No help lurked in the darkness of shattered lights overhead.

Where are they? Come on, this isn't fair. This thing is too powerful for me. I need help. She wriggled again, but froze, whimpering at the pain in her side. *The Seraph poked through because Charazu did. This thing feels even stronger. Where are they?* Kirsten wobbled, arms trapped by the strut as if it held her in some kind of full nelson. Only fatigue and pain kept her there, but at the moment, it was enough.

I don't know this thing's true name. I can't read stick figures. It's gonna kill me, eat Dorian, and destroy the Moon. She started to cry, but crying hurt too much as well. *Nothing. No 'guardian angel,' no silver light.*

Something warm and spongy poked her on the cheek. Time seemed to slow; the sounds of war faded to a meaningless, indistinct auditory blur.

Kirsten let gravity pull her head to the side. Evan—at least Astral-Evan—floated there. The silver cord ran from between his eyes into the floor. She stared at the glowing amber figure of a scrawny, nude boy hovering at her side. His transparent energy-body shimmered with urgency.

"E-Evan? Is t-that really you, or am I slipping away?"

He grabbed her hand. "Mom, you're scaring me. Stop it."

"How did you get to the Moon?"

"I flew. Why are you napping?"

"How did you find the moon?"

"I wanted to go to you."

Sound, pain, and the frigidity of the air all rushed into her mind at once. Time restarted. Kirsten flailed. "Evan, what are you doing here? There is a big demon, get out of here. It can hurt you."

"I'm not leaving 'til you get up."

"It's gonna…" *No Seraphim. I must be able to do something.*

Kirsten reached up and grabbed the top of the C-strut, lifting her weight off her back while screaming. Without the band snagged on her arms, she slipped forward until her butt found metal. *Ow. Ow. Ow.* Eyes closed, she lay as flat as possible and fumbled at her belt for a stimpak. Demonic roars and objects crashing about provided an amusing mental play-by-play of a solid demon chasing her intangible partner. Heavy support equipment went skidding out of the way as it swatted obstacles he simply ran through.

Tingly warmth touched her left cheek as Evan kissed her. "Come home soon."

Her fingers found the case release and slipped in around the beautiful red cylinders. She reached across her chest and stabbed herself under the right arm—a little too close to the break. Wailing, she clawed at the vehicle under her while the coldness of stim fluid spread over her side, engulfing the pain. Synthetic adrenaline made her eyes wiggle in their sockets as nanobots swarmed to the site of trauma and knit the rib. A faint *crunch* paralyzed her for a few seconds while a million tiny machines dragged bone splinters back into place.

Dorian ran past, within five or six feet. "Incoming. Might want to consider moving."

"Crap." She swung her left arm over, using the momentum to spill the rest of her body to the ground.

Astral-Evan spun, silently mouthing 'oh shit' when he finally got a good look at the creature. Sensing the soul of an innocent, it stopped in its tracks and drooled at him. Before the abyssal could take a step, the boy grabbed the silver thread and blurred out of sight.

Enraged at missing such a treat, the demon roared and swatted the missile cart into the air. It struck Dorian, dragging him forward by virtue of the knife in his hand being solid. He slipped away, the missile carrier not striking the ground until it had flown most of the way across the cavernous chamber.

The Nano knife lay on the ground, four of Dorian's fingers coming up from the floor the only sing of him. Demon-Konstantin stomped over to it, but Dorian sprang out of the ground. He slashed and stabbed, shortening two of the demon's claws before it caught him with a downward left-handed rake.

His ghostly body smeared out to five or six times his usual height, turned into a puddle of ethereal vapor for a second, and came together with him face-down about ten yards from where he started.

Kirsten stood, favoring her right side, and forced the lash into existence. "I don't think we can beat this thing without knowing its name."

"Thanks for the reassuring words," said Dorian, staggering upright, a faint transparency to the edges of his body.

"I think you're right. *Konnie* won't translate it for us." She advanced.

The shifting energy of the lash attracted the creature's attention. It turned in a slow series of steps that sounded like giant plasticrete blocks falling to the floor. It towered over her, making little effort to hide its lack of concern for her weapon.

Kirsten drew her arm back, coiling the tendril and grinning. "I know who you are." With a sharp intake of breath, she tapped into her fear and rage. Every ounce of anger she felt at being a sycophantic thrall to Konstantin's charms poured into a blinding thread of blue-white light.

"Back to the abyss, *Avarazel!*"

The spoken name struck the abyssal with the force of a blow that knocked it down to one knee. She swiped the lash at the ten-foot monstrosity with a two-handed crossing slash from shoulder to hip. Rather than a pale grey burn mark, the scintillating cord melted its flesh open like a laser cutter. Kirsten spun from the force of her swing, using her momentum to rake the whip across the enormous chest a second time.

Dark crimson vapor spewed out along with jet-black blood. Huge puddles splattered to the floor, steaming and reeking of rotten eggs.

"Begone from this world, Avarazel!" she screamed.

Kirsten pictured the terrified look on Evan's face when the demon made eye contact with him. Anger at it for scaring her son poured yet more emotion into the lash. Anger at herself for coming so close to giving up made it thrum. She whipped her arms around, coiling the energy tendril into an overhead swing that split the creature wide open from face to stomach. Roaring disintegrated to gurgling. Two seconds later, it erupted in a pillar of dark red flames, cutting loose with a shriek of pure agony that knocked lights off the ceiling.

A blast of hot, black ichor knocked her over. She slid and spun in the torrent, coming to a halt in a steaming pool of awfulness. It might have smelled of sulphur, were the stench not so overpowering her nose gave up trying to interpret it. She lay motionless, staring at the giant charred skeleton surrounded by chunks of flesh that had blown away from it. Magmatic orange crept along the bones as they flaked away into ash particles.

Dorian, acting like a ghost, floated over the tar pool and hovered at her side. She shifted to look at him, not even nauseated by the sensation of her hair sticking to the floor.

"How the hell did you figure out the damn thing's name?"

"Heh." Between the heat, the stickiness, her fatigue, and the lack of urgency, she couldn't make herself sit up. She did manage to get a fingertip to her earbud. "Nina, you can come in now. I need an adult." She let her head sag to face Dorian.

"How…" He blinked.

She closed her eyes. "Apparently, true demons have surface thoughts."

FAMILY

E van sat at the table, swinging his feet while shoveling cereal into his mouth. Covered only by last night's underwear, which would soon be in the wall-machine, he didn't care about neatness and wore about as much OmniSoy milk as he drank. Kirsten smirked at him. He flashed a 'so what' grin. Early morning sunlight created a shimmering orange aura around his spherical mop of shaggy, light brown hair. The soap-scented humidity of a recent shower clung to Kirsten. A little dampness lingered in her hair, out of reach of the tube's dry cycle.

"Try to eat like a civilized human at least."

He bubbled milk at her, breaking up into giggles only two seconds into the gesture. Kirsten laughed. The boy still vibrated with joy at her safe return from the Moon two days prior. He didn't sleep at all the first night, likely due to a thirteen-hour nap caused by the sedative Nila gave him while Kirsten was gone. She kept smiling, despite the serpent of guilt tangling her guts at the thought of how terrified he must've been. The timing of him needing to be knocked out coincided with his astral visit.

Cereal finished, he wiped his chest off and trudged to the bathroom. Briefs hit the rug on his way into the tube. After reaching up to poke the control screen, he closed his eyes and gripped the head-level railing. Warm jets of water sprayed him down, followed by the soapy mix, and then more water. He cheered as the swirling rush of warm air came close to lifting him off his feet. When the turbines settled down and the safety lock disengaged from the door, he jumped from the tube to the small throw rug in an effort to avoid stepping on cold tiles.

Scooting the rug underfoot, he shimmied across the room, pausing to grab his dirty briefs, and climbed up on the sink to reach the white box. Dirty went in a hatch at the top, and clean, wrapped in plastic, came out the bottom. He pulled them on, wadded up the wrapper, and pushed open the bathroom door.

He stopped, dead in his tracks, gawking at Kirsten.

She smiled, having donned a loose-fitting black dress uniform while he showered. The E-90 sat in its holster, affixed to a thinner belt without all the other utility pouches. Her skirt ended an inch or so above the knee, plain and black like the top. Gold rank insignia glimmered on both shoulders, matched by a pin on a folding cap. Shiny black kitten heels replaced her usual boots.

"You're pretty," he blurted.

Kirsten laughed. "Why, thank you." She lifted a box from the bed, handing it to him. Before he burst with excitement, she winked. "Don't go through the roof, it's clothes. Get dressed."

He smirked at the offering, but took it. "You said you were off work for a while."

"I am. They gave me a whole month unless something crazy happens."

Evan squinted at the box, suspicious at the contents. He took a seat at the foot of the bed, and unpacked a long-sleeve charcoal-grey shirt with a Chinese collar. Fabric loops clung to buttons from the shoulder to the hip to keep it closed. Still underweight for his age, he swam into it without undoing any of the fasteners except for the top two to get his head out the top.

A plain pair of black pants followed. Kirsten intervened, pulling the flaps of the shirt out and letting them hang. Evan emitted an odd squeak as the belt adjusted itself to his waist. The face he made set Kirsten laughing again.

"These are the same way," she said, handing him a pair of dark, lace-less shoes halfway between sneaker and formal. When he looked up at her, she bounced a pair of socks off his head.

Laughing, he dropped the shoes, put on the socks, and spent a moment staring back and forth between her and his new footwear.

"They won't hurt, come on... we're late."

One foot tested one shoe. "Where are we going?" He held in the urge to squeal when it adjusted to fit. Since it didn't hurt, he stepped into the other.

"Oh, just some official thing." She took his hand and walked to the door.

He grinned. "They givin' you an award for beating a demon?"

"Something like that."

"Sounds boring."

Kirsten's lip quivered. "I'm sure it won't be."

KIRSTEN BARELY MANAGED TO KEEP HERSELF OUTWARDLY CALM WHILE driving. An hour or so in the future, she'd either be thrilled—or destroyed. Evan kept quiet, but grinned the entire ride to the Police Administrative Center. After a bit of concentration, Dorian had managed to shift his appearance to his best memory of a dress uniform. He grinned as broadly as Evan as they walked across the parking deck to the elevator.

When they went right past the hallway that led to the school, Evan twisted to look at it, letting his weight dangle on Kirsten's handhold. She tugged him upright, smiling.

"You don't have to go to school today, Ev."

His walking became bouncing, which faded to a cautious stride when they also went straight past the Division 0 wing without entering. He tugged on her hand. Kirsten glanced down at him, but her happy expression calmed him.

Several hallways later, Kirsten's shoes clicked on dark tiles in a corridor with a big fancy window along the right and black faux marble wall on the left. Evan leaned close to her, seemingly frightened by the expansive place full of important-looking people with grim expressions. She stopped by a door and took a seat on a bench against the wall. Evan hopped up next to her, the light thuds of his heels on the seat drew smiles from some people and annoyed glances from others.

Dorian sat to her left. Evan leaned forward, looking past her at the holographic panel floating by the door.

"Hearing Room Eight?" He blinked. "Is the room listening to us?"

"Probably is," said Dorian. "They have microphones everywhere."

Kirsten's laugh had more nervousness than mirth. "No, hon. People inside it are."

A few minutes later, Danita Reed emerged from the crowd at the far end of the corridor, entering from the other direction where the PAC connected to the West City Municipal Center. Her grey business suit was, as usual, clean and neat, and she kept a small case tucked under her left arm. Kirsten couldn't help but stare at her as the woman walked all the way down the curving hallway and came to a stop in front of her.

"Oh, I thought you'd like to know. That girl you referred my way, Brooke? I managed to find a paternal aunt. Her father had a younger sister who is married with two of her own. The girl's got some work ahead of her from a counseling standpoint, but she has a nice home. I got the feeling those people will be good caretakers. The girl wanted me to pass along her thanks for what you did for her."

"She helped more than she knows. I don't even want to consider what could have happened without her witnessing that…"

A familiar scent wafted past a second before Kirsten's father exuded out from the wall. She choked up at the sight of him and smiled her thanks, as she couldn't talk.

"They should be ready for us in a few minutes," said Danita. "You look adorable, Evan."

He blushed, fidgeting with his fancy shirt, sticking his finger into the small gap at the front of the collar to tug it off his neck.

The door to Hearing Room 8 opened. A white-haired older man in uniform, white shirt and black pants, gave Kirsten a nod. She stood, taking Evan's hand before walking down a pale tan carpet into the courtroom. She approached a single long table in front of the bench. Few Division 0 cases ever made it into an Inquest in front of a judge. The unfamiliar, foreboding surroundings added to her nerves and got her hands trembling.

A middle-aged Asian woman in a black robe sat upon the elevated bench, and offered a pleasant nod of greeting. 'Hon. Maria Yuen' glowed in gold letters at the top edge.

Once everyone arrived at their spots, she spoke. "Good morning, everyone."

Captain Eze ducked in the door, offering a wincing smile. "Apologies, Your Honor, I was delayed by a meeting." He moved at a brisk walk to the table.

"Are we expecting anyone else?" asked the judge.

"No, Your Honor," said Danita. "Myself and Captain Eze are acting as witnesses."

Evan twisted to stare up at her, Kirsten, Eze, Dorian, and back to Kirsten. He looked terrified.

Kirsten squeezed his hand and winked. The gesture might have calmed him if she could've stopped trembling.

"Very well." A shift in color from a concealed display bathed the judge's face in lime green glow. "I have reviewed the findings from the caseworker... That would be you, Ms. Reed"—the judge gestured at her— "as well as the findings of Dr. Loring, and the *exhaustive* communications of support from Captain Eze and even Director Carter." Judge Yuen raised an eyebrow. "I see no reason to delay this process any further." She tilted her head forward, peering at Kirsten, as if looking over glasses that didn't exist. "You have made the necessary arrangements as stipulated by Ms. Reed?"

"Yes, Your Honor," she rasped. Eze handed her a cup of water from the table. She took a sip, cleared her throat, and spoke again in a clear voice. "Yes, Your Honor. It should be in the case notes."

"Good. In that case, my ruling is that Miss Kirsten Wren, holding the rank of Agent (W4) in the Division 0 bureau of the National Police Force, is hereby awarded custody of the minor born Evan Dawson."

Speechless, Evan burst into joyous tears and clamped his arms around his new mother.

Seeing him cry was too much for her. She took a knee, embraced him, and wept.

Judge Yuen spotted something on her terminal and looked up. "There is one small issue."

Kirsten's heart almost stopped.

"The records are incomplete. The boy's medical file doesn't contain an official date of birth."

Kirsten almost melted into a puddle of relief.

Danita leaned forward. "Your Honor, the child's birth mother was off the grid. They were squatters living in an stolen apartment, no employment history. She didn't deliver him in an approved medical facility. No records were made at the time."

"Well, what's your best guess?" asked the judge. "I have to put something in here. The boy needs a birthdate."

Evan wriggled free from Kirsten's grip enough to speak. "Judge lady, can it be the day she found me?" He looked between her and the judge. "I want my birthday to be the day she found me."

Kirsten shuddered, clasping a hand over her face. Speechless, all she could do was squeeze him and sniffle, crying harder. Her father's ghost put a hand on her shoulder. Dorian smiled, wider than she had ever seen him smile.

"I have no problem with that…" Judge Yuen gave the table an expectant look. "Any objections?"

Danita flipped her case open and swiped her hand over a datapad. She went too far, having to back up two pages. "The inquest Agent Wren filed to terminate parental rights of the birth parent is 24180414A3. That puts it on April 14th, about six months ago. The boy is nine, so…"

"Official date of birth: April 14, 2409," muttered the judge, while typing on noiseless holographic keys. "Done." She tapped the desk with a gavel. "Congratulations, Agent Wren. This is a big responsibility, I hope you are prepared for it."

Don't say I hope so too… She swallowed her emotions. "I am, Your Honor. I am."

EVAN DRAPED HIMSELF THROUGH THE GAP BETWEEN THE CAR'S FRONT SEATS, grinning at everything. With the anxiety of worrying which way the verdict would go gone, Kirsten's head throbbed. Despite the pain, she remained too elated to speak. It had taken her almost fifteen minutes to compose herself enough to drive after hearing Evan's request for a birthdate.

He squinted at the NavMap. "Are we visiting Nila?"

Kirsten smiled at him.

"'Kay. Shani was worried about you." He slid into the back seat, making sputtering noises with his lips. "Prob'ly 'cause I was acting like a dork."

"You were worried." She nudged the patrol craft into a graceful descent, sliding in over the parking deck in search of a spot.

"Not gonna park on the pool this time?"

"Hush, you."

He squeezed past the gap into the front seat. "I wanna hit the button for the wheels!"

His finger found it before she could tell him it was okay. She set down in an open space—well, space and a half—finding it a bit boring not to have to position the car just right to balance it between ventilation pumps or ducts. Landing on a flat, clear surface intended for hovercars felt... strange.

Evan followed her out her door, holding hands as they walked past rows of civilian vehicles toward the building. He checked out a handful of expensive, sporty models and glanced back at the armored black behemoth with clear bar lights.

"Your car's the coolest in the lot. Bet none of the other ones ran over a ghost-ninja."

Kirsten giggled all the way to the elevator. Evan hit the button for the thirty-ninth floor. Kirsten squinted, pushing the one for the forty-first with telekinesis. He didn't notice until the elevator stopped descending.

"Hey, why did we stop on this floor? Nila's place is two more down."

His expression went from quizzical to confused as Kirsten tugged his arm and led him out.

"Do we know someone else that lives here?"

"Yeah."

"Do I know them?" He seemed gripped by a sudden bout of shyness.

"Yep."

"Oh." He discarded the bashful affect, following her in silence until they stopped at a door marked 4140. "Who lives here?"

Kirsten swiped at the hand-sized silver panel on the wall. The door opened. "We do."

His jaw dropped.

She took a step inside, leaning on the wall and grinning as a nine-year-old missile zoomed from room to room.

"It's got two bathrooms," he yelled during the brief instant he appeared in the hallway. "Do I get my own room?"

"Yes, sweetie." She shoved away from the wall, walking across the living room area, past the kitchen, and down the hallway to the bedrooms.

"Whoa!" he gasped.

She found him gawking at the far wall of the master bedroom, almost entirely amber-hued window. It created a balcony effect, extending four-feet out from the room to form a glass-enclosed patio. The bedroom had a stunning view of the city, streams of passing hovercar traffic, as well as a glittering train of advert bots.

He spun into a hug. "This is ours?"

"Yes," she said as she picked him up, "but this is my room."

She carried him into the hallway, stopping at the first door on the left and setting him on his feet outside. Evan smiled and put his hand on the panel. The door slid open, and his jaw dropped for the second time.

The furniture, despite the requisite modern amenities such as a holo-terminal, appeared as if lifted from a Monwyn video. Two medieval tapestries hung on the far wall opposite a reality-enhanced window that replaced the outside with a rolling forest, complete with wizard's tower and the occasional passing dragon. A novelty holo-projector created false cobwebs, castle-stone texture on the walls, and random creepy-crawlies scuttling in the shadows. He ran in, circled the room once—touching everything—before grabbing a replica of Monwyn's quarterstaff from the wall by the bed and sitting with it across his lap.

"This is awesome!" he cheered, holding his arms over his head.

"Oh. Forgot something." She pulled her hand out from behind her back. He gawked at the holodisk case bearing Monwyn's face.

"Is… that… *Lure of Shadows?*" He almost dropped the staff. "That… *just* came out."

"Wanna watch it?"

He raced past her. "I'll make the popcorn"

HIGH SOCIETY

K irsten studied the images of food gliding along above a silver rail. Burgers of several shapes and sizes led the way as if train cars on a track, followed by a few blobs claiming to be chicken. Something unidentifiable, labeled fish, brought up the end of the chain after some hand-snacks like nuggets or fried pickle chips.

Every time she ducked into a CyberBurger, she never failed to wonder at how OmniSoy could taste like so many different things—at least if she ate it fast enough before it degenerated back into beige slime.

Samuel Chang rubbed his chin, oblivious to the impatient stare from a Class 1 doll on the far side of the register. The ersatz teen couldn't help but smile at him, a corporate-polished face that had no range of emotion other than cloying pleasantry. A potbellied man behind them, white button-down shirt marked with years-old coffee stains, stood up on tiptoe to wave over Sam at the doll. Kirsten glanced at the thick, twitching moustache on his face as he searched for the courage to speak. Her eyes fell to a gold nameplate hanging from his coffee-stained pocket with the logo of the Imperial Hotel on it: Milton Swanson – Network Administrator.

"Umm, excuse me..." he whispered, waving the tips of his fingers at Sam's back. When no one noticed him, he looked at the floor and muttered under his breath. "I'm on lunch break. I only get forty-five minutes for lunch break. I'm going to be late because this man cannot place his order. Why do they only give me forty-five minutes for lunch? I'm the head of the network operations team. I should get more than forty-five minutes for lunch. I'm going to talk to Courtney in HR. This is not acceptable. I should get more than that since I've been there for six years now. It's shameful how they treat their employees. Shameful."

Kirsten leaned on Sam's shoulder. "Just pick something. It's all the same stuff."

Sam bit his lip. "I can't decide what flavor milkshake to get."

She stared into the kitchen, mind lost for a moment, until she remembered something Evan said over a week ago. She winked at him, grinning. "Get strawberry."

Orders in hand, they went around Milton each on a different side, leaving the mad mumbler free to approach the counter. The poor man proceeded to assail the doll with complaints of his insufficient lunch break, which it had no ability to react to.

Sam took a seat, stiff and uncomfortable, at one of the small red plastic tables by the front window. As Kirsten settled down across from him, still smiling, she got into a staring contest with an old man leaning on a broom.

Like an Old West showdown, he dared her to drop one thing on the floor. Bushy eyebrows quivered over narrowing eyes. Just one fry, I dare you.

"What the hell is his problem?" She looked away, blinking.

Sam barely noticed him. "Sorry, I know this isn't the kind of place you're used to going."

Kirsten suppressed the urge to feel sick at the thought of the ice swan and the man that took her there. CyberBurger didn't make her feel out of her element. Here, she was just an ordinary young woman out on her first date with an ordinary young man. The elite could go to hell.

She reached across the table to hold his hand. "No, Sam, it's fine. It's more than fine. Honestly, I'm much happier in a place like this. I'm sorry it took me so long to keep this promise to have dinner with you. I had an umm"—she rubbed her empty wrist where the ouroboros bracelet wasn't —"paranormal issue."

He blushed, unable to keep eye contact. "You shouldn't be sorry. I still can't believe a girl like you even looked at me twice."

"You'd be surprised how difficult it's been finding someone who isn't a shallow, judgmental prick. You're a sweet guy, Sam, but I have to do this to you."

Samuel Chang stared at her, seeming about to cry.

"I'm psionic."

He furrowed his brow, eyes shifting left to right. "Umm… yeah. You're in Division 0 right? Isn't that like, required?"

Kirsten leaned over the table, pushed his milkshake to the side, and kissed him.

She loved the taste of strawberry.

---

fin

ACKNOWLEDGMENTS

Thank you for reading Thrall – Division Zero Book 3 (revised edition).

Additional thanks to Alexandria Thompson, for the superb covers.

I'd also like to thank the people at Curiosity Quills press for publishing the original edition and helping me get started on my publishing journey.

ABOUT THE AUTHOR

Originally from South Amboy NJ, Matthew has been creating science fiction and fantasy worlds for most of his reasoning life. Since 1996, he has developed the "Divergent Fates" world, in which *Division Zero, Virtual Immortality, The Awakened Series, The Harmony Paradox, and the Daughter of Mars series* take place. Along with being an editor at Curiosity Quills press, he has worked in IT and technical support.

Matthew is an avid gamer, a recovered WoW addict, Gamemaster for two custom RPG systems, and a fan of anime, British humour, and intellectual science fiction that questions the nature of reality, life, and what happens after it.

He is also fond of cats.

Visit me online at:
    Facebook: https://www.facebook.com/MatthewSCoxAuthor
    Amazon: https://www.amazon.com/author/mscox
    Pinterest: https://www.pinterest.com/matthewcox10420/
    Goodreads: https://www.goodreads.com/author/show/7712730.
Matthew_S_Cox
    Email: mcox2112@gmail.com

OTHER BOOKS BY MATTHEW S. COX

Divergent Fates Universe Novels

Division Zero series

- Division Zero
- Lex De Mortuis
- Thrall
- Guardian
- Harbinger
- The Shadow Fixer
- Neuroshock

The Awakened series

- Prophet of the Badlands
- Archon's Queen
- Grey Ronin
- Daughter of Ash
- Zero Rogue
- Angel Descended

Daughter of Mars series

- The Hand of Raziel
- Araphel
- Ghost Black

Virtual Immortality series

- Virtual Immortality
- The Harmony Paradox

Prophet of the Badlands Series

- Prophet's Journey

- Prophet's Mercy

Divergent Fates Anthology

(Fiction Novels - Adult)
The Roadhouse Chronicles Series

- One More Run
- The Redeemed
- Dead Man's Number

Faded Skies series

- Heir Ascendant
- Ascendant Unrest
- Ascendant Revolution

Temporal Armistice Series

- Nascent Shadow
- The Shadow Collector
- The Gate to Oblivion
- The Queen of Discord
- The Burning Alchemist

Vampire Innocent series

- A Nighttime of Forever
- A Beginner's Guide to Fangs
- The Artist of Ruin
- The Last Family Road Trip
- The Phantom Oracle
- How Not to Summon Demons
- Ordinary Problems of a College Vampire
- A Vampire's Guide to Surviving Holidays
- An Introduction to Paranormal Diplomacy
- A Vampire's Guide to Adulting

- How to Stop a Vampire War in Six Easy Steps
- Ancient Vampire Death Cults and Other Annoyances
- Hunting Vampires for Fun and Profit
- A String of Seriously Unlucky Events
- The Summer of Completely Usual Strangeness
- Demonic Crisis Management for the Modern Vampire

Standalones

- Wayfarer: AV494
- Axillon99
- Chiaroscuro: The Mouse and the Candle
- The Spirits of Six Minstrel Run
- Sophie's Light
- The Far Side of Promise anthology
- Operation: Chimera (with Tony Healey)
- The Dysfunctional Conspiracy (with Christopher Veltmann)
- Of Myth and Shadow
- The Girl Who Found the Sun

Winter Solstice series (with J.R. Rain)

- Convergence
- Containment
- Catalyst
- Catacombs

Alexis Silver series (with J.R. Rain)

- Silver Light
- Deep Silver
- Silver Quarrel
- Silver Crucible
- Silver Heart

Samantha Moon Origins series (with J.R. Rain)

- New Moon Rising
- Moon Mourning

- Haunted Moon

- Moon Master
- Dead Moon
- Lost Moon
- Vampire Destiny
- Infinite Moon
- Vampire Empress
- Moon Elder
- Wicked Moon
- Moon Blade

Maddy Wimsey series (with J.R. Rain)

- The Devil's Eye
- The Drifting Gloom
- Dark Mercy
- Primal Wrath

Samantha Moon Case Files series (with J.R. Rain)

- Blood Moon

Immortal Operative (with J.R. Rain)

- Broken Ice
- Broken Wing

Four Elements series (with J.R. Rain)

- The Elementalist
- The Black Rose
- The Wakefield Curse

Witches series (with J.R. Rain)

- The Witch and the Hangman

Zeb Clemens series (with J.R. Rain)

- The Beast of Devil's Creek
- Wanted: Undead or Alive

Young Adult Novels

The Eldritch Heart Series

- The Eldritch Heart
- The Cursed Crown
- The Sapphire Soul

Evergreen Series

- Evergreen
- The World That Remains
- The Lucky Ones
- Nuclear Summer
- The Nuclear Frontier
- The World We Make
- The Threat Unseen

Progenitor Series

- Out of Sight
- Out of Mind

Diary of a Teenage Fey
(Short story series)

- Elder Horror
- The Hag of Barrow Falls
- Babysitter's Nightmare
- Lharakki
- Bauble for a Soul
- Simulacrum

- Amorphous
- Manticore

- Caller 107
- The Summer the World Ended
- Nine Candles of Deepest Black
- The Forest Beyond the Earth

Middle Grade Novels

The Adventures of Ubergirl series

- My Dad is a Mad Scientist
- Aliens Ate My Homework
- The End of all Halloweens
- Dr. Infinity and the Soul Smasher

Tales of Widowswood series

- Emma and the Banderwigh
- Emma and the Silk Thieves
- Emma and the Silverbell Faeries
- Emma and the Elixir of Madness
- Emma and the Weeping Spirit

Standalones

- Citadel: The Concordant Sequence
- The Cursed Codex
- The Menagerie of Jenkins Bailey

www.ingramcontent.com/pod-product-compliance
Lightning Source LLC
Chambersburg PA
CBHW060216030726
47499CB00004B/1070